THE
EXPLOIT

ALSO BY DANIEL SCANLAN

The Ericka Blackwood Files
The Hacker

THE EXPLOIT

DANIEL SCANLAN

HEAD
ZEUS

An Aries Book

A catalogue record for this book is available from the British Library.

ISBN (PB): 9781801107877
ISBN (E): 9781801107853

Cover design: Head of Zeus/Ben Prior

Printed and bound in Great Britain by
CPI Group (UK) Ltd, Croydon CR0 4YY

Head of Zeus
5–8 Hardwick Street
London EC1R 4RG

WWW.HEADOFZEUS.COM

To my wife Tiffany, and my Uncle Pat (1944-2023)

A child of Erebus and Nyx, Nemesis was the Greek goddess of retribution, Invidia to the Romans. She rendered judgment and meted out punishments to those who perpetrated evil or amassed great fortune beyond what they had earned. Nemesis ensured a balance of happiness and sadness, good and bad luck. Often invoked against people whose hubris and arrogance dominated their lives, she was a force of divine reckoning. She would descend to Earth, winged vengeance, to deal with mortals who thought themselves better than the gods.

D.S.

1

Resurrection

He flinched at the sound of ricocheting bullets striking rock just above his head, the impact preceding the sounds of the rifle firing them. The whole squad lunged for cover in unison. His back pressed against stone, Captain Bradley Morris of the U.S. Rangers hunched over, scanning for his men in the shadows, his guts tight, fearing casualties. The six he could see were uninjured; the other three reported in hushed voices— no one hit. All peered through rifle sights, trying to locate the attack's source. He couldn't tell who spoke. "I have eyes on at least two fighters, two hundred and fifty yards, bearing..." a short pause "...two-seven-five."

Morris glanced down at the gravel between his legs so his men couldn't see his eyes while he squeezed them shut— just a few seconds, permitting himself the luxury of a few deep breaths. Stone dust caked his nostrils, the source of the pervasive stink of these jagged hills, like stale sweat of a thousand years. Stones dug into his ribs as he crawled closer to his men, fearing any sound would draw more fire. *Christ, that was close.* Men firing from a concealed vantage point ahead, their pursuers not far behind. They were blown.

This was where the covert mission ended and the fight to survive began. *Think it through.* Discovered as they made their way towards the target concealed in late evening shadows, light towards the target, or maybe the intel they were following was bogus and this was a trap. Something for the asset handlers to figure out later. There would be no ambush of the man they'd been sent to apprehend, no intelligence bonanza, no feather in the squad's cap. Now, it was about getting his men out for another day. A stab of pain from another stone made him flinch, cramps in his guts, cold fear suppressed by force of will.

Motion from between two jagged boulders caught his attention, his man watching the rear crouched under them, waving for attention, white eyes contrasting face camo smeared on in the style of war paint. Enemy approaching from the north, twenty plus. That made the decision easy. No way they could fight their way out, and no sense in bringing in backup to be shot dead by concealed fighters as they arrived. The ISIL fighters, if that's who they were, would be expecting that. An arriving helo would be a sitting duck. He glanced at his watch; it would be night in half an hour.

Morris could see the relief on the men's faces, hear the soft chorus of sighs as he yanked the sat phone from its pouch. Another burst of automatic fire ripped above their heads, a heavy gun this time, forcing them to duck as showers of stone chips tapped on helmets like hailstones. Stretching to peer around a rock, he could just make out the outline of a battered Toyota truck on the road blocking their retreat, heavy gun mounted in the back, what soldiers called a technical. Morris held the phone's hooded screen close, unsure if the green glow was visible from above. Since the withdrawal, Afghanistan was a different place, dared only by elite troops on short-term missions. Speed and stealth were all that kept them alive.

Ensuring the connection, Morris double-checked the GPS lock then keyed the mic. "Pac-Man, this is Snakebelly, over." *The bastards better be on their toes. No time to wait for goddam gamer drone pilots stateside to finish their avocado toast.*

An unbearable few seconds of static preceded the answer. "Snakebelly, Pac-Man, go ahead."

Morris's shoulders sagged, voice hoarse from a parched throat. "Pac-Man, Snakebelly. We're blown, aborting our mission. I say again, mission abort. Are you in position to clear a path to an extraction point? Hostiles on all sides. Road blocked with a technical, looks like a fifty-cal. If you can see a Hilux, that's it."

Morris waited again, tension stretching the length of each second, digging grit from the corners of his eyes with a knuckle. "Snakebelly, firing position in two minutes, got two JDAMS on board, scanning for the technical. Tell me where you want them."

Two JDAM guided munitions—smart bombs—would clear a path but might not get them all the way out. "Pac-Man, we may need a little more ordinance for the way home."

A longer pause preceded the answer this time. "Roger that. Two more Reapers inbound."

"Take out the technical first. We'll proceed to extraction that direction with whatever cover you can provide. Too tight in here for a chopper." *Call for that once I'm sure we can get somewhere it can land.*

A few seconds of waiting forced him to look at the screen, concerned it had stopped working before it hissed back to life. "Reapers two and three, twenty minutes out. Think I have your technical approximately three hundred meters south of your position?"

Morris gestured to his sergeant, pointing to the man's M151 spotter scope, curling his finger at him to bring it. He wedged it against the rock for stability, squinting into the range finder, keying the mic. "I get two-eight-five meters, one-eight-seven degrees from our position."

The reply this time was instant. "GPS lock on that. Keep your heads down. Great and mighty bang inbound."

Morris hadn't realized he was holding his breath. Forcing his shoulders down, he gave his men a ferocious smile and a thumbs-up. All eyes were on him, stark white contrasting painted skin, dark with shadow now the sun had slid behind the toothy ridge to the west, peaks silhouetted against the last red light. Brave men, all of them; the trust on their faces forced him to again steel his features. No fear could show but he was more than merely aware any mistake would cost all of them their lives. Nothing to do but stay low and wait for death to fall on their enemies, Thor's hammer from the night sky.

Technical Sergeant Alex Kingsley, USAF, went numb, knowing what was coming, seeing what was happening in front of him, realizing here was where it all ended. He'd waited for it, but anticipation made no difference to the horror. Not dread at raining death on enemy targets unfortunate enough to be visible to his MQ-9 Reaper. He had done that many times and was becoming almost hardened to it. No, now it was time to pay the piper, time for the final betrayal to play out on the screen in front of him. Sweat ran under his uniform shirt, tickling him. His jaw ached from clenching.

Stationed at Creech Air Force Base in Nevada, crew on an armed Reaper drone, call sign Pac-Man, he was accounted by his superiors a talented weapons officer, a young man of iron nerves, one whose calm focus allowed him to react and fire with deadly accuracy, time after time. He was thought to be going places, but he hid a terrible secret: he was a traitor to his country and now his malfeasance had caught up with him.

It wasn't like Kingsley didn't have the best of reasons for taking the money, or at least as good as such reasons got. He surely wasn't the only enlisted man serving in the US armed forces with a close relative needing medical attention they couldn't afford. But he was the one who'd sold it, information about the USAF drone systems and operations to a person he didn't know, for sale to whichever country bid the highest. When he'd heard it had gone to the People's Republic, it brought tears and a wave of nausea but by then money had changed hands and his sister's surgery was done. Experimental, no guarantees, but seeing her in recovery, still a child really, sleeping without pain, color in her cheeks, the guilt drained away for a time.

It might have ended there, but it was not to be. Caught, not by police or the intelligence services, but by an unseen wraith lurking in darkness, spaces he didn't even know existed. He bit his lip at the memory, forgetting where he was, stifling the groan just in time.

The voice from the darkness had found him. He had not sought him out nor had any warning. One minute engrossed in a role-playing combat game, his VR goggles creating an immersive environment, cutting a bloody swath through legions of digital foes. The next the display went dark, his headphones silent. His first thought was he'd lost power. Before he could tug the headset off, words came out of the void, a rich baritone arriving the same time a shape became visible, a human shape, indistinct, ethereal. All Kingsley could make out was the seated figure of a man, but with wings, dark angel's wings, shadows on ink. One hung at an angle, broken, incapable of flight.

There was a hint of movement, perhaps its head turned. "Alex, my son, do you truly feel nothing, no guilt, not the slightest remorse?" The question hung in air as if it had echoed from unseen walls. Kingsley didn't answer. This time he was sure, a look in his direction. "Do you not fear the special hell prepared for traitors? For those like you who have abandoned honor. Or do you not even appreciate what you are?"

The full-body chill was instant and instinctive, but Kingsley was sure he was dealing with some idiot who knew what he did for a living, maybe a friend feeding him a joke video. The drone program had many enemies and he had idiot techy friends. That's all this was. He was breathing again. "Fuck you. If you want to call me out, have the stones to say it to my face."

The voice sounded amused, dripping irony as the head tilted up. "Ah, but Alex, you have so many faces. Which one would you like me to say it to?"

"Kiss my ass!" Not a recorded video then—this was a

conversation. His guts tightened. It could be real, his secret out.

The figure grew indistinct for a moment, as if a mist had passed between them, then it reformed, almost solid now, the tone harsh. "Before you think to do it—if you power down, I will expose you tonight."

Oh shit, this is bad. Try to bluff. "Expose me for what?"

A hint of reproof in the tone, perhaps even annoyance. "You will find playing games with me is a dreadful mistake. The three hundred and fifty thousand dollars you took to betray your oath. Shall I bring up the hospital receipts for you to see? A video of you visiting after the surgery? I have more. Did you think a name change for her and traveling abroad for surgery would change anything?"

Chilled as if plunged into ice water, goose bumps all over, Kingsley couldn't help the quaver in his voice. "Who the fuck are you?"

"Call me Dantalion—many do. I will remain silent, no one will know. I will even erase all records anyone might ever find, but two things you will do for me first. For me and your family."

Despair and panic flooded him, drowning his senses, tears pooling, salt taste dribbling from under the goggles. He could barely force the whisper. "What?"

All warmth was gone from the voice, transforming to repressed rage, even ferocity. "Soon, you will receive a package containing a device. It will load data inside the Reaper control systems and find its own way from there. The code in the device will encrypt after use."

He has no idea how tight the security is... or does he? "They'll figure it out. They're not idiots. What's the other thing?"

"I'm sure they will, but you will not care if they do. The second thing you are going to do to buy my silence is restore your own honor, your family's honor. Bring yourself to an end. How you do it is no concern to me."

Kingsley sucked in a breath, terrible knots growing in his stomach. Was this a joke? "You can't be serious." But he knew he was. There was no way out.

"But I am. It's not like you haven't thought of it before. Or so you've told your doctor. And the meds your brother takes. Perhaps he simply buys them so there is no record to point to that which would disqualify you from your position?"

"What do you want?"

"The device will be there in two days. If my software is not loaded within the week, expect me. As will all your family, the authorities, the media. All will know the misdeeds of their hero, their defender, their faithful servant. Of the depression, the medicines you hid, how you lied to get into the program in the first place. I will give you a few hours' warning of when I will activate. It would be very unwise of you to outlive the result by more than a few minutes."

2

Retribution

The package contained a watch, an old-looking analog quartz timepiece from another age and a USB stick. As directed, Kingsley had worn the watch every day while on duty.

After three days, following his instructions, he stood next to a maintenance terminal while the technician left to speak to a colleague. He set the watch to four minutes before midnight, pushing the adjustment dial in with an audible click. His eyes widened as the network symbol flashed on the laptop for an instant, showing it had connected. Whatever it had done had taken mere seconds. When off duty, he was told to plug the memory stick into his home computer and leave the watch near it. After several days, his tormentor bade him to burn both, which he did, turning the insides to ashes. Now it was happening.

Driving to the base for his shift, a single word flashed on his car's infotainment screen: "Today." Thirty seconds later, the screen went dead, defying his efforts to turn it back on. Distracted, Kingsley found himself on the shoulder, tires chattering on the pavement's edge, making him yank hard on the wheel to avoid the ditch, teeth clenched. The bland yellows and browns of the desert slid by, glimpsed through slitted eyes. He forced himself to gulp short breaths. It was over, all lost now, and he was as alone as he'd ever been. He shook his head, pulling himself together. Now, it was all about protecting his family, completing this final task, these all that he would be permitted. The gate to the base appeared around the bend of US 95 and he shivered despite being bathed in sweat.

Kingsley gazed over his left shoulder, searching for the mission coordinator—Captain Phillips. The officer was nowhere in sight, so he turned to face his screens. Pilot and weapons officer were both ensconced side by side in a two-person pod, heavy armchairs with a center console between them, three walls of screens complimenting the control systems directly in front, the array for flying the drone a gamer's dream. His pilot, First Lieutenant Schneider, call sign Pac-Man, seated to his left, stared focused on her screens, paying attention only to the equipment and the mission, awaiting final clearance to fire as requested. Time to see if he still had weapons control. Kingsley flipped the toggle down, switching the drone's firing system to manual mode, nudging the control column to aim. Nothing happened. The drone's camera did not respond. He tried again with the same result. Another look around him—still no one watching him. Several flashes on his main screen snapped his attention back to the skies of southern Afghanistan.

The screen showed weapons activating, but he wasn't doing it. Another glance behind for the captain before turning back to his targeting screen. The Reaper made a slight turn, bringing the target just within visual range. Schneider's eyes bulged and she swore under her breath. *God no!* The targeting controls were changing, moving up the rough canyon scrolling below, three hundred yards from where he'd programed impact. *Jesus Christ!* He lunged forward, scrambling to shut the weapons down with no effect. Nothing altered the drone's course or weapons lock, now focused on the unit who'd called in the strike.

Kingsley pressed his eyes shut, bowing his head before a bolt of pain and rage forced them to snap open. Rage flared like a match to gasoline and he pounded both fists on his main screen, cracking the glass to an anguished shout. "Fuck no!"

All eyes in the control room were on him as he lowered his head onto bleeding hands, red smears on the glass. Fingers gripped his shoulder, digging into muscle, hauling his head up to look into Phillip's brown eyes. "You're relieved. Stand down now!"

He wouldn't be asked twice. Kingsley stood, his gaze fixed on the monitor. The weapon launched. A JDAM with five hundred pounds of high explosive was on its way down. He fell to the ground, cracking his head on a pillar, thrown out of the way by his superior as Phillips lunged for the weapons seat. Holding the wet patch on the back of his head, skull throbbing, Kingsley turned for the door. Schneider's hands flew over the switches as she tried to regain flight control.

Phillips's voice was shrill. "Turn hard, break the weapons lock!"

Schneider's tone was pure anguish. "I can't—no control."

★ ★ ★

Morris lay on his back, sheltered between two large rocks, the stench of his own sweat filling his nostrils, staring skyward. He knew he would see nothing before the flash of exploding ordinance lit the surrounding area but waited to give the order to run until the truck with the heavy gun was neutralized. He craned his neck to peer at his men, his concern for them his last thought. He looked up. The sky was dark, the first few stars just visible. A beautiful night in different circumstances. He held on to the sigh. It was just morning at home. *Be there soon,* he told himself. None of the squad saw or even perceived the explosion that tore them to pieces, scattering their burning bodies amongst rocks and gravel.

Phillips sat back, his spine snapping erect, breath lost to an explosive gasp like he'd been gut punched. "Jesus no, we just hit our own guys." At the edge of his vision, he perceived faces twisting in his direction, mouths open. The cracked screen displayed an expanding detonation cloud, larger pieces of debris beginning to rain down, dust obscuring the carnage on the ground.

He shouted without taking his eyes from the disaster unfolding half a world away. "What the fuck happened?" No answer. He spun around with a second demand. "I said, what the fuck happened?" He was speaking to no one. Kingsley was gone. He scanned behind him. No one was there.

The other crews leaned back from their pods staring wide-eyed, their own machines ignored for the moment. One jerked his head towards the entrance. He stood, intending to run to the door before realizing he couldn't leave the controls. Dropping back into the chair, he keyed the mic on his lapel, calling the MPs. Before he could speak, a single muffled gunshot rang through the room.

This was all going sideways. *What the hell now?* He heard but didn't process the shouted words from the adjacent station, his horrified focus still on the drifting dust cloud, the edge of the crater just becoming visible. "Chief! I need you to listen, now!"

"Yes, what?" His voice cracked as he said it, spinning to look.

The pilot leaned from her chair, waving as she spoke. "I've lost flight control of my bird. No response to flight commands or weapons inputs."

A male voice from farther down the line. "Mine too. Completely frozen out."

Phillips forced himself to take several deep breaths. They sounded like gasps as he drew them. *Concentrate—can't lose it now! Work the protocols.* Losing contact with a drone happened all the time, but he had at least three of them happening at once and one that had targeted and deployed weapons in a controlled manner. This wasn't a lost telemetry link, they were still getting video feed from the birds. The unthinkable had happened.

The same pilot called again, her voice elevated. "I'm turning south towards Pakistan, losing altitude."

A male voice came from farther down the line. "Mine too, no response to inputs. Shit! Lost video and location feed now!"

No decisions to be made at all then. Only one possible

course of action was open to him. He clicked the mic again, speaking now in a steady voice, paging his superior.

When he answered, his commanding officer's voice was soft. "Go ahead."

"Sir, we have an emergent situation. Three birds rogue with full weapons loads. One just took out a unit of Rangers without any input from us. All armed and descending on the same heading south towards friendly territory and assets. We're going to need an intercept and shoot-down. I recommend base lockdown. I think this was an inside job. Someone's looking now, but I think our mole may have just shot himself."

Shoulders hunched and tense, Joseph Maxwell of Homeland Security waited for his director to answer. There had never been any question in his mind that this day would come, nor did he feel any particular surprise at where it came from. The FBI was pretty confident he'd survived and escaped, and there was no escaping the implications of what he was looking at. He would have expected nothing less. Worse, he knew he was outgunned and alone. All the signs were there, things he'd seen working with the FBI two years before, first in the Philippines, then Brazil.

Maxwell's team leaned in from the stations around him. They needed to know, better they understood what they were facing. Two more rings and she picked up. "Andrea Riley." Even jolted from a deep sleep, the director of Homeland's National Cyber Security Division was always all business.

"Maxwell here. Sorry to wake you, ma'am. I had no alternative."

A male voice swore in the background followed by cloth rustling and footsteps. "Yes, go ahead."

He nibbled his lower lip before speaking. "The air force has simultaneously lost control of three Reapers over Afghanistan, now flying below radar but last known heading was for the Sahiwal in Pakistan. One targeted and fired on an American unit. Wiped them out."

"Jesus Christ, they trying to shoot them down?"

"No American assets in range, but the Pakistanis are scrambling jets."

"What do they need from us?"

"Any advice or assistance in identifying who's controlling them. Looks to us like they've gone fully autonomous and silent. Nothing to jam or intercept. They've lost them on radar."

She interrupted him. "What assistance can we provide? Where are the NSA?"

This would wake her up. He was sure of his conclusion. Time to spit it out; Ericka had been right. "They're working on it too, but there's more. We received data fragments from Creech that appear to have been used to insert malware into the drone control systems before they lost them. God knows how he got it in there. Most of the malicious code on their servers encrypted itself, bricked right up before someone thought to pull the plug, but there's no mistaking who wrote it."

Maxwell could make out the sound of forced breathing. "Jesus Christ, you're sure?"

"As sure as I can be, ma'am. First high-probability Dantalion sighting since São Paulo."

Riley was silent for a few moments. When she spoke, it was

with her usual forceful authority. "Okay, I'll report up. Any idea how he's doing it?"

"I think it's a preprogramed mission. The drones appear to be sending him short data bursts, but he uses a different set of satellites to receive each communication. We can't triangulate. NSA has drawn a blank too."

"Analysis?"

"The only reason I can think of why he'd need that uplink is to try and defend the drones until they complete their mission. He clearly isn't steering them in real time." He waited for the inevitable question.

"Which is?"

"Last known trajectory was for Sahiwal, but I think what he may want is the prison. Lots of human sources, terrorist prisoners held there. Old habits are hard to break."

"Is there anything you can do?"

He'd thought through all the angles before he called and come up dry. "Nothing the military isn't already trying. Try to get some control back and order them to fly where the interceptors can get a lock on them. A very long shot. It isn't like he's going to have programed them to fly in a straight line, and he's picked a night with no moon and some really nasty terrain."

A few moments passed. "Do whatever you can. When the incident is over, engage the Dark-Web Intelligence Unit at the FBI. They've got the most experience with this target."

Wing Commander Yusef Abidi of the Pakistan Air Force kept his eyes on his fighter's nav screen, scanning flight instruments to maintain control of his machine. A member of the air force reserve, retired from regular service, tonight he was a long way from the operations desk at Inter-Services Intelligence, pulled from his bed to get all possible warplanes in the air. The Chinese-made JF-17 was their latest, guided by China's state-of-the-art BeiDou navigation system.

As he concentrated, the noise of the engine faded into the background, as did the faint scent of heated electronics and jet fuel. His two wingmen flew behind and just below as he followed a satellite-guided grid pattern, searching for these rogue American drones. The night was ink black and he flew solely by instruments, waiting for the fighter's radar to find the target, but there was nothing in the mountain air below. Two other three-plane flights searched adjacent areas and he listened as they reported negative results.

The Americans built these things to be hard to see, but they weren't stealthy, they had to be here somewhere. Even flying low and close to terrain, they didn't have endless range. His flight controller was guessing based on a last known trajectory that was ninety minutes old. Abidi glanced at the nav screen, right on course coming out of rougher terrain. He should be able to see lights from the towns. He lifted his head to peer into the black. Nothing in sight. Must be low cloud. That wasn't going to make this any easier. Abidi couldn't see the expected glow of the city to the south either. He double-checked his position, but BeiDou had him exactly where he should be.

It was going to be hard for the Pakistani Air Force to find them. The terrain was rough and they were flying junky Chinese-made fighters. Maxwell shook his head, drumming his fingers next to the keyboard, raising his eyebrows in mute inquiry as he glanced towards his team. All shook their heads before looking down, each screen's glow lighting their faces, accenting tense expressions.

Someone's machine chimed. "Another encrypted data burst. Really tiny and one way going up, no response back."

Maxwell posed a question to the team. "Why does he have them transmitting anything? Even with these microbursts, he's taking a risk we'll use them to find the drone. If he's preprogramed his instructions, what does he need data for if he's not sending anything back?" Thoughtful looks, eyes focused in other directions but no one answered. "How long until he could be in firing position?"

The analyst's head was buried behind her monitor. "Ten minutes if he flew in a straight line, which he wouldn't, but not much longer than that either way."

Another voice came from behind him. "Does he need to know where the drones are to time something else?"

Maxwell sat up straight, spinning towards the man. "Good thought; work it. Even if we can't stop this one, this may not be his only move tonight."

His second in command stroked his goatee but his eyes never left his screen. "To protect them somehow? To know when to set something else in motion? I'm just guessing."

Maxwell gave him a thumbs-up before turning back to his own screen. "Keep it coming. Guessing's all we've got."

Something was very wrong and he flew with teeth clenched almost to the point of pain. Abidi could see a few points of light in the dark below, but it didn't add up. If his nav screen was correct the lights of two towns should be obvious even through broken cloud. The running lights of his two wingmen were visible, holding station one hundred and fifty meters to either side. Nothing on radar, but down low in this terrain there was little chance of a lock until they were close. He wished he had one of their older American fighters tonight, the F-16 he remembered from his years of active service.

No help for it, Abidi toggled his mic. "Down to five hundred meters. We may have to do this visually." He could hear the tension in his flight's terse acknowledgment. In this mountainous country, they could run out of flying room very fast.

Time to report in. "Minhas control, this is flight six. No contact. Any further direction?"

The reply crackled through static. "No target sightings. Note, you are not visible on radar." *That's peculiar.* Even at this altitude, they should be visible on radar with transponders running. He refreshed his navigation screen, confirming his position. He shook his head, wishing he could reach the dreadful sweat itch tickling his lower back.

The intense flash of red to his left came from a fireball, formerly his wingman, the explosion's flash illuminating the cliff as he spun to look. Hauling back on his stick he ordered his surviving wingman to pull up, staring down as tumbling bits of debris lit the rocks they struck, disintegrating into ever-smaller fragments. He went numb all over. Allah be merciful, the pilot's first child would be born in the next few weeks. White noise. A roar filled his headphones as his mic picked up his ragged breathing, amplifying the sound. He forced his eyes to focus. They were lost and those drones would be in firing position any minute. This was over. *Why no terrain warning from the nav computer? Was anything working?*

Air Commodore Kashani lowered his head over folded hands as he absorbed the news of the loss. A good man and a new fighter gone. He would be regarded by his superiors as responsible for both. He dragged the back of his hand across his forehead, dislodging the headset. As he tugged it back into position, a flash on his screen caught his eye. A small window with a blinking red border displayed near the bottom, overlaying the radar feed, displaying the title US Homeland Security. It held a message in English. "*Tell them to use GLONASS or GPS. Use their phones.*" He reached for his keyboard to type a response, but the window disappeared, leaving him staring at the feed from Pakistani air defense radar. He tugged at his beard. His planes were circling lost. What was the harm?

He switched on his mic. "Flight six, Commodore Kashani here." He broke protocol, using his name in the clear for effect, to ensure obedience.

Abidi answered, his tone sounding puzzled. "Sir?"

"Do you have your mobile with you?"

A few seconds of silence. "Pardon? Say again."

It was against the rules to carry them while flying so Abidi was probably reluctant to answer. Kashani deliberately sharpened his tone. "Your mobile, do you have it?"

"Yessir."

"Switch it on and use it to verify your position."

"Sir?"

"Humor me."

★ ★ ★

Abidi kept his gaze focused in front as he fumbled for his iPhone, fishing it from the inside pocket of his flight suit. He held the mobile at eye level while he switched on, careful to keep his focus on flying, worried about ruining his night vision with the bright screen when it started up. He pointed it down, illuminating his booted feet on the rudder pedals, waiting until it was ready. Diverting his gaze, he tapped the maps icon, waiting again, seeing good signal and several satellites.

His eyes widened as he shivered. *That's not possible!* A glance at his cockpit nav screen confirmed his mobile and aircraft were showing two different locations, not even close. If his mobile was correct, he was still over the mountains just passing an escarpment. God, it was a wonder they hadn't all ended up black stains on the cliffs. *Can I trust anything this plane is telling me?*

He shook his head, mouth dry as he transmitted. "Sir, if this is correct, we are nearly one hundred kilometers off course. That accords with visual references, or lack of them. Turning for our assigned area now."

He toggled switches, turning off his useless cockpit nav and slid the mobile into his kneeboard where he could see it before issuing orders to his remaining wingman. "Follow my lead, light your afterburner, speed nine-five zero knots." He banked and pulled back on his stick, instant Gs shoving him into his seat hard enough it felt like his face was stretching. This was going to be a very tight race between fuel supply and arriving in time to have any chance.

★ ★ ★

Maxwell leaned back, his chair creaking. They were going to lose this one, never going to break these microbursts. They had nothing more than guesses what they were for. The bastard was going to win another one. How had Ericka put it? He was all but invincible technically, but the man underneath was weak and flawed. If Dantalion hadn't found spying on his ex-wife irresistible, she'd have never had the data to locate him. Not like he'd make the same mistake twice, not this one.

He lost his train of thought remembering the look of determination on Ericka's face as she left for São Paulo, wondering if she was even alive.

And there they were, close enough now Abidi could just make out the outline of two drones silhouetted against the city lights, dark birds of prey. The third one was somewhere ahead of these, but he had a lock on that one with a heat-seeking missile. The area below where he thought the last one must be was unlit, hopefully clear of civilians. He bit his lip, hoping, but there was no way to be sure. He had to bring it down either way.

He ripped off his oxygen mask, gulped a deep breath and fired. The heat seeker's rocket motor made an audible hiss as it leapt from its launch rail, spiraling into the black to become a gyrating point of light. Mere seconds passed before a painful flash of light caused him to glance away. *Closer than he'd anticipated.* When he looked, flaming pieces arced towards the ground. "*Allahu Akbar!* Got one."

Kashani's tone made it clear there was no debating his next order. "Bring the others down now. We can't risk a weapons launch."

He understood the order—they would just have to risk ground casualties. Whoever was controlling these things knew that, damn him. The fact that all three had converged here right now meant the drone's target was close. He flipped on his fighter's 23mm cannon, firing a quick burst trying to detonate the first one's weapons in the air. Another enormous flash demonstrated his success and he banked hard to avoid the explosive debris hurtling towards him before arcing down.

His wingman had less luck with the last one. Abidi watched, teeth clenched, as the Reaper's engine exploded with a tiny puff of fuel, causing the drone to spiral, mostly intact, towards the surface. No time for a second shot, its bombs exploded on impact, the glaring flash of detonation lighting up what looked like a warehouse. They'd had no choice. He offered a silent prayer for anyone who might have been on the ground before glancing down at his phone to vector to the nearest airport, dreading the call he must make on his wingman's widow, then a quick prayer for vengeance.

Someday whoever did this would pay for this reckless atrocity, and tomorrow his hunt would begin.

"Well, that was some outstanding work! How did you know?" Director Riley's beaming face filled the video window.

Maxwell peered into the webcam, baffled, expecting to be hearing news of a mass casualty event somewhere in Pakistan. "Sorry, ma'am?"

Her expression looked bemused, then she leaned back, her forehead wrinkling. "That he'd scrambled their nav? Your message to the Pakistanis to use GLONASS. They're crediting your team with this one. They think they shot them down seconds before weapons release. Outstanding work!"

He knew he must look stunned to his boss, but there was no avoiding it. "It wasn't us. We didn't send any message; we didn't do anything."

3

Awakening

Well, that was mostly blind goddammed luck, and a damned good guess very late in the day. Ericka melted back into her seat. Most of what she'd thought he'd been up to turned out to be wrong. That was so cocky. Not content with ordinary hacking and smuggling anymore, now he'd decided to tweak his old country's collective nose by screwing with a significant military asset. *Every bum in the American defense establishment will have clenched tight to the point of pain all at once. He'll be loving the thought of that.* Soon her quarry would turn his mind to who might be behind the happy ending, not the one he intended.

Lank strands of hair stuck to her forehead so she finger-combed it back, not caring how oily it felt. She avoided mirrors these days, cringeworthy events providing graphic evidence of how far she had let herself slide, pale and gaunt, looking years older than the birthdate her numerous fake identities had her. The apartment was clean enough, spartan, a place to work and rest, but not to live. Living would have to wait for another unimagined time, a time always anticipated but which never seemed to arrive.

There could be no going back to her old life, nor could she imagine a way forward. She'd returned to her old habit of embracing obsession to salve pain, finding out that insight and release were not the same thing after all. She'd been so very wrong. Relief came only one way now.

Ericka tugged the screen of her laptop shut, folding her hands over it as she leaned back, sighing with fatigue. She'd known he was on the move, seen where he was probing, had a shrewd idea what he had in mind, but no idea of time or place. She'd even considered trying to warn someone back home but wasn't confident they wouldn't be able to run a trace back to her. She'd learned much from studying his code, playing with his hacks, but Dantalion she was not. Her former colleagues were not idiots either.

Ericka had found several desperate postings, people looking for any information on someone using the handle of Dantalion, military pilots and maintenance people it turned out. It was clear where he was probing but not what he was planning. Clusters of traffic in Pakistani servers told of her his likely target location. Once under way, frantic communications between air traffic control and lost civilian aircraft provided the final piece. He was spoofing satellite nav signals somehow, simultaneously making sure his hijacked toys weren't shot down. Newer Pakistani Air Force planes used Chinese satellite systems so he wouldn't have bothered disrupting the Russian system, and iPhones, beloved of an entire generation worldwide, could use GLONASS. With any luck, her target would worry she'd penetrated his system rather than the fortunate inference it had really been. She'd never get that lucky again.

She arched her back, stretching muscles tight from hours of seated tension. Doing this was brazen, even for him, risking one of the national intelligence services getting a line on him, not to mention goading American authorities to redouble their efforts. No longer a mere criminal, his stunt with the remotely hijacked airliner had branded him a significant terrorist threat and made him a legend among the internet's underworld.

Two years of near-absolute silence and now he'd appeared again, leaving no doubts who was behind this stunt. Perhaps he'd come up with something new, or maybe his narcissism wouldn't allow him too much time in hiding without the reaffirmation of the limelight. There'd be time to analyze both possibilities. Even he wouldn't dare poke his head out of his hole soon after stirring the hornets' nest like this. She'd have some time, but not forever. He'd be doing a bit of failure analysis right now and might soon be on the hunt for her.

She could smell her own sour sweat. She grimaced and stood, walking to draw a cool bath against the heat in the shuttered apartment, gasping as she settled in. Getting into Creech had to be a mole; all the critical control systems of drones were surely air-gapped. There was no defense against an inside man and that was one of the things that set him apart. Dantalion had an unerring talent to find and get into the deviant or vulnerable minds of people who could give him what even his enormous hacking talents could not. Much of his past success had been manipulating and extorting his way past unsolvable technical problems by exploiting faults in the wetware of the weak rather than a target's robust software.

Even so, stealing drones was another groundbreaking feat, however he got in. Iran claimed to have done it, but nothing on this scale. Disrupting the signal should have just put the aircraft into autonomous mode, rendering it harmless. At the very least, he'd thought how to set both programed flight and weapons release. She chewed her lower lip. Maybe another mole on the ground with the Reaper.

The sat nav work was something new and more worrying. The air force would patch whatever hole he'd found in their security, but if he'd found some way to remotely fool geolocation equipment or, heaven forbid, mess with the satellite system itself, this was going to get nasty. She'd have to try and hack the investigation reports of the national agencies. She wasn't the only one watching for him.

Not today though. Chilled now, Ericka stood up dripping as goose bumps rose from her skin. Feeling cold here was a rare treat. She toweled off before tugging on a short robe, stopping to stare at the row of pill bottles lined up on the chipped counter, tiny sentinels standing between her and madness. She squeezed her eyes shut at the wave of guilt. *It was a kind of chemical happiness, if numbing pain was truly some dreadfully pathetic version of happy.* For now, it was all she had. Ericka shook two of the small blue pills and one white into her hand before downing them with half a glass of water.

She settled into her nest of pillows, aware for a few minutes of the rising noise outside, before the welcome caress of Morpheus relaxed her neck, then her shoulders, before conferring on her at last the priceless gift of dreamless slumber.

* * *

He leaned back, keyboard ignored, enhanced reality rig lying next to its cradle. Teeth clenched, he toggled through the various news feeds, but there was nothing breaking from the area. Perhaps it was a bit early yet, so he paused on an American channel. A lovely reporter was conducting a video interview about the prospect of a manned mission to Mars. The equally pretty talking head answering the questions was doing so on the sole basis he had starred in a movie about going to Mars. Doing what he did would really be a lot harder if people were not so profoundly stupid. He should be glad. He shook his head. Give it a few minutes. He nudged his control column and gave the button a slight squeeze, turning the display off.

He turned to another screen, scrolling through the coded bursts of drone data. A moment's anxiety spurred him to replot the tracks of all three of them. In the oppressive silence he could hear his own breathing, a slight whistling as he exhaled, random noises from a flute. The terrible air didn't help—bad enough at times he could smell it. Soon time to move again.

The aircraft had followed exactly the route he had set them, following the jumbled terrain, cruising low to avoid radar, where possible keeping them over populated areas to deter efforts to shoot them down if they were spotted. Each taking a different route in case these stupid tribesmen turned fighter pilots got lucky. The drone's weapons were precise enough that only one needed to get through. The rest were just for bragging rights and entertainment.

He was hunted now by every intelligence agency and

police force in the world, though for different reasons, and this would properly announce his return. From the briefings he'd stolen, it seemed many thought him dead, claiming no one with an ego like his could stay hidden for so long. They were right of course—he had to give them that. It killed him lying low, and it still grated that the FBI of all hidebound dilettantes had found him, or at least one had, but she had vanished.

He'd been smugly satisfied when the first of her victims had washed up near a Baja fishing village. His end hadn't taken very long; he knew Ericka would never be able to contain it. A very elegant pursuit using the tools he'd left when he'd had to run from Brazil. The second hit had been surprisingly public. Very risky right near a town square on market day, cheeky bitch, and she accused him of having an ego. That had been over a year ago and the third one remained alive and well when last he checked a week before. The idiot hadn't put it together, strutting about in the open, confident that fear kept him safe, and it seemed he would get away with it. Perhaps he should take the last one out for old time's sake. It had taken some doing to find them for Ericka; shame if it went to waste—the three men she held responsible for her sister's death.

Rather astonishing that Ericka had been so cocky, and it appeared to have cost her. If her target's cartel colleagues had found her, he expected she would have vanished with no one the wiser. Her former associates and the other American services were still looking for her, but they didn't know where she'd been heading, or who she was pursuing. He'd fully expected Ericka would take out all three of the men he'd handed her in quick succession, then come searching for him.

He'd been counting on it, looking forward to it. Sighing, he reached for his water, taking a sip, wrinkling his nose. It had gone warm while he was engrossed. He glanced at the clock. Yes, they had to be there by now.

He activated his largest screen, toggling to Al Jazeera, Pakistan, waiting, heart starting to race, causing his breath to shudder. There it was, explosions and flames, excited-looking people in the background, an ultra-secure prison on fire. Except it wasn't. The translation said it was a crashed aircraft, just missing a warehouse, one of three shot down just north of Sahiwal. Aircraft of unknown origins.

Blinding rage exploded in his head. He pounded his fist down before hurling his steel water bottle straight at the screen, smashing the glass, knocking it from its mounts to lie sparking on the floor. *How? How did they manage to find all three?* He sat for a few minutes, forcing regular breathing, waiting for the red mist to clear. To get ahead of his plan like that, someone would have to have been watching his preparations. They couldn't have known about his mole at Creech, or this would have ended with an arrest before it ever started. Someone watching perhaps, but not seeing the whole picture, just enough to anticipate the response needed once he revealed himself.

The thought came to him in an instant. If anyone else had thwarted him, any one of the national security services, they'd be crowing to each other. *Funny that I was just thinking of you, my nemesis. So, perhaps you are out there after all.* That was some compensation for this disaster, but it meant a change in schedule. *No one without your intellect and talent could have done this. Bravo, Ericka, well played! I hope you're alive.*

4

Anagram

Special Agent Tim O'Connell didn't bother to open his eyes or even lift his head from the pillows. With his right hand he groped for the IV controller, clicking it twice with his thumb for more numbing painkiller. Antiseptic smells complimented the hum of machines and ventilation. This was all getting to be monotonous as his doctors had scheduled a series of surgeries to reconstruct his face, arm and hand from the debilitating burns and scars. This should be the last one. He was used to the pain now, at least that kind, but it would be a lot easier to endure if his sacrifice hadn't been in vain, if it had meant something. He bit his lip and sighed.

That's what he feared this had been, a way for his best friend, a sister in spirit, to indulge her own obsessions under cover of a career based on pretense. In Brazil, she'd come into his hospital room and told him she'd be back, then vanished like she'd never existed. A stab of guilt accompanied the thought, but where was she? If she'd gone to do what he expected, she'd have had to lie low, but that didn't explain how months had stretched into years. He couldn't have been that wrong about her, just discarding him like this.

The slow-burning resentment was back so he squeezed his eyes tight to force the doubt from his mind. It didn't work. Ericka left him burned and alone, facing no small amount of suspicion from above that he'd helped her with whatever she was doing now, at least to escape detection. He hadn't, but covering for her was just as bad and he had done that. By rights he should have disconnected all her old equipment, air-gapped it to preserve evidence, knowing perfectly well she'd be back to hide all traces leading to where she might be now. Better for her that he'd left them open to whatever Ericka had in mind, than be found to be actively doing something that might create suspicion he was helping her. She would find a way to get rid of what she didn't want found on FBI servers and she hadn't disappointed.

Part of it was the mental haze as painkillers began their work, but the stab of guilt crinkled his face, bringing a jolt of pain from under bandages and releasing tears to dribble from between eyelids pressed shut. She might be dead and here he was bad-mouthing her in his mind. The people he believed she'd gone after were likely protected by men who were trained and lethal. His stomach clenched, guilty at his anger, at his loss of faith in her, his mentor and comrade in arms. Where was she? Why no communication at all? Again, the vision of an unmarked grave in a Mexican desert made him gasp. He forced himself to relax and the drugs again granted him the mercy of sleep.

When he woke, it was sudden, almost a jolt of alarm. Like someone had poked him but no one had. His eyes opened to the ceiling and the burning pain of reconstructive surgery surged back, searing for a moment before fading enough he could open his eyes. He saw just the hospital ceiling fixtures with the lights off, a smoke detector with blinking green lights, but with the sense something was wrong. The instinct was overwhelming. Teeth clenched to endure the pain of movement, he turned his head to look to his left. The bed next to him was empty as expected, but the intense gaze locked on his eyes confirmed his instinct.

The man was tall and thin, seated, hunched and unmoving between the beds, leaning in his direction, eyes unblinking. Not a visitor he'd been expecting, no one he knew. So far from home at the Mayo Clinic in Arizona, he'd expected no one at all. It was another reason to travel this far—he didn't have the will or the energy for well-wishing visitors.

The man leaned closer seeing Tim was awake. "I'm sorry to intrude but I saw your name on the chart in the hall. Tim O'Connell?" The soothing tone belied the intense gaze and scarred face. He'd been sitting in the dark staring at him, some kind of nutter. *Who the hell does that?*

Tim forced himself to speak, his voice hoarse with a dry tongue and chapped lips. "Do I know you?" Speaking made him flinch. The words made his throat hurt where he'd been intubated. He reached for the plastic cup, cool water soothing as it went down.

A slight smile accompanied a shake of the shaved head, the aura of menace gone like a switch had been thrown. "No, and I know you only by reputation. I'm a friend of Ericka's from years ago. Sorry to intrude. When I saw the name on the chart, I put two and two together. I was just wandering the halls, couldn't sleep."

A shot of annoyance jolted him. *Shitty time for a social call—an industry geek with no social skills. Where do they find these guys?* "You're not catching me at my best just now."

A tilt of the head but the eyes remained locked. "No, and I apologize for my intrusion. I won't take up any more of your time. I'll leave you my card and perhaps you can contact me when you're feeling better." A bony hand appeared over the edge of his tray table, placing a card where he could reach it.

Tim raised his brow in inquiry, leaning, trying to read the card, Ian Dalton, CEO, Deepweb Cyber-Security. He made no effort to keep the irritation from his voice. "She's never mentioned you?"

A small shrug of what looked like affected disinterest. "It was a long time ago, but she'll remember, I'm sure." He leaned in again. "Let me get to the point. Setting aside all the rumors, I'm familiar with her current predicament and I can help. Contact me when you're ready."

Tim stared at the card, annoyance forgotten. His interest was piqued but he was fighting the drugs beginning to tug on his mind, dragging him back to sleep. He leaned back into the antiseptic-smelling pillows. "You'll have to excuse me now."

"Of course. Please be well." The man had a soothing tone, a trained voice, perfect tonality but lacking the slightest sincerity.

It was the odd squeaking that made Tim force his eyes open, a noise different from the anticipated footsteps. He caught a fleeting impression of the man wheeling himself out of the room, a hunched figure framed by the doorway and the hallway beyond. Sleep claimed him but not for long.

Like many, his mind often worked while he slept, waking him up with conclusions that eluded the focused efforts of his waking mind, drawing inferences out of apparently thin air. More than once in his career, he had bolted awake, the evidence in his current case making sense, but never like this before.

The thought took him like a slap across the face, so hard he sat halfway up before the pain forced him to relax back, eyes wide open, almost bugging out from his head. *Ian Dalton? That bastard! That evil bastard!* A simple anagram for Dantalion. He groaned. *Really right here, within throttling distance? Fuck me!* He fumbled for his mobile, almost dropping it. Hours had passed. There would be no trace he knew, but they had to try. Luck had to swing their way some time, didn't it? He made the call—the forensic team from the local FBI office would be here soon—before buzzing for the nurse and asking for hospital security.

His mind churned while he waited. *Could that have been him?* After the attack in Pakistan, the betting was he was holed up somewhere in China. Bloody hell, the balls on him coming back to the States. He let the other inference settle in his head, heart racing as it sunk in. He wouldn't be here looking for Ericka if he thought she was dead. She was out there somewhere.

"Ooh, cheeky bastard, that is some massive set of stones he has on him! Where does he find trousers to fit?" O'Brien shook his head before taking a sip from the large whiskey glass in his hand. He looked like hell as usual, offset by his cheerful energy and exuberance. Tim gave him a jaundiced glance, face tingling as he flushed with embarrassment. He would be a long time living this down.

Tim took a sip of the lightly watered Laphroaig, letting it burn down his throat while he thought. He glanced up to see the portly lawyer peering at him, scanning his features. *Probably wondering how much he can trust me.* He leaned back, making the worn chair leather creak. "Why has he started looking for her now? Something must have triggered his interest, never mind the colossal risk he took doing that. He never shows up for anything. He can't have seriously thought I would tell someone who shows up in my hospital room in the middle of the night where Ericka is, even if I knew."

O'Brien turned his gaze to the office window and the low September sun. "No, that makes sense. He's clean away as usual?"

Tim mentally ran the checklist as he spoke, palms sweaty with angst. "All the hospital security video is bricked up, nothing from the surrounding area, but get this: there was DNA on the card. It was him."

O'Brien shrugged, pursing his lips. "He knows we already have that. He just wants us to be sure, so we know he's serious. It isn't like we can use it to find him."

Tim sipped, having already reached the same conclusion. "This is very unlike the previous Dantalion." O'Brien held up the bottle, brows raised in inquiry. He nodded watching, holding up his hand as the generous pour reached halfway. "Thanks."

O'Brien had another sip before speaking. "What do the behavioral unit think?"

"No idea. They're keeping me firewalled from everything to do with the investigation. I'm pretty sure they're watching me to see if Ericka pops up." A stab of anger. If she was alive, why the hell hadn't she let him know what was going on? "They never could get a read on this guy anyway."

O'Brien's gaze was intent. *He's analyzing me and I'm really bloody sick of being analyzed.* The lawyer guessed one of his worries. "They can't bug a DOJ office. What's said in here, stays in here."

Tim fought down a bark of sarcastic laughter, but no way he was spilling everything in here. "Where is she? Vanished for two years. Not a peep. Now we hear from this bastard." He cringed, realizing he'd let go some real heat in his tone. He hadn't meant to.

The lawyer's eyes narrowed, seeming unsurprised. "I'd be pissed with her too. You guys were close." He sighed, seeming lost for words for a moment. "There has to be a reason. She wouldn't put you through this, or that old aunt of yours for that matter."

Tim cringed at the pang of guilt. "I thought she was dead."

"We all did and she might still be, but something has led Dantalion to believe she isn't. That's worth something. You're not getting briefings, right?"

Tim looked away, teeth clenched in annoyance, but they had no idea why she went anyway. "Nothing—just rumors."

"That thing with the runaway drones is being attributed to Dantalion."

"I heard that much. He loves to play with other people's toys." The whole hacker community was agog at the accomplishment.

"But not loving how it ended, I'm thinking. Or who helped end it."

His guts tightened as he stared at O'Brien. "Yes?"

"Someone penetrated the Pakistani Air Force comms

system with a message from an unknown source telling them how to find the Reapers. No one knows who sent it, and no one's admitting they themselves did it."

It took him a moment to identify the emotion chilling his whole body. It was relief, a giant weight lifting from his thoughts. "So, is this any more complicated than he thinks it's her and wants us to get her off his back?"

O'Brien snorted with laughter before his expression became serious. "She can't contact you. For your own protection. Think about it. Any indication you're in touch and they'd string you up and hunt her down."

Tim looked away so O'Brien couldn't see his eyes. *Yes, but who cares. The whole FBI thing is going a little flat and it doesn't look like it's going to improve any time soon.* "I'm halfway strung up as it is. Kept on a very short leash."

"Where's the problem? The new boss?"

"She's the least of it. Used to run the local forensics lab in Seattle. NSA before that. She's all right." Someone well up the food chain from her was managing things on this. "They're treating the file more as a terrorism threat. That brings a whole different reporting structure that gets pretty murky the farther up you go."

O'Brien cradled his glass near his chest, almost cuddling it. "Are you having any luck deciphering the message?"

He locked eyes with O'Brien for several slow breaths. *I can't do this alone. I have to trust someone.* "It's not a message and no one else is even close as far as I know." He hesitated as the lawyer's eyes probed his. "What he wrote on the back of that card, it's something of a math riddle and the answer is a set of numbers, almost certainly a set of coordinates leading to a server."

"Have you told anyone?"

Tim rolled his eyes. "Do I look stupid? No."

"Okay."

He glared at the lawyer. "We need to go for a walk sometime soon."

A fleeting expression of annoyance crossed O'Brien's face. "The DOJ doesn't wiretap itself. We can talk."

He doesn't get it. This isn't his gig. "It's not you guys I'm worried about."

"Anyone else you willing to trust with this? Clarke? That expensive haircut from Homeland? Maxwell?"

Tim shook his head, squeezing his eyes shut for a few seconds. As soon as he brought others in, he lost control. Way too early for that. "Not at this point. Maybe Steiner if things progress."

"To try and draw a bead on Dantalion?"

Tim stuffed down the anger again. *Have faith in her. She had a reason.* "I think she might need Steiner's help."

O'Brien's eyebrows rose, his eyes wide. "She left me with the distinct impression she had no use for his help. And no use for him except for the entertainment she got from tormenting him. You know her views on shrinks."

Tim locked eyes with O'Brien. "Steiner's talked her off the ledge several times and given us the only useful profile on Dantalion since this started."

O'Brien's brow wrinkled, surprise all over his face. "Well then. Impressive. I had no idea. Let's have a chat with the good doctor."

5

Pied Piper

Calling the fog thick didn't do it justice. It was as if the ship existed in its own universe, surrounded by a narrow band of iron-hued water that faded into gray oblivion within a few meters. First lieutenant Liu Wei of the Chinese People's Armed Police Force Coast Guard Corps, or Haijing, had the night watch and was not enjoying his first shift in command of the Shuoshi II-class cutter, 2502. Like countless junior officers before him, he was finding out that making decisions was vastly different from watching more senior officers do it. Far more experienced crewmen manned the stations around him, eyes averted except for shared glances with each other, their contempt for his youth palpable.

He contented himself with staring out the front windows of the ship's bridge at the impenetrable wall of gray, back to his curt subordinates. The ship was twenty-nine nautical miles off the mouth of the Pearl River on an anti-smuggling patrol making under five knots, navigating only by satellites. Even at reduced efficiency, radar gave them the location of larger ships in the busy shipping lane, but smaller boats were lost in wave clutter. The bridge was warm, but he kept his jacket on rather than have the bridge crew see his sweat-stained shirt.

Wei turned to glare at the radar officer. "Target location, speed and position please?"

The woman spoke without looking up. "Same heading as before, holding twelve knots and closing on our position off the port bow."

Wei gritted his teeth at the breach of protocol in failing to use the correct honorific for his rank but chose to ignore it this time. "Turn to intercept, bring us to visual range, speed two-five knots."

The helmsman spoke without taking his eyes from the navigation screen, multiple targets showing within five nautical miles. "We should wake the captain."

Wei gritted his teeth at the insolence, not letting it go this time. "I will make that decision. Carry out my orders and address me in the appropriate manner."

The man paused, appearing to consider his options before deciding on compliance. "Yes, sir, steering to one-eight-five degrees, increasing to two-five knots."

Wei ignored the glances between bridge crew, settling into the captain's chair where he could see the navigation and targeting screens marking their target as they closed. Coordinates from the AIS, automatic identification system, should match their target's radar tracks, but they didn't. Their screen flashed red as the intercept distance closed to within the warning parameters of a proximity alert. He knew the speed he'd ordered bordered on reckless in this fog but was determined his first intercept in command would show the kind of aggression rewarded by his country's armed services.

Wei turned to the ship's communications station. "Try again." Then he listened as the crewman began hailing the ship.

The radar operator's voice rose in pitch as she spoke. "Getting clearer now, estimate two-hundred meters in length. Still no corresponding AIS." Had to be a smuggler running without the international automated system, which broadcast the ship's name, GPS, tonnage and course. *Locking onto him had just been blind luck. A smuggler for sure.*

Wei needed a look at what he was dealing with and to appear like he knew what he was doing. "Helm, bring us alongside and match their speed."

"Aye, sir, coming about."

As they approached, Wei pulled the heavy night binoculars from their cradle, opening the door to the outside deck where the heavy fog added heft to the stinging wind's slap to his face. The air lacked the crisp scent of open ocean, holding instead the heavier smell of coastal outflow, sullied with the mud and pollution of the nearby delta. He regretted failing to pull on a heavier coat but declined to face the embarrassment of running back inside shivering. He pressed his belly against the icy railing as he leaned into the fog, scanning for the target, cold radiating through his uniform and into his abdomen. There was nothing out there. He keyed his headset. "Range?"

The response time was acceptable this time, a mere moment's pause before the answer crackled in his headset. "Three hundred meters alongside to port."

Even in this soup he should be able to make out the shape of something that big, at least see the running lights. He could hear and feel the deep rhythmic throbbing of the target's propellers, like the ocean's heartbeat coming from all directions at once. Eyes watering from the wind, he squinted as the dark shape hove into view. "Pull in closer!"

"Sir?"

"I said closer."

"Yes, sir."

His stomach lurched as the ship's course changed, leaning the ship's hull. The hulking shape filled his field of vision and solidified, the blunt bow of an older freighter accompanied by the muted roar and hiss of its bow wake. "Search lights, look for a name!" He flinched, blinking tears as the powerful beams converged on the target. There it was, *Tasmin Clipper*. "Run that name."

The response took only seconds. The radar operator's tone was puzzled. "Sir, AIS shows that ship docked in Tokyo."

"What the hell do you think you are doing?" The roar came from the open door to the bridge. Captain Xiping leaned out, aroused from sleep, his uniform thrown on. "Idiot, you risk my ship playing games? Helm, back off and take up station five hundred meters to the target's stern. Follow them."

The voice of the helmsman sounded almost smug as he acknowledged the order before he was cut off by the radar operator. "Sir, now showing correct location for the target AIS matching our radar and a second ship close alongside the first, no AIS. Running close so the radar couldn't tell them apart."

What he'd just heard made absolutely no sense. Wei closed the door, taking care it would make no noise as he came back inside, standing behind the captain who was leaning over the radar station. The captain gave him a foul look that said there would be further discussion. "Follow the AIS for the original target and call in the other one for intercept. They were probably running close to give only one radar signature."

"Primary target now veering to port and increasing speed." The radar operator peered at the captain over her shoulder.

The captain glared at Wei again before issuing his orders, his voice rasping from a lifetime of cheap cigarettes. "Match speed and course, bring us to within two hundred meters of her stern." A finger rose, stabbing at Wei's chest. "And you are leading the boarding party. Break out the weapons, prepare a team. Move!"

Wei issued the orders, then strode into the locker area behind the bridge to don a survival suit and body armor. He returned to stand behind the captain, holstering a pistol as he did. "Ready, sir." He choked down his fear at the thought of clambering up boarding lines in these conditions. Any course change by the target's helm and they would all end up in the heaving water in near-zero visibility, perhaps caught by the ship's propellers.

The captain gave no sign of acknowledgment, his stare fixed on the helm and radar screens.

"She's veering to starboard again, now making one-nine knots."

Captain Xiping gestured to the radar operator, leaning towards the helmsman. Before he could say anything, the navigator spoke, a slight rise from his normal pitch giving an edge to his voice.

"She's making for a series of sand bars. At the current tide they're likely barely three meters down, dry in a few places."

Wei looked into Xiping's demanding gaze, answering the unspoken question. "Even lightly loaded, the target will draw eight to ten meters. Unless they know a way through, she's going to run aground."

Xiping pursed his lips before turning his attention back to the helm. "Back off and slow to fifteen knots. If they want to make it easy for us by running themselves aground, let's give them some room to do it." He glowered at the helmsman as he watched him work.

Wei walked to stand behind the radar operator. "Where is the second target?"

"Same heading, now making…" she paused, her forehead crinkling "…three-eight knots by the AIS. That can't be right." She worked her equipment, eyes never leaving the screen, a brief sigh before she spoke again. "There's something wrong. Now showing a partial AIS and a speed of four-five knots. No radar signature at all. There is no way."

Wei studied the screen, the pit of his stomach signaling danger where none was apparent. "Captain, we may have an equipment malfunction. That speed's not possible. Recommend we call for an aerial asset to track the second ship."

Xiping's brows went up, his lips curling in a sneer. "Don't talk nonsense. In this soup? What good will air support do?" He appeared to think for a few moments. "What kind of malfunction?"

Before Wei could answer, the radar operator interjected. "The primary target is through the sand bars, maintaining one-eight knots."

She was followed by the navigator. "Confirmed, their position is past the charted hazard."

Wei watched the captain's hands clench into fists. "Flank speed in pursuit, follow his track exactly. They draw more water than we do. These fucking smugglers know every hole between sandbars and rocks." He stood with clenched teeth as the captain turned to him and barked his orders. "Get on deck and stand by to board."

"Aye, sir." He took one more glance at the nav screen, showing their ship making over twenty knots, no more than one hundred meters from the marked hazard. He wasn't halfway down the gangway when the hull rumbled with a low grinding sound, throwing him into the bulkhead, causing him to cling to the railing. The shuddering stopped and the lights went out for long seconds before batteries took over. The engines had stopped, they'd run aground. He took the stairs back to the bridge, two steps at a time.

The captain's roar filled the bridge. "Idiot, what have you done?" Xiping stood over the helmsman who was on one knee holding his forehead, bright blood oozing between fingers. The smear on the console's edge made it clear where he'd hit it.

The man struggled to gather himself as he drew erect. "Sir, I followed the target's course exactly."

"Idiots!" Xiping activated his mic. "All hands, damage and casualty reports, see if we are holed." He glared at Wei. "What are you looking at? Get below and make yourself useful!"

Wei was leaning in behind the radar operator who was trying to staunch a bloody nose as she worked. "We need to call in the targets and get other ships in front of them." Xiping waved him off, nodding his consent. Wei turned back to the screen, reading the speed and heading from the target's AIS when it vanished.

The operator's eyes widened, and she shot him a puzzled

glance while she worked. "I can't get the primary target on radar either. It's gone."

Wei rubbed his shoulder where it had impacted the bulkhead. "The radar may be damaged from the impact. Can you give me a read on the second target?"

Practiced hands flew over the controls while blood dripped from her nose, leaving crimson streaks on her sweat-stained white shirt. "There." She gestured at the screen with her chin. He read the numbers, seeing the second target was now displaying AIS numbers showing it moving away at an impossible seventy-five knots. Her eyes bugged wide as she turned to him. The target vanished, the screen was empty.

He squeezed his eyes shut in frustration. "Not your fault—the radar's obviously damaged."

She shook her head. "None of that came from our radar. All of that was from the AIS uplink. Something has gone very wrong. I think somebody is manipulating it."

Wei stood erect, thinking through the implications. "Explain?"

"This isn't the first time this has happened. Something is making our ability to track targets at close range unreliable. This isn't the first time."

The room was characteristically dark except for his screens. He sighed and leaned back, leaving the enhanced reality set on, eyes covered, tension in his shoulders forcing him to hunch. The shipment was through the coast guard perimeter and would be unloaded into smaller boats over the next few hours. From there, it would disappear into the immense warrens of China's markets. No one had told him of the cargo and he hadn't been interested enough to ask. His task was to ensure his client's ship wasn't boarded. He didn't care what they were smuggling, and they didn't care how he cleared a path through the increasingly tight cordon the People's Republic threw up around the coast.

He allowed himself a smile. Evading was one thing. Getting the Chinese coast guard to follow a ghost onto a sand bar was downright funny, like a dark-web Pied Piper leading digital rodents over a cliff. The reports said the warship was still there awaiting both a larger tugboat and a higher tide to float them free. The thought of the many heads that would roll was pleasant and relaxing. *Stupid people should be made to understand they're stupid, then pay a price for it.* When it came to a choice between trusting their own senses and a data feed, people made the wrong choice time and again. *You can only trust the data if the data is trustworthy, and you can't tell if it is or isn't. That's what eyes and brains are for.* So much of the world lived in this overlap of the digital and physical realms that doing what he did was sometimes almost too easy.

Despite the final outcome, his benefactors had been impressed with his hijacking of the American drones. He was pleased they were impressed but couldn't bear to think about it, suffering a searing jab of shame to the guts every time it came to mind. This would reassure any doubters of his ability, but it came at a price. It was a two-way street and a delicate equilibrium. With every intelligence agency in the world baying in pursuit, he needed the cover the criminal organizations provided him. He needed to be skillful enough to be indispensable while posing no threat to the leadership and their heirs. His days of melting into the shadows were finished. Pakistan was unfinished business that would have to wait for now.

His communique to his client sent, he pulled off his headset, running his hand along the ridges of scar tissue crisscrossing his scalp, his face tightening into a scowl. Involuntarily, he glanced down at his wasted legs, an ever-present reminder of the great betrayal that had torn him from the path that had been his—from his rightful place, made him an object of derision. The people who had cost him tasked his days with a blistering hate he couldn't contain, even though his old partner, Bromwich, was now several years in the ground. His former wife, Claire, would follow in time, but before then he wanted her fear to age and mature, become part of her every waking moment, pollute her dreams. Fear the slightest sound, panic every time she stepped out, dread every face, never knowing if it was the last she would see. Then on to the final act, his legacy.

If he was being truthful with himself, the vicious hate and volcanic anger had always been there. What she and her lover had done was to remove the slightest inclination for him to control it. *Why the hell should I? Look what happened to me!* He'd always known he was better, smarter, entitled to the adoring compliance of women. All lost now—the company, the prestige, the status, the burning humiliation of being less than he was, less than he was entitled to be. Bromwich had no idea how lucky being dead made him. He'd been far too hasty using his Porsche to push Bromwich's Ferrari into the ditch. The resulting disfiguring accident, the years of paralysis were something his bitch of a wife would pay for and it would not be quick. That he had betrayed her in the same manner starting the week after their wedding never entered his mind.

A man of his caliber had certain entitlements, and she'd been very lucky to have him. Existence as an adjunct to him was all she deserved. He could have had any woman he wanted. *Bitch!*

He leaned back, reaching for his water, the first sips a balm to his dry throat. When on the hunt, he forgot all else, consumed by lust for his chosen target, his prey. He would need to call for some food too, then perhaps a few hours' sleep before some entertainment. Best to be fresh for that.

Truth be told, Claire had released him. When the time finally came, he would tell her, regale her with the tale of how her treachery had allowed him, forced him, to be truthful to himself, what he had done since. The psychological profiles written about him were very funny, though his real reason for stealing them was he couldn't bear to leave anything written about him unread. The narcissist label was almost laughable. What else could he be? A childhood trauma of some great magnitude they suspected. They had it dead wrong. The incandescent anger, the lust to see pain, and thrill to another's terror had been there since childhood. It had always been there. He couldn't remember a time without it. Fantasizing about it was often the only way he could sleep.

As a boy he had giggled at the part of the movie supposed to bring gasps of horror. His ferocity had won him fights as a teenager, pulled off victorious by onlookers while he was fantasizing about tearing at the facial features of his defeated foe with his teeth. Losing was never possible. A lost fistfight with a large high school football player ended at night a week later with him driving up on the sidewalk in a stolen car, his erstwhile opponent suffering in hospital for many months, giggling every time he envisioned Anderson's body tumbling over the hood into the ditch.

Yes, he was content and whole now, but Claire would still pay at a time of his choosing. His current career would be brief but spectacular. He'd known that since conceiving the digital hijacking of a passenger plane—a one-way trip. Now his reputation was secure, he was free to do whatever he liked, see just what he could do, knowing the end was already written, work on a legacy for after he was gone. He looked down again at his legs, this time without the stab of anger that had always brought. Things were changing and the final act of the play was about to begin. He would write it. The future was his. *Not long now.*

6

White Rabbit

Ericka's eyes snapped open but it was some time before full awareness returned. The combination of pills carried a price, dreamless slumber purchased at the cost of mental clarity. Worth any price to stop the dreams, seeing it again, recollections altered by her sleeping mind and blended with a lifetime's memories, events scrambled into an unintelligible blend fueled by waking guilt. Her compulsive habit, bordering on addiction, was the only defense against the constant threat to sanity. That wasn't working out so well. Jolted awake, she rubbed her eyes and the dam burst, bringing an icy flood of perception. She drew a full breath, tightening the sheets knotted around her chest, the sounds of the city flooding her mind as if someone had turned on a television at high volume.

The windows were dark but the ubiquitous rumble of life in the great metropolis was constant. Despite the valiant efforts of the Mexican government, the air in the capital city remained thick with soot, foul enough she kept a small herd of air filters constantly on duty. Originally planned as a safe house if the second hit all went wrong, it was now a permanent abode, a small suite above a warehouse and tiny grocery store. Her deal with the shop owner for the suite included groceries in exchange for rent at almost double the market. That no questions would be asked was presumed in a place where secrecy could be enforced by very direct means. After she was set up, she'd led her landlord to believe she was fleeing a violent husband who would not thank him for concealing her.

She could have everything delivered and never go outside, but she didn't. Her swarthy complexion and dark hair allowed her some freedom in her neighborhood of exile. She spoke the language without accent, walking only in places where she was sure she wouldn't be recorded, hats, sunglasses and twilight outings a hedge against unseen cameras. One image clear enough for facial recognition and she was done. Ericka had no doubt Clearview would have been deployed against her by her old employer. This technology matched photos of a wanted subject against a gigantic database scoured from the clear web and social media. Any tourist or kid taking a selfie and posting it publicly and they could have her.

Ericka swung her feet to the floor, holding still for a moment against the dizziness, her empty stomach cramping. She pushed herself to stand for a few wobbly seconds, biting her lower lip, knowing the toll exacted by her habit, or—let's face it—addiction. It wasn't like it was her first battle with substance abuse. *I should be better than this.*

She fell hard into the chair, almost spilling her coffee, staring at the several monitors arrayed in front of her. Her work area carried the blended odor of sweat, spilled food and sticky fear. She was losing this fight. There was no way she could outmatch her adversary like this, brain half addled and without a fraction of the resources she'd once commanded. Haring off like that had proven a terrible mistake with Dantalion still on the loose. She should've stayed. He'd gotten into her head and she was only now beginning to understand just how far, how deep. She'd always fantasized about finding Patty's attackers and what she would do, but he'd made it real, shown her how to wield the power to do it. She'd walked into the trap like a half-starved rat, taking revenge her sister would never have approved.

Back now to questioning herself about the Spokane incident. It had been easy to tell herself after the fact she hadn't meant to kill, just a lash of anger. Maybe she hadn't, but there was no stretching the truth to herself that could erase the savage thrill that had coursed through her as she watched the handcuffed child molester tumbling down the stairs. Had guilt and revulsion rewritten memories to something she could live with? Were her memories real?

Sweat tickled her neck, converging into a rivulet between her shoulder blades, her head leaning forward to stare at clutched hands. All that time telling herself it wasn't actually the real her and she'd done it again, not once but twice. Pushed far enough, it really was her. There was no denying it. She'd lacked the courage to withstand the anguish, then let that evil bastard fan the flames, a fleeting kind of madness. What was it about Dantalion that he could spot the flaws and weaknesses, filling gaping voids in someone's character with his own desires?

The sun would be down in an hour. If she were going to get out in the light, it would have to be soon. Always business first, Ericka toggled through the day's surveillance, scanning items flagged by her crawlers. She saw several segments of traffic likely his, all encrypted beyond her current resources to pierce. He was out there, active now, but where and what he was doing would elude everything she had at her disposal. She'd only tracked him to his lair the one time due to a slip he'd made and the enormous resources of the US government. *What kind of arrogance made me think I could take him down from here, alone?*

Time for a shower to get rid of this horrible sticky feeling. She started to stand, then stopped, unable to resist. She brought up streams of several webcams of home, images of her old life, imagining one day she would see Mrs. Donnelly or Tim in a grocery store security cam. On public webcams, people went about their business, oblivious to her attention. More longing, without consolation. She could never go back. Ericka clenched her teeth against the sigh, forcing herself to power down the monitor. No way forward, no way back, caught in a trap of her own making. Self-pity was eating into her, consuming her, dissolving her focus.

Toxic stuff even when you knew you were doing it.

"Can it really be that simple?" Special Agent Sheila Clarke looked puzzled as she stared at Tim. She leaned across the table, laptop turned so he could peer at her work. A half-eaten sandwich lay within arm's reach next to a paper cup of cold coffee.

Tim's instincts wouldn't allow him to believe it. "No, I expect it isn't. He wanted to make absolutely sure we got this far, but what we find there, who knows?" He was more worried about what they were missing, having cracked the code himself and come to the same solution two days before.

He picked up the exhibit bag holding the business card now stained and missing clipped notches where material had been removed for forensic testing.

New wrinkles encircled Clarke's pale eyes, an unfortunate legacy of the last two years at the bureau. Her clothes were crumpled as if she'd worked all day without moving. The untidy workstation was set up away from other analysts using the same room, all gone for the day now. "It wasn't even that hard. Any computer science grad student could have solved it given time and a fast enough computer. If this does lead us to her, how can we avoid reporting up? Others are going to figure it out. If they haven't already. The brass will wonder why we didn't."

Tim had been waiting for that exact question since Clarke's text telling him they needed to speak. She was no fool. She'd obviously duplicated his earlier work, results he'd stored on a secure thumb drive so they couldn't be found on any searches or audits. *Say it.* "Maybe this is a trail we don't want to follow right now." Her brows shot up. She was by the book, this one. "I'm not asking you to hide anything, but you can't hide what you don't know."

He let that sink in, seeing her eyes narrow, a slight clench of her jaw. She wasn't liking what she was hearing. "What are you suggesting? We're not the only ones working on this."

Choose your words very carefully. She'd been Ericka's protégée, even bent the rules a little, but that's a long way from concealing information about an agent most believed had gone rogue, if she wasn't dead. That was career-ending stuff, or worse. "I'm suggesting we consider all our options before we create something we're obliged to report. We have every justification for caution. This might be a lead to her. It could just as easily be a trap. Remember who we're dealing with."

Clarke shook her head before puffing out a small sigh through pursed lips. "He probably wants us to find her so she's no threat to him. Why did he do this? She must have done something that scared him. I think she's alive."

That was exactly what Tim thought as well, but this had to be played in a way that Clarke could continue with defensibly, without professional jeopardy. His continued career hung in the balance too. "We need to separate what we think from what we know. We don't know if she's even alive. We have no evidence she is or isn't. All we have is a short conversation with this bastard while I'm drugged up and a scribbled, half-assed math riddle that seems to point to a server farm in Pakistan. The balance of the math could be the key to a decryption algorithm. Yes?"

Clarke was studying his features, *looking for the lie.* "Sure, but that's not what I think. What other possible reason could he have for communicating with us if it doesn't have to do with her? He's left something on a server he wants us to see."

Time to speak plainly. "Granted, but our well-reasoned conjecture isn't something that obliges us to report to Shingen."

Tim watched as Clarke's features set, eyes hard. "Isn't it? Dantalion himself tells you it's to find her, and the next step in his little hide-and-seek leads us to Pakistan, a place chosen by him for his first serious escapade in two years, one that is ultimately unsuccessful, thwarted by information from a source unknown to us. Sound like anyone you know?"

Clarke wasn't biting. She wasn't stupid. *Go for broke—no choice now.* Tim's voice cracked as he said it. "If it's going to lead to Ericka, I would really like to get to her first. Assess the situation. Make sure the first thing she gets is help."

That drew a short laugh. "Shingen will have our asses for doormats. Look where this cowboy shit of Ericka's has got us!" SAC Hikari Shingen, the new unit commander, kept a much closer eye on things than her predecessor Abara ever had, with good reason. Tim grimaced, catching Clarke's eye as she read his expression. Her gaze probed him. "You knew her best. Did she play us as well?"

Tim turned his chair, unable to meet the look, a question he'd struggled with since she'd disappeared. *Had she indeed?* His gut said no, something was wrong; his analytical skill set screamed the opposite. He chose the comfort of blind faith over pain supported by evidence. "I don't think so."

Clarke shook her head, toying with her mouse. "None of this makes any sense. Dantalion, here on US soil, just to give us a handwritten puzzle scribbled on the back of a fake business card. He could have sent his little puzzle to us from anywhere without the risk. This is way out of character."

The same thought had galled Tim since that night. "I don't think he knew I was going to be there. I think whatever this is, he hatched it on the fly. That's why the riddle was so simple. He was there for another reason."

Shaking her head in disbelief, Clarke raised her voice. "That makes no sense. What are the odds? All the hospitals in the world and he shows up at the one you're in on one of the four nights you're there. Then why is he there? Nothing in the hospital records. He wasn't there for lipo' or a chin cleft or anything. If he just wanted to steal something, he'd use a flunky."

"I know, not like him at all." *She's right, Dantalion had known and was playing games.* Tim turned at the scuffing of shoe leather on linoleum.

Dr. Claus Steiner, company shrink and counsellor to Ericka, stood just inside the doorway. "If you are speaking about Dantalion, I agree and there may be a reason for it. May I?" He pointed to a chair, eyebrows raised.

Tim looked down the hall past the open door. *No one else there.* "We were having a private conversation."

Steiner sighed as he settled into the chair, folding linked fingers over his belly, as usual wearing an overworn suit too tight for a man his size. "My apologies, but it's necessary that I intrude on it."

Brow furrowed with irritation, Tim glared at him. "Were you listening?"

Steiner held his palms towards Tim. "Not intentionally, but I heard some of it as I approached, yes. Most people go somewhere private if they want to have a private conversation."

Tim clenched his teeth in annoyance, opening his mouth to ask him to leave when Clarke grasped his wrist, making eye contact, shaking her head. This wasn't going to work if too many people knew, too dangerous, but he was here now. Best to hear him out. "What's on your mind, doctor?"

"Many things, first Dantalion, then I would like to speak about Ericka." He paused, but Tim said nothing. "Given what has happened, don't expect your quarry to act as he did before. After the events of two years ago, his psychopathy will have progressed, taking him down different roads."

Tim and Ericka had always maintained a healthy skepticism

of profilers. He had seen Ericka warm to Steiner's thinking but remained dubious himself. "Like?"

"His ability to completely hide in the dark was lost with the hijacking. He will be pulled now between the sadist's desire to see continued fear and pain and a wanting to feed the narcissist's insatiable need for heightened grandiosity. He will be closely following every time his exploits appear in the news or intelligence reports. He has a substantial following, a fan base if you will, in the underworld."

Fair enough, he's got that right. Tim gestured for him to continue. "What does that give us in terms of predictability? The man who came into my room was in a wheelchair. Just before I passed out in São Paulo, a man in a wheelchair took off in the elevator with Ericka pounding the doors. You knew that?"

Steiner smiled. "I did. Up until the hijacking all his violent crimes were through a proxy. Stealing the plane in flight was him directly. His coming out? His return? Stepping back onto the stage, as it were, after his injuries. To his thinking, he now steps back into the limelight of entitlement, returning to the attention he thinks he deserves. He will no longer be content with private violence where no one sees his dominance." Steiner paused before continuing, pitch elevated as if nervous straying from his assigned role. "His need for grandiosity takes the forefront in his thinking, particularly since his enormous intelligence tells him capture or death are now inevitable as resources are brought to bear on him. He will take more risks now, increasing all the time, seeing the inevitable end but always wanting one more notch in his belt."

Clarke stared, eyes narrowed as if intrigued. "Yes, I see that. But what was he doing in the hospital then?"

Steiner shrugged, lips compressed in a flat line. "Perhaps he has a medical issue?"

Tim snorted. "Yes, that's one way to put it. We've obviously followed up every patient, all check out."

Steiner was smiling now. "Not everything that happens in a hospital ends up in a record or stays there. I imagine all the security video was put beyond use?" Clarke raised her eyebrows and Steiner continued. "Doesn't that imply he had some purpose there? I'm not technical, but don't you have to plan these things?"

Tim glanced at Clarke. *He's got a point.* Dantalion took the time to get into the security system so he must care enough to leave no record of something happening in there. He shifted his gaze to Clarke. "We perhaps need to concentrate on what isn't there, rather than what is?" She flopped back in her seat to look at the ceiling, appearing lost in thought.

Steiner wasn't finished. "And now to Ericka if I may?" Tim gestured to him to continue. "Without a body, I will not presume her dead. I do think there is reason to believe she has suffered something of a breakdown, perhaps a reactive psychosis. Given my role and reporting obligations, she would never open up to me fully, but it was clear to me terrible past trauma augmented by her experience here at the bureau left her in an extremely vulnerable state. Without violating any confidences, does this ring true to you?"

Just how much has he guessed? Ericka had said she'd underestimated Steiner. "It's certainly possible, yes, but she's a lot stronger than you credit her for."

Steiner flushed a brighter shade of pink, holding up a hand, shaking his head. "I have rarely met anyone stronger, but no one's fortitude is endless. If she has suffered a psychotic break of some sort, delusions are common. Rational decision-making may not be possible for her just now."

Tim controlled his expression, not at all sure he trusted him. He seemed sincere but he had no idea how long Steiner's resolve would last if things heated up. "What do you propose?"

Steiner rubbed his chin, nibbling his lower lip. "That depends on what we are willing to risk. If she's alive, she needs help or we would have heard from her. This is self-evident, yes?"

Tim had other ideas. "What if she has a plan and just doesn't want to risk us if it goes sideways?"

Steiner shook his head. "Possibly, but just because she thinks she can do something alone doesn't mean she can."

Clarke raised a finger to interject, giving Tim a look to shut him up. "What do you propose, doctor?"

"If you are going to find her before someone else does, I will need to speak to her and determine her condition."

Tim tried to picture it and couldn't suppress the smile. "Doctor, you don't have much field experience."

Clarke chuckled, but Steiner didn't flinch, his face studied neutrality. "Perhaps we can borrow from our opponent. He seems to manage. Can you reverse-engineer it?" He pointed at the collection of VR headsets on their workbench.

Clarke looked downcast, appearing almost embarrassed as she always did when admitting something was beyond her ability. "Partially—we can certainly do a secure VR conversation with facial mapping, if not with his bells and whistles."

Steiner smiled as Tim chuckled to himself. "Will it work?"

Tim shrugged. "Not if we don't try."

7

A Question of Honor

Hamza made sure he was alone in the house before taking his treasure from below the floorboards of his bedroom. He satisfied himself that his parents would not return—he did not expect them for hours—before powering up his prized gaming VR set and connecting it to the satellite Wi-Fi of their wealthy neighbors. At seventeen he was almost a man and chafed at the restrictions placed on him by his rigid, traditional parents. Anything to have the freedom to do as he liked without having to defer to the staid traditions of his forebears. His VR connection to the world was his way to wander outside the confines of Pakistan and his parents' rigid boundaries.

It was not his only break with tradition. He smiled at the memory of Sanaya's dark-eyed beauty, their moments together, chilled by the consequences of their illicit union. No fear tonight, she was safe in her home—the picture of innocent chastity expected of her. His father's position in the country's intelligence service was respectable, but far beneath the station of his love, his ethnicity beneath her family's contempt. So far apart that she would be in real danger from her father if he knew.

Hamza pulled on the Oculus headset, holding down the power button until the maker's corporate logo appeared, waiting until the unit placed him in the lifelike penthouse apartment he'd chosen as his home environment. The view of Los Angeles was startling, realistic. He relaxed, sinking into the soft wool blanket covering his unseen chair, leaning back, moving his hands until the controllers appeared in virtual form, hands accurately portrayed, capturing and rendering the movements of each finger. He licked his lips as he pondered his choices, a virtual Tokyo dance floor, beautiful girls in club dresses dancing close or perhaps a racing game, a difficult choice between competing young male fantasies.

The nightclub it was. The canned three-sixty scene began with being led by the virtual hand past an interminable queue, young women at the bar giving him interested glances before abandoning their drinks and turning to follow. Then it went black, all sound lost. He tore off the headset. *Shit, I'm busted.* His heartbeat fell to normal. His room was empty, the house silent. He stood sticking his head into the hallway, no sign of his parents. His phone showed the pilfered Wi-Fi was strong. He turned the VR set around, seeing the LED's glow. He rubbed his nose, staring at them. *It can only be a network outage.*

He could barely hear the words from the headset speakers. "Hamza." Mouth open, he stared at his rig, dumbfounded. "Hamza, you must listen to me." He could see the screens were glowing now so he tugged it back on, securing the headphones before opening his eyes.

Hamza stood open-mouthed in a raging sandstorm, fighting

for balance, hands out in front of him. Swirling browns and yellows clearing for seconds gave him glimpses of jagged rock as if he stood in a shallow gully. The wind's roar was like a waterfall, punctuated by percussive gusts like drumbeats. Sand churned and eddied around sandaled feet not his. A hint of movement to his right and he sucked in breath as he spun to stare.

This was good, very good. The apparition stood just out of arm's reach, hooded, robed like a desert tribesman, features obscured. He flinched as a gust blew across hidden features, darkness gone, replaced by the face of death, skeletal features, tatters of desiccated flesh fluttering in the wind. His nose wrinkled at the imagined smell before the wind subsided, leaving the hooded face obscured in shadow. He was smiling now. This was excellent, an immersive environment and a jinni so lifelike it drew a visceral reaction deep in his guts. Lifelike, ha! A monster was drawn from his Arabian heritage, but his family had moved generations ago. Who knew and cared enough to create this?

He spoke in Urdu, voice muffled by the wind. "This is great, but I'm a little old for genies."

The wind rose, bringing a longer glimpse of death's visage, a grinning mouth, the voice a rich baritone, timbered like a mullah preaching, words in English. "You may think so, Hamza Bukhari, but for you it could not be more real."

Safe in the knowledge he was in his bedroom, he snorted his derision. "Then show me—cast your spell, whoever you are." Apprehension tempered bravado. The specter knew his name and that he had a VR rig. That alone was more trouble than he wished to contemplate.

"You may call me Dantalion. Time now to show you where illusion ends and reality begins."

More forced bravado. "Do it!"

The change was abrupt. He stood in a rocky valley, the sun near the horizon, dawn judging by the clarity of the air before the day's heat raised dust. The ground was a mixed collection of small, sharp stones and sand. A group of tribesmen stood in a semicircle, throwing stones at something in front of them he couldn't see. A hand from the man with the camera rose and settled on the shoulder of one of the men, moving him so he could pass. The one-eighty view created a fisheye look, but the center was all too clear.

Buried to her shoulders, arms pinned to her sides by earth, was a young girl no more than sixteen or seventeen. Her head lolled to the side, her once beautiful features bloodied and crushed, mercifully on the edge of consciousness. Tears jetted in his eyes, obscuring his vision, his mouth now dry. Bound by sheer horror, he stared as another stone struck the delicate features, the impact sending up a spurt of blood, adding to the small puddles scattered around her. Her head flopped onto her chest, a lifeless doll.

A rasping voice growled from behind him. "Enough! For honor's sake her father must finish it. Only then is dishonor purged."

A man stepped forward, muttering prayers, clutching a huge stone. His anguished cry echoed from the rocks, "*Allahu Akbar!*" and he struck. Hamza barely made out the impact, but the sound of stone on meat was agonizing. The camera moved forward, focused at his feet. The man closest to his left squatted, reaching for the head, turning it over by the hair. The bloodied features shimmered, blurred for a barely perceived moment and Sanaya's dead eyes stared into his.

Hamza tore the headset off just as the contents of his stomach exploded from him, striking the wall and fouling the carpet. He bent over, retching as he inhaled the rancid stench, unable to see through the flood of tears. Breaths came in long, shuddering gasps.

The voice rose again from the discarded headset. "Hamza. It is time now for you to listen very carefully to me."

Uncontrollable sobs took him, his body racked, childlike sounds rising unbidden, forming in his throat. *No choice, none at all.* This monster knew, and the knowledge was enough to make it come true. He pulled the goggles back on and the jinni stood before him, a wraith half seen through blowing sands. "Do you wish to mock me further?"

Hamza shook his head, staring at the monster's feet. "Was it real? Who?"

The tone was stern, condescending. "Don't be a child, you know that it was. She died a few months past and now lies in an unmarked grave, food for worms."

He forced the words. "Sanaya is alive!"

That brought a short chuckle just as the gust faded, features retreating into shadow. "She looked like it to me when I observed her a few moments ago. Playing with her fat, orange cat."

Hamza's stomach knotted. *This fucking monster knew who she was and where to find her.* "Then what was the shit you just showed me?"

There was a pause before he answered. "Something I participated in for entertainment. I merely changed it ever so slightly to give you a view of what might be, what will be unless I have your unstinting cooperation. Her father, after all, prides himself as a man of honor."

"Never!"

"So sure are you? Then why does she tell you in her messages how she fears him, how he can never know about you? A girl's fantasy of running away to another life."

He pictured Sanaya's father in his mind, chiseled features cloaked by a full beard, fierce eyes, expression always harsh as if he lived to find things to be angry about, to force him to righteous action. Hamza had only ever seen him at the mosque. If he had ever smiled, his features recorded no trace of it. "Why would you do that to her, to me? What did we do to you?"

The jinni's voice was rich with restrained fury, dripping contempt. "I would do it for the pleasure it would give me, but my silence can be bought, though I'm afraid my price is rather dear."

The monster had him. There was no way out. "Tell me what I must do."

A sigh of satisfaction accompanied a step forward and now he could see the crusted remnants of eyelids draped over empty sockets. "Your father is a member of the intelligence service."

It was not a question, but the compulsion to answer was irresistible. "Yes." He couldn't suppress the tremor in his voice.

"My offer is one great betrayal to avoid another. Many days, your father brings a computer home from work. In three days' time, you will receive something from me. Where you and Sanaya last met, taped to the underside of the same bench. Your task is simple. When you are sure your father will not return for at least an hour, plug it into his computer and switch it on. Then you must burn what I send you so only ashes remain."

"He locks it up." *How does he know all this?* It was as if he looked on the world through the eyes of the divine, or a demon.

"You appear to me to be a resourceful child. Do you need to view the consequences of failure again?"

His shoulders sagged as the contents of his stomach rose into the back of his throat a second time. "I'll find a way."

"See that you do. You have fourteen days from today. If you succeed, you will never hear from me again. Failure will bring my undivided attention." The wind rose to a higher pitch, obscuring his vision. When the surge abated, the apparition was gone leaving only blowing sand and rock, its sound a keening dirge.

Agent Yusef Abidi's dark eyes never left his screen, left hand tugging his close-cropped beard as he thought. What was it in Pakistan that had riveted this one's attention? First the drones, now he is hacking into servers all over the country, leaving almost no traces and where he did, his work defied all efforts at decryption. American intelligence spoke of a previous association with jihadis and some apparent fascination with them, but that wasn't what he was doing now. He reached for his tea, the spiced blend filling his nostrils, then leaned back. This Dantalion, Mr. Frank London, was placing relay points all over, capable of ensuring he had almost full use of servers when he wanted. Far more bandwidth than required even for something as hungry as high-resolution gaming. *Gaming of a different sort perhaps.*

He leaned forward to scribble some notes, clenching his teeth as he did so. Tracing him back to his lair wasn't possible. Intercepting the traffic was far beyond the capability of his agency and—he was quite confident—anyone else's. The Americans believed he was in China anyway, beyond the reach of even their vaunted special forces. Why the Chinese hadn't dealt with him was itself an interesting question, doubtless having to do with the right allies to hide him and profit sharing to avoid someone taking a real interest. There was no help for it. Until the target made his move, telegraphing intent, there was nothing to do but wait and watch.

He wasn't the only one. Crawler activity was high, some of it penetrating beyond the public-facing portion of local servers and networks. Almost certainly the Americans and likely the French were looking at the same activity he was. Dantalion's willingness to help jihadis made the Israelis very nervous so Mossad, too, was likely on the prowl. *Everyone was watching.*

"It was never going to be that easy." Clarke looked over her shoulder at Tim, gesturing with her chin at the strings of numbers and code symbols filling her screen. "You were right; it was a decryption key and the data block opened, but what's inside makes no sense at all." She tapped a pen on her chin, shaking her head.

Tim's shoulders dropped a notch, almost relieved. "So, nothing you feel obliged to report up?"

Clarke rolled her eyes as she turned to glare at him. "We

don't need to keep going around on this. I'm with you. Unless we find something in his data that gives us a shot at him, or they actually issue a warrant for her, I'm good to keep going." She pivoted back to her monitors, speaking without facing him. "You might try trusting our new SAC. She's all about loyalty and the team. I think she'll be all over getting Ericka back, if only because she'll always be our best shot at getting this bastard."

Tim dropped into a chair beside Clarke, avoiding eye contact. No one in the FBI would support having Ericka back, except in a cell, if they knew where Tim believed her to have gone, but only he and O'Brien knew that. Maybe it was worth a shot. All bullshit if they couldn't make sense of this jumble of numbers that he'd fed them. Why would he make it so easy to get this far and then leave them hanging? Or had he?

A thought crossed his mind as he scanned the lines of code, nearly dropping him to the floor. Controlling his breathing, he leaned forward to peer over Clarke's shoulder, mouthing his conclusion to himself. *Yes, it could be. The pattern was right.*

Clarke turned to glare at him. "Do you mind? I'm not your type and the old heavy breathing on the shoulder trick doesn't work on me anyway." She paused before smiling and gesturing as if shooing off an irritating pet.

Tim smiled back at her, knowing Clarke's wife had little fear of him. "Everyone's my type, Sheila love, but I'm going to head out. See you tomorrow."

She was eyeing him, eyes slitted with suspicion. "What?"

He could barely repress the idiot smile, wanting to babble like an excited child, but this had to wait. It wouldn't be long before she figured it out herself and she might not be willing to hang on to it. He had to be sure, move now if he was right. "You just blew me off so I'm off to call on my second choice."

She rolled her eyes and turned away with a dismissive gesture. "Shingen's going to want a briefing soon. Better think about what lies you're going to tell her about why we haven't cracked this." She spun her chair to look but he was gone.

"Jesus! You look like you've been up all night." O'Brien didn't look surprised. Someone must have told him on the way in that Tim was camped in his office—nothing remarkable about FBI agents coming and going at the DOJ. He watched as the rotund lawyer fiddled, unpacking his briefcase, all but glowing in the early morning light pouring through the window. Tim didn't try to control the smile. Carrying a briefcase in and out of the office was good for image, but from what he could see everything inside it was edible.

He couldn't resist. "Wow, never seen a Maxwell-Scott lunch kit before."

O'Brien had a hide like a rhino, showing not the slightest reaction to the barb. "Food for thought. Just what you need when you make your living doing everyone's thinking for them." He sunk into his chair and leaned back. "You signed in downstairs at 6:14 AM. Something on your mind?"

"I've cracked it."

O'Brien drew in a long breath through his nostrils before leaning over to shut his office door, glancing into the hallway as he did. "Who else knows?"

"No one, but it won't be long before someone else figures it out." He tugged his computer from its case, setting it up on the desk's corner where both could see it. "He made it just hard enough so any idiot who found it couldn't do this, but not so hard it would stump us. This is a message directed at us."

O'Brien's expression changed, the jovial façade gone, replaced with cold stone. "Before you go any further, let's have a chat. We'll call everything that happens in here today privileged legal advice, but that's not going to save your ass if you're sitting on something you have an obligation to hand over. Everyone wants this guy, like nothing I've ever seen. With good reason."

Tim's voice rose as he spoke. "Nothing in this gives us him. You're her friend. You and I are the only ones she's ever trusted." The flash of anger surprised him.

The lawyer held up his hand, shaking his head, unperturbed. "I'm not worried about my own ass. I've lost the stomach for this place anyway." He leaned forward. "What I mean is this might be the only chance we have to get her back. If I'm sacked and you're in jail, she's got nothing. We have to handle this carefully, consider our moves."

Tim found he was holding his breath. It had never crossed his mind there was a way back for her. A muddy plan to find her and get her to help was as far as he'd gotten. "I'm listening."

O'Brien rested his hands on his belly. "The way you sell something to the sweaty herd of nervous suits upstairs is to convince them that what you're proposing solves a bunch of their problems. It's all they care about. Sorry to be blunt, but problem one for them is they have no one else who can touch Dantalion. When Ericka went over the wall, the FBI's collective IQ dropped measurably. She's their best shot."

He was waiting for Tim to react. *Don't give it to him.* "No two ways about that. Keep going."

"Nothing harder on an organization than someone going rogue. Everyone wears that. No one's ever announced she's gone. That's the main reason there's no warrant. If she's back, no one ever has to know. Move along, nothing to see here. Ericka gets put out to pasture, the minute this bastard is in the bag."

Brilliant, he'd never dared hope. "She might not be the same Ericka. Steiner reckons she could be in pretty rough shape."

O'Brien shrugged. "A problem for another day. First, we lay the groundwork, an immunity agreement for whatever the hell they think they can prove she's done in exchange for Ericka putting her shoulder to the wheel and pretending, no she didn't go off the bloody rails and fly the black flag for two years."

That would take some serious footwork. "You can sell that?"

O'Brien shrugged again, raising his brows. "Too early to tell. It's our best shot. Now we've come to an understanding, I think you have something I need to look at."

Tim's shoulders were tense, absurdly eager to show what he'd found, like a kid with a science project. "Do you know how facial-recognition software works?"

Up went one eyebrow, O'Brien's voice heavy with sarcasm. "Wouldn't be doing this if I could do something useful like run a computer."

Tim smirked, opening up his laptop. "Okay, the small words version then. Details, like distance between the eyes and the shape of the nose or chin, are converted to a mathematical representation, a model if you will. The program looks for matches in its database. Good?"

The lawyer's thumb popped up. "Right with you."

"What looked at first to be a bunch of code is in fact just such a representation. Not a kind I've seen before—he's probably using something custom. I'm sure he didn't want it to be too easy, and I was able to convert it. Watch!" He turned the screen to one side where they could both see it. Several lines formed a graph, a stick drawing of a woman's face. "Now the next layers."

O'Brien leaned forward as the first layer appeared, now a CGI avatar of Ericka's face. A second picture displayed beside the first, a grainy image, bad lighting, shot at a distance. The graphic diagram overlaid both images at exactly the same points. He gasped. "Jesus Christ, it is her!"

Tim sighed, blinking back tears. "The first one I think is something he got from the VR goggles when they were talking two years ago. The second one was taken about three weeks ago according to the metadata in the image. He's found her."

O'Brien's face was flushed, mouth open. "She's alive then. Fuck me, do we know where?"

Tim hesitated. His stomach heaved but there was no alternative to trusting him. "We do, not exactly where, but close enough. I know where the camera is that took this." He ran his thumb along the edge of the screen before closing the lid. "I don't know how Dantalion did this. It's similar to stuff we have, but we couldn't have done it ourselves. He's miles ahead of us."

O'Brien settled back, staring out the window into the rising sun, pupils tightening to pinpricks. "We have to move fast, but everything has to happen in just the right order. We're going to need Steiner. Do you trust him?"

Not really, but what the hell choice did they have? "We're going to have to."

"Ericka is close to that aunt of yours. Are you prepared to work that angle?"

Tim flinched, his breath catching for a moment as he pondered. "I'd hate for Dantalion to somehow become aware of her importance to Ericka."

"Fair point. Then we'll just have to work this with what we've got. Time for a little tradition before we get to work." He reached for his worn copy of *The Art of War*, thumbing for a moment before the raised finger announced he'd found what he was looking for. "Here's the one for today. 'Strategy without tactics is the slowest route to victory. Tactics without strategy is the noise before defeat.' Keep in touch, all the time. Let me know when you're ready to leave."

8

Reunion

Ericka was out of wind, wiping away sweat from walking in the late evening heat. Her clothes itched where they stuck to her skin. She was thinking only of a cooling bath as she dumped the cloth bag of groceries on the counter. She snatched a glass from the shelf, running the water over her hand, waiting for it to run cool before she filled it. She dropped it into the sink, hearing it shatter, but her focus was the Glock taped to the underside of the cabinet. No idea what had alerted her, but she was not alone.

The surge of adrenaline reduced everything to slow motion. Ericka dropped as she spun to get behind the counter's cover, gun in both hands, pistol rising as she squeezed the grip to activate laser sights, placing the red dot center of mass on the dark shape reclining on her couch. As she stared down the barrel, the laser light moved up and down his chest an inch or two in time with her breathing. He didn't move, no sign he was aware of her.

She barely recognized Tim's voice when he spoke, his Manchester accent heavier than usual. "Really bloody sloppy.

You didn't so much as scan the room when you came in. You're going to get killed if anyone serious really does come for you."

She raised the barrel, took her finger off the trigger, slowly placing the weapon on the counter, as if worried it might still go off. Not possible, Ericka knew, but her shoulders were a knotted mass of tension, her hand shaking. "Jesus, I could have shot you."

"No, I unloaded it before you got home, worried you might've gotten trigger-happy." She could see the magazine on the table in front of him.

She squeezed her eyes shut. The moment she'd dreaded for so very long had arrived. *No hiding from it now. He was never going to leave without an explanation.* "How did you find me?"

His voice held some real heat, but his face remained hidden in shadow. "What, the chosen one is shocked her peasant lackeys aren't as stupid as she supposed?"

The dark rose, blotting out her thoughts, making it hard to breathe. She remembered who she was talking to. Tim was the closest thing she'd ever had to a brother. "How the hell did you find me?"

Tim leaned back, putting his feet up on the table, his tone insolent. "First, my friend, we have something we need to discuss." *That was hurt talking. Let it go.*

She had no doubt what it was and had no answer to the question she knew was coming. The answer, if she told him the truth, sounded as terrible now as the hundreds of times she'd rehearsed it in her head. She turned away, her back to him as she filled two glasses of water, fighting the surge of panic. She placed the two glasses on the table and settled into the worn chair opposite. "I'm not going back."

She could see his features as her eyes adjusted, set and angry, expression hard. "The time when you're going to have any choice on that is almost over. Do you have anything a little better than water?"

"I don't drink—you know that!" She hadn't intended the snap.

"No, I wouldn't either if I was hoovering fucking pills like you are. Jesus, Ericka, what the fuck?"

Out came the first lie, unbidden. "Just temporary until I get my head on straight."

Tim looked away. "Have you looked at yourself in the mirror lately? Who d'you think you're trying to shit?"

Change the subject. He was never going to buy the nonsense. "What do you mean no choice?"

He was glaring at her now, punishing her. "The information that led me here is in many hands now. I'm almost surprised I made it first. You've gotten sloppy."

The jolt of adrenaline raised goose bumps all over. "Who?" She knew the answer from his tone.

Tim was almost shouting now. "Who do you fucking think? You thought you could take him on, just you, working with this? The great and powerful Ericka!" He gestured at the stacked computers, appearing to be connected in complete disarray.

She didn't try to bite back the jolt of anger. "I've shut him down twice. How've you been doing without me?"

His face was puzzled, hurt. "What the hell is wrong with you? We were partners. You left me burned in hospital, told me you'd be back and then nothing for two years. And don't try to bullshit me about where you went."

Guilt flooded the anger, quenching the heat. "I'm so sorry.

I couldn't—there was no way. And I can't ever come back now."

He was shaking his head, eyes locked on hers. "It's me you're talking to. I was there in Spokane. I've watched you burn with anger for years. I know what he offered you. Maybe you're done at the FBI, but what about me? I had no idea if you were dead, or alive but being held. Two years of hell and you're standing there without a scratch. You fucked me over!"

Yes, I did. And everyone else who believed in me. "I can't face it, not anyone, especially not you. You've no idea what's happened. If I'd been talking to you, they'd have thought you were helping me. It didn't go as planned. I wasn't taking you down with me."

His clenched teeth told her he wasn't buying it. "So, your plan was to sit here in this bloody shithole, forget about everyone else and hope Dantalion accidentally sends you his whereabouts in the clear? Bump into him at the market? Good thinking. Is that the pills talking?"

The mental paralysis gripped her again, fueled by a toxic combination of angry pride and overwhelming humiliation. Of course, the fucking pills weren't helping, but she had to sleep. *I'll get better, think straight again. I can do this, can't I?* How could she go back and face the people of her former life with the mental images of what she'd done swirling through her mind, haunting her nightmares. She forced herself to make eye contact, voice rising in volume and pitch. "Don't you realize what I did? I took his thirty pieces of silver. He was so far in my head, I had no idea, all compass lost. All those years looking for those animals and nothing. He wanted me to leave the bureau and I told him to go to hell.

As soon as I was looking at their faces, the pictures of their lives, I did exactly what he wanted. I may not have sent my resignation but I stepped so far out there's no going back. The evil bastard knew that. Seeing their lives, like the one Patty never had, broke something in me. There's no redemption for Judas. It's a one-way trip."

Tears welled in Tim's unblinking eyes. "Christ, Ericka, what did you do?"

She shook her head. Articulating it would just bring it back again. "Don't you see what he did? He knew this would happen. It's why he did it."

The anger was gone from Tim's face, replaced with a focused gaze. He looked heartbroken. "Come back. There is a way. No one but you knows what happened down here. Keep it that way. For what they can prove, O'Brien thinks an immunity deal is doable as long as you retire as soon as we've got him."

She bowed her head, looking at clenched hands, her voice choked by uncontrolled sobs as she spoke. "That's not the part I can't do. I can't face myself, you, your aunt, my former life. I betrayed Patty. I betrayed everything I was and an immunity agreement is just a fucking piece of paper. It doesn't rewrite history; it's just a way of ignoring it for the greater good."

He hesitated, appearing to consider his words. "Steiner thinks you've suffered something of a psychotic break and, forgive me, listening to you here I think he's right. He's convinced he can help. You're hardly in any shape for an objective look at yourself."

The jolt of anger made her gasp, face tingling as she flushed. Thoughts jumbled like multiple videos overlaid, a muddled whirlpool of memories. She spat her words at Tim.

"You didn't see it, you didn't live it. How the fuck do you know what's in my head?"

His features hardened again. "We've done this before. One thing I'm pretty clear on though. I've never seen a crazy person who thinks they're crazy."

"Fuck you!"

"Swear at me all you like. You know perfectly well you're ill. Does this seem like the you from before? Can't think straight, ineffective, living in the bottom of a pill bottle. He's lit you up. Dantalion showed us how to find you. You're not fighting him anymore. You're kidding yourself while he toys with you. Now, he's getting bored. This's over. Time to choose how it ends!"

Now the dark again, like a weight on her mind, got to sleep. The pills flashed in her mind, the craving irresistible, her last refuge from facing the truth. "Get out!"

He leaned forward, speaking through clenched teeth. "Sure, have another fistful and wait for the next person to decipher the invitation. You can't stay here."

Teeth gritted, seeing through red haze, she stabbed a finger at the door. "I said get the fuck out! I'm not coming back!"

Tim looked down, sighing, rising from the couch. His face showed the hurt, his facial scars livid with emotion, shoulders slumped in resignation. "You're not the only one who's sacrificed." He leaned to lift a satchel from behind the couch, reaching into it to place a familiar object on the counter. The matte black VR set chilled her guts. "We've paired two of them. I have the other one. Fully secure and we can talk wherever you are. We can't stop him without you. The real you."

She stumbled to the bathroom, clumsy fingers prying at

the lid, several tries before popping three into her mouth. Lukewarm tap water made her feel like retching. Relief would come soon. Panting, she leaned to look out the door, but Tim was gone.

9

The Gift

Sometimes in this business you didn't have to look for it, sometimes it just came to you. Yusef Abidi adjusted his tailored western suit as he strode the hallway to the interrogation room, centering his tie, hearing the crisp echo of his footsteps return from bleak concrete walls. Prisons had a smell. All similar but no two exactly alike, decades of fear-driven sweat overlaid the tang of industrial cleaners. The central prison in Sahiwal had an odor he'd always found distinctly distasteful, but it would have to do for today. There was no risking being followed to where this one was being held. Even bringing him here might not have escaped detection.

He was burning with curiosity, perspiring despite the relative cool of the prison's depths. As he approached the door, the guard drew himself erect, standing to the side, fist banging on the metal door to announce him before shoving it open. The man seated at the bare wooden table was smaller than he imagined him. One always pictured towering jihadis with full beards and fierce expressions. This one looked like a sickly academic, dragged from his lab to sit peering wide-eyed at the guards leaning against the walls around him.

Yusef gestured to them as he pulled out the chair facing the prisoner. "Gentlemen, please wait outside and close the door behind you!" He sat without looking around him, staring at the man until he heard the heavy, metallic clang of the door, followed by the thud of thrown bolts.

He scanned the man's face. In every organization there were men for all roles. With groups such as this one, it was rare to see the brains, the minds that led the others. Their presence in a group's actions was unmistakable, clever strategy, not spontaneous, but the faces that everyone saw were the brutes, the thugs, those who must dirty their hands to bring about the final objectives. This man's deep brown eyes stared back from under furrowed brows, the trim beard failing to cover the tight muscles of his controlled expression. His cultured appearance stood in contrast to his shabby prison clothes.

"Good morning. I am Wing Commander Yusef Abidi and I believe you asked to speak to me?"

The man's faint smile did not touch his eyes. "These days I go by Aalem Mirza. My former names are unimportant. And yes, it had to be you."

Spare me the stroking. "May I offer you anything?"

The bland smile again. "No thank you, but it is good to speak to someone with manners after all this time."

Yusef looked for any clues as to the man's thinking, but the wall was impenetrable. "So, we shall speak, as they say in the west, frankly. You cannot have expected gentle treatment when you turned yourself in. I can think of no reason why anyone in your position should do so unless they needed our protection having run afoul of their comrades. So, what do you want? Protection is for sale. It is not a gift and the price is very dear. This, I expect you know."

Mirza's head dipped in acknowledgment of the statement's truth, maintaining eye contact. "I am hoping to do a little better than mere protection, but I bring a great deal in exchange."

Yusef sneered. "What, you will perhaps tell me where you are hiding a few boxes of explosives, an AK-47 or two? We shoot you down like dogs wherever we find you. The Americans circle overhead like *shaheen*, incinerating you whenever it pleases them. We do not bargain with rats peering at us with a leg already in the trap. Do tell me what you offer that I have wasted my time for."

He watched, pleased to see Mirza struggle with his anger, an amateur to this game. "The great struggle will continue until Allah in his wisdom sees fit that we shall triumph. For every single one who falls, two more rise to take his place. But I do not offer the lives of holy warriors, but rather something else. A poison that has tainted the cause. A monster who at first offered help, but who now infects us all with his sin."

Yusef couldn't restrain the snort of derision. "How could you tell who is sinful, awash in your own sins as you are?"

Mirza's eyes blazed with rage as he sat up. "I, at least, am not a running dog of the godless Americans and Chinese!"

Yusef laughed out loud, a sound without humor. "You are worse. Having been given the true faith, you pervert it to support the wants and lusts of men little better than common criminals. You disgrace Islam!"

The men glared at each other, unblinking, before Mirza at last looked down. "There is no denying we lost our way dealing with this one."

Yusef didn't need to ask. *Make him say it.* "Who?"

"You know him, by deeds if not by name. The one who flew the French airliner like a toy and who stole the Americans' prized drones. Calling himself Dantalion, a fitting name. Do you know what he was after, when he was thwarted?"

Yusef fought to steel his expression, not daring to hope. "Please, you have my attention."

"Me."

Yusef's lips curled in derision. "You? That is a great deal of effort for such a minuscule prize."

Mirza's lip formed into a snarl. "That, fool, is because he knows what you do not. That I have something very valuable he does not want me handing over."

He glanced towards the door as if about to call the guards. "Are you going to tell me? I do not share your taste in drama. This grows tedious and I am a busy man."

"Him. I can give you him. And he knows it."

Yusef's heart missed a beat. *Play this very carefully.* "He may have other ideas about that. What do you seek in return?"

"To live out my life in peace. Somewhere in America or perhaps Canada. A new name and life. I will even need a new face. Allah knows even that may not be enough."

Time to see if this was genuine. Yusef leaned in, stroking his beard. "Give me something that shows me this is real. I'm not going to haggle with you like a carpet seller on market day. How is a small man such as you able to give me a devil who can do these things?"

Mirza broke eye contact to look at the dirty table. "I was his student. At first, we paid him to act for us, to tell us when the Americans would strike, who our traitors were, who could send us weapons. After he stole the airliner, he needed to hide, plot his next move. He sent us equipment so we could meet him in a virtual madrassa he built. There were other students present but I have no idea who they were or where. He provided tools, taught us how to use them. Things no one else had. Securing his legacy, he called it."

Yusef fought to control his expression, to speak without betraying his emotions. *This might just be true.* "I'm still waiting."

Mirza scowled at him. "He underestimated me, as many do. He thought of me as a novice when I was already some distance down the road he himself has traveled. I saw things he thought were lost on us. He is blinded by his arrogance that one. I learned more rapidly than he taught, drank deeply from the well."

Yusef placed his hands on the table, smiling to put his prisoner at ease, his mind racing through the various scenarios. "Then it appears that we shall be able to do business after all." One thing needed clarifying. "Forgive my curiosity, but why now?"

Mirza's eyes bulged, mouth open, like he was speaking to an idiot. "He knows what I know. He has already moved heaven and earth to try and kill me. He will have seen me brought here and you must expect he will come for me again, soon. This one misses nothing. With what he has built, it is as if he looks down at the world through the eyes of God."

10

Overkill

They were just going to have to wait in the radar shadow of the rocky islets until the Chinese warships passed out of range. *You can't always smuggle on a timetable like a Japanese train schedule.* He was masking the client's AIS so it would only be dreadful luck that would take the navy around the far side of the island where the smugglers might be visible. If anyone had the urge to look it up by AIS, the MV *Kunming* was tied up awaiting repairs near a Vancouver shipyard. He had several juicier-looking ghosts prepared, ready to go if the navy needed a fatter target to distract them. He was only half watching. Moving smuggled cargo in and out of China was getting so easy it was becoming tedious.

As soon as he had the ship safely in the maze of Guangdong's harbor, he would see to the payment. He ran his eyes over the code, a genuine smile of pride lighting his features. The indistinct reflection in his center monitor returned a ghostly reminder of his face as it once had been.

There were many *hawalas*. They had been in use for centuries, but not like this one. Like all such constructs money would be transferred from one party to another, but it was the nature of the transaction that money would never actually move. Hawala to Islam, *daigou* to the Chinese, a system so ancient it was employed by the Templars to move money for pilgrims safely to the Holy Land. Taken up in principle by PayPal and other similar services, profits were enormous. His coupled the process with crypto-currency, servers hidden and protected by multiple layers of encryption. It made a mockery of police efforts to keep drug money from crossing borders. They had never even come close.

It was simple in principle. To pay for their shipment of illicit goods, the buyer deposited the agreed amount in the specified crypto to his account on a web node, the location of which moved and which was only provided to customers on an 'as needed' basis. When the delivery was done, the hawala paid the seller from currency stored in another node. The buyer's money never ended up in the seller's hands, different money did, and so left no trail for police to follow. No movement of funds to trace, no chain analysis of the blockchain to worry about, nothing to tie payment to goods. No digital wallets stuffed with cash linked in any way to any crime. If the various nodes became imbalanced, he moved the money around, slowly and in small amounts, buying and selling legitimate commodities, at market prices.

He took a hearty bite from every transaction he handled, plus his fee for getting the ships through borders. He paid gang associates a percentage for his physical security, secure facilities and for feeding him the business. It covered the bills, allowing him to plan his next steps, build what he needed, pay for the very best of black-hatter help to do the heavy lifting.

He drummed his fingers as he stared at his hospital

checklist, scowling as he read it to himself. The minimal video security was simple and he could brick the whole system up at will. Getting into patient records and implanting the software to add, delete or modify as he wished would take a little more time, but he was well ahead of schedule. The code was written and required only that he debug it. Transportation in and out and later to remote convalescence would be the real trick. He would be vulnerable for a period of time, dependent on well-compensated and above all, most trustworthy minions. No help for it. It had to be this way. A necessary step to where his journey would take him.

Three quick chimes sounded in his ear, drawing his gaze back to the South China Sea. He tugged the enhanced-reality rig from its cradle, sliding it down over his eyes and ears, waiting a few seconds while it activated. His breath caught as the display flashed on, causing him to lean back. The Chinese ships had vanished and his client was now transmitting their actual AIS, showing them tucked into the small cove, obviously to avoid surface radar. They might as well have transmitted a description tag as a smuggler ship along with their position.

Where the hell were the navy ships? His hands flew over the keys as he tried to reestablish his connection to the command servers. Getting in there had been both difficult and expensive, but the benefit of being inside the Chinese government's vehicle traffic system was beyond price. He stole nothing, he changed nothing, all his software did was duplicate a stream of data it was generating anyway, providing him with the same information as their command center, a classic man-in-the-middle attack.

A jolt of anger tore through him. The stream was still

active but now it was encrypted, a layer he could certainly break, but it would take time and the navy ships could be anywhere. To do this someone would have to be inside the Chinese military structure or be using his own gateway. He closed his eyes, lips pressed together as he thought. Blocking him meant someone knew he was in there in the first place. He gasped as the answer flashed through his mind. Mirza! That slithering worm. He'd shown him the process, inserting small bits of his software using legitimate software updates not secured, then hijacking the process when someone did an install to assemble his own components. *He's seen far more than I meant. Traitorous bastard!*

He needed to be dealt with as soon as this was over. For now, where were those ships?

Yusef paced behind the stations of his team, posture erect, his demeanor deliberately projecting calm. He paid particular attention to the center of the five positions where Mirza sat hunched, flanked by two of his own, watching his every move. The room was darkened and cool, air conditioning running flat out. Today, they would see how invulnerable this Dantalion really was. No playing around, this would be a stand-up fight.

He placed his hand on the back of the chair of one of his team members to get her attention. "You have him engaged?"

She turned to look at him. Dark eyes flashed over glasses perched on her nose, eyes wide, clearly thrilled by what she was doing. "I believe so, sir. The naval ships appear to be moving to intercept, like they are now aware of the smuggler. They have changed course and increased speed. No signs of countermeasures being deployed, but our target will be aware of our attack by now."

Yusef smiled before moving to the next station. He leaned over the hulking agent. "Try it now. He should be distracted."

The man spoke without looking up. "Yes, sir. I am still concerned taking off this many layers of encryption will take more time than we have. Even with the help." The man jerked his head towards where Mirza sat with his minders.

Yusef nodded, placing his hand on the man's shoulder. "Be careful to change nothing. Just an intelligence scan of his financial assets. When in doubt do nothing rather than let him know where we have been. Create as good a map as possible."

Mirza overheard, speaking loudly enough for the whole team to hear. "He is going to know. He always knows. I am telling you to strike now. You'll not get another chance. Not against this one. Once he knows I am helping you, he will change everything. He will counterattack!"

Yusef walked back down the line, standing over the prisoner, his voice projecting menace. "You will do as you are told and nothing more. If he is tipped off, I am going to assume it was you and that I have a mole on my hands instead of an asset. Do you understand the consequences of that?"

Mirza blanched despite his dark skin. "Don't blame me if this fails. I have warned you. Strike now."

Yusef inhaled, holding his breath for a moment. No, the targets could keep the money. He had to know where the tentacles reached, then strike a killing blow later, taking all the heads of the hydra at once. Never leave a wounded enemy in your wake to recover and fight again. He didn't have the means for a death blow now.

★ ★ ★

Ericka shook her head, trying to clear her thoughts, caffeine gaining the high ground over sleeping pills, the contest's outcome yet undecided. She leaned into her screen, tracing her finger along the lines of data. Something had changed, none of this made any sense. Encrypted data, scattered portions of servers, dark-web nodes she was sure were Dantalion activity abruptly visible in the clear like someone had just switched the encryption off, data packets now readable. For some of what she was looking at she could even discern physical location of currency.

She nibbled her lower lip. *Was this him baiting her or law enforcement somewhere trolling for bottom feeders?* He was wide open. Nothing was ever this wide open, but this looked real and it wasn't only his data that was hanging out in the breeze. He had control of enormous amounts of money. *Is he running hawala?* Nothing on its face to identify who this stuff belonged to, but the transfer mechanisms were gaping wide open as were the feeder accounts, wallets with digital keys lying there for the taking. Whoever had it open wasn't doing anything. Were they waiting to see what he did? *He's going to shut this down and go to his failover any second.*

She giggled as the thought crossed her mind. *It had to be him. On the small chance it wasn't, it was another large-scale criminal organization, maybe several pooling their resources.* They might find her, she might have to move. She thought of the contents of her go bag—a small collection of essentials she kept ready in case she had to travel without time to pack— sitting in a locked box in the warehouse below. All she would need if she had to make a run for it.

At the very least, the bastard would have some explaining to do, maybe have to make good the loss from his own resources. *So, this is what he's been doing to make ends meet. The dark web's overlord has been whoring himself out to keep everyone's money safe.* An amusing thought, but it was likely how he'd been financing himself all along.

Her skin tingled, mouth dry as she perched on the razor's edge of indecision. Her breathing shallowed, not believing her eyes. She read again, mouthing words as she did. Multiple smaller transactions going into a single account right after all the larger ones. Her hands were trembling. *That's his piggy bank, sure as hell. It's how he pays himself.* She moved her cursor to empty it, then snorted with laughter as she thought the better of it. *After all, a genius like him deserved the money for all his good work. He deserved all of it, every last penny. Last reports were he was in China somewhere. We'll start with giving him theirs. All of it.*

She began entering commands, opening digital wallets and moving all of the client's money into her target's account as rapidly as she could. She could lose access at any second. As soon as it appeared in his main account, she dispersed it into what were certainly hidden holding accounts. She could barely gulp each breath, gripped with fear he would retake control before she was done. She was also planning her route out of Mexico City. This would all but paint cross hairs on her forehead. She'd need to move the minute she was done. And that was it, done—no money left to move. One more step.

She'd taken and modified several so-called ransomware programs for a moment like this. She couldn't get at all of it, but bricking up even parts of it might slow him down from moving any of it back to its rightful owners. *Let his customers think he's stolen it. It was worth a parting shot.*

Finally, a page out of Dantalion's own playbook. It was time to go, she'd exposed herself. She entered a password, lingering a few moments to ensure it was running as intended. First, it encrypted all of her data on the machines linked together in front of her. Then it would methodically overwrite the computer's storage and memory with random binary digits. Then, a remote server would do two further wipes, leaving nothing intelligible to anyone who might find these machines. All the data she needed when she got where she was going was already backed up, dispersed and encrypted in locations all over the world. Reassembly was tedious, but she had nothing now but time.

Ericka stood at the top of the stairs staring back at her self-imposed cell, seeing all the telltale signs of a disordered mind, not caring. She'd created it primarily as a safe house to lie low before leaving the country, safe from the heat created by the reason she was there in the first place. It had become a prison, one where her mind served out a never-ending sentence as she grappled with overpowering guilt and self-loathing. A surge of energy coursed through her, making her feel giddy, realizing only now how much she loathed this place, how good it would be to be gone. Not gone home of course. There was no way home. A familiar jolt of panic and she was chilled, feeling she needed to hide again.

She ran down the dirty stairs to where her go bag lay open. Money, documents, a few changes of clothing, a gun she would discard before she got to the small, regional airport she had selected, two clean burner phones and nothing else. Keys and passwords to recover her data were every second letter in every seventh word starting on page twenty-six of the trashy, dog-eared novel in her carry-on. If she lost it, any copy from a used bookstore would allow her to retrieve and restore. She tossed the bag into the trunk of the decrepit wreck of a car she had for the purpose. She spared the place not so much as a glance in the rearview mirror.

The ship had appeared from nowhere on the AIS, then they'd found it on radar minutes later. Now, the old freighter was visible against the rocks where it held station, shadowed from probing radar. Captain Feng Chan, commander of the Type 54 class frigate, *Wenzhou*, squinted against the sun as he stood on the outside deck above the bridge, the thrill of the hunt making him tingle with excitement. He lowered his field glasses, glancing at the officers behind him. "Come alongside, two hundred meters, and train the main gun on their bridge to ensure we have their undivided attention! Tell the boarding party, I need the captain and the officers alive, but if there is any resistance from the crew, he is free to deploy weapons at his discretion. Anyone on board who touches any computer or other device is to be shot!"

His first officer turned away to issue orders over the comm system. Chan lifted his glasses back to his face to examine his prize. *It was a typical aging freighter, nothing remarkable about it, rusting with black smoke dribbling from her stack as she idled, looking like any good storm would sink her.* He forced himself to take slow, deep breaths.

What he wanted was not on the ship, her smuggled cargo was of no relevance to him. What he wanted was in the heads of her bridge crew, the answers perhaps? How it was these last months the sea was filled with ghosts? Ships that appeared and vanished when approached, reappeared on tracking systems thousands of miles away, appearing to know how to stay just out of range of surface radar. Something had changed, now instruments could not be trusted, only eyes and ears. How and who would not be known to the thugs running this ship, but they had to start somewhere. His standing orders were very clear. He was to capture the bridge crew and preserve any device containing navigation data at all costs.

Teeth clenched, eyes bulging with rage, it took several seconds before the alarm tore his attention from the pending disaster at sea. His client's ship messaged they were about to be boarded with no time to get the illicit cargo over the side. The warships were too close to be decoyed away with phantom AIS signatures. This one was a dead loss. Remembering his cockiness from minutes before intensified his fury. He tilted his VR headset back to look up at the virtual menu before toggling to the alarm's source, gasping at what he saw.

All the money was gone. Everything he was holding for his clients in hawala had been moved first to his transfer account, then to his dispersed holding accounts where it would take days to retrieve. Worse, his system had been used to send his clients messages that he had transferred the funds to his own account as he normally did when he took his share. His mouth open, he was panting with rage. Someone had used a childish ransomware program to brick up his credentials. Safeguards in place against such a move had been switched off. No way to open them quickly. In the weeks it would take, he would be in real danger.

He spun his chair, turning his back on the unfolding disaster behind him, iron will quashing anger in favor of the icy cool he would need to see his way through. He looked down at his legs, like sticks, pathetic. It was too risky to stay. Everything would be in jeopardy. He sighed, no help for it. First see if his attackers left anything he could use, then run his failover. Every bit of data would move as would the money he could still access, then he himself would vanish to one of his safe houses until he could find a more permanent base. He had several in mind.

While he was there, he would see whoever did this was repaid in similar coin. His breathing became more regular as the prospect played out in his mind. He'd been complacent, gotten caught with his pants down. The path he'd chosen was too difficult for anything but unwavering concentration, unhesitating decisions and he'd gotten cocky. *The final result would be worth it. No one would ever forget him. His final act like nothing anyone had ever managed before.* The exhilaration of adrenaline settled into a warm glow. Time to get on with it.

Two attackers at once, interesting. Were they acting in concert? There was no evidence in the code traces that showed any similarity. One was easy to follow and what he would have expected. They weren't making the slightest effort to hide themselves, Pakistani intelligence using stolen code from that worm, Mirza. He would need to think of something special for that one. *Him dead, the threat from that direction would be eliminated. Not like those idiots were a threat without Mirza.* For their trouble, he would pay them a visit. They would regret this. Their meddling meant he would have to change everything Mirza might have had access to or might have inferred, and they would pay a price for that too.

The other attacker showed a much higher level of sophistication. The raid had been quick, the actions decisive. Contingencies had been thought through, software prepared. It had all happened in minutes. Even if he had been aware it was coming, he would have been hard-pressed to defend against it. The little bit of routing information left behind told him no more than it had come from the southern portion of North America. It told him nothing he'd not already deduced.

A thin smile played across his face while a hand rose to trace his scars. She must have just been sitting there waiting, watching, prepared for the slightest slip. When Mirza peeled off the shielding layers of encryption, she must have fallen off her chair but wasted not a second. *Good to have you back, Ericka. No way I'll have a go at killing you. I need you to keep me honed, and you're just too much fun alive. But there will be a price for this in the dearest coin. There is no doubt about that. Time for that later.*

A deep breath drew in cool air. He forced his shoulders to relax and he was moving again. He was done with this place anyway. Being in China meant staying out of sight, never free to go outside. *A few last things to get rid of, got to be absolutely clear his fail-safe was working and his remote data intact.* His projects were never stored locally anyway. All was working as he'd designed. When it was done, software would activate and his equipment here would be beyond use. Satisfied, he wheeled himself to the door. The car would be here soon.

★ ★ ★

"Give me a reason, any reason, why I shouldn't just leave now and let Achmed here indulge himself? I can see he very badly wants to." Yusef gestured to the heavily bearded, hulking brute standing behind the seated and handcuffed Mirza, thick arms folded, his humorless smile displaying gaps in his teeth. The cell's painted cinderblocks were stained reddish-brown with what looked like old blood, no windows with a single tiny air vent. The light fixture hummed and flickered giving motion to shadows.

Mirza peered over his shoulder at Achmed, eyes bulging, while a gasp forced its way through his teeth. *All treachery but no courage in this one, truly a rat in human form.* Yusef's stomach knotted with distaste before the smaller man finally answered, his voice little more than a squeak. "I swear to God, I did nothing but what you told me."

Hands on the rough table, Yusef leaned in, face inches from Mirza where he had to fight to avoid his face wrinkling in disgust at the smell, pure fear. *Coward!* The one thing he could not abide. "And yet within less than five minutes from the time you opened him up, someone swiftly took every rupee, dollar, euro, yen and crypto and moved it where we can't find it. Someone just waiting, it would seem, with just the right software, who happened to be ready just as we attack, an operation no one should have known about. It almost seems like magic. I think you tipped someone off to steal it, give you your share later."

"I swear I did nothing! I am not his only enemy. All the world is looking for Dantalion." He flinched at the sound of Achmed's frustrated sigh, followed by the scuffing sound of boots as the man behind shifted his immense weight. Mirza could feel the thug's eyes boring into the back of his neck, yearning for the slightest approval from Yusef.

Yusef stood up straight, stroking his beard, strong jaw set with determination, turning his back as he took a few steps away. No denying that, but none of the world's police had been able to get anywhere near this Dantalion. This was someone lying in wait, a hawk circling on raptor's wings waiting for the rat to emerge. "In your time as his disciple, did he ever mention any concern about any of those looking for him?"

Mirza shook his head with exaggerated vigor. "He regarded them all as idiots worthy only of contempt. Except the one who found him after the hijacking, and he said she was dead."

Yusef's tone conveyed his contempt. "An evil spirit then, no mortal can touch him?" Achmed snorted derision from the back of the cell. Yusef gave him a look to silence him.

Mirza's eyes were wide, forehead now beading with sweat. "Oh, he taught caution and prudence with multiple fail-safes. He would often quote the infidel Sun Tzu about battles being won before they are fought through preparation."

"And you have said you never once saw him in person." Yusef's eyes narrowed as he scoured Mirza's face for truth.

"Never, we all appeared in his madrassa as avatars."

Yusef turned to glare at Achmed, pleased to see Mirza quail. The guard took a step forward, placing his hand on the back of Mirza's chair. "As the money disappeared, all the links went dead, vermin running for their dens. You, of course, would know nothing of who they were?"

Mirza looked away, rubbing his nose, craning his neck to give Achmed a fearful glance, receiving a feral smirk in return. "I don't, but he was hardly discerning from what he said. Anyone willing to pay his tithe. He needed the money to pay his minions, buy his toys."

Yusef affected an expression as if he had tasted something very sour, filling his words with contempt. "And this evil whoreson, you welcomed his support in your jihad, giving you the purity of purpose that cloaks a martyr in righteousness?"

Mirza looked down at his hands as if interested only in his filthy nails, his voice subdued, almost difficult to hear. "We had no idea what we were dealing with. That I am prepared to admit."

"You can explain your sins to Allah in due course. You will be leaving here in a few days, as soon as the Americans have their paperwork in order."

Mirza's voice became a squeak. "Americans?"

His eye-bulging shock forced a smile onto Yusef's controlled interrogation face. "Isn't that what you wanted? I believe you asked to go there? I am led to believe they are always greatly pleased to send a plane to collect people in your line of work. How can you be surprised?"

Mirza's expression was pure desperation. "What do I get in return?"

Yusef's barked laugh was purely theatrical. "Nothing! Any time you fancy yourself ill-treated, just say so and you can go. Perhaps ask them to deliver you somewhere your old master will spot you quickly. The question is what you can give them that will make it worth the effort to keep you alive. For your sake, I hope it is more than you have told me."

"They will have me? You are giving me to them?"

"One of their team who have been seeking this Dantalion is coming himself. Better him than Achmed, believe you me."

He glanced over Mirza's shoulder to where the enormous brute wore an expression of great disappointment, fingering the truncheon worn on his belt.

Yusef studied Mirza's features, seeing hope flicker, forcing the scowl of disgust from his features. Two quick steps and he stood leaning over the prisoner, holding Mirza's jaw, pulling his head up to force eye contact. "Never come back, ever. There will be no arrest, no protection. Do we understand each other?"

Without waiting for an answer, he gestured to the waiting guard, spinning on his heel to leave.

11

Judas Risen

Six flights, six stopovers, each just long enough to book the next leg, each using a different name and nationality than the one before, all identification single-use, one flight only. She'd moved using regional airports and airlines, flying on planes that had a good, thick patina of rust on them from the time she was a girl. Ericka's eyes stung from acrid smoke, burning plastic, watching the last passport burn in a flowerpot, her newly rented property a cash deal, nothing that could lead to her. She'd be there for only a few days while she found something a little more secure in nearby Panama City.

Ericka sighed, running through the checklist: source new equipment, find hidden access points, prepare go bag ready for the next one, fill it with another little stack of fake identification. They cost a fortune, but it wasn't Ericka's money, just poorly secured drug profits left lying where they were easy to steal, money well spent, like Robin fucking Hood.

Eyes heavy, she stared at her luggage, little bottles of chemical solace beckoning to her, the need to sleep all-consuming. She rooted through the soft-sided bag, yanking out clothes as she burrowed to the bottom. Something hard brushed her hand and she grasped it, tossing them onto a patio chair; the VR goggles. Her throat went dry. They looked exactly like his. She knew they weren't, they had to be recreations. They brought back the encounters with the monster, slipping unhindered past her defenses, sowing thoughts and desires that had flourished in the fertile soil of anger and obsession.

Ericka swallowed hard, looking away at nothing. Tim said there was a way back, that she could come home, but they didn't know. She'd spent the thirty pieces of silver on herself and there was no redemption for Judas. If they had any idea what she'd done, they'd see her as she saw herself. She dropped into a chair, head in hands, trying to clear the memory, but it played out again, blood on a child's tiny hands where it had no place being. She let a few sobs escape before she choked them down, standing to jab her hands into the bag again, a full-body chill spreading up her arm as her fingers clutched the pill bottle's familiar shape. She swallowed them dry, knowing she was minutes from peace. The line between sight and her mind's eye blurred, faces appeared, voices that said nothing. *Tim, Mrs. Donnelly—I'm so sorry. You may think you want me back, but you don't, not if you knew. I didn't know it, but this was a one-way trip. How could I not have known?*

"So, you are satisfied they will abide by this agreement?" Steiner nibbled on an arm of his glasses as he held them to stare at O'Brien. His shoulders ached with tension, nervous still despite meeting in the security of the lawyer's office. His professional gaze took in the man's flushed face and gray complexion, visual clues to the toll taken by long hours and distilled self-medication.

A tiny smile played across O'Brien's face as he returned the look. "No, don't be silly. They will abide as long as they see it as in their interests. That's how these things work around here. Promises are for kindergarten kids at Christmas time. We'll make this work by making sure they think it remains to their benefit."

Steiner linked his fingers, palms sticky with sweat. "Convincing Ericka of this with the assurance they will probably not try to jail her as long as they feel like it may not be that easy."

O'Brien's smile broadened, an infectious one, making Steiner return the expression. "You shrinks have convinced people of things a lot harder to swallow than that. You can do it. I have faith."

Steiner stifled the giggle, looking down at his valise. "Being described as such a skilled bullshitter by a lawyer of your caliber is a tremendous compliment. You flatter me."

O'Brien chuckled, never happier than when verbally sparring. "Over the years, I have suggested to many—judges, politicians—that when you shrinks testify in court you should be required by law to wear fishnet stockings and cheap perfume so no one is misled." He leaned in, lowering his voice as Steiner chortled. "Funny thing is no one ever laughs. They just nod their heads like it's a good idea."

You are not getting away with that. "Yes, well I can do no better in riposte than to paraphrase Winston Churchill. 'Lawyers occasionally stumble over the truth, but most of them pick themselves up and hurry off as if nothing had happened.'"

O'Brien held his sides while he laughed, unfazed as always. "How is it all these years and I've never heard that one?"

Steiner smiled for a few moments before his shoulders tightened again, the tension flooding back. "This is still going to take some doing. Take me through the supervision component again. I need to know what it means."

O'Brien leaned forward, tapping the multi-page document lying on the leather writing pad. "The suits upstairs left this deliberately vague and they're giving me the hairy eyeball for being the one to approach them about it, so I'm limited as to how I can play this."

Steiner's brow wrinkled with surprise. "They don't trust you?"

O'Brien responded with another snort of derision. "You've no idea. These bastards don't trust their right hand to scratch their own arses unless they can see it happening in a mirror and review the video later. What has their knickers in a twist is they don't have any read on my role in the lines of communication to former agent Blackwood. Makes them nervous about leveling with me."

Steiner sighed. "I suppose it will have to do. She cannot stay where she is. It will finish her. This is the best chance we can give her."

O'Brien shrugged heavy shoulders. "They don't give a shit about that. All they care about is having her back in the tent where they have no explaining to do and shutting down Dantalion before he does something again that has people getting hoisted in front of congress. Immunity for all past crimes she may have committed anywhere in the world, immunity from extradition. She plays by the rules once back, acts under supervision and retires when they say so. They were very clear with me: take it or leave it."

And so, it will have to do. "Then I shall do my best to see she takes it."

O'Brien leaned forward, linking his fingers on the desktop. "I don't think you know the specifics of what took her to where she is. Better for you that you don't. I can hide behind legal privilege, you and O'Connell can't. Be careful what you ask. If you don't know, you don't have to lie. But she's the best of us—she didn't ask for this. We have to get her back."

The cringing little slug had turned out to be a useful child after all. Well worth the effort beyond the delicious thrill of terrifying and controlling him. His father's network access had been all he needed. Almost a pity he'd delivered, depriving him of the sport he could have had with the girlfriend—she looked like a real screamer. He could always tell. Sighing, he turned back to his screens. There were always others.

It had taken some time to implant the components of his software all over the Pakistani intelligence network. Slowly, piece by piece, his AI inserted segments of inert code at times and places calculated to avoid scrutiny by the agency's layers of software. The program learned as it went. It took advantage of legitimate software updates like hiding drug shipments inside the tires of imported cars from a trusted manufacturer. When all was in place, he used the credentials a final time to access a secure area of the network and manually assemble key elements. Now he simply reset the security system to ignore his actions before altering the audit function, relabeling his actions as belonging to an administrator currently on leave. For a short period of time, he had all but unlimited access and it was time to present his bill.

He stopped to stare out over the grassy expanse of Kazakhstan's open plains, the vista drawing a sigh. His new allies had kept their word and done very well for him. The old Soviet facility was spartan but comfortably refurbished, once a listening post for their vast tracking network. The walls were concrete giving the place an austere feel, contrasting with sumptuous appointments and superb climate control. Unlike China, he could even go outside in daylight to hear the constant wind rustle grasses under an unlimited sky, an appetizer, a taste of what was to come. It wouldn't be too long now.

The loosely knit Russian group seemed to have accepted his explanation for the debacle of his hawala. An underling had sold him out. Not entirely untrue, just a properly limited subset of the truth. *All the very best lies closely mirror truth, an axiom that has done me well my entire life.* As the code required, he'd made good the losses after locating and unlocking the remaining funds. The loss of face with his former allies was irredeemable. He took several deep, calming breaths. The welcome and familiar surge of heat always present before a kill immersed him in restorative anger, a self-generated and addictive high. Mirza's end would go some way to restoring his reputation, but far more important, it would bring a return to balance.

He had no equals and could not be bested. This must be demonstrated to anyone who might think otherwise, but first things first. He shifted his useless legs under him, sipping his water. Always steal the most sensitive data first, in this case the identity and location of the rats, the human sources, the core stock in trade of any intelligence service. The filthy rodents always did the most damage and were accordingly worth the most to those seeking them. He worked with complete focus, sifting through data parsed by his crawler's AI. You never knew when some bright light in the target organization would get wise and kick the plug out of the wall. The smart money was on taking everything now and doling it out to clients later, then take the lower value data in small doses, leaving the impression with his customers he could pop in and out of protected areas at will.

The jolt of anger made him gasp as he scanned the material. Mirza gone, taken away three days before, now in the hands of the FBI. He toggled through stolen documents. Signed for by Special Agent Tim O'Connell, Ericka's old running dog. Teeth gritted in frustration, he considered his options. No matter, an inconvenience only. He'd gotten through FBI and WITSEC security before and would again. He would deal with Ericka's minion soon enough. O'Connell had been one of the agents who'd burst through his door in São Paulo, meriting special attention for that reason alone. It would be a nasty shock for Ericka too. Visiting him in the hospital to sic her old colleagues on Ericka had been just too much fun to pass up, truly delicious irony. *And you, Ericka, have no idea where that is going to lead you.*

He looked out the window again, seeing a cat's-paw of wind drag through tall grasses, a pleasing sight. It was important to his motivation to have things to look forward to. Isn't that what idiot motivational speakers and tiresome life coaches said? Always gift yourself with small rewards? He chortled at the thought. *Oh, I will. And then on to much bigger things.*

Almost absent-mindedly he dropped the stolen information about several jihadi rats into his processing folder. Like all intelligence agencies, the Pakistanis did not keep full files on human sources where they could be stolen. Locations were usually known only to the handlers and committed to writing just in locked-up paper files, if recorded at all. It was the greatest irony of the digital era that the most secure information, the kind that can never be stolen, now existed only on paper and then never copied. *How else to be sure?* He activated the find function and the Providence symbol appeared on his central screen. It really didn't matter where people put anything. As long as he could specify what he was looking for, the all-seeing eye of God could see it and then so would he.

And finally for you today, Wing Commander Yusef Abidi, a little bit of a heads-up about who you are annoying. He opened his portal into the intelligence network one final time, inserting prototype software for its first operational use. A type of program commonly called ransomware but with a significant difference. There was no way to undo it, no key that would ever open it again. Similar to an encrypting tool he'd used in the past to cover his tracks, this one perpetuated self-propelled along a network, rendering all data within reach forever beyond use while proactively disabling defensive software. It combined worms and other network-penetration code with significant machine learning and encryption abilities. He called this one Oblivion. Smiling to himself at his own sense of drama, he watched the attack unfold.

Insistent pounding jarred his teeth, forcing him out of a deep sleep, opening his eyes to stare at the only thing visible in his office, the hallway lights framing the door. "Sir, there is an emergency requiring your presence!"

Yusef pushed himself erect, lifting his feet off the desk before leaning to switch on his desk lamp. *Damn, didn't mean to do that.* His voice was hoarse, throat dry. "Yes, what is it?" He was watch commander today, requiring him to remain on premises for a full twenty-four-hour shift, responsible for all operations and decisions required until relieved from duty, or a higher-ranking officer took over.

The hinges creaked as the heavy door swung inward, the head of security leaning in, maintaining his grasp on the door handle. "We are under attack. Our entire network appears to have been compromised. The analysts believe it is him: Dantalion."

"Allah preserve us." Yusef lunged to his feet, pulling his uniform jacket from the back of his chair as he ran.

Oh dear, look at that—they used a set of servers for backup instead of physical media. Very amateur hour and it will cost them. He adjusted his enhanced reality headset where it pinched his scalp, peering at the network chart displayed as if it floated in the air in front of him. He pointed, selecting a single component, expanding his view of his invasive software's progress. Oblivion was through the barriers and working its way through contents, using co-opted processing power to overwrite or encrypt all the data it could find.

There we go, some bright light in the ISI has remembered that computers need electricity and has started unplugging them. Well done, Einstein! Good thing he'd told Oblivion to begin with the servers in easy physical reach. The ones going dark on his schematic were finished and beyond use already. *Now for some fun*. Savage heat coursed through him, his mouth dry as he moved to the next stage of his attack, taking manual control of their physical security system. Like most well-designed premises, it had a lockdown feature that activated backup power sources. He selected the rooms he wanted, triggering the sealing of armored doors, flipping on the failover to batteries. Designed to keep intruders from overrunning the facility, it would take them some time to cut through their own doors. Imagined mayhem fueled a smile as he reached for his water, his physical hand appearing virtually in his goggles' display.

The man turned to look over his shoulder at Yusef, his eyes concealed by welder's glasses. "At least another fifteen minutes to cut the bolts."

Yusef pounded the wall in frustration, catching himself from cursing him just in time. This would be over long before then. He took a moment to contain himself and steady his voice. "Thank you, please proceed with all haste." He spun on his heel, striding down the hall to where two dripping men pounded the wall, trying to break through concrete with fire axes. The stale air was thick with the stench of sweat and cement dust.

Achmed glanced up, his wet uniform stuck to bulging shoulders. Seeing Yusef's stare he shook his head. "We can't find the cabling. We are just knocking holes in the wall like blind men. Sir, does no one know where they run?"

Calm descended on him like being dipped in ice water. *This was over. Taken down like fools, completely defenseless.*

He slapped the man's shoulder, the solid mass unmoving, like patting a horse. "Not anymore. Thank you. You have done all you can. The wiring chart like everything else was somewhere on the system this great bastard has just destroyed." *He has won this battle. All we can do now is be ready to win the next one.*

They had chortled to themselves two years ago when this same Dantalion had battered down the FBI's defenses and stolen their data. This was worse. It appears he was now able to propagate malware through an entire secured network through a single entry point. As the doorway to the stairs clanged shut behind him, he bent over—hands on his knees—taking deep, measured lungsful of air. Briefing the brass was going to be unpleasant, but the upside needed to be considered and a plan made. Heads would roll for this but not his. He had advocated for measures that might have prevented this or at least minimized the carnage. All this was on record. Offices on the top floor would soon be vacant. This could be his time to rise.

Her brain was coming alive at the trickling pace of a melting ice block, the cloying effects of chemically enhanced sleep melting away. Ericka slouched in the cushioned depth of the old wicker chair, feet up, her nose in a mug filled with the aroma of thick, black coffee, sun streaming through the window. She scowled at the VR rig, wondering who was on the other end. The fact that they worked meant someone back at the ranch had puzzled out at least a little bit of Dantalion technology, probably Clarke. Tim had already tried to bring her back so unlikely they would use him for the second try. It had better not be Mrs. Donnelly, Tim's aunt and her confidante, counsellor, mother who never was. A stab of anger accompanied the thought they'd stoop to try it. No, it would be O'Brien or Steiner.

Everything that has gone profoundly wrong for me in the last few years started with blinking lights on one of these things. Ericka had set them on the corner of her new table, the row of green LEDs blinking their unwelcome invitation every twelve hours. She'd considered throwing them out, but she'd have to dispose of them with enormous care, not easy in a vacation rental in the resort town of Turicentro de Veracrúz. Her presence here would require less stealth and the large chain hotels nearby offered easy rotating network access for her to pirate. This place was better, but it was unlikely she'd be here long.

She leaned over, grasping her laptop one-handed, flipping the lid open against her knees. *Everything green, no intrusions or scans detected.* She opened the modified browser to carry out her morning ritual, flipping through pirated reports shared between intelligence services. She gasped, eyes wide at the highlighted line at the top. She sat up, putting her mug down to read, 'Confirmed Dantalion Attack on Pakistani Intelligence.' *What is his fascination with them? Either they've got something he really wants or they've profoundly pissed him off.*

She shook her head as she scoured the briefing, nibbling her lip. *Previously unknown malware capabilities? Did no one read my analysis of his attack on us? Sounds like he's made some improvements, but this should have been preventable.* Perhaps her report and recommendations hadn't been shared outside of Five Eyes, a mistake he'd exploit. She was pondering the risks of trying to communicate with the Pakistanis directly once again when the headset chimed the end of their twelve-hour cycle. She looked up. It had been her plan to simply let them run out of battery without her doing anything that could trigger a detectable response. It might be trying to tell them where she was, but they'd found her once already.

Perhaps there was no harm in it. She couldn't go back but why not talk? Longing filling her, she didn't bother to wipe the tears running down her cheeks. They'd never take her back now, just a stupid fantasy. She turned the VR rig over in her hands, so much like his, complete with facial mapping to display expressions. The lights were blinking but it wouldn't be long before shutdown. The midmorning sun streamed through her window warming her legs, and the impulse took her.

Ericka tugged them on, banishing all outside influence on her senses, dark silence welcoming this time, rather than ominous. She could hear her own breathing, still feel the sunlight. There were a few flashes of green light as code ran accompanied by a noiseless hiss, flooding the headphones.

The voice sounded tinny, pitched high with excitement. "She's connected. Really? Are you sure?" *Steiner? Interesting.* An unintelligible murmur answered, then Steiner again? "I must have privacy. Please leave and lock the door behind you." *Yes, Steiner for sure.* "Ericka, if you are there, wait one moment while I put these on and get settled. This is unexpected."

She'd come this far. "I'll wait."

"It is so good to hear your voice." There was a rustling sound, then chair legs scraping a hard floor. "There we go."

The lights came on and a room appeared, a passible CGI replica of an FBI interview room. The impressive avatar of Steiner sat behind a much nicer desk than the cheap government furniture she remembered. On the walls, wood paneling replaced tired white paint. The thought of how she must look made Ericka want to giggle.

His voice now sounded as she remembered it. "You seem in a better frame of mind than I'd been expecting."

Oh, was that so? "Expecting drooling wreckage?" *Trying to engage her by pissing her off? Good idea!*

"Yes, drug-addicted and on the verge of mental collapse was what I'd been expecting." His tone was level. He might be restraining his avatar's expressions.

"What do you want, doctor?" Her tone was sharper than she wanted, but she wasn't sitting through a lecture.

He was using his clinician voice now. "Personally, to continue with your therapy. I believe I can help. On behalf of the organization, I am to relay an offer that has come from the considerable efforts of Mr. O'Brien."

Ericka sat upright, surprised. If O'Brien was involved something had happened worth listening to. "Recommendations on Scotch at the duty-free?"

The avatar's face gave a cartoonish hint of annoyance, but he maintained iron control over his voice. "Time to be serious please. The government is prepared to offer you an immunity agreement." Steiner repeated the terms, while she tilted her head in concentration.

Buy time to think. This was unexpected. "For what? Am I charged with anything?"

Steiner responded again in a deadpan tone. "Not that I am aware of. Nor do I wish to be made aware of anything that you might someday be charged with. Medical help is never tied to a bargaining process."

"Very noble. I'm not coming back. I can't. Ever." Ericka heard her own voice crack as her shoulders knotted with tension.

Was that a sigh, stifled before he answered? "I will leave you to consider the offer on your own. What we speak of from here on is between me as your physician and you as my patient."

She wondered whether the facial scanning was good enough to show her eye roll. "I'm familiar with the limits of patient confidentiality."

"Tim has assured me there can be no interception or recording of what we say. He has seen to it personally."

Ericka wondered for a moment if he was being deliberately obtuse. "I meant the limits governing you."

His voice carried a hint of something—eagerness? "Yes, let's discuss that before we go further. We will discuss your mental health, but it must be done without relaying to me any of the events that have occurred since São Paulo. Simply put, Ericka, don't leave me in the position of having to choose between violating a confidence or lying to the FBI. Yes?"

Okay, I'll play. "Who says anything has happened that would interest them?"

"Quite so!" He paused for a moment, seeming to gather himself. "So, let us begin. The description I received left me gravely concerned. Opiates, a flat in disarray, looking ten years older. Hostile and uncommunicative. Do I have this right?"

The flash of anger made her catch her breath. *Thanks, Tim. Jerk.* "Sorry, I think we've missed a step. The part where

I decide whether I'm interested in remote shrinking for an unknown purpose."

Ericka could imagine what he was thinking, but the Steiner avatar was motionless until he spoke, mouth out of phase with words. "We have established in the past that your intelligence makes much of what normally constitutes therapy, shall we say, difficult to administer. As always, all I propose to do is assist you with insight and the tools for self-analysis. Allow you to peer where your ego and stubbornness usually won't let you look."

Goose bumps rose from the sudden chill. *Asshole!* "For what? What do they want from me? Maybe I just want to be left alone."

That put some steel in Steiner's voice. "You want to spend the rest of your life hiding, on the run? Having conversations in your head with people long gone? Picking imagined fights with people not present? Sleeping only with the benefit of abused medications?"

Ericka struggled to inhale, like she'd been gut-punched. His read was uncanny sometimes. She rasped a response. "That was low. Go to hell!"

"Forgive me if the circumstances dictate that I be unduly direct. Your behavior is what people often do after they have suffered some sort of psychotic break. I am not trying to torment you, but self-perception is always impaired and prevents recovery. You must face yourself as you are."

The black was rising again, smothering her ability to think. "For what? You think I'm going to ride back into the FBI and vanquish this monster? I'm all used up. Someone else is going to have to do it."

This time there was a pause before Steiner spoke. "Ericka,

as I have said, this is not an effort by me in asset recovery done on behalf of the FBI. It is to make you whole. You must overcome what has happened. When you left, you suffered from events in your career—some I knew of, some I didn't. You had tremendous unresolved anger from your sister's death."

Oh, I've resolved that in a big way. If only you knew. "Just leave me alone."

His avatar's hands rose, palms up. It would have been comical in any other circumstances, a machine parody of the real man. "You can't imagine your current course of action is going to end well. You'll never run him to ground on your own."

Fuck this, I'm out of here. "Here's my answer. Work your way up the food chain, find the stuffed shirt who set this in motion and tell him to kiss my ass!"

"Ericka, that isn't what this is about." The VR was good enough to give his avatar a look of dismay. She tore the headset off, tossing it to the couch where it bounced to the floor before spinning to face the window. Her heart drummed against her ribs as she raised her feet to the ledge. The window was open, the cool breeze welcome. She sat watching the tops of the palms dance in the wind, thinking of possibilities. Anger, self-isolation, intrusive memories, she could read the shrink textbooks as well as anyone. Awareness didn't make the pain stop.

Shame was a dreadfully effective motivation to rewrite history, creating memories that never were, convincing yourself that they're true. It wasn't an enormous leap to writing an alternate history in your head. Ericka had done that for years. It was nothing new, wishing something hadn't happened, that you'd not done what you remembered doing, a gut feeling you can never put the past fully behind you. How could she be forgiven when she couldn't absolve herself? How could Judas repent when the memory of spending silver rose unbidden in the mind's eye?

It wasn't killing she couldn't process. A dead pervert in Spokane she'd lived with. She hadn't consciously decided to end his life, but there was no denying it was a possible outcome of kicking a handcuffed man down a flight of steps. She had agonized at how it reflected on her, mortified what her sister Patty would've thought, but the end of the man himself did not weigh on her. The world was better off without him. The second time she'd taken a life, in the heat of battle in Dantalion's São Paulo lair, produced no recriminations. Abs lay dead on the floor. She and Tim would've been dead in seconds if she hadn't. There was nothing to forgive and the world wouldn't miss another thuggish killer. Police sometimes had to kill. It was an unavoidable part of the job.

Frederico Martinez was something else entirely. The thought froze her soul as she replayed events in her head. The opportunity was too much to resist. All those years of anger and hate for what they'd done to Patty burst open the minute she opened the files Dantalion had given her. The instant transition from wanting to having and the opportunity overwhelmed all restraint. The malware she'd taken from Dantalion's servers wasn't hard to modify, such elegant simplicity. All too easy to manipulate data, steal cartel money, create an iron-clad trail of breadcrumbs to Martinez's door then keep the chase rolling. When he drove across the desert to elude his former colleagues, all too simple to point the hounds where the bastard was hiding. *He had it coming in spades*. Seeing him the last time through a hacked bank security camera, she'd thought he looked like a frightened rat. Contempt and hate overwhelmed all restraint, the thrill driving her to move on to the next one, making her plans without reflection.

Next was Antonio Rojas. The memories were less distinct, almost like they weren't hers at all, emotions alien to her, more like a blurry video of something someone else had done. Like a movie where she could feel the emotions behind the camera, but they weren't hers. *Did it even happen like this? Was that what true insanity felt like, the psychotic break Steiner was on about, when you felt like someone else's thoughts were in your head?* Self-diagnosis really didn't help. Steiner was of course right: the retreat into isolation bred anger, addiction and led to risk-taking behavior, anything to salve a wound that would not close. There was no stopping and no turning back.

Rojas, she would see with her own eyes, stand beside him while he died, see life's light flicker and disappear. That was the plan. Ericka could remember parts, not sure the memories were accurate or even in the right order. *Had her mind scrambled them, allowing a neural rewrite as a matter of self-preservation?* It was a colossal risk. She took it knowing she might be joining her quarry in the ground at the end of it. This other person, whose memories now shared her head had sneered at the risk, wanting revenge so very badly.

She'd watched Rojas for a time and knew his pattern. He had a different name now, Juan Gómez, a common name bringing him the gift of obscurity. It wasn't the first time he'd changed it since they'd raped Patty. In his profession, being connected to your past was always a hazard. Occasionally, his work took him into the maze of Mexico City and into the Ciudad Neza district in particular. Poor and crime-ridden, it provided an endless supply of recruits for the gangs and that appeared to be what Rojas did there on his periodic trips, besides whoring. She'd never seen him travel with family.

His itinerary in hand, lying in wait for him posed no hurdles. Ericka's dark hair and dusky skin, combined with her language proficiency, had always allowed her to travel south of the border unremarked. If she kept to herself, her lack of a local accent would not single her out for curiosity. Getting out afterwards was the challenge. Any sudden flight could light her up for Rojas' colleagues, so she decided to stay, but the bolt-hole suite she'd set up had become her prison for months. She'd barely set foot outside.

No amount of trying would do it. Some of the memories were either gone or repressed, drowned and washed away in a sea of chemicals. She could still see on her own computer some of how she'd prepared, how she'd stalked him. A private plane would bring him to Mexico City Airport where a rental car waited, a Cadillac Escalade. He'd booked a large suite at the same hotel he always used. His credit card bills from previous trips had been stored in a desktop folder where she'd put them. Creatures of habit, people's GPS trails alone showed them following the same routes to the same places time and again. *After all, that's why people bought mobiles, to record everything they did, all day, every day, right?* She had no recall of actually doing any of it but clearly, she had.

Ericka opened her eyes, surprised at where she was, so complete was memory's immersion. She squeezed them shut, clenching her jaw, irritated with herself at the nihilistic compulsion driving her to rerun this mental home movie.

Involuntary flashbacks were part of daily life, a cerebral video set on an endless loop. Like a bad song on a car radio, once heard it can't be dislodged. When she closed her eyes it started again, lights dimming in the cinema as the show starts.

Another hazy, isolated memory, sweat dripping on concrete, installing components, minor modifications to a car's circuit board allowing remote control, then tweaking software so she could drive it from a burner mobile. Any car that could change lanes on its own would do. It only had to work once. Then, eyes watering from bleach, scrubbing the interior ensured no DNA traces. How long these took or when she did them were forever gone to her.

Sitting on a bench across the street, she looked like a tourist immersed in her phone, one amongst many thousands. A reflection in a window, she wore dark glasses, a headscarf, a blond wig protruding from underneath. Fully charged, the car was near the hotel in a place away from any security camera.

And there he was. She could see him from the shoulders up as he made his way out of the hotel, walking slower than usual, the smile on his face boiling her blood. All her muscles tightened, her breathing shallow as she focused down the street where the car waited, remembering the burning rage, feeling it again, letting it fuel her, exulting in it. Another glance at Rojas as he emerged from the entrance looking behind him, gesturing, and it was time.

The car's tires chirped as it accelerated, the whine of electric motors lost to the city's din. A glance at Rojas—he was moving, mere feet from the crosswalk. Concentrating on the car, tilting her mobile to steer it, gritting her teeth as it came up to freeway speed, head up to watch, a final surge of adrenaline. There was the final reward, a look of wide-eyed horror on Rojas' face. He had time to pivot backward before it struck, catapulting him into the air, spinning, to fall limp to the ground like a ragdoll, striking the pavement headfirst.

Then a short silence before screams filled the street, shouts to call an ambulance. She slowed the car, allowing it to make a preprogramed turn into an access alley where in a few seconds it would overload and burn, taking her modifications with it. Just another gang hit, if a little more creative than usual.

It was not over, now the worst was to come. Cringing as it played out, this part a clear slow-motion replay—getting up, walking to see his dead face, to gloat. All tension lost now, breathing easier. Rest easy, little sister, only one left now, then they're all gone. No answer. Patty's answering voice had ended, vanishing as Ericka pocketed the thirty pieces of silver two years before. Rojas was obscured by the line of parked cars, but she measured her pace. He wasn't going anywhere. *Don't draw attention.* She rounded the last one. He was sprawled face down, a large pool of blood spreading from a split skull. This was as she'd planned, but there was more.

Ericka doubled over, choking down a cry. The little girl kneeling next to the corpse was dressed in a frilly dress, no more than six. Small fingers clutched handfuls of shirt, shaking him. Shrieks became words. *"Levántate, Papi, levántate!"* Unable to turn away, she took hesitant steps. He'd brought his children. Why this time? The girl looked up, eyes bulging wide with devastated horror, bloody to her elbows, staring into Ericka's eyes. *"Ayuda a mi papi! No puede despertar."*

Christ, what have I done? Her eyes! I've condemned a child to live my life. Become another me? Or worse, like him. The world went black and silent.

Back to the present. She didn't blink, staring out the window at the tops of palms now dancing in the breeze. Her memories were unclear after that, impressionistic like video shot with a Monet filter. Sitting on the curb staring until the ambulance arrived. Someone—probably one of the attendants—asking if she knew him. She shook her head, pushing to shaky feet, the man's grip steadying, asking if she was okay, just the presence of mind to answer in Spanish.

It must have taken hours to walk to her bolt-hole, sitting staring at the wall, unmoving until long after dark. The image of the child's stricken face would not leave, playing over and over and over. Now, almost a year later, the vignette of horror had run again. Her shoulders slumped with exhaustion. She turned to stare at the VR set lying where she'd thrown it. Trapped in a mental loop, no way forward, no way out, no escape from the past. *So, this was what insanity felt like.*

12

Backlash

Tim bit his lip to force down the chuckle as he looked in the side mirror. Mirza's eyes were wide, aghast at the scene out the window. It was named the Hoh rainforest for a reason. Wind whipped the torrential rain until it became gray streaks running almost parallel to the ground. Enormous cedars crowded the gravel road, thick moss dripping from lower branches, forming a dark wall, impenetrable to sight more than a few feet in. Jarring potholes shook the vehicle every few seconds. Ahead, the road opened out into a small clearing, revealing what had once been a small hunting cabin, one that had clearly seen better days. The cedar siding was weathered to a washed-out gray, shaded by damp. The roof sagged visibly.

Tim shared a look with the local agent who was driving the battered SUV before turning back to stare at the back seat's sole occupant. The vehicle had long since been stripped of all digital technology. "Your villa!"

Mirza's mouth gaped before he answered in accented English. "Are you joking? I am not living in this hovel."

The driver turned to hide his smile as Tim continued. "What's not to love? You are miles from a working cell signal, this place is completely off-grid, lots of fresh air and exercise."

"Exercise?"

Tim gave the knife a turn. "You don't have to. Only if you want heat. Wood for the stove. It isn't going to chop itself."

The window in front of Mirza fogged from his breath as he peered out at the sodden ground. "Here, by myself?"

Tim was having trouble keeping a straight face. "Things are different here in America. We trust you. Besides, even if you walk out, every place you can get to will have cameras. Nasty if you popped onto someone's radar."

Mirza's mouth hung open in disgust. "What am I going to do out here? I will go mad."

Enough with the whining. Tim stepped out and opened Mirza's door. The chill was the kind of damp cold that went straight through clothes to the bone, a feature of Pacific rainforests that always surprised newcomers. "There are lots of books inside. If it was me, I would put some thought into how I can be helpful, the better to earn more palatable accommodation and a permanent relocation."

Mirza craned his neck to peer up at the circle of dark, uniform clouds framed by trees turning black with approaching twilight. "You can't be serious!"

Tim grasped Mirza's arm to steer him inside, feeling the bony shoulder under the several layers of clothes. Time to remind him where he stood. "You're not under arrest or anything. If you don't like it, tell us where you'd like to be dropped."

He pushed the door open to reveal a dark interior. Mirza's voice rose in pitch. "There is no power?"

Tim lifted the hurricane lantern from its perch, not answering while he fiddled with it, finally coaxing a usable flame to life. "There's a generator in the shed behind and plenty of oil for the lamps. We keep a week's food here, but someone from the local office will be by every day or two to check on you. We don't want too much regular traffic drawing attention." He handed Mirza a small yellow Garmin device. "It's been modified. Press the panic button on the side only if absolutely necessary. Remember if you do, we may not be the only ones who see it."

Mirza zipped up his fleece, tugging it tight around his neck. "It's freezing in here."

"Nippy, isn't it? Hope the firewood's dry." Tim turned for the door. "I'll be back when we're ready to start debriefing." Mirza stood in the doorway, his face a portrait of self-pity. Tim turned to watch as they pulled away, but Mirza didn't move, standing looking abandoned. They rounded the first bend in the road and he was gone.

The small drone perched motionless on the roof where a hooded male figure had placed it the day before, all identifying features removed, protected from sight by the raised roof edge, invisible from street level. A light coat of matte black paint rendered it a small shadow in the evening light, unnoticeable unless the observer were standing next to it. Without warning, it burst to life, all four rotors at full throttle, the sound like a squadron of meth-driven hornets, startling a group of crows into panicked flight. It lurched from the worn asphalt tiles, hesitating, seeming to search its surroundings, motors straining against the payload. It rotated on its vertical axis as if scanning the area, looking for threats before sending a quick burst of encrypted data signaling readiness. The answering instructions came an instant later and it was moving.

Without haste it crossed the edge of the roof, flew to the center of the intersection five floors below before choosing a street, following its preprogramed course towards its target two miles away. It maintained altitude down several streets, slowing to make ninety-degree turns at intersections, arriving at the edge of the park where it paused, performing one complete rotation like a petty criminal doing a heat check. The high-pitched whine was lost to the rumbling din of city traffic. No one so much as looked up.

The motor's pitch dropped several tones as it descended, flying scant feet above the highest leaves of the park's canopy, noticed only by nesting birds. Halfway across, responding to code embedded on its chip, it took a new GPS reading, confirming its final bearing before accelerating. Engines whining at a feverish tone, all considerations of battery life overridden, it streaked towards the target, a tiny wraith against evening sky.

Tim was late getting home, walking without haste as he grazed from the bag of deli pastries held in the crook of his arm, carry-on duffel slung over one shoulder. The strudel would have to serve as dinner tonight—he was too tired for anything but a whiskey then bed, regretfully alone. A long day, a late flight and he was in no real hurry, treating himself to an unhurried stroll to enjoy the warmth of the evening. Their new asset Mirza was as safe as they could make him.

He could stew there with the bloody horseflies for a bit before they started work on him.

Sleep tonight would be short, and he'd be in the office before the sun rose. Sleep was a rare luxury anyway, his attention focused by the chemical kick in the ass well known to all Red Bull junkies. Anger and relief wrestled each other, a common emotional theme since his return from Mexico City. If Steiner was right, Ericka was ill and needed help, but he had to consciously lower his knotted shoulders to dispel the angry notion she'd abandoned their cause, leaving him to take the heat. Maybe he should talk to Steiner. He snorted at the thought, him talking to a shrink. *As if.*

He stopped, looking at the pavement, lost in thought as he meandered. Ericka wasn't the first he'd seen crack over the years, but he suffered from seeing a personal hero fall. No one was immune. It wasn't like the obsession that led her away was news to him. He would see her again—he was confident now. Answers would be had in time. He looked up to see a woman with a small dog staring at him, eyebrows raised in concern. He smiled, turning the final corner before home, looking at his balcony, brow knotted. *Hard to tell in this light, but it looks like the lights are on.* Attention diverted, Tim didn't see the tiny shadow burst from the trees.

Its target was the front window of the third-floor apartment, a modest two-bedroom suite with a view towards the park, a tranquil scene from a welcoming deck. Split seconds to go, another line of code ran, activating the device fastened to the drone's underside, arming the fuse. The shape flashed above the street, skimming deck furniture before striking the main window beside French doors, blasting glass shards inward to tumble across the floor.

The two and a half pounds of Semtex and phosphorous encased in a magnesium shell detonated exactly as planned, little more than twenty feet from point of entry. Special Agent Tim O'Connell wasn't there, having missed his commercial flight home, hitching a ride on a military plane. He was late, not yet where he was supposed to be, where his stolen itinerary implied he should be. His aunt, Mrs. Margaret Donnelly, was there, minding his home, watering plants in the living room, her back to the street, thoughts on dinner, her final thoughts. She didn't even have time to register the noise of impact before it exploded two feet from her head, blowing her and the contents of the home into burning fragments, collapsing floors above and below.

Tim was staring at his home from the sidewalk below when the drone detonated. Eyes bulging, barely time to draw a gasping breath before the shockwave slammed him backwards, his tailbone striking concrete followed by the back of his head, filling his skull with flashing lights. His sight went black for a moment, returning just as burning debris rained down around him like hailstones. He rolled behind a parked car, covering his head until the impacts stopped.

His legs wobbled as he pushed himself to his feet, mouth agape, not feeling the sting of glass fragments embedded in his skin, vaguely aware of bloody dribbles on his chest and head. He staggered a few steps forward, bracing himself against a retaining wall, gripping the rough brick as he scanned the yawning hole in the side of his building. If either of his neighbors above or below had been home, they were dead, crushed under layers of concrete still settling as the structure burned. He took a few unsteady steps forward, back aching, before he noticed.

His attention was diverted from the wreckage by the familiar, eyes coming to rest on the car. The small white electric Nissan was his aunt's pride and joy, parked crooked to the curb as was the old lady's habit.

"Oh, no!" The words burst from his lips as tears blurred his vision, mouth parched. He looked again to be sure, but the bumper sticker, the flag of the Irish Republic, left no doubt. He slid to the ground, his back against her passenger door, tightening his gut muscles, fighting the urge to vomit. He could taste it in the back of his throat. There was nothing he could think of to do so he sat with his head hanging between his knees, watching as tears formed a puddle. He was still there, unmoving, when the emergency crews arrived.

The phosphorous-fueled magnesium ensured the fire would burn long and hot, leaving no traceable evidence and very little of the old woman to bury. It took six hours of concentrated firefighting work before the blaze was out, and they were unable to save the building.

If there was one thing American news networks could be relied upon to do properly, it was to locate and relay bad news, the nastier, the better. The warmth spreading through him made him tingle as he watched the video, verging on mild euphoria. He drew in a deep deliberate breath, his excitement producing an audible shudder as he exhaled. *If they thought him neutered because he'd had to move, think again. Let anyone think themselves safe now.*

As always, no loose ends. Time to send the richly deserved payment to his man who'd placed the drone for him. Someone who was not only a mid-level drug dealer, but also an addict in debt to his boss for heroin that had gone into his arm instead of to customers. That made him pliable but dangerous. *Never trust a man with a needle in his arm.* He sent the digital key releasing funds, which in turn would send the promised drugs to his man, along with a little something extra. He had no doubt some of the payment would be in a well-used syringe within an instant of arrival. The cocktail of bonus ingredients would kill him within minutes. Just another opioid death amongst many. Sad, but hardly worth anyone's attention. Certainly not his.

Interesting to see if American authorities told the truth. They were going to be very reluctant to admit a wanted cyber-terrorist was capable of picking off one of their precious FBI on American soil without leaving a trace. Seeing the screen change he unmuted, leaning back, fingers steepled, staring at the pretty reporter perched wide-eyed with the police tape behind her, fire crews still hosing down smoking rubble. It was axiomatic to the dogma of American news coverage that a pretty person standing with their back to an unfolding disaster and reacting with exaggerated emotions was better news than conveying real information. He turned the volume up, absently sliding a hand along his ridged cranial scars, cocking his head to listen.

"Authorities aren't saying much, but sources on the scene have told us the fire was unusually hot, burning persistently, in a manner they haven't seen before. The explosive power

can't be accounted for by any source known to be present."
Pausing for effect, features frozen to look serious and credible,
she continued in deadpan. "Foul play is suspected."

He doubled over as the unexpected belly laugh erupted,
holding on to the surface by one of his keyboards. It was
several minutes while he reran the clip, wiping his eyes and
blowing out a sigh. Yes, this was so much better than hiding
in the dark, letting others claim his acts, his triumphs. Who
cares how it would end? It was only ever going to end one
way. Above all, he would be remembered and feared.

He shoved his chair back, looking at his wasted legs,
rearranging his trousers to hide the protruding bones. *Not
that long now, and things will be better.* For a moment the
rage subsided and without warning he relaxed, a familiar
moment of tranquility following a successful kill. Fingers
drummed on the desk, a few moments of indecision.
Always nice to check in. His screen filled with video from
hacked webcams and security video. It took a few minutes
to find her, perched on a picnic table at the edge of the
parking lot camera's field of view, staring towards the
small lake.

*Curious, Claire looks so relaxed. Who would have thought
witness protection would suit her? Perhaps her husband
leaving her for fear of him had actually cheered her up?* Maybe
his former wife fancied herself safe, hidden just outside the
small city of Aberdeen, Washington. *Sorry, Claire darling, or
Sandra as everyone is calling you now, this silly notion might
have worked before the days of cameras everywhere, before
web crawlers and facial-recognition software, but not now.
All too easy, some of the idiots hired to protect you weren't
smart enough to turn off their phones when they came to*

visit. Can't stay off social media for a single shift. Apologies, ladies and gentlemen, not good enough!

What mostly worked to hide people from thugs and gangsters wasn't going to suffice with someone existing in the overlap, the place where the physical and the digital coexisted. Not against someone who slid without effort between the two, increasingly master of both. The overlapping space between the digital and physical realms was the world's blind spot.

His back stiffened as he watched, his mouth going dry. A man stood next to the table where she sat. Too far away to see expressions. His imagination supplied the smile she gave him, sliding into his embrace, forehead nestled on his chest. His hands pulled her to him before one slid down, holding her ass as they kissed. His lips curled into a snarl. That was his! Bubbling rage reddened his vision, adrenaline kickstarting his heart rate, covering him in a sheen of oily sweat. That bitch, she thought she was free to do whatever she liked. Fuck whoever she pleased, while he was left like this!

He sat there gasping with impotent rage, incandescent he had nothing at hand to strike at them in the instant. But no, for her something special. Not the quick, clean death of a bullet or an explosion. Discipline, he must maintain his discipline. He closed his eyes and forced relaxation with deep breathing. Her end was one to be savored above all others and be all the sweeter for his forbearance. He snapped off the screens and reached for his VR rig. *Time to get back to work*. He activated his new software, one he'd never shared with clients or followers, and never would. He called it the Eye of Providence after the Masonic symbol, the eye of God. Thinking the name curled his lips with a thin smile, for who could hide from the eye of the Almighty.

13

Reboot

Ericka hadn't heard until CNC news displayed the smoldering wreckage of Tim's home. When she read the names of the five dead on a local newspaper's website, she'd literally stopped breathing for a few moments. Ericka leaned back in bed, unable to see, eyes flooding with tears, lower lip trembling. Then it stopped. She leaned forward, ice cold inside, goose bumps rising. The fog evaporated and her mind was clear.

Cold purpose flooded to fill the void left by fleeing madness, driven away by rage, new purpose drowning lingering self-pity. She welcomed the return of cold anger, so long her companion and well of strength. She'd been clutching her hands together with such force it was painful. Unclenching them, she stared at her palms like they belonged to someone else. She stood to peer at a hallway mirror. Sallow, exhausted eyes stared back, not hers at all, no visible hint of her former strength.

How had Seneca said it almost two thousand years ago? "We are more often frightened than hurt; and we suffer more in imagination than in reality." That was the dark land where she'd lived for so long. Fear clogging her thoughts, every foreseen outcome a catastrophe. No path chosen and pursued, always fearing where it led, dragged under, sure in the knowledge she could never go home, not after what she'd done. Home lost in every sense, self-loathing guilt robbing her of her core belief that her purpose was righteous, her well of strength dry. What she'd done wasn't righteous. Without that, she'd not had the will or strength of purpose.

But here was the light she would follow out of her personal Elysium, a purpose requiring absolute commitment of everything she had. Because of this atrocity, she would find him and end him at any cost. No thought of after. There might not be an after, probably wouldn't be an after, but that didn't matter. Dantalion gone, deeds good and evil might balance. She'd become his Nemesis to restore her balance. Perhaps then, there was redemption for Judas after all, though not the sort that brought the sinner back into the light. There was no light.

She took hesitant steps away from her bed, glancing around the place she'd hidden, but seeing it now through different eyes, like staring around the home of a stranger. The clutter around her mirrored her mind as it had been these last months, a barely functioning quagmire. Turning back to her screens, Ericka chewed her lip. *Time to go back, to finish this whatever the price.*

The old bus rattled and shook as it hit a pothole, sounding like something had hit it, shaking her awake. Ericka's teeth chattered and she clutched her jacket tight, trying to stay warm in the ninety-degree heat. Her empty stomach roiled and heaved. She sat up, forcing her eyes open to peer at the parched hills of the Baja as they rumbled by. The highway was a darker ribbon through a dusty landscape, parched hills dotted with scrubby bush and cactus. Ericka lay back against the hard seat back, trying for a moment to stop her hands trembling before giving up and closing her eyes.

"*Estas bien mi amiga?*" The old man's smile was kind, eyes submerged in the type of wrinkles that take a lifetime of sun to burn into skin, gray hair and whiskers protruding from under an ancient cowboy hat. He leaned back over his seat staring at her.

She managed a tiny smile. "*Gracias. Demasiado tequila.*"

His smile broadened with an understanding nod. "*Tómatelo con calma la próxima vez!*" He wagged a fatherly finger in her direction before settling back into his seat.

Ericka glanced at her watch. Four days she'd been taking alternating short flights and bus trips, making her way towards the American border. It was going to be a few more days of living hell, but the initial withdrawal symptoms had to subside soon. A few days in a Tijuana hotel, then fly into southern Ontario before driving the last leg home. Her head had to clear sometime. She uncapped her water and took several large gulps before drifting off into blissful sleep, the rumbling bus unnoticed.

The polished white headstone glistened as rainwater dribbled down its side, illuminated by the light of Ericka's mobile. The patter of rain on the nearby oak drowned any sound of distant traffic. The earthy smell of the Virginia cemetery's immaculate gardens verged on oppressive. She knelt on the sodden grass, cold and wet unnoticed as she traced her fingers over the name of her confidante and mentor, carved into marble in final remembrance. Her hand shook, no amount of effort would hold it steady. To her right, an identical stone stood over the grave of the old woman's husband, dead years before her. Her faith in being reunited with him had been a constant source of strength to her. *What a comfort it must be, complete assurance of a happy ending beyond death. What great fortune to have a faith to lean against.*

She pulled herself to her feet, one hand on top of the stone, and walked away, now at the end of her time with the old woman, her friendship and guidance, mothering. Ericka determined she would return to mourn properly one day, but not now. Now was the time to honor the sacrifice and use the strength it gave her. There was no avoiding the stab of guilt at the pain she knew her disappearance would have caused the old lady, and now she could never make up for it. She mentally added the price to Dantalion's tally. Now she would find a way to present her bill. *If revenge and anger were her way now, then so be it.* A few more moments of silence and she turned on her heel, wiping away rain and tears, striding towards the street, looking forward to the walk.

She'd never been to Steiner's home, a top-floor apartment in an older brick building, surrounded by overgrown gardens at the end of a cul-de-sac. Dense trees obscured streetlights that projected wind-driven shadows on the pavement, the uneven surface a labyrinth of rain puddles. All the buildings were of the same era, the street a time capsule, the feeling of permanence a comfort lost when she walked to the front door to be confronted by security bars and a camera. Someone's best efforts at removing the graffiti had left an illegible outline of the tagger's name.

Surely, he could afford better than this hole even on what the bureau pays him. He was a complicated man driven by things she'd yet to understand. Ericka shook her head, adjusting her hood so it touched the rim of her sunglasses. Stupid really wearing them, part of a bad habit she didn't need now. She tugged them off. It was a great risk coming back before the agreement was signed, but now was the time for risks.

Her finger wavered over the keypad only for the time it took to sigh. This was never going to happen without risks, this one just the first of many. She swallowed rising panic, stabbing at the old-fashioned button next to his name, pressing for a count of three. One step away from the dirty console, then a pivot to face the camera as she tugged off the hood, staring right at it. She was lifting her hand to press again, surprised to see trembling fingers, when an electric hum and metallic click signaled the door was unlocked. Perhaps the intercom was out of order but she preferred the theory Piggy was dumbstruck. Right now, he was almost certainly wondering if her late night visit meant he should run out the back door and call for help.

She took measured steps up the staircase, giving Steiner time to gather himself. The railing was smooth to the touch, the hardwood worn bare in places. The musty smell from the carpet was short of obnoxious but spoke to the age and condition of the building. A pang of annoyance as she found herself winded when she reached the top floor. That wasn't going to do. There was movement to her right as a door cracked open, silhouetting a man from behind. That wasn't how a field agent would do it. She approached, stopping ten feet away, giving him a chance to change his mind.

A creaking hinge accompanied the door's slow opening. She couldn't entirely hide her smile at the pajamas and housecoat. Just as she would have imagined. Stepping closer, she fought the urge to hug him. "May I come in?"

Steiner nodded without expression, standing to the side. "Of course."

She still had no read on him. "My apologies for intruding unannounced."

A tiny snort of laughter. "Announcing yourself these days seems to me unwise, but no apology needed. I would offer you a port if you drank."

"I'd love one, thanks." She clenched her jaw as a single eyebrow rose. *He's watching me like a hawk. Can't blame him though.* He took her coat, gesturing to his couch before turning his back to pour while she glanced around. Again, everything old-fashioned but immaculate, a well-stocked bar laden with crystal glasses of every type, never to sip a particular drink out of something wrongly suited and uncouth. Her drink arrived in proper cut-crystal stemware filled exactly to halfway.

He'd aged more than he should have in two years. Pale, as always, but he'd lost a bit of weight giving his eyes a gaunt look. His nails and remaining hair were groomed to an uncommonly high standard that required constant attention, but it wasn't vanity, she didn't think. It was fear of being thought anything but proper. Like all shrinks she'd ever met, Ericka suspected he could use some time on the couch himself and wondered what was in there behind the public construct.

She stuck her nose in the glass, drawing a chortle from Steiner. "Don't bother. It's plonk. I'm not wasting the good stuff on you. It's too expensive."

"Then cheers!" She tipped half the glass into her mouth, the drink thick and sweet, smiling back at him.

His eyes lost the smile first and she stiffened as he scanned her eyes, face, body language. A few awkward minutes passed as each took another sip, eyes diverted. He put his drink on a side table and leaned forward, linking his fingers around one knee. "Can you do this? Are you ready?"

She had no illusions about what he meant. "I'm off the pills. I'm clean."

A tiny wrinkle twisted his nose before he caught it. "Not for long by the look of it. You'd hardly be the first to relapse when things heat up."

That was fair enough but, she was sure. "I guess I'll have to rely on you to keep an eye on me."

"I think you'll find in the fine print of your immunity agreement that you are now peeing and providing blood whenever someone snaps their fingers and points."

She watched his eyes narrow, waiting for her reaction. "I'm completely committed to finding this bastard and ending him."

Steiner's expression was devoid of any hint of the thoughts behind his eyes. "That isn't the same thing as being able to do so. And forgive me but time has shown you to have more than one agenda."

Ericka choked down the retort, squashing the anger behind it, looking down at her glass. Of course, they would all ask now. *Fair enough.* "I came back for only this reason."

She could see him struggling to hold all expression from

his features before he spoke. "Again, that isn't the same at all. This monster has defied all efforts to date. Even yours. Why should anyone take the risk of trying to help you?"

He was provoking her and it was working. She let the flash of anger show, her voice rising. "I don't know if I can get him. No one's ever encountered anything like him before. All I can tell you is he will have my undivided attention until he's taken down or I'm dead."

Steiner leaned back, taking a sip, seemingly gathering his thoughts once again. "And that, Ericka, is one of the more intriguing aspects of all this. He's had several opportunities to see that you do die trying, seemed willing to do it if you proved less than the worthy nemesis he expects. And then once he is sure you are defeated, he lets you live to fight another day. Why?"

"You tell me, you're the goddam shrink!" *Steiner was an ass sometimes. None of that Socratic shit.*

"Indeed." Another sip, visibly relished before swallowing. "Pathological narcissists will usually tolerate no rivals and quickly seek to eliminate them. As far as we know, you are the only one he even regards as a rival. The only one worth killing, but he doesn't. No drone through your window."

She flinched, almost spilling her port. "Fuck you, that was a cheap shot."

Now there was anger in Steiner's eyes. "If you don't have spine enough to absorb that, then this is over before it's begun."

She lowered her head, hiding her eyes, fearing she was tearing up. "Fair enough, but I am going to see that old woman's death play in my mind every day until I die."

"Which won't be long if you can't discipline your thoughts better than that."

Where is the anger coming from? He must feel betrayed too. "Why'd you help me, make the effort to get me back if you don't think I'm up to it?"

Irritation flared on his face before the mask slid back into place. "You're my patient. For that reason alone I'll help you, whatever you've done. That isn't the same as bringing you back into the fold."

Ericka found him almost impossible to read sometimes, so hard to tell where his professional persona ended and the real Piggy began. "I'm the only one who can do it."

He chuckled. "Oh very good, only colossal arrogance like that can sustain the confidence you'll need to see this through."

That drew a cackle of laughter she couldn't repress, the unfamiliar sensation surprising her. It felt good. When had she last really laughed? Some of the tension lifted and they both leaned back. "This evil bastard can do things most of his colleagues haven't even thought of."

"It isn't just his ability I worry about. I fear his psychopathy is progressing in a very dangerous direction." Steiner got up to fetch the decanter, pouring each of them another glass. "It isn't his technical prowess that concerns me most. Most of his greatest accomplishments haven't begun with writing code, but with co-opting those who can give him what he wants. His own depth of deviance is such it is like he can reach into their inner being and stir fear and want corresponding to his purpose. He then uses that to manipulate them into giving him things even he might not be able to hack on his own. In this sense, he hacks minds as much as technology."

Ericka's breath caught as she worked through the implications. Steiner was the only shrink in the lot who'd ever had any real insight into Dantalion. He'd been endlessly labeled and categorized by others, but none of them had produced anything that helped investigators anticipate him. Piggy's analysis always displayed a greater depth of thought. She gestured to him to continue.

"Consider his choice of handle. It is not just a display of megalomania. His daemon namesake can see into people's minds and plant his thoughts there, making his victim see whatever he wants them to see, want what he wants. Through sometimes astounding technical feats and diabolical manipulation and fear, our suspect does exactly that."

That very insight had made it clear to her before, barriers impermeable even to Dantalion's abilities would fall. He'd penetrated the minds of people made weak by deviance and fear of discovery long before he wrote a single line of code. His own depravity gave him the power over his minions, fear-driven obedience absolute. They followed him because he was one of them. In his success, they saw themselves triumphant, shared his glory. "I think it's more than just fear. You've heard them. These people admire him, something akin to worship."

He tilted his head in agreement, his round face displaying the intense smile he gave when engrossed in his craft. "Agreed. They imagine what they themselves could do if they had half his ability. They want his power for themselves, basking in his glow. They are disciples as much as anything."

"And this new direction. What am I missing?"

Steiner leaned back in his armchair, steepling his fingers,

unknowingly mimicking their target in a manner that made her swallow hard. "He knows the end is coming. Dantalion is no one's fool. At the start, he was content to hide in the shadows, feed his hunger vicariously, always safe and free to strike again. Now, he is regarded as an international terrorist and all the world's intelligence agencies hunt him, albeit perhaps not for the same reasons. His end is inevitable and he knows it. Far from constraining him, a mind plagued with his kind of psychopathy will find that irresistibly freeing. Motivating even. The pursuit of him now has the opposite effect it would on a normal personality. He will not dive for cover. He will lead his pursuers a merry dance then turn at bay to confront them, going out in an unforgettable blaze of triumph. To his thinking, it will have to top all he has done before, giving him a glorious legacy to carry on after he's gone."

Ericka had wondered at his endgame. "So, he'll keep trying to top himself, ending in a great final battle, a predator without equal, one for the history books."

"Precisely. And not make any attempt to hide who is behind it. No more letting his minions face the law. His purpose in hiding now is so he can strike again, but never concealing what he has done. Not anymore."

He was watching her again, evaluating, calculating. *So, the moment of truth, let's get it over with.* "Are we good? Are we going to do this?"

Steiner sipped the remnants of his glass. "You'll forgive me that I had to be sure. Your brilliance as an investigator would not be enough this time. I had to be absolutely sure. Sure, that the iron core will be repaired, forged to the temper required. If you wish to stay, please feel free to use my spare bedroom. I will call Mr. O'Brien in the morning."

* * *

SAC Hikari Shingen was almost impossible for Ericka to read. She'd met her in passing before, but never since she'd replaced Abara as head of the Dark-Web Intelligence Unit. Shingen's reputation preceded her. She was said to be as technically accomplished as those she commanded with a talent for motivating her team, maintaining focus until the job was done. Dark eyes, framed by graying black hair, projected a cool self-confidence. She said nothing while Ericka settled into her chair, then flipped through the small stack of papers on her otherwise clear desk. Ericka could see it was a copy of the immunity agreement she'd signed the day before, but she doubted Shingen was reading it for the first time now. A glance around showed the office to be free of clutter, not a trace of dust, no rings from coffee cups, much like her predecessor.

Perhaps a little levity. "I don't know what it means either, but my lawyer said to sign it."

One eyebrow went up as Shingen's eyes crinkled. "Well, I do, and I keep having to read it to remind myself it's real. Someone way up near the top of the DOJ or the bureau really thinks you're the only answer we have to our target. A divine gift to us mere mortals."

"More like someone a little farther down with a silver tongue and a keen mind convinced them it was in their interests." O'Brien's jovial face popped into Ericka's mind.

"Good to have friends of that caliber." It was clear to Ericka that Shingen knew who'd made this happen. Their eyes locked. "Now we'll have a frank conversation, shall we?" Hands almost delicate folded on the desk in front of her slight frame.

Here comes the leash. "Please."

Shingen's voice was soft yet crystal clear. "I'm not going to repeat the errors of SAC Abara. Leaving you to do as you please out of sight resulted in you going rogue right under his nose. All your previous open files were wiped some time ago by an external source, which I'm sure you know nothing about. I suspect this   " she pointed at the agreement with her chin "—would never have happened if anyone had ever gotten a look at what was in them." She waited, peering at Ericka.

Ericka mentally rolled her eyes. *Yes, as if, let me explain everything for you. Do I look stupid?* "Go on."

Shingen cocked her head to the side. "If you fancy this a career restart, think again. You're not back in the fold. You're here to carry out a single task, then you get your gold watch and ride off into the sunset."

Ericka forced a smile. "I'm quite clear what I'm here to do, thank you."

Shingen's voice held an edge. "You and I will have daily briefings where you will outline every investigative step before you take it."

Jesus, that's going to be tiresome. "Done."

Now a hint of a smile on her face. "And we'll be working closely with your old friends at Homeland and some new ones from the NSA."

Ericka expected no less. "Gods not the CIA too?"

A genuine smile lit Shingen's face, showing her for the real beauty she was behind the professional mask. "No, not the CIA. I'm not cruel." She leaned in, propping her chin on both fists, silent for a few moments, her expression neutral again. "You'll understand, I don't know what to make of you. All

I heard for years was wide-eyed, breathless accounts of your abilities and what you'd done. The bad guys you'd crushed. Then a bunch of rumors and gossip following the raid in São Paulo. Then this." She tapped the agreement with a perfect nail.

Ericka gave her a bland smile. *Well, you're just going to have to keep wondering.* "I'm not playing coy, but I'm not filling in the blanks either. Expect my undivided attention to be on finding this bastard, nothing more, nothing less."

Shingen didn't appear impressed. "Given the events of the last while, I would have to be some sort of moron to take that at face value. I'm not an idiot."

Ericka flinched, swallowing. *Yes, fair enough.* "I think we understand each other." She stood and extended her hand. Shingen took it, her grip firm but damp, some nerves behind the steel perhaps. The two women maintained the clasp, eyes locked before Ericka pivoted, turning to leave.

14

Reformation

Ericka stared at Tim, his expression telling her he wasn't going to speak first. "Can this Mirza really give him to us?"

He shrugged, staring along the edge of the boardroom table at his feet on the chair next to him. "He's certainly selling himself as the way through Dantalion's defenses. No one is going to be able to just give him to us." Tim didn't look up.

Ericka took a sip of coffee to bide her time. This was going to take a very careful approach to not end up in a shouting match. She quailed inside, realizing again the pain she'd caused this man she considered a brother. "Have you debriefed at all?"

"I tried to make a start on the flight back. He wasn't in a talkative mood." Tim stared back, not volunteering anything.

Ericka walked down beside the table, dropping into a chair in his line of sight and leaning towards him. She was going to have to force it. "I can't think of what happened without wanting to throw up. She was like a mother to me."

There was the anger. Just a flicker before he hid it. His tone was hard. "Like the real one, the one you didn't like?"

Take the hit, she had it coming, he had to know, no other way to regain his trust. "If I'd tried communicating, I'd have lit you both up. You professionally, but if he'd known I was alive and talking to her, I might as well have painted a target on her door!"

Ericka could see Tim's jaw muscles clench before he spoke. "Well done, how'd that work out?"

She dropped her head towards her knees, looking at the floor, not knowing if she wanted the answer. The patterns in the carpet blurred as tears filled her eyes. The closest thing she had to family and she'd caused them nothing but pain. "Was that about me? Did that fucking bastard put it together?" He didn't answer. "I have to know."

Eyes squeezed shut, not able to bear looking at him, Ericka waited, then heard a sharp intake of breath from Tim. "No, I think it was a shot at me for taking Mirza. You know how he is about traitors. I took that away from him, however temporarily. He was trying to kill me and she was in exactly the wrong place when he took his shot."

"I'm so sorry. If I'd stayed and hunted this bastard down, she might still be alive." Ericka still couldn't look up and he wasn't talking. Was Tim protecting her again, from the guilt, lying to keep her intact? Had the attack been to punish her? Very hard to believe otherwise. "Remember who we're talking about. He could well have known you missed your flight and figured out who was taking care of your place. She lived in the same building I used to. Hell, she was on the deck when his drone flew to my place two years ago."

Tim stared at the floor, expression flat, his shoulders giving the tiniest shrug. "Could be. Either way, she's dead."

"We can't work together like this." Stomach in knots, heart thumping, she raised her head.

Tim's head snapped up, staring at her, expression controlled. "No, we can't. But I'm having a hard time understanding what the fuck went on these last two years. We were partners. Friends."

Tell it like it was. He deserves the truth. "I can't tell you what happened, what started it, but I snapped. Not for a few minutes. Not an anger thing. Living in a very dark place for a long time, and yes on the pills in a bad way."

His expression said contempt. *Ouch.* "Oh good, that's going to make this easy."

"I'm off them."

Tim's tone contained heat now. "Bullshit! Who do you think you're trying to kid?"

How to convince him, but she hadn't touched them since she found out about Mrs. Donnelly. *I haven't even felt the urge until now.* Time to feel it now, and with it came the guilt that had helped drive her in the first place. Tim had to know she was genuine. "Fair enough but you'll see over time. I'm to spend plenty of time with Steiner, daily pee tests, blood every week. Seems I have a credibility issue." She smiled, hoping.

His eyes flooded with tears, but he was smiling. "Fucking right you do. Are we going to get him this time? This has to mean something."

Again, not a time for bullshit. "I don't know, but it's either that or I'm going into the ground trying." She reached out and they clasped hands, eyes locked, tears running down the cheeks of both.

★★★

Shingen gestured to Clarke. "Go ahead."

Ericka glanced across the table at Tim seeing he had no idea what this was about either, both responding to a text summons. They'd walked into the briefing room at the same time. As always, it held the mild tang from generations of sweaty cops, worn furniture lit by buzzing fluorescent lights.

Clarke's gaze lingered on Ericka for a few seconds, before she turned to address Shingen. The look wasn't friendly. "Mirza, says we have to move him to a secure facility. Leaving him in one place too long, especially out there, is going to get him killed."

Tim drummed his fingers on the metal table. "Rubbish. He's full of shit. He bitched about that place the second he saw it."

Clarke tilted her head, eyebrows raised. "He claims he had no idea we were going to leave him out there. He's telling his minders Dantalion will find him. Some new toy he boasted about called Providence."

Ericka was about to ask but Tim responded first. "He mentioned that on the flight back but wouldn't tell me what he was talking about."

Shingen broke into the conversation with an uplifted hand. "It seems we're going to have to move him anyway." She waved towards the open doorway. O'Brien lumbered in, tossing his bag behind a chair before dropping his bulk into a seat across from Ericka. He raised his eyebrows as he looked at her. They hadn't had a chance to speak in private since her return. O'Brien glanced at Tim who wore the same hard-eyed expression, staring at his mobile. Another glance back to Ericka confirmed to her his assessment of the team's morale.

Shingen looked at Ericka as she addressed the meeting.

"I've asked the DOJ to join us today. It will come as no surprise we are doing things a little differently going forward. Mr. O'Brien?"

He leaned onto the table, hands clasped. "We're going to need to fully debrief this Mirza guy, under oath, to get this rolling, warrants and wiretap for both you and Homeland. If you ever want to prosecute or extradite him, you need them. I know that's the last thing on your minds, but you need to keep all possible endgames in play. Not everything ends with a drone strike or shootout."

"This one certainly should, if there's any justice." Tim's comment drew a look from Shingen.

O'Brien looked away. "Can't disagree with you, but this has to go by the book from here on. We got Ericka back in carefully controlled circumstances and you need to understand that there will be oversight." He gave Ericka a quick smile. "That may require some modification from the standard operating procedures of the last while."

Not getting away with that, smartass. "Always good to have lawyers on board, like a shovel full of nice, gritty sand in the wheels of progress."

The gauntlet down, O'Brien perked up. "Yes, well someone needs to remind cops and spooks that what they actually do for a living is uphold the law."

"Looks like everyone is going to get their wish." Clarke held up a hand, staring at her mobile in the other. "Mirza's minders just texted. A drone just made several slow passes over the safe house. He's blown and they're moving him now."

Tim's eyes were wide. "Out there in the middle of nowhere? Where did the damned thing launch from?"

Clarke shrugged. "One of his guys with a backpack or an ATV? Doesn't matter now. Mirza was right."

Ericka shook her head, tension flooding her shoulders and neck. "It does matter. He didn't do this by randomly overflying the whole US with little biddy drones flown by his idiots. He knew where to look. How?" She looked around the room. "We need to speak to Mirza as soon as we can."

Shingen's brow creased as she stared back. "Shouldn't we get him somewhere secure, then spin him down?"

Ericka clenched her teeth. She's not getting it. Too much procedure manual, not enough thinking it through. "I don't think so. We need to proceed on the premise that we may not actually be able to protect him."

That got her a tilt of the head and an eye roll from her boss. "That's maybe a bit dramatic."

Ericka shook her head, locking eyes with Shingen. "Is it? How can you determine if facilities are secure enough when you've no idea how he found the last one?" She let it hang in the air long enough to establish no one had an answer. "I don't want to be pedantic about it, but he doesn't have millions of drones sitting in little, tiny silos all over the country waiting to do his bidding, yes?"

Shingen raised a single brow. "Your point?"

"That's three times now he's been able to use a short-range drone to get to a target. That we know about. He found my place, attacked Tim's home, and now a supposedly fully analog safe house miles from the nearest computer or phone. He isn't guessing. Hacking gas station security cams in town doesn't explain it."

O'Brien inserted himself, both hands palm up, gesturing. "Security aside, the sooner we debrief, the sooner I can get us in front of a judge and get the authorizations in place. We're going to be asking for some pretty intrusive surveillance that will tag a lot of people so the more we have for the judge about what this guy can do, the more likely we are to get it."

Clarke leaned over the table, turning to look at Ericka. "You're seriously suggesting we can't protect our witnesses?"

Tim craned his neck, speaking to Clarke. "My home wasn't in any public-facing database. He put a drone through my front window and detonated a bomb over my dining room table. We can't even protect ourselves."

Clarke looked down, flushing red. "Sorry, I didn't mean…" Tim glared for a few seconds before staring down, letting out a long sigh.

After awkward seconds, Shingen spoke to Ericka. "I take your point, but if you're right, how can we even move him?"

"Whatever our suspect's doing, it can't be instant. Assuming he's gotten in somewhere that gives him a hint or starting point, he has to collate and then focus his search before he'll have the precise location he'll need to strike. He needs time to move assets into position and prepare."

"Yes, and?"

Why does everything need to be spelled out like this? "At least until we get what we need from him, we'll have to keep Mirza in motion. And us too. No point obscuring where our source is if all he has to do is track us. He knows how we work." She stared at O'Brien. "He probably even knows we have lawyers slowing us down, inserting themselves in the middle of good police work."

O'Brien glanced at Ericka. "And making sure you have evidence you can use when you're all done with the Hollywood stuff."

Is he serious? That's an interesting fantasy. Ericka stared at him. "You're never getting a prosecution or a trial of this one."

Shingen sounded shocked. "That's most certainly our goal!"

Ericka fought to control the eye roll. "Sure, it's what we're always after, but my bet is this one proves a little bit difficult to arrest. At this point, the best we can do for his location is get the continent right."

O'Brien maintained eye contact with Ericka, his shoulders turned away from Shingen. "So, what's our play?"

Ericka glanced at Shingen whose cheeks were beginning to redden. "First, let's get him to a military base somewhere and shake him down. Figure out if we can protect him afterwards."

Shingen's tone was sharp as she leaned on the table staring at Ericka. "We have to be sure of the asset's safety."

Oh good, dominance games already. Show us who's in charge. "Dantalion takes out traitors for amusement, tortures them to death. This one betrayed him personally. He's dead already. It's just a matter of time."

Shingen looked baffled. "Well, we're going to do our best!"

"The longer we succeed, the more time he'll need to get creative."

Shingen raised her voice, intent on asserting her authority. "Agent Blackwood, if you got the idea that what I said was optional, you need to go back and read your agreement again."

Ericka looked down, avoiding eye contact, gritting her teeth. *Just take it. The important thing is to get what we can out of this Mirza before he's taken out.* She looked up into Shingen's fierce eyes, holding her gaze. "As you wish."

★ ★ ★

Maxim Semenov's mouth dropped open as the VR screens glowed to life, nothing like a little bit of fun to break up the tedium between gigs. There was only so much a man could drink and whores he could have before it was time for something new. He squirmed in his armchair, moved by the same tiny surge of adrenaline familiar to him from every time he'd ever gone into combat, not enough to fluster him, just enough to ignite his senses, allowing him to savor the violence of battle. He knew his life might have been very different, but understood he was the product of his beginnings. Insight into one's nature was the proffered gift of intelligence if one chose to take it. Growing up poor in Moscow in the days after the Soviet Union collapsed required a certain mindset and toughness to thrive.

Thuggish street behavior at the behest of the rising mob had led first into the hands of the police and from there into the army, the time-honored place for young men whose nature needed taming, anger focused and honed into something useful. Semenov's ferocity, reckless bravery and brains had not gone unnoticed by his superiors and he was duly permitted to join the Spetsnaz, or Russian special forces. Sadly, it had turned out that he couldn't contain his violence within the disciplined confines required by life at the tip of the Russian spear. That was the past. Now, he had come into his own, he and a loosely knit group of like-minded colleagues, offered for hire to anyone needing a job done outside the confines of society's normal structure. Semenov got to decide which gigs he took, Semenov got to carry them out as he saw fit, and Semenov got the wealth to live the life that was his due.

Semenov had, of course, heard of this one. Who had not? When the unsourced message appeared on his mobile, telling him to expect the VR kit and inviting him to speak, he had been thrilled. Here was a man worth following and to make things even better, this Dantalion shared his love of theatrics and showmanship. Life tended to settle into gray monotony if you let it, and it was far too short to let that happen.

The room was like something in a palace at St. Petersburg, sumptuous furniture surrounded by art depicting the czars, set at night and lit by candles in wall sconces. The hulking figure in the chair facing him was built much like he was, thick-framed and muscular, head shaven, wearing what looked like the ornate clothes of the prerevolutionary era, scaled up to much larger than he should be. The gloom hid all features except the silhouette of the oversized head. Looking down made him chuckle. He was dressed as a late-imperial-era Cossack. *So that's how things stood then.*

With a tilt of his head, the giant spoke, his voice rich in timbre. "Greetings, Mr. Semenov. I have long been an admirer of your work."

Semenov nodded his thanks. "I am honored. Of course, your reputation precedes you." No point beating about the bushes. "I am surprised my services are of interest to you. You are reputed to operate in, how shall I put it, different environments than I do."

The head bobbed once, the tone sounded amused. "Correct, but there are some things that do not happen at the push of a button. Sometimes a man of your unique skill set is best suited."

Semenov dipped his head in acknowledgment. This was going to be very entertaining. "Do you mean my military skills or my reputation for employing methods often distasteful to my thin-skinned competitors? My fee varies accordingly."

The massive form leaned back, bringing his features partially into light. Semenov could make out the hint of a smile. "You may name your fee. I expect I will have several tasks for you. Tell me, have you ever traveled to the United States?"

"I have not, but I have always wished to see it."

"You will like it, I expect."

Steiner put the worn hardcover book down as she walked in, settling back into his chair, appearing apprehensive like he had no idea how she was going to react. Ericka glanced at the title. "You're reading Seneca now?"

He smiled. "I always did, but our discussions before you left and your interest in his writings drew me back."

She looked about the room. He had an office now, not working out of a borrowed boardroom anymore. *Good, he deserved it, a shrink who actually had some insight should be cherished. Who would have thought?* "And what does the venerable Lucius Seneca have to say to us today?"

Steiner picked up the book, flipping pages. "I read one last night that made me think of you—yes, here." He glanced up before reading. "'No man has been shattered by the blows of Fortune unless he was first deceived by her favors.'"

An odd choice among many Seneca gems. "You're shrinking me already? No pleasantries? Why aren't you asking me about my experiences and feelings from the last few years?"

The laughter was spontaneous. When he dropped the professional façade, his humor and sincerity were truly charming. "I gave up trying to shrink you, as you put it, a long time ago. And, no I'm never going to ask you what has happened since our last professional meeting. You are going to heal yourself, I'm just going to provide you the tools."

Ericka held on to the chuckle, settling into her chair, readying herself for one of their duels of wit. "How, when you don't even know what happened?"

"I think I do. I just don't know what caused it. That will be enough."

Time to give him a poke. "We're not going to do that cognitive behavioral shit again are we?"

Steiner laughed. "We'll do whatever we have to." He leaned with his chin on his hands. "I'm not going to lecture you on psychosis, but guilt can become delusional. It can enhance the severity of what we hold to be misdeeds. It can lead to psychotic, disordered thought stimulating the belief that punishment is both deserved and looming. You can read the symptom list for PTSD yourself. Uncontrolled reliving of events will be the worst for you, I suspect."

Ericka closed her eyes, squeezing them shut, a small Mexican girl's shattered expression flooding her mind's eye. "What if, for the sake of argument, the deeds were real, not exaggerated at all?"

Steiner's expression changed, back to the neutral professional. "A disordered mind can't make that assessment. Concentrate on the healing, not on the self-diagnosis. That leads nowhere."

This isn't going to help me if he doesn't understand what's happened. He's assuming I'm exaggerating. "But if correct, then what?"

Steiner took the time to draw a slow breath before sighing.

"Then atonement may be the key, a return to balance if you will. A true function of becoming someone's nemesis, not revenge. Not in anger. You must satisfy yourself that the good you do now outweighs the evil you blame yourself for. Remember your Seneca, anger is a form of madness. What you do must be justifiable through logic, not merely feed your lust for revenge."

He really did help, drawing her out of her own tortured, circular logic. Some of the weight lifted. Inside her head, it seemed brighter, like fresh air and sunlight through an open window. *There is a way forward.* "I thought you were a shrink, not a philosopher."

His eyebrows went up as he tilted his head to the side. "There is much overlap, and one often slips seamlessly into the other. Or so I've often thought. Nothing in modern theories of anger management would have surprised the stoics." He was smiling again. "Rage is too toxic, for you in particular. It will burn you into nothing before you complete your task."

Ericka sighed. He was right. A long slow-burning anger, planned and executed with great care. *A decade yearning for revenge, then I live it. Now, I can't bear even to bring it to mind.* "Go ahead."

Steiner leafed through the book to where he'd dog-eared a page. "This one. Seneca might have written it just for you. 'No man becomes braver through anger, anger does not come to assist courage, but to take its place.'" The ancient words summed it up. Her muscles tightened, forcing her gaze down. He'd hit it right on the head. Her greatest fear, that she was fundamentally the same as him.

How does a sick mind make that judgment without straying

into paranoia? If she couldn't redeem herself as good, then perhaps counterbalancing a great evil was enough, absolution and balance a poor substitute for forgiveness. *It would have to do.*

15

Prodigy

Aalem Mirza was no idiot and this wasn't going to be a standard interrogation. Ericka could sense the keen mind behind the weary eyes, evaluating and considering in the same manner she did. The fact he'd been selected as one of those to be trained by Dantalion spoke to both his intelligence and to some form of deviance, the latter necessary for his former teacher to maintain control. He was not as trained as he should be at hiding his thoughts, a common problem with criminals who used computers to commit crimes. They were used to having a screen between themselves and whoever they were speaking to, they didn't know how to make themselves difficult to read. They hadn't the personal skills to respond with someone staring in their eyes. No time to Google things then craft a lie before typing. That was one weakness.

Another was the obvious contempt for her and for being questioned by a woman. The fanatics, misogynists in particular, underestimated the person facing them, always to their detriment. It would be difficult to articulate what it was in his expression that signaled disdain, but Ericka saw without difficulty. She glanced at O'Brien, his cue to begin the plan they'd discussed. They faced Mirza over what looked to once have been a mess hall table, now sitting dead center of a room once used for troop barracks. He'd been brought to the middle of Fort Lewis, Washington, at night in the back of a military truck, his fatigue obvious from red eyes and haggard features.

Mirza glanced back and forth between them, eyeing the video equipment behind them before speaking. "Are we going to sit here all day or are you going to get on with it?"

O'Brien read him the standard warnings about lying, then swore him on the Quran. "Do you understand you are under no compulsion to speak?"

Mirza snorted his contempt. "Am I not? I am not even provided a lawyer."

O'Brien answered, "You don't need one. You're not detained and you're not charged with anything. Any time you want you can leave. Just say so. The door's behind you."

Mirza looked away before answering. "I would be dead before Tahajjud prayers and you know it. Compulsion enough I think."

Time to make the first cut, albeit an obvious one. Ericka leaned towards O'Brien, her tone drenched in contempt. "If he knew anything, Dantalion wouldn't have let him live. The fact he's here and alive means he knows nothing."

O'Brien gave a dismissive shrug, pretending to be unconcerned with Ericka's opinions. "We'll see." He leaned back, silent, waiting for her to continue, an impatient man apparently waiting for a minion to get on with it.

Feigning the appearance of being chastened, Ericka

turned back to Mirza. "If you think we're under some sort of obligation to protect you, think again. You get witness protection for telling us everything."

Mirza's lip curled into a sneer. "I'm sure you mean a plausible attempt to protect me, just enough to protect yourself from any blame when he kills me. That's what you mean. Or do you have some other plan than putting me in the forest somewhere and hoping for the best?"

"If you think you've got a better option, just say so." *Keep reminding him of the alternative, of the fact he has none.*

Mirza smiled before he spoke. "I don't or I wouldn't be speaking with an infidel. That doesn't mean I have nothing to bargain with, like what he has in mind."

That was O'Brien's cue. "Spare us. He doesn't share anything very important with his minions. We know that."

Ericka piled on. "If he gave a damn about what you know, you'd be dead already."

She watched his body tense followed by flaring nostrils. "And yet you waste your precious time with me! Spare me the games."

Ericka gave him a scornful half-smile. "Then start with telling us what you have. An inventory of your very valuable wares."

"First my conditions must be met."

Time to rile him a bit. She leaned back to glance at O'Brien again, as if seeking his approval. "Maybe you need to go back to that cabin and think for a month. Think hard about what you've got to sell. It's quiet out there, you'll probably hear the drones coming."

Mirza's face flushed, lip curling to bare his teeth. "*Ya Shar-Moo-Ta!* Go to hell!"

Ericka turned back to O'Brien, affecting a puzzled look. "Did he just call me something rude?"

O'Brien raised his brows, his expression serious. "It sounds like he thinks you're a bitch."

"Oh!" She turned back to Mirza, pausing a moment for effect. "Try a little harder. I have that one printed on my business cards."

"You are wasting my time!"

"Oh no, time out of your busy schedule? I feel awful." Ericka pointed to the door. "If you have somewhere you need to be, one of the soldiers will take you to the front gate."

His shoulders slumped accompanied by a long sigh, his voice now weary. "How do you think you can keep me alive?" He gestured to the room. "Other than in places like this?"

Time to hit him with it between the eyes. "Stupid question. We can't. Your only hope for a longer life not buried in an old mine shaft is Dantalion dead or in a cell."

Mirza glanced up. "His untold secrets are your motivation to keep me safe. I feel the need to keep you motivated."

O'Brien slapped a hand on the table, his face red with feigned anger. "Enough with the bullshit! Let's talk about someone else for a minute. You, of course, know Yìchén Ho?" He let that sink in, the only other name they had from Dantalion's cadre. "The Israelis have him. Think it through!"

Mirza paused before answering. "Liar! Even if the Jews had him, he would never talk."

Ericka stared at him for a few seconds, considering. This was confirmation of the one name she'd seen when Dantalion's security had been breached, tied to gangs in southern China. The lie was a small card to play. "Trouble with Mossad is they don't give a shit about niceties like jurisdiction and procedure. Ho got on the wrong plane. I've never seen it myself, but they're said to use direct interrogation methods. Especially on jihadis or their lackeys."

"He will never talk. His own people would see to the revenge if he betrayed their trust." Mirza's voice held the tiniest quaver.

Ericka leaned in. She was close. "How much are you willing to wager on that? If Ho talks, we have no interest in you. Perhaps Mossad would still like to speak with you though. You'll find we're a bit more reasonable."

That got him. She watched Mirza's hand tremble as he lifted his water to drink. He was quiet for a time, staring at nothing on the worn table, like they weren't there. Seeming to come to some conclusion he snapped into an erect posture. "If I share some of what I know, you will guarantee no extradition to Israel? More will come later." He stared at O'Brien.

O'Brien shrugged, keeping the play going. "That'll be a tough sell. We owe them a lot. I can't do that deal without knowing what you're giving us."

Ericka lifted a finger to get his attention. "Start with Providence. You mentioned it to our ISI colleagues?"

Mirza shook his head, a subtle smile reaching just his lips. "What I know about that is, how do you say it, my retirement plan. I do not wish it to be written on my tomb. Let us start somewhere else. What if I could tell you where he plans to be in the next few months?"

His words rippled through her like an electric shock. Not daring to hope, she modulated her tone, removing any hint of emotion. "Then we might have something interesting to talk about after all."

Mirza smirked. "He too thought he was dealing with a

fool. I saw things he never intended me to see. Things he was planning. This was one of them."

Ba Lian Ming, now the boss of the Dragon Warriors, stared at his screen waiting for a response. He felt sticky, as he always did when he spoke to this one, not fear but rather a palpable sense of unease like being in a room with a wild animal, always unpredictable and dangerous. He settled his bulk, causing leather to creak, then lit a cigarette. Sun streamed through the window behind him making his screen hard to see. He was years away from his former role as one of the gang's enforcers, no longer at the peak of fighting trim, still a hulking, dangerous figure.

He had done business with Dantalion, as he was now openly calling himself, for many years, paying him exorbitant sums for information available nowhere else. He had rooted out traitors and rats. They had shared in the spoils of the enormous success of smuggling, paying his price. He'd seemed invincible at getting boats through any navy or coast guard interference. Now, something was wrong, there was a change.

The text answer appeared on his screen. *No system is perfect. Occasional losses are inevitable. One interception by the navy and they are worried enough to want to stop?*

Something was different. This was not a time for niceties. Ming was losing face with the other leaders. He needed to be clear. Finally, a stab of fear at what he was about to say and the reaction it might bring. *Would that it was the only problem. They have heard stories that one of your men has left, stealing your secrets, then there was the matter of the banking.*

That brought an instant response. *I made good on that. Ask yourself who else is as capable?*

Ming hesitated before typing. *Don't mistake my intent. Ours has been a long and profitable association. I wish to preserve that, but it is now not without difficulties.*

Tell me.

Is it true the Americans have your traitor?

Yes, but not for long. And I have taken the necessary steps to limit any damage he can do. He is aware of the consequences.

Ming rubbed his chin, wondering how much he was willing to risk. *I need to know one more thing today.*

Of course.

Ming was quite sure he knew the answer already and that his associate knew that he knew. *Ask anyway. The bitcoin mine I am pretending to own for you. What is it really?*

A place where I can hide the enormous processing power I need for something else.

Ming knew he was pushing his luck. *Then how is it that I'm still getting my cut of bitcoins you are not mining?*

I am providing your share from another source. All clean. It is finished and, soon, I will demonstrate the full potential.

Ming spun his chair to look out his window. *No lies, just a refusal to answer. Fair enough. We can continue to do business, Mr. London.*

Not with him you can't. He ceased to exist years ago, whatever the FBI website says.

Let him know his secret is not as secret as he thinks. As you wish, I will look forward to news of our continued endeavor. As I'm sure will my customers. They are very keen to see if you can do as you say you can. Many among them have waited decades.

The answer was again quick. *Their time is at hand. A few*

months and I will be ready to proceed. Perhaps I will arrange for a demonstration so they won't need to doubt. Send me some names of their enemies.

Ericka pushed herself away from the granite-lined wall she'd been leaning on as O'Brien lumbered from the elevator of the DOJ's building, home to an inexhaustible supply of pompous windbags in suits. Going cap in hand to the brass here just went against the grain. Bad enough, she'd endured the granular scrutiny of Shingen before it could even go this far. "Will they go for it?"

He shrugged as they turned to walk towards the door to the street. "I think they will, but they're going to need some time to wrap their heads around it. Sending commandos onto an ally's soil doesn't faze them per se but sending them in and then having the mission tank in time for the news makes them all shit themselves."

Ericka had been expecting them to balk. She scanned O'Brien's features as they walked. "The information isn't getting any better and the clock's ticking. He's probably there already. What can we give them?"

O'Brien pushed the door open, standing aside to let Ericka pass, old-school in his manners. "Nothing. They're hung up on why we can't simply let the local police take him down."

She glared at him, knowing full well this wasn't his doing. "Because he'll read the communications we send to them before they do. Are they dense?"

O'Brien shook his head as he scanned the street for Ericka's Audi. "Farthest thing from it, but in their world covering your ass trumps all other considerations. They have to think it through and be satisfied that if it fails, the shit will stick to someone else. Best if it's you. Then they can pin the whole idea to bring you back on me and kill two birds with one stone. Where did you park?"

Ericka turned to face him, brow knotted with exasperation. "Forget about lunch for a minute. What's it going to take?"

He raised one brow as he stared down at her. "Knowing exactly why he's there might help? Why there? Why now?"

Ericka blew out a frustrated sigh. "I don't know. Something surgical with time nearby to recover is all Mirza knows and there's private hospitals and clinics all over the area." She turned, walking towards her car. "The fact that he's going dark for so long means it's something major. Something that needs recovery time under medical supervision before he can fly. I want to go in with the team."

O'Brien chortled before answering. "You're going to have to grow a foot or so taller and maybe 'roid up a bit to be considered for the SEALs."

Ericka glared up at him, fighting the smile forcing itself on her. She'd always been very fond of him. "Idiot. No one but Tim and I have seen him. All the pictures we have are years old." She thought for a moment, running her modified plan through her mind. "Let's try this on for an ops plan, I'll write it up. A dispersed team looking like tourists, combined agents and commandos. We'll take mobile facial-recognition rigs that will pass for camera equipment. If Thai customs flags any of us, he'll hear about it and rabbit so we'll have to move slowly. He won't trust his flunkies with his best toys so he may be a bit blind while he's there. We cruise around everywhere, walk around, go into all the hospitals for consults. If we get a hit, we call back and these scared-shitless suits on your top floor can put their heads together with our director and the military and make the call. They can extract or put a kill team ashore."

O'Brien paused, rubbing his chin as he thought. "That call will go up to the political level, but I like the plan. I like it a lot. Brilliant as always. We can sell it as leaving the final call as to whether we extract or drop him until we have the best information. They'll like that either you'll wear any fuckup or the politicians will. If it works, they'll claim the glory."

Ericka smiled. "And if we don't pick him up, the team can just leave looking like a bunch of sunburned tourists, with no one the wiser."

"Will facial recognition work like that?"

She shrugged her shoulders. "Hard to say, but it's worth trying. Facial surgery might be why he's there and there are countermeasures. Tim and I will have to wear them so he doesn't pick us up. It's usually pretty obvious, so we'll have to take some chances. He may have some local capability of his own."

O'Brien was beginning to puff at the brisk pace, his cheeks flushed. "What's your guess why he's there?"

Ericka nibbled her lower lip. "I'm worried he's there for facial surgery. The kind so we don't pick him up every time he wheels under a camera from now on. He may be planning something where he needs to expose himself. He may have arranged for local facilities and just fly in a surgeon of his choice."

O'Brien sighed, looking back up the street towards the justice building. "Where the hell has he been these last two years? What's he been doing?"

Ericka's stomach tightened, flinching at the thought. "If I had any real idea, I might be able to sleep at night."

"Can we go for lunch now?"

She gave him a small shove towards the passenger door, rolling her eyes. "Get in!"

Steiner's face was flush with excitement as he spoke to her, but his eyes never left her face. Ericka sat across his desk in his ridiculously comfortable client chair. He'd replaced the nasty, government-issue ones with his own. "So, they are letting you go, for sure?"

She leaned her chin on her fist and settled in. "Completely expendable assets like me are always a good choice for missions like this."

Steiner pointed to his teapot, brows raised. At Ericka's nod he poured the dark brew into elegant cups, sliding one towards her, giving her a mischievous look. "You don't have to do these sessions anymore, you know. What are they going to do? Fire you?"

Ericka giggled before sipping the scalding tea. "Yes, I think I'm a bit of a lost cause for shrinking anyway. You have the best tea in the building." The thought brought an old woman's face to mind, and with it, a stab of guilt, making her squeeze her eyes shut.

Steiner saw her expression, guessing the source. "Let it flow, don't bottle it. That wound will be a long time closing."

Ericka looked up. "If ever." *Time to change the subject.* "What is this bastard doing in Thailand? Has he gotten so cocky, he thinks we can't touch him?"

Steiner sat with cup and saucer in his lap, legs crossed.

"Possibly, or it's something he wants so badly he's willing to chance it. I remain convinced of what I said earlier. The inevitability of his end is going to make him reckless. I suspect he's enjoying himself too much for restraint."

She stared into Steiner's gentle eyes. Never any ulterior motive, he really just wants to help. "He's not stupid enough to think we can't get a kill order now he's being called a terrorist."

Steiner lowered his cup to the saucer on his lap. "No, the profile the behavioral unit has built since you identified him contains many interesting facts from when he was London. His IQ is well into the genius range. As to being thought of as dangerous enough to shoot on sight, I expect he is reveling in it, if anything. Any chance you're being baited in for something? He knows you have one of his men. Having all of you arrested by Thai police would be very tempting to him."

Ericka all but spat out her tea, ending up coughing. "Yes, the thought had occurred to me, but my guess is he didn't know Mirza was aware of his plans."

He gave her a cheeky smile. "Best pack your toothbrush in case."

Ericka giggled at the thought. "Yes, thanks, did they teach you that in shrink school?"

Steiner placed his teacup on his desk, folding his hands in his lap. "Speaking of shrinking, I would be remiss if I didn't inquire as to how you're feeling on your way out on your first ops since your return to the fold?" His expression was now that of the focused professional.

"About what?" He sat, waiting her out. *Playing silly bugger isn't going to work.* "I'm looking forward to some sun, good food and catching up with my old pal Dantalion."

One eyebrow went up. "Ericka, I'm not writing."

Ericka looked down, clenching her teeth, reluctant to open her thoughts to where this would lead. "I can't think about what happened to Tim's aunt without seeing red and wanting to throw up. I dream about how close I got in São Paulo, elevator doors closing in my face. I'm very sure none of this surprises you."

His stare was intense. "It doesn't, but it leads to the real question. Can you manage it?"

Ericka stiffened with resentment. "Why are you asking? You think I can't?"

Steiner paused, seeming to search for words. "Before you left for Brazil, you were like a boiling pot with the lid duct-taped on, always on the edge of an explosion. I will never ask what you were doing when you disappeared, but you needed an immunity agreement to return. Most FBI agents don't have an immunity agreement to do their work, I have noticed. Now, one of the very few people you were close to has been slaughtered by the very target you're pursuing. Forgive me if I turn my mind to anger management."

The snort of laughter exploded unrestrained, followed by a flash of pain. Ericka loved his sarcastic wit, but it bit deep sometimes. "I'm not going in alone. The military people have overall command. They're the only ones who can arrest on foreign soil anyway."

His voice was deadpan. "Of course, but under your guidance as lead investigator. I expect they will shoot whoever you tell them to."

"Tim is coming too."

Steiner's brows went up at that. "Yes, I know. I expect he is rather angry himself."

She scanned his features looking for clues from behind the mask, seeing nothing. "I don't want to guess. Please say what you need to."

Steiner leaned forward. "Remember your Seneca. Remember what anger is and what it does to reason. If you cannot look in the mirror and tell yourself this is about ending a threat and not about revenge you shouldn't be going in."

"The brass don't seem worried."

He shook his head with some vigor. "I expect they are very worried but have little choice. They don't have, how shall I put it, my direct opportunities for insight." His face held the tiniest smirk.

She couldn't resist a small poke. "Or the ability all shrinks have to read minds."

His smile was genuine and open. "That too. I trust you do not need me to remind you your superiors will assign some of the team members as minders for you?"

Her eyes bulged open. The thought hadn't occurred to her. "Who?"

Steiner's expression remained neutral, but his tone was now layered with sarcasm. "Not Tim probably. Other than him, watch your back."

"Good thinking."

"Ericka, medicine has changed in the last two thousand years, but human nature not at all. Anger control and cognitive therapy have nothing on the stoic philosophy. Reading it in a book is easy, governing your behavior, channeling your thoughts, is hard. The part that is very difficult is aligning your thoughts and emotions. Remember, your character is the sum of your thoughts. You will never be free of it until you manage that."

Ericka had no answer. She stood, squeezing his shoulder in thanks as she walked out into the hallway.

16

A Bleeding Wraith

SAC Hikari Shingen stood at the head of the enormous boardroom table, hands gripping the small lectern, glaring at those still speaking to shut them up. The room had no windows, lit by recessed ceiling lights, the air was stale. Around the table sat a mix of uniforms and civilian clothes, SEALS and FBI, broken into the smaller groups who would go ashore. Shingen scowled and picked up a large binder, held it high over the table and dropped it. The noise made several people jump, halting all conversation. She glared at the offending group. "We're going to start now, thank you." She glanced at the uniformed man sitting next to her, Lieutenant Commander Flaherty USN, the officer who would have overall command once in the field. He smiled.

Shingen took a moment to find Ericka, as far from the podium as possible, staring at her as if to assure herself Ericka was listening. Shingen cleared her throat, then spoke, projecting her voice to the end of the room. "Before I turn this over for the final operational briefing—" she turned to the naval officer next to her "—let me address the parameters of the mission from a policing and law enforcement perspective. If at all possible, bringing him back alive remains the highest priority. To have any chance to undo the damage this one has done, we require him alive. Bringing back a body is a very poor second."

She paused to scan the room before continuing. "I cannot overemphasize the abilities of this target. Once ashore, you must maintain absolute comms blackout. I know you've read the briefing materials, but it can't be said too many times. Unless the need is dire, all reports to the field commander must be delivered in person. If you have to use a phone of any sort, speak in the clear using just the code phrases. Once we have local confirmation we've acquired the target, we will seek final authorization to take him. Any arrest must be made by the military. Failing that a kill team will come ashore. Only two of our agents have ever seen the subject, so initial confirmation will be largely reliant on facial recognition alone. Agent Blackwood, do you have anything to add at this point?"

Ericka stood, pushing her chair from the table, trying to keep the emotion from her voice. "I won't repeat what's in the materials, just a few things I want to emphasize. Stay away from every camera you can. You were selected for your lack of online presence, but everyone has some. If he gets wind of any SEALs or FBI in the country, he'll rabbit. Don't count on a soft target. In São Paulo, his men fought to the death to get him out and took out more than twice their number. Expect them to be as fanatical as any jihadi."

She paused to find Tim before continuing. "Speaking from the police perspective, this one is very different, the kind of criminal we've always feared existed. He's a cruel and vicious killer whose command of technology is something we've never seen before. None of the world's intelligence agencies have been able to latch on to him. We got our first shot two years ago when he screwed up. We're getting this one from inside intel. If we miss it, who knows when we'll get another shot and who'll pay the price in the meantime.

"Those cameras you've been issued capture a lot more image than stock ones and can hold ten hours of video. All Wi-Fi and other connectivity have been removed so you can't accidentally turn them on. The internal facial recognition is limited but should work, if you're close. Once you dump your data with us, the full processing will be quick. The laptops have something like a desktop version of Clearview, but it's only scanning one source, so it's fast. Agent O'Connell and I will stay with your commander until the target is located. We're just too easy to spot to be moving around, but we have to confirm identity." She stared around the table. Several dozen pairs of unblinking eyes locked on hers, before sitting down.

Flaherty stood and moved to the lectern, working without notes. "First, let me emphasize Agent Blackwood's warning. This target is capable of severely damaging the people and infrastructure of the country, probably more so than the cyberwar capabilities of some of our adversaries. There can be no stone left unturned. We have the opportunity to catch him here while he's vulnerable. We're in a friendly country without permission so there can be no collateral damage. CIA staff in the embassy will preposition a limited supply of weapons. You will enter the country like any other tourists and act accordingly. We'll issue specific flights, accommodations and target areas tomorrow."

Tim held up his hand. "If we find him, how long do you expect before the kill team is on site if needed?"

Flaherty glanced at one of his subordinates before he answered. "The kill team will be offshore and realistically we can only put them ashore at night. Anywhere from a few hours to a day depending. Any other questions?"

No one spoke so Flaherty gave them a casual salute. "You'll have the final briefing materials tonight. Good luck and we'll see all of you at the wrap party."

Tim was leaning against the stark cinderblock wall outside, staring at his shoes. Ericka knew he'd wanted to talk again for some time but had been avoiding more than professional contact with her. A painful distance for a brother. He glanced in her direction, his facial burn scars emphasizing the pained expression. He'd lost weight, though none of his athletic build. What seemed to be gone was the constant wisecracking of the old Tim, the new one was somber, almost sullen.

She squeezed his arm, feeling the thick bicep tighten as she did. "It's time brother. We can't stay like this forever." He started towards a door leading outside. Ericka followed, moving her hand to his shoulder. He turned just enough to dislodge her hand, not quite shrugging it off, but the meaning was clear.

They walked in silence out of the complex at the Naval Amphibious Base Coronado, California, where the military component of the teams would stage from. There was no conversation as they walked across the parking lot and drove away, stopping for beer before driving down the thin, sandy neck of the peninsula joining the base area to the mainland.

Ericka drove onto the sand-covered shoulder on the ocean-facing side where the sun was descending towards the waves. She ventured a glance. "Here?"

Tim didn't look back, reaching for the door handle. "Good as any." His accent was always thicker when his emotions had the better of him.

He led the way to the beach, little more than a football field. Behind him on the narrow path, Ericka shielded her eyes from the sun as her boots dug into damp sand. They threaded their way through small dunes before settling on a grass-covered hummock. Squinting against the glare, she tugged on sunglasses, staring at gentle surf, the breeze moving rivulets of sand through miniature dunes, carrying the scent of seaweed and salt air.

He picked up a shell, turning it in his fingers before speaking. "I don't think he did it to get at you. He wanted to take me out. Unless he was listening to phone calls, there's no way he'd have known she'd be there. It isn't like she worked a schedule. Just god-awful luck."

Her eyes ached as they welled up, picturing Mrs. Donnelly's last seconds. "Whoever he had in mind, she'd be alive if not for us."

He turned his head to glance at her, the first real eye contact. "Yes, no two ways around that." He paused to sigh. "She wouldn't have us sitting feeling guilty, she'd have wanted us after him with all we've got. There was a very hard core to that old woman. You know where it came from. You were there for part of it. She'd want us off our arses, not feeling sorry for ourselves."

Ericka did. Growing up in Northern Ireland's Troubles, Mrs. Donnelly had buried brothers and her first husband there. She wasn't one for shying from what she considered necessary violence, a pacifist she was not. "I do. Then what is it?" She knew, but it had to be said so there was no mistake.

Tim's glare held real heat, features contorted by his scars, face flushed. "Playing bloody games isn't going to help!"

She shook her head, holding his gaze. "No, it isn't. I'm not playing. I'm saying it so we can have a frank conversation with everything on the table. Say what you need to! Then I will."

Some of the anger faded from his expression but the flush remained while he took a few breaths. Ericka couldn't tell if it was anger or the reddening light of the setting sun. "Right, I will. I'd no idea if you were dead or alive. It still hurts and you're still holding out on me." He paused, eyes narrowing. "But I had a pretty fucking good idea where you were going!"

Ericka looked down, not trying to hold on to the tears sliding down her cheeks. "Do you want to know? We can't keep going around and around on this."

"No, I don't! I covered for you once and I told you I'm not doing it again. Don't put me in the position of having to lie for you again. It's not really about what happened anymore. I'm having a hard time trusting you."

Ericka bit her lower lip, pausing to wipe the tears with the back of her hand, feeling the grit of beach sand under her eyes. "I don't have to tell you what I was doing. You know."

Tim shook his head, scowling. "That isn't what I asked you! The issue is trust."

Ericka watched a rivulet of sand flow around her boot in the rising wind. *Here it goes.* "I know that. Recognize I wasn't in a rational state of mind. Not an excuse, but an explanation. I own what I did. I started on the pills and made it worse. People who are crazy don't know they're fucking crazy or at least can't tell how crazy they are. So many times, I started setting up routing to send you something, but there was always a good reason not to."

"Like what?"

Ericka dropped her forehead into both hands. *How do I describe something I can barely remember? A swirl of thoughts that never made sense.* "For one thing, I was worried someone would backtrack it—him or the agency—and find me. I was scared I'd light you up if the brass found out we were talking. But you know what it was mostly? I thought none of you would want me to after what I did! A lot of the time, all I wanted to do was track the bastard down and then die there!"

Tim was silent, lying back on the grassy hummock to stare at the sky. She glanced over, waiting. He linked his hands behind his neck before speaking. "It was fucking hard. They all assumed we were talking and cut me out like I was some sort of traitor. I was cut out of the Dantalion investigation, and I could see they were running audit trails on me nearly all the time."

"I'm so sorry."

Tim's laugh was short and devoid of humor. "Are you? From all I've heard, it sounds like you're feeling pretty bloody sorry for yourself more than anything."

She clenched her jaw. That was the hurt talking. *Take it and move on. It hurts more because he's right. Give him that. There can't be any trust without truth here.* "I can't change what's happened. That evil bastard got way under my skin. I knew what was happening, but I couldn't stop. He knew where every button was and pushed them all at once. I cracked, completely fucking cracked. That's the truth."

The hint of a sneer curled Tim's lips. "Right, all his fault! Not like you weren't chasing those men before Dantalion stepped into the picture. You were pure as the driven snow until he turned up. Never stepped out of line, not once."

Ericka winced, turning to look at the waves, now backlit in the twilight. *Ouch, he knows me so well.* "You're right. He led, but I chose to follow. What I'm trying to tell you is that once there, I was in a very bad spot." She paused, taking his hand, warm and calloused. "I'm sorry. That's all I've got other than I'm back and I will be on the bastard one hundred percent until we take him down. No more hidden agenda. I'll do whatever it takes."

Tim took several deep breaths before sitting up, drawing knees to his chest. "You're done with the pills?"

"Yes, Steiner is going to stay on me while I'm still with the bureau. I feel bad. I used to go to those psych eval sessions and just torture him for fun. He's really helped and has a very solid read on Dantalion." Ericka leaned in, making close eye contact. "Are we good? Is this behind us?"

Tim looked down before leaning towards her, drawing her into a powerful hug. "Can't stay mad at the only sister I've got. Not like I'm Snow bloody White. This ends here. We're good."

They lay in silence, staring at the emerging stars for a long time until it grew cold.

Ericka tugged on the string, lifting the old blind just enough to peer under it, arms covered in goose bumps despite the failing efforts of the room's ancient air conditioning. The rooms they were using as an ops center were on the wrong side of the rented cottage, catching heat from the afternoon sun. She chewed her lip, staring out at what a real estate agent would call a peekaboo view, other cottages with glimpses of beach and water in between. Looking forward to tonight's walk, she spun her chair back to her monitor, the middle one of five in the room. The air had the expected miasma of hot electronics, old food and bodies that had done little but sit staring at screens for weeks. Her back was stiff from sitting hunched, and they had found nothing.

She racked her brains for anything else they might do, but she had been over this ground hundreds of times since arriving in Pranburi Beach. This was all they could do without lighting themselves up, either to the locals or their target. The only way to be absolutely sure they left no digital clues as to their presence was not to send any at all. Occupying the seat to her left, Flaherty had repeatedly pointed out that his team sitting offshore waiting for a command to come ashore were the ones with something to snivel about. The combined SEAL FBI teams onshore were on holiday, some posing as couples, others as groups of friends wandering the tourist areas, casually finding the various medical facilities, wandering where they hoped their equipment might catch a glimpse of the face they were looking for.

It was a long shot, a weeks-long, tedious long shot based on information from an untested source; but it was all they had. *Mirza isn't lying to us, but he certainly wasn't telling everything either.* It was their best hope and always had been. Dantalion didn't make mistakes, except relying too much on his disciples, and there he had no choice.

Tonight, two of the teams would arrive after dark to report in and get new orders, dumping their video into servers for full processing and scanning, servers covertly brought ashore farther down the coast. The ones coming tonight were posing as vacationing couples. Scrutinizing the body language on their last visit, Ericka had formed the view one of the SEAL FBI "couples" might have buried themselves in the part. It probably gave them better cover anyway, so she decided to say nothing and live through them vicariously.

The protocol she'd insisted on had made the whole operation slow and cumbersome. With no idea as to the security Dantalion might have, they had eliminated all digital traffic that might give them away. It was a huge shift. Much early dark-web technology had been developed for the US Navy as a way of communicating covertly while onshore. The TOR network was now ancient history to them and their opponents alike. Covert communications were exactly what she would expect her quarry to be looking for. Her solution had been simple, don't use it. If it wasn't feasible to wait until they could report in person, the teams would call, using selected code words to convey both their observations and the urgency.

Now, Ericka knew what it was like to be a Zoomer. For the past weeks, she and the command-post team had spent their days scanning nothing but social media. The field agents had been instructed to take all the photographs they could and post them to Instagram and Twitter. The command team scanned the selected accounts along with all other open social media data from the area. The pictures had the usual location data embedded in them and the team's captions were code phrases reporting progress. 'Wish you were here' meant nothing to report. The phrase they were all waiting for was 'you just have to see this,' posted to social media for anyone in the world to see. That meant the surveillance team had a likely contact and the next group of pictures would contain a facial-recognition hit. Then things would get interesting.

The teams would converge on the target to try and contain him, while the kill team would surface and come ashore. Then it was up to the suits and brass in Washington to order either a capture attempt or a kill. The final order would come from the political level, but either way, they were not letting him go. Dantalion was no longer a mere criminal. His abilities and willingness to use them had elevated him to merit far greater attention.

The chair next to Ericka creaked as Tim dropped into it to begin his shift. The low-angle light emphasized the gray that was now creeping through his beard. He grew it longer to help cover the burn scars that several rounds of cosmetic surgery hadn't been able to completely hide. He caught her stare and his smile forced wrinkles around his eyes. "What are you staring at? Not your usual?" Tim gestured with his chin towards the chiseled profile of Flaherty who leaned into his screen, head cocked, listening to something through his headset.

Busted. She glanced down, reddening, trying to change the subject. "Sleep well?"

Tim wasn't letting it go just yet. "You must be feeling better. Are you?"

Ericka didn't want to meet his eye. *No avoiding the scrutiny.* "I think maybe a bit. I get some sleep. The walks help, but it'd be nice if they were in the light."

Tim turned to his station to input his credentials. "One way or the other, this will be over soon. The two agents rotated in yesterday say Shingen's told them the brass are angling to pull the pin."

Ericka wasn't surprised. This had always been a long shot, and their target might well be gone by now, if he was ever here. She turned to log out as she spoke, weariness weighing on her motions. "I think he was here. If this turns out to be a bullshit lead, he's been very quiet doing something else."

"Head's up, there's a problem!" Flaherty tugged off his headset, staring at them, eyes wide. "The *Bangkok Post* is quoting an unnamed source in the Royal Thai Police that they've arrested members of a foreign national security service, as well as members of a mercenary unit."

Gritting her teeth, Ericka spun to her screen, making her chair squeak, the chill of goose bumps rising on her neck and arms. *Fuck, this could be a disaster.* She brought up the social media feeds of the field teams, scanning them one by one, before leaning back to look at Flaherty who was focused on his laptop. "They're all logged on as scheduled. We've got to figure out which of them has been busted and start the remote encryption protocols. How long has the story been up?"

Tim answered. "Twenty two minutes."

Ericka gnawed on her lip as she thought. "We're blown. All we can do is get the rest out and brick up our stuff so Dantalion doesn't steal it from the local police if they find it. How the hell did they get caught?" If their target had detected them, tipping off the local police would make for a good defensive move. *What the hell did the team have to do with foreign mercenaries?*

Flaherty shrugged. Tim was slow answering, frowning at his screen. He rubbed his chin, not looking up. "I don't think they did. Look at this!"

She stood, holding the back of Tim's chair as she leaned in close over his shoulder. Flaherty stood behind, bulging arms folded over his chest, showing ink. "What?"

Tim's finger slid over the touchpad to click on an image. "Al Jazeera claims this is security video of the foreign team being arrested. Look!"

Ericka peered at the video, knuckles white as she gripped the back of Tim's chair. Three dark, bearded men kneeled on the pavement, hands up, glaring at uniformed police holding them at gunpoint.

Flaherty let out a heavy sigh from behind her. "Not ours."

Ericka nodded without looking back. "No, they're not." She felt heat flush her face, drawing the obvious conclusion. "We've been stepped on. Someone else is here too. Shit!"

Flaherty stared, compressing his lips. "Any guesses? They look like they might be Indian or Pakistani."

She glanced back at the screen. "Our target has hit the Pakistanis pretty hard and that's where we got our source from. They must have gotten the same intel and decided to have a stab at picking him up." She looked from Flaherty to Tim. "We're screwed. We'll have to bail. The locals will be on high alert and looking now."

Flaherty was on his way back to his terminal. She watched as he plugged a small thumb drive into his machine and entered a password. The extraction protocol required breaking digital silence. A few minutes of two finger typing and he turned back to them. It seemed much longer than the four minutes it was before the new message chime from his device. He read for a moment. "Full emergency bugout. Too risky to disperse through the airports. Pick up on the beach in eighteen hours, Khao Sam Roi Yot National Park."

Ericka entered the final password, scrutinizing her machine as wiping protocols began to run. There was no time to dispose of the larger equipment and carrying it to the extraction point could light them up. Best she could do here was brick them up, bleach every surface and shove them into the crawl space under the cottage where they might stay hidden for years. Burning would be best, but torching computers in the backyard might strike the neighbors as unusual.

She glanced through the open door into the next room. Tim wore protective goggles and a mask and was using a spray bottle to spritz each surface with a mix of bleach and water. One of the SEALs, his face covered, followed behind with a mop, spreading the mix evenly to destroy any DNA left behind. They had to do everything they could. Anything the police got here, Dantalion could soon have, never mind the diplomatic incident.

Ericka peered out the window, watching Flaherty bend to load their scant luggage into the back of a rented Hyundai SUV. He stopped to scan the area around him, no doubt worried about prying eyes.

Tim leaned in from what had been their local ops room. "We're done." He looked at her mobile. "Everyone on the move?"

Ericka glanced down to check, flipping through all the social media accounts. "All but two showing social media pics from en route." Before they left to drive, they would encrypt their mobiles. If they were caught, the browsing history would lead local police to the rest.

Flaherty pulled open the back door, his heavy frame filling the hallway. "Sun's down in ten. Ready? We should go dark now until we get to the beach."

She nodded. "Five more minutes." Her mobile vibrated in her pocket and she saw Tim reach for his at the same time. She held it in front of her face as she selected the Twitter account broadcasting an update, one of the teams posing as a couple, the "Engels." The picture was very clear, showing a walkway above the beach, couples and families strolling, but it was the upper right hand that was framed with red brackets. She expanded the image, zeroing in to show the deck of what looked like an apartment complex above the promenade.

Muscles tight, her breathing shallowed as she stared. A comment popped up under the picture and it took several tries to open it, her mouth dry as she read. "Beaches here so amazing, you just have to see this!" She slid the image back to the area the software had flagged. There was no mistaking it. Leaning towards the railing, seated in a wheelchair, his face glowing red in the setting sun. It was him. She had him.

Captain Dane Lewis stared over the front of the bouncing zodiac, through the spray and towards the black shore beyond. The rushing air was hot and damp, but this kind of trifling discomfort had no effect on him or his team. He glanced at the other two boats, following to the side and behind. They were still too far for details, but lights on the highway were visible now behind a white line of breaking surf to the south of the park. He waved to the driver to slow down for the last kilometer. Even the special engine with its hush kit made some noise. Ninety minutes until twilight.

They had to make it onshore without detection. The SEAL and FBI teams onshore would head back to the waiting ship, while the two snipers would join the last of the shore team, one FBI agent and the mission's commander. One boat would take them close to the target where they would wait out the day in concealment before making the attempt near sunset the next day, then straight to extraction. Their briefing made it clear local authorities were on heightened alert. People near the top must really want this guy. If they couldn't extract him, they'd been told to expect a kill order.

Lewis pivoted to the man driving, slicing his hand across his throat, glancing at the others. The motor went silent as they reached for paddles lying at their feet. With the silence, the sound of the surf dominated fifty yards in front of them. First a gentle crash, then a low-pitched rumble trailing the sibilant hissing of countless bubbles. As he leaned out to dig in his paddle, he could smell rotting seaweed on the beach, a long familiar mental cue that action was about to begin. A light flickered from the black wall of foliage above the beach, all clear.

Once through the breakers, Lewis slid over the side, grabbing lines to drag the boat up the beach, lifting to minimize noise. The water flooding Lewis's boots was cooler than expected. Several of his men ran along the beach in each direction, hugging the tree line, forming a perimeter. There were no buildings in this area of the park, but all it would take is a restless sleeper with a dog, and this would get much more exciting. Seeing his pickets were in position, Lewis strode up past the high-tide line, dried seaweed crunching under his boots, to where he could see the hulking silhouette of Flaherty lurking in the vegetation. Beside him stood a smaller figure, a woman whose slight but muscular frame he could just make out.

Lewis spoke to his commanding officer in a subdued tone. "Sir, no issues coming ashore."

"Thank you. This is your number two, Special Agent Blackwood."

So, this was the FBI super spook they'd all heard of. The one he'd been briefed to watch like a hawk and be ready to intervene if she showed any sign of going off the rails. Only one of two people who'd recently seen their target up close. He'd been told they would hold the second agent in reserve if this attempt failed. Lewis pulled the duffel bag from his shoulder, handing it to her. "Ma'am. Your gear."

Ericka gave the sniper a smile he probably couldn't see in this light, taking the proffered bag. She turned, picking her way back into the trees to change into fatigues, stuffing her civilian clothes into the bag. She shivered as she glanced up, seeing the remaining surveillance teams mass on the beach next to the two boats taking them out to sea. Flaherty and his spotter bent to load equipment cases into the third zodiac. She clipped on the webbing holding her gear, then bent to tighten her boots before hurrying down the beach to toss her bag into a departing boat.

She found Tim leaning on the bow of one, arms folded over his chest. He stood as she approached. They stared at each other for a few moments, but she could barely see his eyes.

He reached out and they clasped each other's wrists, no hugs going into battle.

Ericka could hear the emotion in his voice, whispered as it was. "Don't fuck this up! Get the bastard this time."

She had to choke down the laugh, still grasping his wrist. "This time, I won't be weighed down rescuing you." There was just enough starlight to see his broad smile. He grasped her shoulder with his free hand, then turned to stand next to the boat, gripping a line, ready to help launch.

Ericka turned to stand next to her boat, leaning on the flotation tube, watching as the SEALs pulled off dark coverings, revealing their in-plain-sight camouflage. Their boat had been painted and kitted out as a small, commercial dive boat, allowing it to loiter during the day hopefully without drawing unwanted attention.

His task complete, Flaherty leaned to the middle of the boat, his voice just audible. "Let's get moving." He turned to Ericka. "Sun's up in two hours and we've got a ways to go yet."

She dug her boots into the wet sand to help push as a wave lapped up her legs to mid-calf. The boat made little sound, its hard bottom grinding over sand before it floated clear. Ericka ignored a proffered helping hand as she clambered over the side. She lowered night-vision goggles to scan the beach a final time, seeing nothing. She grabbed a paddle, smiling to herself in the dark. Now she knew what the big deal about joining this unit was; being a SEAL was enormous fun.

Sun filtered through the small camouflage net dangling inches above her head. Ericka and Lewis lay on sand and gravel in what was probably a stream bed after rain, but now it was bone-dry. Cut banks concealed them from casual observation should anybody wander through the dense stand of trees and foliage where they'd been since the sun rose. At even the smallest sound, Lewis would sit up using a small periscope to scan for the source. So far, nothing but birds. Next to him, its action covered against the sand, lay his M25 sniper rifle, fiberglass stock gleaming in the filtered light. It was the final option if they were unable to take him. In a pouch attached to the left shoulder strap of her webbing was a kit that would allow her to inject sedating drugs, ensuring a silent trip back to the beach.

They were wedged together in a small sandy patch, bodies inches apart. Close enough to smell sweat as the day grew warm. Lewis suggested she sleep, but there was no way, this close. Dantalion was no more than a few hundred yards away. She stared at the rifle, perhaps with too much longing.

Lewis gave her a quizzical look. "It's good. Had that rifle for a long time."

She turned on her side to hide her expression, busying herself cutting at a root that had been digging into her arm. "All good. Just itching to get this done."

Ericka turned on her back and shut her eyes. Time to focus. Sitting here fantasizing about shooting Dantalion, blowing the top of his head off, wasn't contributing to her effort. This was going to require razor-sharp thinking and ice-cold concentration. She heard Steiner's voice in her head, lecturing her about what she already knew. The road back doesn't start with revenge, it starts with success, controlling the rage. She managed her breathing, taking slow deep breaths, holding for a count of three between inhaling and exhaling. *The heart rate will come down when the mind is clear.*

Once more the plan. Flaherty and the fourth team member, Baird, were very close to where they believed he was holed up, by himself in some sort of long-term vacation rental often used by people recovering from surgery. He seemed to be in the habit of coming out to the large ground-level deck at sunset. It was there they would try and take him. She would provide final positive identification while Lewis provided lethal oversight should Dantalion have security close enough to interfere or should they receive the order for a kill shot.

Ericka suspected Dantalion was alone. A person with a resident security detail would draw attention. He would have men here somewhere, but they would be some distance away. Her bet was on a local, commercial security service rather than risk bringing people in. Tourists traveling with guns was a dicey proposition.

Lewis had his radio out, not military-issue, rather the small walkie-talkie kind tourists use to keep in touch when they split up to go shopping. Any significant traffic using their normal, encrypted military comms might be detected if not read. Military comms within a few hundred yards would mean only one thing to their target. The encrypted system was reserved for obtaining orders in the mission's final stages.

He depressed the button and spoke, the sound muffled by the added face seal. "So, is there a liquor store down there?"

Ericka could hear Flaherty's voice through her earpiece. "Yes, but they don't have it. Try the other one near the beach." The code meant no sign yet, but that they were going to move their position by a few yards for a better look.

Lewis raised his brows and smiled. "Nothing to see, go back to sleep."

"I wasn't sleeping."

He rolled his eyes, smiling at her. "Right, you were just snoring while meditating."

Ericka gave him a perfunctory glare, before smiling and settling on her back. *These guys were all comedians.* This time she woke to dimmer light, the gentle patter of rain on leaves, and the scent of damp soil. "Shit, how long was I asleep?"

He was wearing a black watch cap now, scanning through the periscope. He answered without turning. "Maybe an hour. Looks like this will end just before sunset. Perfect timing. Another half an hour, we should get into position. Rain's almost done."

Ericka shivered, tugging her camouflage jacket tight, pulling on her cap. She sat up, opening clips on the case containing the spotter scope and sat phone. If Flaherty and Baird weren't able to get their target in hand and tranquilized, it was her role to make final identification and convey any new orders to Lewis. SEALs didn't employ spotters with snipers as a standard procedure, but identification was too important. She tugged the scope out, checking it a final time.

Crawling through brush without making noise was a slow, meticulous art. Every twig was a potential snap that would give them away, each unintended shake of a bush might draw attention. Timing was everything. When a gust of wind or heavier rain raised the ambient sound level, time to move. Wait and listen in the quieter moments in between. The jungle was thick, making it difficult for anyone else to see them, but more prone to making noise. A gust rustled leaves overhead, treating them to a spattering of dislodged rain.

Before it subsided, Lewis slithered two body lengths on his belly, Ericka following suit. She lifted her head to peer over his back. Fifty more yards to go.

"Did you find a place for dinner?" There was no tension in Flaherty's voice as it crackled in her earpiece.

Lewis answered. "I think so, just looking over the menu." He turned to glance at Ericka, brows raised in inquiry.

"One sec." The rain had stopped and the low sun was behind and to the side, just about to dip behind the trees. They lay on a low ridge at the edge of the undergrowth. In front of them an unkempt lawn stretched for about one hundred yards before ending in a long-untrimmed hedge. A further one hundred and twenty-five yards away lay the deck's edge overlooking the coastal road and the ocean beyond. She could make out the back of several wooden benches facing the sea, bracketing the spot where they'd seen him. Ericka slid the scope forward so just the tip penetrated hanging branches. One last look, the spotter scope's laser range finder two hundred and forty-six yards to the bench. Child's play for a military sniper. "Clear shot?"

He nodded and keyed his mic, speaking into the voice suppressing mouthpiece. Ericka heard his voice in her earphone. "Dinner here is good. Let me know when you're close and I'll order you a drink."

Once they had him spotted, they would dispense with the pretense and code phrases. At that point, precision was needed. Ericka closed her eyes, forcing tension from her shoulders, biting her lower lip. A glance at Lewis told her he was feeling it too, if controlling it much better. His jaw was clenched but his body relaxed as a sniper's must be. Muscle tension, breathing and a racing heart could all send a shot wide of the intended target, or turn a kill into a wounding. Controlled breathing slowed the heart rate. At the point of taking the shot, he would follow the time-honored procedure of taking three regular breaths, exhaling and holding for a few seconds while squeezing the trigger in a way to avoid sending the round left or right of the target. It was a dark art and she'd heard Flaherty say Lewis was the best he'd ever seen.

Something inaudible crackled in her earphone. She made out the word 'problem' but nothing else.

Lewis transmitted back. "Say again, all after problem." The pretense was gone. This was starting.

Flaherty sounded out of breath, his speech clipped. "I say again, we're not the only ones here. We just captured and sedated someone I think was set up on the same target. May have attracted some attention. Going to have to sit still for a bit. We're not in position to effect the grab."

"Shit!" Lewis transmitted. "Any sign of the target or probable security?"

There was a pause, perhaps Flaherty was popping his head up for a look. "Nothing. Baird is hurt, busted jaw. The guy we took down was a professional."

Ericka looked down at her hands clutching the spotter scope, groaning inwardly. How the hell to do a capture now? Her nostrils flared. She knew her face was flushing, thrilled at the thought of the alternative. Steiner's face barged in to fill her mind's eye. She closed her eyes to concentrate, willing that savage part of her back into its cage. Focus on getting this done, forget the kill.

She touched Lewis's wrist, leaning in to whisper near his uncovered ear. "I think we need the brass to update our orders. The sun's down in thirty minutes. This's going to happen fast."

He transmitted to Flaherty. "We clear to seek updated orders?"

That was Flaherty's call as on-scene commander. His answer was immediate. "Yes, do that."

Ericka pulled out the small touch pad, typing in the cryptic request for uplink. "Capture unlikely, request authorization for lethal force." It took a few seconds for the encrypted signal to uplink. No telling when they'd get their answer.

Flaherty again, his rapid speech the sole hint of emotion. "Eyes on the target. Middle-aged white male in a wheelchair, by himself, heading to where we expected."

Lewis answered before settling his face into the rifle. "Roger that. Call it out. No contact here."

Ericka's mouth went dry, her breathing shallow. Her mind flashed back to São Paulo and the last time she'd gotten near this bastard. Right there in front of her, two-arms' lengths away, gone before she realized who she was looking at. Not this time.

"He's mixed in with civvies right now, taking his time. Couple of minutes until he gets to the ramp."

"Jesus Christ!" Lewis's face was away from his scope looking at her with wide eyes.

"What?"

"Someone sitting on one of the benches in the kill zone. Elderly woman, came from the upper path, using a walker."

"Let's hope they don't get cozy."

Flaherty's voice filled her headset. "Lost sight of him. Last seen on the path going up, using electric motor. Correction, got him again. Bushes in the way. Definitely on his way up to you."

Lewis kept his eye to the scope. "Nothing yet. Getting dark, lights on the deck are going to mess with the night vision."

"Lost him again. Still heading your direction."

Lewis pulled back to look at her, shaking his head. Ericka put down the comms unit and leaned into her spotter scope. The deck lights were off but it was still lit with the ruddy, indirect light of the sun now behind the trees. There was movement. Someone stopped down the hill, maybe for a better view of the water there. She could see just the top of his head, too far away for any details.

"Do you have him?" Now there was tension in Flaherty's voice.

"Negative." Lewis's voice was cold, devoid of any emotion.

Minutes passed, then Ericka gasped as she heard a noise behind them. She and Lewis turned as he drew his sidearm and slid the safety off, chambering a round. A few tense seconds passed before he spotted the source standing under a bush looking at them. "It's a fucking rat." They shared a look for a moment, before he shook his head.

Ericka spun back to her scope. The woman was still there but no longer alone. She was seated and the gloom now covered everything but her head. A man sat next to her, no more than an arm's length away, heads bowed as if they were chatting.

Lewis's tone was ice cold. "Is that him?"

She took a shuddering breath. "Has to be. Right build, hunched, barely make out his features when he turns, but

I'm sure." As she said it, she shivered. *How fucking sure? No innocents!*

Lewis keyed his mic. "Did he come back down?"

No delay in Flaherty's response. "Negative, disappeared, your direction."

Ericka transmitted. "Did you get facial recognition as he went by?"

"Negative, too dark, but looks like the same man it picked up last time."

Now there was a hint of excitement in Lewis's voice. "I've got a clean head shot. He's silhouetted against the sky beyond the deck."

The comm link vibrated in her hand. *There's timing for you.* She leaned into the hooded screen, reading aloud to Lewis. "Deadly force authorized."

It was getting too dark to see Lewis's features. "Understood. Kill shot is authorized."

Ericka transmitted again. "The shot is authorized."

"Understood. Calling in the boat now."

Ericka leaned back into the scope. The heads of both the man and woman were black cutouts against red sky, as if speaking but not intimate. With the backlight, the night-vision setting didn't offer any better detail. "Have you got a shot still?"

His voice was just above a whisper. "Clean shot, just waiting for him to lean back a little."

They leaned away from each other as if pausing in their conversation.

"There we go!"

Adrenaline made her hands tremble, ruining her view. *And*

here it ends for you, you evil bastard. She held her breath waiting for the shot. Lewis was inhaling again, two more and he would stop and fire. She counted them, focused on the back of Dantalion's head, two, three, silence. The man stood up and stretched his arms to the side, taking a few halting steps, before turning to his companion.

Ericka lunged to the side shoving the rifle just as Lewis fired. The shot went wide, striking sparks against the stone wall enclosing the deck, no more than a foot from the target's skull. The light from the nightscope lit Lewis's features enough she could see his eyes bulging with surprise. Unlikely he could see her, but she shook her head. "Not him."

A woman's high-pitched voice shrieked in English for someone to call the police while distant shouts raised the alarm. She peered through the scope, seeing nothing. Both the man and woman must be below the retaining wall taking cover.

Flaherty's voice pierced the static. "Confirm target is down."

Ericka could hear the controlled heat in Lewis's tone. "Negative!" He paused. She could hear him taking deep, controlled breaths. "We have lost visual, target is uninjured."

Flaherty paused before answering, no doubt indulging in some choice words in his head. "Roger that, bug out and head for the beach, RV2. Boat is inbound. Stay in the bush, expect local law enforcement in minutes."

Ericka pushed herself up, grit between her fingers, under her nails, stuffing her equipment before flipping on night vision. She glanced at Lewis, unable to read his expression in monochrome green lighting.

He returned the look. "We're cool, got to be sure on a kill

shot." He stood, slinging his rifle over his pack, bending to scan the ground. They couldn't leave anything behind. He gave her the thumbs-up before turning to pick his way down the dry stream bed. In the dark, the risk of being seen was reduced and all she could see was a few yards ahead. She looked down trying to place her steps on sandy patches, avoiding stones and twigs, pushing herself to keep up with Lewis. He glanced back, checking she was there, but remained focused on the path ahead.

Ericka flinched as an unseen branch scraped her face, leaving her to pull spider webs from her eyes. The wail of sirens echoed from the trees sounding like they were coming from all directions at once. Her mouth was parched, this could get ugly. It wouldn't take long for responding police to fan out. "Much farther?"

Lewis glanced at his wrist. "Three hundred meters to the beach, then one-point-five clicks to RV2."

They increased their pace. With the noise of arriving police, stepping on the occasional branch wasn't going to give them away and they had to be gone before the search expanded to the beach. The smell of seaweed and the surf's low rumble told her they were close. Lewis held up his hand, squatting to lean into low bushes marking the edge of the forest right over the high-tide line. Satisfied, he gestured to follow. "We're running from here on."

Ericka followed close as they rushed along the edge of the trees. High tide left little bare beach. She turned to look behind, adjusting her night goggles. *Nothing in view.* She almost ran into Lewis where he'd stopped. Peering past him, she watched as Flaherty stood up from the shrubs he'd been using as cover. On the sand next to him, sat the fourth team member, Baird, who held his jaw in stoic silence staring out to sea. The dark shape beyond him was the man they'd captured, tied and looking sedated. Peering out, she could see the track where they'd come out of the foaming surf. They'd dragged him through the water just below the tide line to avoid leaving a track.

Flaherty leaned to whisper to them. "The boat is inbound, two or three minutes. What happened?"

Ericka answered, her chest tight at the thought they'd almost executed an innocent man. *Or had they? What if that was what the surgery was for?* "Last second, the target stood and walked. Can't be him. Maybe we got our wires crossed somewhere."

Flaherty's head dropped to look at the sand. "Fuck, where the hell did he go? Could the facial recognition have been wrong?"

She was very sure the software was right. "Anything's possible, but I don't think so. The bastard's here somewhere." *Even if he has nine goddamned lives, he has to run out soon.* She looked up as the hum of the inflatable's motor reached them.

A breaking wave slapped her side, making her gasp as she held the boat steady, the chill always unexpected. Baird hauled himself over the side and slouched near the bow as Flaherty and Lewis dragged their captive in, laying him on the floor on his side. Ericka jumped, pushing on the side line down to lever herself over the side. A hand touched her shoulder and she turned to follow where Lewis's finger pointed. Up the beach from the direction they'd come, intersecting white beams of flashlights crisscrossed. Ten minutes later and they would have had to either surrender or shoot a few shots over their heads to buy time. She cringed as she thought of Dantalion watching the video of her and the team being led away.

Saltwater drops from the bow sprayed her face as they got under way, heading out to the unseen sub, lurking miles out, black sky merging with dark water in an indiscernible horizon.

How the hell were they going to find him again?

The sub was running submerged until they were well away from territorial waters. A faint hum came through the steel decking, setting her teeth on edge. The air coming from overhead vents seemed fresh, but the walls and ceiling were tight. Ericka was not comfortable in confined spaces. Flaherty leaned over the medic's shoulder, watching as she hooked their captive up for vital signs before turning to frown at him. "How much did you give him?"

Flaherty shrugged, looking unconcerned. "Probably too much, but I couldn't have him waking up. He's fast and a damned good fighter. Took Baird out before we knew there was any fight in him. Speaking of whom?"

The medic answered without pausing in her work. "The doc's got him in the next room. Dinner through a straw for him for a while, but other than that, all good."

Lewis stood in the doorway, Tim behind him in the passageway leaning on the bulkhead, brow knotted with a puzzled expression. Their prisoner lay on a gurney, his wrists shackled, still unconscious. He was tall, barrel-chested with heavy shoulders, black hair, trim beard shot with gray. Blood seeped through the white dressing covering the left half of his face, obscuring strong features. He wore dark fatigues and military boots.

Lewis addressed Flaherty. "Chief, any idea who he is?"

Flaherty shook his head in response. "No idea. It looked like he was trying to get the same shot as us. He was carrying a HK MP5, not a civvy version either. No ID. This may take a while."

"Perhaps not." They all turned to look at Tim.

Brows raised, Flaherty looked at Tim. "You got any guesses?"

Tim smiled as he squeezed past Lewis to peer at their captive's face. "No, no guesses at all. Meet Colonel Yusef Abidi of the Pakistani ISI. Colonel, meet Private Flaherty." The man on the table didn't move, showing no sign of consciousness.

All chortled except Flaherty who scowled. "That's not very fucking funny."

Tim beamed at him, not intimidated. "I'm not joking. This is the man who handed us the asset who gave us the intel to be here in the first place."

Flaherty's face drained to pale under his tanned skin. "Shit, the paperwork for this is going to reach the ceiling."

17

Enemy of My Enemy

Diego Garcia was a place Ericka had never thought to visit. A flyspeck in the middle of the Indian Ocean, owned by the British, home to a large military base shared by the owners and the US military. First lifted off the submarine by helicopter, then two days on an aircraft carrier before being flown here, a paradise of bright blue water and white sand uninhabited except for the occupants of the joint base. Despite the extra distance, someone had made the decision to get all of the team out of the operational area as fast as possible.

There was something so very calming, compelling even about the isolation of such a place. The heat drove a constant wind, churning wind waves on top of ever-present swell and surf. It was never silent, a soothing low roar and hiss. In the three days since they had arrived, Ericka felt like she'd slept more than the last several months combined. Flights here were infrequent, leaving them marooned for a few more days.

This was the first time she'd had a chance to speak to Yusef without other eyes and ears keeping a constant watch. They walked along the beach, far from the base, leaving even Tim behind in the hope their former captive would speak to her alone.

She glanced up at Yusef who did not follow her lead, staring back with a half-smile still obscured by bandages. "Agent Blackwood, are we having a picnic or talking business?"

Ericka smiled back, strolling back up to where the white sand was dry. "We only get vacation every ten years, so I take advantage of every opportunity." Despite herself, the walk in the sun and the enforced days of downtime had her feeling something unfamiliar, almost relaxed.

Yusef raised an eyebrow, holding her gaze. There was something very compelling about him. "And yet, I have heard you were 'away' from your duties for over two years, and work now on, how shall I say it, a very short leash?"

She stopped, teeth clenched, wrestling a flash of anger. She let out a slow sigh, looking at her sand-covered feet. "Well, aren't you well informed."

He started walking, turning his head back over his shoulder. "I came out here to speak frankly. Can we do that?"

"Yes, let's."

Yusef waited until she caught up, tugging his hat lower against the sun. "The first time Mr. London takes any risk that might expose him, and we tread on each other trying to kill him. That tells me two things. First, we are the only ones capable of getting close to him and second, that we need to not trip over each other again. Getting another shot at him may be very difficult."

That was annoying. "We didn't get a shot at him. It wasn't him, if he was ever even there."

Yusef looked back down the beach with narrowed eyes.

"You're going to have to forgive me if I seem untrusting of your people, but I don't, it is as simple as that. London, I will not call him Dantalion—that just plays his game—has no difficulty compromising people with any kind of security clearance."

Ericka shot him a glare. "My people are good."

He responded with a gentle snort of derisive laughter. "I'm sure the people in your drone program thought so too. And yet I myself had to shoot them down in our own airspace."

Ericka's eyes widened in surprise, impressed into forgetting his disdain for FBI security. "That was you? All that work to get Mirza and you shut it down. I bet our target doesn't like you very much."

The smirk widened, showing dimples. "I sincerely hope he doesn't like me at all." He paused as if thinking. "What I am going to say now is going to be very difficult to hear." His face became a rigid mask.

Fuck, now what? "Go on."

"For a very brief moment we had his security down, Mirza's doing. Because someone stepped on us, using the opportunity to steal some of London's money, we didn't get all we'd hoped, but what we did get led us here."

Ericka could feel her face flushing, deciding now was not the time to fess up. "I'm listening. What did you get?"

"That he was communicating with a surgeon and we got that doctor's identity. Getting into the surgeon's records was not easy, but we got a few emails I expect were eventually routed to Mr. London. Medical opinions. Telling him essentially that he had checked himself out of hospital in Mexico too soon, that the damage to his spine wasn't as catastrophic as first thought, more of a compression injury than severance. The doctor thought with a series of operations, and a new type of shock therapy, he might walk again."

In the few seconds it took to sink in, Ericka bent over, hands on knees, panting, fighting the urge to throw up, her vision dark. *Just what I feared.* Yusef's hands gripped her waist, preventing her from going over. She shrugged him off, straightening, grabbing his shirt to glare up into dark brown eyes, shaking her head, but no words would come out. Her gaze fell and she dropped to sit in the sand. After a few moments, Yusef lowered himself next to her and they both stared at the breakers crashing on the submerged reef just offshore. Clouds bubbled up on the horizon, wind carrying the scent of rain.

He placed his hand on her shoulder, leaning in to speak. "You acted to avoid shooting someone you thought an innocent man. You didn't know. There is no shame in that. I spoke simply because we cannot let lack of coordination allow this evil bastard to slip away again."

Ericka stood up to walk away, taking off her shoes, holding them dangling in her hand as she meandered down the beach's incline to where the last of the spent breakers slid hissing up the sand.

"You followed protocols. You'd lost sight of him and there was some evidence you were about to kill an innocent man. If you'd been right, we'd have a serious international incident and Thailand would be making noises about extraditing your team to face murder charges right now." Shingen rested her chin on her fists as she spoke, giving Ericka what looked like a sympathetic smile.

Ericka reached over to shut the door to the small boardroom before pivoting to look out the window, not wanting to meet Shingen's gaze. The series of flights back to Virginia had left her exhausted and irritable. "I bet the SEALs have printed off a special series of range targets in my honor." She turned back towards the head of the table. "The intel was good. We had him. I feel sick every time I think about it."

Shingen's head tilted as she spoke. "But now we know Mirza has the real goods and he says he has more to sell. Who knows what that fellow from the ISI still has up his sleeve? He had better stuff than us."

Ericka glanced at her. "Part of his team is still in the bucket in Thailand. Maybe if we can convince them to release his people, he will feel generous with his intel."

"Already under way. Yusef will be sticking around here for a few weeks. It could be that his welcome home won't be as warm as he'd planned. He gave us Mirza, he knew how bad we wanted Dantalion, why the hell was he sitting on this?"

Ericka shrugged. *We didn't share either. He's always slipped through the cracks between jurisdictions.* "I'm not sure we're very popular in that part of the world."

"Not sure we're popular anywhere anymore." Shingen scribbled a few notes and snapped her valise shut. "When you are ready to have another go at Mirza, I'd like you to include our ISI colleague. Keep Mr. O'Brien in the loop."

Why don't you just send me back to basic and make sure I eat my veggies? "Yes ma'am."

Captain Jorge Jimenez leaned back in his old wooden chair making it creak, certain he was the butt of someone's idea of a joke. It was a good one. He stared across the scarred surface of his desk at the man sitting in front of him. His visitor's hair was unkempt, pale under his swarthy skin, the smell of old sweat at odds with the expensive, tailored suit he wore, wrinkled like he'd been wearing it for days. The office blinds were closed against the day's heat, leaving the overhead fan to move warm air around, rustling the few papers on his desk. He stared into the man's watering eyes. Whoever the joker was he had gone to a lot of trouble to make this look real.

The man had come to the gate of the Guardia Nacional at Blvd. Francisco Medina Ascencio, Puerto Vallarta, and politely asked to speak to the officer in charge, claiming he wished to confess to several crimes. Behind him, pulled to the side of the road was a new Cadillac Escalade, displaying the typical gang mods of dark glass, ostentatious wheels and thin, rubber-band-looking tires. Jimenez knew it had to be a joke when the man handed him a very old driver's license showing his visitor as a young man and bearing the name Enrique Hernández, absolutely sure it was true when he typed it into the police database and found it contained pages of criminal history, numerous aliases and several outstanding warrants. Several of the entries were restricted above the permissions Jimenez had and he couldn't read them. That restriction meant cartel leadership.

Jimenez was supposed to believe the inky, late-thirties pretty boy sitting in his guest chair was in fact a career criminal who'd worked his way up through his organization, leaving a bloody trail of unsolved crime in his wake. Jimenez stared at Hernández waiting for the punchline to the joke. "Who put you up to this? Diego?"

The man's brow crinkled, and Jimenez thought he detected a flash of anger. "What do you mean?"

Jimenez folded his hands across his toned stomach, trying to be good-humored. Someone had put a lot of effort into this. "I've been a cop a long time. This is the first time someone so well connected has walked into the police station in broad daylight and told me they want to confess. Usually, they try to shoot at me. Or threaten my mother or my kids. Today is my lucky day. Why?"

"You thinking I'm fucking joking? Run my prints! Scan my face. I'm who I say I am."

He had. If it was a joke, it was one to remember. While Jimenez watched, the results from their facial-recognition software flashed on his screen accompanied by various blinking alerts about warrants and how dangerous this man was. Comforted by the weight of his holstered HK USP, he leaned his elbows on the desk. "Humor me. Why?"

That drew a scowl and a real flash of anger or was it fear? "Why is none of your fucking business, pig. I'm here to confess. Or do I need to see if I can find a smarter cop in this fucking building?"

"Yeah, good luck with that—you're already talking with him."

The corners of Hernández's mouth twitched up, but his eyes remained hard. *He's not doing this because he wants to, he's terrified.* "Give me some paper and I'll start writing."

Jimenez pushed a pad across his desk and tossed a pen on top of it. "Don't start writing until I've told you your rights!"

Hernández pulled the pad towards him and picked up the

pen, tense muscles radiating stress. "Fuck off! I don't give a shit about your rights."

Jimenez shrugged and leaned in as Hernández began to write. He first wrote a series of numbers down the side of the page, then began to fill them in. Turning his head to read them upside down, he gasped at the first one, very unexpected: rape, American girl, Patricia Blackwood, apartment in Puerto Vallarta. The crimes after that were more what he would have expected, the usual violent thug work young men undertook to rise inside a gang. In a few minutes the page was full and Hernández turned the pad around and slid it back across the table. "There, I want to be charged as soon as possible so I can plead guilty."

"You are going to put me out of a job. Anything else?"

The man's speech was rapid, pressured, his eyes now displaying terror. "Yes, if the Americans want to extradite me for any of the drug stuff, I consent to extradition!"

"Jesus, what, you think the food in jail there is better or something?"

That got Jimenez another flash of anger as the man's eyes filled with tears. "If things were different, I would shoot your greasy cop ass dead for fucking with me like this. Just get it done, asshole! Especially the first one. Until that's entered in the system, I can never sleep."

"Okay, señor, no problem. I'll call the prosecutor's office and get you in front of a judge. I do have a question. Why here? Why come all the way back here to PV to confess. Only the first one on your crime list was here."

Hernández looked down, playing with his fingers, unable to sit still. His speech slow, voice cracking, he didn't look up. "It just has to be that way. Anything else and he'll know."

"Who?"

Hernández leaned back in his chair, folding his arms across his chest. "Just get the fuck on with it."

18

Scent of the Quarry

Ericka tossed her keys on the kitchen counter, hanging her bag on the back of one of the stools. She walked to the sliding doors leading out to the rooftop deck, her former refuge from the day's stress. It was looking a little overgrown but not like it should after the two years she'd been gone. Mrs. Donnelly had kept it until she was murdered. She cringed at the thought, the mental image of the old woman's life snuffed out. It took several minutes of deliberate measured breathing before she felt her heart slow and the red tinge left the edges of her vision.

She'd seen no reason she shouldn't live in her own place now and wasn't minded to give the evil bastard the satisfaction of running her out of her own home. It wasn't like he couldn't track her, he had something new. She was determined that Mirza would give them what he knew or he could go back to Pakistan with Yusef and see how long they could protect him. Flinging her work clothes on her unmade bed, she leaned into the en suite to run a bath before heading back to the kitchen for her mobile. Walking back, she keyed in her PIN and scrolled through her texts. One stood out. *Look at you strutting about in the clear. Feeling pretty cocky for someone who doesn't even recognize an old friend. Listen for the beeps!*

Ericka's chest tightened and she had to force herself to breathe, the colossal cheek of this motherfucker! *What the hell was he talking about?* Then she heard them. Triple beeps coming from the pile of things she'd thrown in her closet and not touched since. She froze in the midst of turning for the front door, pausing for a moment. If that was an explosive or something else as nasty, she was dead already. She clutched the bedroom doorframe, peering into the room. The pile looked as she'd left it, nothing had been moved. *Jesus Christ, the VR rig Tim gave her. How the hell!*

She sat down hard on the bed's edge, staring at the source of the noise, her stomach muscles tightening as the rage bubbled up, her vision blurred by angry tears. She found herself clutching handfuls of the comforter as if doing so could anchor her from responding. No chance of that. Ericka lunged forward, tearing aside clothes, kicking shoes out of the way, before snatching up the VR set. Straightening, she held them to eye level, noting the glow from the internal screens. She strode back to her bed and sat, tugging them on.

Seeing a high-resolution video of blowing sands in a rocky defile, Ericka growled into the mic, so angry she was spitting. "You bastard, knock it off with the gamer theatrics!" For a full thirty seconds, all she could hear was the howl of wind and the hiss of shifting sands.

The voice sounded like it was coming from all around her at once, rising from under the wind's scream. "But then how would I be any different than the petty hacks you find such easy prey?" Before she could shriek her answer, a human shape appeared between gusts, dressed like the Hollywood version of a Bedouin nomad, leaning on a gnarled staff as it approached. Closer now, she could make out the face of a bearded death's head, wrapped in the traditional keffiyeh under the cowl of a robe's hood. The clothes fluttered with each passing gust. "Besides, I have a reason for appearing as my own version of Moses. Guess what it is?"

"You evil bastard, that old woman you killed was completely innocent!" Ericka trembled as she shouted, causing the image to blur.

The apparition's head dipped once before speaking. "That seems unlikely, same for the couple in the apartment below. No one is innocent."

No hint of denial. "What do you want? Say it now, there will be no hesitation next time I have a shot at you."

There was mirth in the voice as it rose to compete with a wind gust. "Yes, that must really sting. You could have watched my head explode but couldn't bring yourself to do it. Ask yourself why?"

Ericka shook her head, forcing words through clenched teeth. "I said, what do you want?"

The hooded figure moved the staff in front of him, leaning on it with both hands. "Why, to check in on my star pupil of course. I was becoming concerned. So much so that I took the fate of Mr. Hernández into my own hands."

"Star fucking pupil, you'll see soon enough." She was shouting again, spitting. The name penetrated the fog of rage. "Hernández?"

He continued, appearing unimpressed. "When I offered you those men, you made a very pretty speech about justice and trials and other nonsense. Then I see two of them have met very well-orchestrated, violent ends. Then you vanish. Imagine my shock and concern that you'd lost your way. Now you are shouting at me for taking a shot at Agent O'Connell, clearly a 'combatant' if ever there was one. So, I acted. Perhaps you truly haven't heard?"

"Heard what?"

"Mr. Hernández has made his way back to Puerto Vallarta, the scene of his crime so long ago, and confessed to Patricia's rape, amongst a long list of other misdeeds. He will plead guilty to all of them on Monday and I expect spend the rest of his life in prison. I thought you'd be so pleased at seeing justice done, like you said, but now I'm worried. Now I wonder if you had something special in store for him that I've gone and spoiled."

Ericka found herself holding her breath, a sudden chill flooding her. "How? What did you do?"

The figure bowed his head as if against a strong gust. "I can be very persuasive when I put my mind to it. It turns out Mr. Hernández has people and things he cares about more than the sentence. By the way, I expect him to consent to extradition to the US, so you may want to think about scheduling your days off to coincide with visiting days at the prison."

That was a thought, to actually be able to confront one of the bastards face-to-face. *Time to figure out what had happened later. First, see if she could get the knife in.* "Finding ways to make ends meet these days, or is that what you want? Running short of cash in hawala?"

The figure bowed over his staff. "Very well played, but no less than I would have expected. Shall we take stock? You deal with your enemies the way I do. You learned how to 'live off the land' from the dark web. Now, you have returned from exile for what? Revenge? On me? My, my, but the apple does not fall far!"

Fucker! "Enjoy it while you can. You have too many enemies now, too few places to hide. And everyone has a bill to present. Your days are numbered."

The apparition spoke again. "Everyone's days are numbered and I have great plans for those left to me. Just wait!" He opened his arms in an expansive gesture, looking down to draw attention to his appearance. "After all, Moses did not live to see the promised land, but he did lead his disciples into it."

Ericka swallowed her bile, keeping the rage from her voice. *What the hell is he talking about? Get him boasting.* "And got run out of town by pharaoh. Where do you think you'll take them?"

"The same place I have existed for several years now, the overlap between the physical world and the digital realm. The place where you can't tell which one you are in. Where in a world of laws based on borders, lines on the ground, is a place where there are no laws? No way to enforce them if there were. Come, Ericka, you are no one's fool. Every new frontier works the same way."

"Enlighten me!"

The figure was leaning on his staff as if weary. *Is that real, is he actually standing somewhere?* The movements looked very natural. "We repeat the patterns of other great changes. The industrial revolution produced coal, shipping, manufacturing barons. It also produced a darker underbelly— protection, bootlegging, brothels, gambling—where almost as much money was made. The pattern now repeats with a few billionaire titans of the digital world leaving all others in their wake. As before, the transition creates opportunities for those who adapt quickly. We never left the jungle behind, Ericka. Its laws still rule our behavior."

Poke him again. "So, you and your little herd of perverts and deviants are going to rule the world?"

His voice sounded amused, at odds with the horrific image speaking to her. "You need to talk to your behavioral unit and update your labels. I have much bigger plans now and a much greater need for gratification. I may even need them to give me a better label. They should think up a new one for me. You'll see soon. They're too reliant now. They'll never see it coming."

Shove him again, maybe he'll get defensive. He can't abide betrayal. "I don't think I feel like waiting. Mirza is somewhere you'll never find him and says he's happy to tell us everything. I don't think he's scared of you anymore."

His head bobbed down, waiting for a moment before rising again. Sometimes motion capture shows things you wish it hadn't. That had bit deep. His tone was too level, too controlled. "The longer it takes me to find him, the more opportunity I shall have to be creative, the more gratifying it will be. Mirza and I will meet soon enough. He is no threat to me. Don't flatter yourself."

Slide the knife in now, followed by a good, sharp twist. Ericka hoped he could see her leering expression. "You underestimate him. What he has given us so far were not things you gave him. They were things he took from you that you didn't know and didn't foresee. You didn't tell him where you were going to be, but he knew, correct? You didn't show him where you hide money, but he knew. You didn't show him how to get through your encryption, but he figured it out. London is a clever boy, but he thinks no one else is, and that makes London cocky and do stupid things. What else has Mirza figured out that you haven't thought of? Who's watching who?"

Ericka pulled off the headset, holding it up to her eyes as she held the power button down, seeing the LEDs wink out. He could probably restart them remotely, but she hoped he was too busy smashing things and shrieking. Narcissists have such gigantic egos but they're so very fragile. That was it for his gloating and boasting, his VR fireside chats. This was a run to the end now. When he cooled off, she expected he would redouble his efforts at finding Mirza. She had no doubt, unless they got him to talk first, Dantalion would eventually end his former protégé in some very unpleasant manner. With any luck, he'd worry that Mirza knew more than he really did and start to take stupid chances trying to shut him up. He was just one man so the trick will be to keep him off balance, failing to concoct his usual intricate plans with multiple fail-safes.

Ericka smiled as she looked at Yusef down the boardroom table. She pointed to the data showing on the room's smartboard sent from her tablet. "You need to be more careful who you lend your mobile to."

Yusef squinted, leaning forward as Tim began to laugh. Shingen appeared unamused. "Damn! Did he really get in or is this just some sort of silly spoofing?" Yusef's tone was full of horror. All stared at him, his face lit by the sunlight streaming through the highest window. He was dressed in what looked like a new suit.

Ericka shrugged, sipping her coffee to hide her laugh, deciding to string him along a bit. "You tell me?" The displayed data showed the text to Ericka from Dantalion had come from Yusef's phone.

Shingen's back was rigid as she sat at the head of the table, features set as she glared at Ericka. "If you are quite done tormenting our guest, Agent Blackwood?"

Yusef turned to Ericka, brows raised. She found his stare disquieting, turning to glance at Tim as she spoke. "He got into your service provider and injected the message midstream. If that's a company phone, you are overdue for a switch."

Yusef looked away. "One of the many consequences of his attack on us, I expect."

Shingen interjected again. "Time for us to discuss how we complete the debriefing of our source."

Tim raised his hand from the table to get her attention. "First off, I know we want to do this as a deposition, but bringing suits through the door again is not likely to get him to spill his guts."

Yusef stroked his trimmed beard, black, lightly shot with gray. "That is for certain. Mirza is a fanatic and is guided in all things by his perverted version of his faith. To him, you are all infidels, fit to be used in pursuit of his goals without second thought. Lucky for us, he is also a bit of a coward and the teachings of his sect about martyrdom have not taken root. That said, we must emphasize the threat London, or Dantalion as I suppose we are going to call him, poses to Mirza and those he cares about. That is the path to emptying him of what he knows."

Shingen glanced around the table before speaking. "So how do we play this?"

Yusef glanced towards Ericka, raising an index finger to point at her. "Much as he may not like me, Mirza sees me as a man of the same faith, however misguided. He knows I control consequences to his organization. You, Ericka, he sees as the one person our target has any respect for. That means something to him. When Mirza speaks of you, I see fear. It makes it worse for him that you are a woman. Together is our best chance."

Ericka raised her brows in mock consternation. "Glad to hear it."

Shingen gestured to Tim. "You're his handler. What's your view?"

Tim shrugged, pressing his lips into a line. "He's not talking to me. This is worth a try. Yusef, we still have no basis to hold him in this country, so any time he decides to leave he can. Though I don't think he'll last a week." He looked to Yusef who nodded his agreement.

Semenov stood on the dock of the Quileute Marina in La Push, Washington. He leaned with his lower back on the sailboat he'd tied up an hour before, glancing up the road as he waited for their vehicle to arrive. He was dying for a cigarette, but some of the boats around him looked like they might be lived in and he didn't want to irritate anyone into remembering him. Up the road, he could see the radio tower of the coast guard station. He squinted at the houses across the road from the marina, practiced eyes seeing no signs of life. His patron had told him to expect to see two vehicles arriving about sunset. In the daylight, too many details were visible and traffic at night was unusual enough to be noteworthy. He approved of the careful, detailed planning behind everything this Dantalion did.

The first vehicle would be a well-used and ubiquitous pickup with a crew cab that the driver would leave in the parking lot with keys in it. The man would go back the way he came in the second vehicle. The driver and Semenov would never meet nor lay eyes on each other. Payment for the truck, delivery and silence had been carried out from wherever his current employer was hanging his hat. It must be transportation that would stick in the mind of no one.

Semenov glanced over his shoulder to ensure his colleague remained below decks for now. Emma Golubev was the perfect choice for this gig. Her skills as a military nurse would ensure Mirza stayed sedated but alive until they got him offshore and onto the Chinese fishing boat meeting them. If it came to fighting, she could more than hold her own. This was not their first time out together, her presence gave him confidence his back was covered.

They had flown into Vancouver separately, met as directed at a marina in nearby Richmond and taken possession of the yacht, moored where they were told it would be. It was provisioned for open water containing documents identifying them as a Polish couple. Few North Americans could tell that accent from Russian. To anyone who wanted to know, they had acquired the boat to sail the Pacific coast to Mexico before turning west into the southern Pacific to wander as they liked.

In fact, the very capable thirty-nine-foot Corbin, named *Aya's Hope*, would go to the bottom in deep water well outside

US waters the minute they were on board their ride. Since they had cleared US customs at Port Angeles, Washington, they had made good time under sail. His encrypted sat phone had beeped sending him a text message that his uncle Pitr was going to be released from hospital and they were just sorting out which convalescence home he would be placed in. Knowing their target had been moved meant they were in no rush. They would have to wait on their moment. They had prepaid for a month's moorage, telling the owner they wished to rent a car and explore the area.

His head snapped up at the sound of tires crunching on wet gravel. The truck was old but looked to be in good condition, far more so than the dilapidated Subaru following it. Semenov grasped the boat's wire railings, pulling himself back on the deck, crossing to behind the mast where he was out of sight from the parking lot. Farther out behind the breakwater, the Quillayute River flowed hard as the tide ebbed. He took a deep breath, enjoying the fresh salt air before knocking on a partially open porthole, taking care the sound wouldn't carry.

Emma's face appeared from the stern, seeing his thumbs-up. Her graying blond hair was tied tight. Combined with her hawklike blue eyes and square jaw, she exuded an air of formidable confidence, perfect for this gig. He stood up straight next to the mast, peering over the mainsail's shroud as two men drove off the way they had come, the battered old station wagon leaving a thin trail of blue smoke.

Semenov slid the hatch open and reached in as Emma handed him up their gear. They would spend the night on the boat here, driving out in the early morning to avoid witnesses. They walked to the truck keeping watch as they did. With the gear stowed behind the vehicle's front seat, they walked down to the beach for vodka and that cigarette he had been craving the last hour. He glanced at his companion, never happier than when facing the thrill of a new mission. As he'd told his new employer, he'd always wanted to see America.

19

Providence

"You tell us, Mirza! How are we going to keep you safe?" Yusef gestured with an open hand, his tone impatient. "You're the one who bent the knee to this fiend you are so frightened of. Now you want us to fix everything for you." Yusef sat back, glancing at Ericka with what she took to be well-feigned exasperation.

Ericka stared down the old mess hall table to where their asset sat, hands resting on the tabletop without cuffs. Mirza was pale, his skin sallow, bags under his eyes, staring back with a sour expression. He constantly wiped his nose with his sleeve. From outside came the sound of troops doing morning exercises to the traditional shouts and insults of a drill sergeant. Life in the Fort Lewis base detention center did not appear to suit him. Mirza's red nose and cough told her the cool, damp climate of the northwest was rather disagreeing with him. His handlers waited in the current mess hall on the other side of the main square.

She let the silence become uncomfortable before she spoke. Time to give him some reason to want to cooperate. "Be reasonable. Your information about where he was going to be was true. We trust you actually have something of value to tell us, but while you're holding out on your old master's capabilities, how do you even expect us to anticipate the danger you might face?"

"Yes, exactly! Much less care enough to go to all the effort." Yusef's tone was harsh, but Ericka suspected it wasn't feigned. She suspected her ISI colleague was used to employing more direct methods to invite cooperation.

Mirza stared at the stained Formica top of the old table, turning a thin gold ring he wore on the little finger of his left hand. "You'll just have to forgive my caution. Now this *'ifrīt* is aware I am here, he will have taken steps to harden himself to areas where I might do him damage." He glared at them both in turn. "Twice I have given him to you, and twice you have failed utterly. You do not leave me brimming with confidence at your ability to deal with him."

Ericka was careful not to let the wince show. Mirza had to be made to believe there was no other way. She opened her mouth to answer, but Yusef beat her to it, voice raised, tone sneering. "And I think our lack of success has far more to do with you holding out. Perhaps secretly pleased that giving us part of what you know is ensuring we don't succeed. And if you truly think we are too stupid for our target, that does not bode well for your future prospects, does it?"

Ericka spoke before Mirza could answer, raising her voice. "It's clear from what your old boss has accomplished lately he now has some tools that we're not familiar with. If you'd told us what we're up against, we'd have had a better chance at putting him down and keeping you safe while we do. Yes?" No point pretending otherwise; their asset wasn't stupid.

Mirza took a deep breath, still fiddling with his ring, seeming to choose his words, speaking in a faltering tone. "Let us not play games then. We are all intelligent people. To his mind, for what I have done already, I have earned the most painful end he can think of. There is no changing that. What little hope I have of staying alive is in your hands. Where I am losing faith is the point where I have given you all that I have and still you fail. No one cares to see to my health and interests."

Yusef spat his words. "We have told you. The American government will honor its contract with you, guaranteeing they will do whatever is necessary!"

Mirza's short laugh was more like a bark. "Yes, I will hand it to you to wipe away your shit, for all that it is worth."

Ericka raised her voice again to drown them both out, glaring at Mirza, seeing his red eyes and flushed cheeks. "You make it sound like there is a third option. There isn't. Either you tell us what we're dealing with and we do our poor incompetent best or you keep your secrets and we don't even have the ability to try. What third choice do you think you're holding out for?"

She caught the faintest glimpse of a smile just as his shoulders slumped. "Quite so. If you must know, I think the third choice is I tell you and he kills me despite your best efforts. I wonder if I should just accept my death and go to my grave happy with the thought he will bedevil you until the end of your days."

Yusef answered, his tone much more accommodating, hands open, palms towards Mirza. "But is that the choice a man of faith would make? You talk a good talk, but you know this shaitan attacks the faithful and the infidels with equal enthusiasm. You might be able to stop that. Think to your own sins and how you might earn forgiveness. You might not have long to atone, remember."

Mirza reddened, mouth open to retort before pausing to consider. He sighed, leaning forward to prop his elbows on the table. "You might have the same thoughts I think, being all but an infidel yourself, but that is between you and God. Much as it kills me inside to think it, you are right." He raised a finger towards Ericka. "I have already signed your paper. I will simply have to have faith you will keep your word."

Ericka smiled, trying to reassure him. Mirza's body language spoke of resignation and weariness, but he was more than smart enough to fake them. She would need to be able to test what he said to be convinced. For effect, she pushed the microphone closer to him. "Please."

"He has accomplished something I would not have thought possible. While I can tell you what he has done, I must be clear that I am not entirely sure *how* he has done it. This was not something he shared, rather things I found out for myself. You are of course familiar with Clearview technology?"

"Of course." Clearview was a commercial AI capable of facial recognition using almost any image available on the web. Many police agencies used the company's services to identify suspects using nothing more than a single image. It was a tool so powerful, several governments had restricted its use.

"Imagine then the power you would have, for yourself and others for a fee, if you could see with the eye of God. That is what he has done. He even calls it Providence as I have told you. In essence it adds to the power of Clearview all of the hacking tools he has used over the years. It doesn't stop at the edge of public domain. Once he has any hits at all, he guides his AI to search for and penetrate private spaces related to his target or the image. For instance, having found a matching picture somewhere, it deploys an array of crawlers and worms to see all it can about the person in the image. If it finds a Twitter image attributable to a location, it will penetrate closed security systems in the area scouring for more. It will look to see what the subject has bought, where he has been, who he speaks to, everything the internet records about him. It will search for any other accounts it can find for the same person. It is like planting software on someone's phone to turn it into a data recorder, like Pegasus, except it goes further, probing into the past, seeking buried secrets. Do you understand?"

Yusef's face flushed; Ericka could see his jaw muscles working. "I thought we were finished with games. We all know there are dark-web sites that can match the faces of undercover police with high school social media."

Mirza shook his head, holding up a hand in protest. "That is not what I'm talking about!"

Ericka held up a hand to Yusef. The dark-web version of Clearview had followed the real one by a few months, smaller, slower but terribly effective at outing police trying to work their way into organized crime. "Go on! How the hell can he run a monster like this without being detected? Where does he get the processing power to run even a limited AI like that?"

Mirza shook his head, eyes wide. "It isn't like he showed me a network diagram. I don't know where it is. Probably many places and can be controlled from wherever he likes. You know how he operates."

Ericka stared at him with narrowed eyes. "That would

require close to true machine learning coupled with semi-automated control of an array of advanced hacking tools?"

"Yes, precisely! That is exactly what he has done."

Yusef glanced at Ericka for a moment before turning back to Mirza. "Fairy tales! This makes no sense. How can he hide such a monster? Where could he steal the processing power necessary?"

Mirza shook his head looking down, resigned, like he was talking to idiots. "This is why you people are always so many steps behind. Maybe it isn't all in one place. Maybe he didn't steal the resources. Who says it has to work that fast?" He turned to point at Ericka again. "Think how you would do it. You who are said to be such a genius."

She leaned back, her hands folded on the edge of the table. *How indeed?* All across the planet, thousands of Bitcoin mines toiled away with all the processing power he'd ever need. Once a match was found, it would be a simple matter for Providence to send data locations to another facility to penetrate their security. Disperse the system. This explained a lot of things: his ability to find whoever he wanted to and deploy against them, the attack on Tim, even finding Mirza where they'd hidden him. How he found dirt and secrets the better to blackmail compliance. "How much of a technical synopsis can you give us?"

Mirza snorted his derision. "Nothing! I doubt he has told anyone how this thing is structured or where it all is. What I know, I inferred from what he told potential clients he could do and knowing the potential of what he has on hand. If I knew more, I'd have stolen it for myself!"

"What traces does it leave? Is there any way to track its use?"

Their asset sneered. "No more than any other competent hacker. Crawlers will find traces of its use. It is the controlling mind that is faster and better. The means are unchanged, a teaspoon of grains in a sandstorm, impossible to discern, but all acting according to plan."

Ericka's mind raced as she spoke. "Does he still make it his business exposing those he sees as rats and traitors?"

Mirza's face lost its smile. "More of a calling for him than a business, almost like a jihad, such is his fervor."

Ericka glanced at Yusef. "I'm afraid you are going to be our guest for a while yet. We might be able to do a little better than this base, but if you're telling us the truth, full relocation with a new identity is out of the question for now." She paused for a sustained look. "I'm not buying your bullshit about how you figured this out on your own. He's not that stupid at all."

Mirza's smile looked genuine this time. "He may be the most intelligent person I have ever known, but he makes the same classic mistake all of you do." The smile widened as Ericka's brows rose, lingering before he spoke, accusatory. "He thinks he's the only one."

"Ever wish you smoked or drank?" The cooling mist driven by light wind was soothing after the interrogation. The sun was out but towering clouds building to the southwest heralded more rain. She glanced up at Yusef who was leaning beside her against the wood siding of the building.

He smiled back, his features lighting up when he did, his harsh, professional persona and face vanishing. "Who says that I do not? With what I have to contend with, I'm quite sure Allah would forgive me if I did." He was studying her features, forcing her to look away. "I have been remiss in asking... How have you fared from the outcome of your Thailand mission? I told my superiors if you hadn't gotten in my way, I'd have killed him."

Ericka turned to look at him, surprised at the kindness in the gaze of someone she'd at first thought a thug from a second-rate service. She gave the standard visual sweep, craning her neck to ensure no one was around. "I'm sure I'm as much beloved of my superiors as I always was. They tolerate me for lack of other options." She paused, staring off across the parade square. "You're really not what I expected."

Another hint of a smile flitted across his features. "What did you expect?"

Ericka prodded him in the side to let him know she was joking. "A man with callouses on his hands from the brass knuckles."

His laugh was deep, resonating over the wind. "Our methods are not perhaps as refined as yours, but we hold our own in all areas."

"You speak English with what sounds like a British accent, but I can't place it?"

"I went to school at the London School of Economics and refined my learning of the language there."

Ericka studied his features, puzzled. "What part of Pakistan are you from?"

Yusef looked down, breaking the moment. "None. My family is Persian and my father was unfortunately a bit too close to the shah to stay in our homeland. So close in fact, that he and my mother were killed in Pakistan by the new regime while I was a boy. Worth hiring local killers. I was in and out of orphanages and when I was old enough to inherit, I used my father's money for education."

The moment's distraction ended, and Ericka squeezed her eyes shut, remembering the back of her target's head against the darkening sky. It could have ended right there. She pushed it from her mind. "And you went back and joined the intelligence service in your adopted country hoping for a shot at whoever called the hit on your parents?"

He was looking at her with wide eyes. "Very perceptive. How did you know? Obviously, orphans make good intelligence agents."

"It's not an unfamiliar theme, but not today." She grasped his wrist. "Where do we go from here?"

Yusef stood straight, turning to face her. "You're the only one he is afraid of. You tell me?"

Her first plan wasn't going to work. Time to adapt. The more Ericka thought through how Providence must work, the more she realized what it might take to keep anything out of view. She sighed, nibbling her lower lip before turning to look back at Yusef. "First, we need a way to keep our asset alive, get him somewhere safe. Even if he doesn't have much more to tell us, we may need him as a witness someday."

"We don't know how he found the worm this time."

She shook her head. "There's only so many things he could have picked up on. There was nothing in the cabin. His handlers were told to power down their phones as they left town."

"Are you sure they did, though?"

Ericka had a hard time believing they'd slipped that badly but shrugged. "Anything's possible, but I doubt it. Thinking out loud, if he has used this thing to identify FBI people and match them to phones, he could scan for clusters of them together. Nine or ten of them showing up in the same dirt-lump town over time doesn't have many alternate explanations. Using rotating handler teams may have worked against us."

Yusef pursed his lips as he stared at her. "So how then?"

If it were very carefully done, his creation might be used against him, maybe make him see things that weren't even there. She tugged her sweater tight around her shoulders. "To start with, neither Mirza nor anyone near him gets to drive, fly in or use any tech newer than nineteen-eighty. We also need to think about what we can feed him without him knowing we've done it."

"Like?"

"Just simple stuff leading him astray. Create fake data and leave it where we hope he'll scan it. Things we know he can find but look like someone went to a lot of trouble to conceal."

Yusef smiled, his eyes crinkling in the corners. "I shall look forward to that. And once we have Mirza safely tucked away?"

"We go on the offensive and chase the bastard down."

20

Diversion

Ericka watched as Mirza rolled down the old Land Cruiser's window by hand, leaning to peer at the grass runway of Cougar Mountain airstrip, thirty miles of rural roads away from Fort Lewis. The old SUV stank of many nights of undercover work, bad food, coffee and cigarettes. Tim drove, treating the ancient Toyota as if it were a much nimbler vehicle, suspension creaking as he took corners without bothering to unduly tax the brakes. She had reached around the driver's seat to poke him in the ribs without effect. The second time, he gave a mocking glance, saying it was how the locals drove and they didn't want to stand out like a carload of tourists from the city.

She was confident that they had passed enough security cameras for anyone interested to pick them up. She had told the younger special agent riding in the front passenger seat to turn his phone on and off to check social media. The balance was critical, to look like they were taking steps to be stealthy while still leaving a usable trail. The frightened-looking man on the seat next to her would have Dantalion's undivided attention, she was sure. He wouldn't bother with having anyone on the ground here, concentrating his efforts on locating where Mirza would be going. All she wanted him to know is Mirza was on the move.

The Toyota lurched to a stop on grass, tired brakes offering a minor squeal of protest, pulling up next to the battered-looking Beechcraft King Air. Mirza's untidy hair blew across his forehead as he looked at the aircraft with sour, undisguised disdain. Ericka shook her head. *Is there anything this guy isn't going to whine about?* True, it was an older plane driven by twin propellers that had started its life moving cocaine, like many aircraft in law enforcement service. It had been refitted to carry five passengers in notional comfort and for this flight, all but the most basic flight instruments had been disconnected from their power source, including the transponder, which would normally transmit a minimum of aircraft type, speed and altitude. Transponder data was visible to air traffic controllers and several web services that made location information available to aviation enthusiasts.

As they clambered through the small door behind the wing, Tim slapped Mirza on his bony shoulder, making the smaller man wince. "Buck up! Robby here used to be a fighter pilot with the marines. I don't think he's ever crashed a plane once! Right?"

The pilot looked up from his checklist, turning his head to smile back at them, sunglasses perched on top of bristling steel-gray hair. "You got it. Always managed to eject first!" Mirza didn't answer, choosing to plant himself in the nearest seat and look out the window, hands trembling.

Tim looked at the pilot, gesturing towards Mirza. "He's shy. Once you get to know him, you can't shut him up."

Ericka ignored them, stuffing their few pieces of luggage into the fuel-smelling rear cargo hold, an odor shared by all old aircraft. She pulled the cargo netting up, stopping to pull the door shut before sitting across from Mirza. A glance out the window showed the Toyota on its way off the field, leaving just the four of them.

Tim buckled himself into the copilot's seat. A qualified pilot himself, he always hogged the right front seat in small planes. Ericka pulled a headset from its hook and draped it around her neck before leaning to tap the pilot's shoulder. "All good?"

The pilot spoke without turning. "Full tanks, flight plan to Portland filed, plane working, pilot sober."

Mirza's head snapped up, eyes wide, his expression suspicious again. "Portland? You said Lexington. Why has the plan changed?"

Ericka was not surprised at his alarm, but tired of babysitting his emotions. She held up a finger to quiet him. "Yes, now we're aboard, I'll tell you. We've filed a flight plan to Portland, but we won't open it with ATC until well after we are airborne. That gives us time to throw you out the door to your new handlers waiting in Lexington and for us to make Portland by the scheduled time. Nothing to trigger anyone watching. We're going to fly low and fast without a transponder so we only appear intermittently on radar. I'm sure your old master has a list of planes like this and will set his software to watch every time one of them is in the air in the Pacific Northwest. We're also obviously hoping that he will have someone on the ground in Portland to try and follow you. We're set to lead them a bit of a chase. Understand?"

Mirza pursed his lips, scowling, and for a moment lost

his sour expression. "You will of course try and intercept anything his men on the ground transmit to him?" She rolled her eyes at the notion she needed reminding. Mirza leaned back, staring at her. "And now I begin to see why he is so wary of you."

Thanks, asshole! Ericka didn't respond, instead leaning forward so she could be heard in the cockpit. "Time?"

Tim leaned back giving her a thumbs-up, his once boyish smile twisted by a complex pattern of facial scars. She bit her lip at the pang of guilt. "Sunset in forty minutes. Let's get shifted."

The pilot cinched his harness, flipped open his checklist and started the engines. Ericka could see him craning his neck to look up and down the length of the airstrip. The gentle push into her seat was simultaneous with the roar of the engines going to full throttle as the plane bounced through the rougher edges of the airfield. The cabin vibrated. The takeoff roll seemed too long, followed by a hard right bank the second the wheels were up, her view out the window containing nothing but blurred treetops glowing red in the evening light.

Fucking cowboy! Ericka keyed her mic. "All right there, Tom Cruise, we're going to call this a fail if you give our quivering cargo a heart attack!"

The pilot waved, glancing back over his shoulder. "Just getting the pinecones and bird shit off the wings." She watched as he handed control to Tim so he could set up his night-vision gear for the Portland leg. Tim kept the turns and twists gentle, following the terrain at about five hundred feet over ground level. As the sun's light faded, lights on the ground became visible, flashing under them, their speed much more apparent than it would be from higher altitude. Mirza held the paper sick bag on his lap, his pallor indicating its use was imminent.

The forests gave way to the high, rolling plains of eastern Oregon, endless brown grasses washed with the pink glow of the last light, highlighting the contours. They approached, flying parallel to the single runway of the Lexington airport before making the two left turns that would line them up to land. The airfield was north of town with just a few buildings nearby, perfect to make the drop without dodging endless security cams. Their local team had switched off the two in the main hangar. Ericka glanced at Mirza who now wore his familiar frightened rodent expression, jaw muscles standing out as he clenched his teeth. She leaned to look out the window for the vehicle waiting for them, pleased she couldn't see it.

The landing was hard enough it made Ericka start, her belt digging into her abdomen as the plane braked hard. She said nothing, contenting herself with a dirty look in the direction of the cockpit. As they turned off the runway, she unclipped and moved to the door, holding on to seats as she did. She steadied herself as the plane lurched to a stop, then opened the door, lowered the steps and peered out into the twilight. The cool, dry air shoved in by the idling propellers washed through the door, making her gasp, raising goose bumps.

She reached for Mirza's bag, tossing it to the waiting agent. He wore the local uniform of worn jeans, matching jacket and well-worn boots. He was tall and muscular, his baseball cap obscuring his features. The agent opened his jacket part way to display his badge pinned to the inside. Ericka leaned from the cabin to ensure it matched the expected name. Silhouetted behind him was an old crew-cab pickup truck, the shape of the second agent just visible against the truck's rear window. She tipped the Stetson she was wearing and waved, staying inside.

Ericka turned to Mirza, shouting to be heard over the engines. "This is your stop. We'll be in touch. Do let us know if your memory suddenly improves." She watched until the two men were at the vehicle before she pulled the steps up, slamming the door hard to be sure of the seal. Crouching, she walked up the aisle to stick her head between the pilots' seats. "Now, let's get out of here and see what we can scare up in the way of bad guys!"

Fifteen minutes out, right on schedule, the pilot switched frequencies and keyed his mic, affecting the Chuck Yeager drawl beloved of all professional pilots. "Seattle Traffic Control, this is King Air November-Seven-Tango-Bravo-Niner, request open flight plan Cougar Mountain to Portland International."

There were a few seconds of dead air before the response crackled in her headset. "Tango-Bravo-Niner, flight plan open, squawk two-two-five-four, cleared on route, altitude five-five-zero-zero."

"Tango-Bravo-Niner, two-two-five-four."

Ericka reached for the overhead handhold as the aircraft banked to hug terrain. Widening her stance, she gazed at Tim. The hunt was on. Her skin tingled as the old thrill gripped her.

Five minutes passed before the expected call came from Seattle. "Tango-Bravo-Niner, please recycle your transponder. You're not showing on radar." Turning it on now would highlight they weren't where they were supposed to be and might generate unwanted radio conversation with air traffic control, conversation that anyone could hear. Ericka clenched her jaw, knowing there was no help for it.

The slow drawl again. "Roger that."

She tapped Tim's shoulder. "How close are we?"

He fiddled with the GPS for a few seconds, before turning to her. "Another ten minutes and we'll intersect the route we filed."

"Tango-Bravo-Niner, Seattle Traffic, we're still not seeing you. Confirm position and check your equipment."

Ericka chewed on her lower lip, staring at the pilot whose features now glowed red from the instrument lights. These open-frequency transmissions could light them up. Tim keyed his mic as the plane banked left to skim over rolling plains, low enough to count individual cows. "Seattle Traffic, Tango-Bravo-Niner, we're on our planned route, give us a moment, just powering up backup equipment. Primary is not functioning."

The pilot turned to glance at Ericka, his expression showing he was well pleased with himself. He gestured at the terrain ahead. "As soon as we're behind that hill coming up, I'll climb to the planned route and switch everything on. Hold on tight!" Minutes later, he pushed the throttles forward and pulled back on the yoke, making Ericka's stomach lurch towards the floor. She bent her knees, tightening her grip on the handholds. Executing a flawless climbing turn on their filed route, the pilot snapped on the transponder and pressed his mic button on the yoke. "Seattle Traffic, Tango-Bravo-Niner, that should do it. Looks like we've found the problem."

A few seconds passed. "Tango-Bravo-Niner, Seattle, have you now. Continue on route; contact Portland Traffic on arrival. Good evening."

Ericka's shoulders dropped with relief. She was dying to contact the agents on the ground but there had to be the absolute silence her quarry would expect. They would pull into a smaller hangar from which an old Range Rover would emerge carrying three agents, one dressed and made up to a reasonable likeness of Mirza. Then the game would be on.

They hunched over the single laptop, heads together as they listened through headsets. The monitor room was stuffy, without windows, but Ericka was focused on the face of the man filling the screen. His name was Alvin Whinnock, pulled out of his truck by the cover team along with two of his brothers. The prisoner's hands were cuffed to the table in front of him and she could only see the back of the head of the agent asking the questions. The officer was dwarfed by the inky thug across the table who scowled at his questioner, wearing a collared plaid shirt with the sleeves torn off. *Christ, was that a mullet? What a hillbilly!*

"Ya, fuck you, you got nothing!" The man leaned back as far as the cuffs allowed, upper lip curled in a sneer.

The agent's voice was calm but forceful. "Think it through. That's not how a judge is going to see it. You're waiting on the off ramp outside the airport—we got you on video sitting there. As soon as a car full of FBI agents goes by, you and your kin up the road take off after them, tailing them until they get out in the country."

"Fuck you, we're just out for a drive!"

"Sure, you were."

"Fuck you, Fed boy, prove it!"

"You wait until you're a little ways out in the country, then you start reeling them in. Truck full of guns. Explain that!"

The idiot was smirking now. "We're doing a little shooting last weekend. Hadn't got around to putting them away yet. Nothing illegal about that, is there?"

Ericka gritted her teeth, knowing there wasn't anything illegal about rifles and shotguns in Oregon vehicles. She turned to the local agent, Chung, sitting behind them at another desk, pleased to be working with him again. "Who is this moron?"

Chung's face was lit by the screen in front of him, highlighting his expression of disgust. "Local hick from just south, hires himself and his brothers out as muscle to collect drug debts, done time for aggravated assault. There's traces of coke under the back seat, all the guns are legal." He looked up to meet Ericka's gaze. "We don't have enough to charge him with anything. Can't hold him much longer."

Ericka rolled her eyes. She'd expected a better class of thug than these idiots. There was no way they'd have hidden Mirza long enough to transport him to their employer even if they had managed to grab him. *How had he expected these goons to get him away from an FBI escort?* She didn't like the conclusion she was coming to and shivered as the implications sank in. "Anything on his phone?"

Chung shook his head. "They just got the warrant so they're still working on it. So far just some texts about heading for Mexico to drink Tequila and fuck Mexican hookers, spend the cash from their last job." His phone rang. He looked at her, holding up a hand. "This is the search team from the trailer park. Lemme take this."

Ericka turned back to Tim who was still listening to the interrogation. "Anything?"

His eyes were wide as he shook his head. "This moron is so stupid he can barely string together a coherent sentence. All he's doing is telling us to fuck off and talk to his lawyer. And he's sticking to that script. Someone whose dad, uncle and grandfather are all the same guy, I think."

Chung's voice rose behind her as he spoke into his phone, brow crinkled. "That's really fucking weird. They must have had some other place set up. Wait 'til we get the phone spun down and see where else he's been. Shit!" He caught Ericka's eye and shook his head.

Ericka turned back to Tim. "Something's wrong. Even if Dantalion had to put it together last minute, it wouldn't be these idiots." *The conclusion was irresistible; he knew Mirza wasn't going to be there. This was a feint.*

Tim leaned back. "No, agreed." He reached over to turn on the computer's speakers so they could hear what Alvin was saying, his face lit by an idiot grin. "Do whatever the fuck you want, pig! I got me a fat, slick-talking windbag of a lawyer and I'm goin' home in the morning!"

There was just no way this idiot was good for anything but a decoy. The pickup team would not break digital silence while they were anywhere near Mirza, so no way to contact them. They'd need another team to warn them, be ready for any attempts on Mirza. She gripped Tim's shoulder, thinking it through. "We're blown. We need to get some SWAT guys out there right now! You go with them. I really hope I'm wrong."

21

Extradition

Semenov shifted his weight, leaning against the truck's door, head on a rolled sweater between him and the window, willing his eyes to stay open, focused with the patience of the hunter he was. It was cool in the old truck, the windows open so he could hear any sound in the absolute still of the night. The air carried the sour smell of a nearby swamp. In the starlight, he could just make out the gravel surface, tucked as they were into an abandoned side road, tape covering all reflectors and lights on the vehicle so nothing would reflect in advancing headlights. His hand slid to where his HK MP5 leaned against the shifter. Any shooting required tonight would be close-range work at multiple targets. He had chosen his spot in a depression in the rolling landscape, allowing him to see headlights coming from either direction.

Golubev stirred in her sleep in the driver's seat. Her watch would begin soon. She was filthy, wearing locally purchased outdoor gear, bloodied-looking bandages tight around her thigh with bruises on her forehead. A torn pack lay in front of the truck ready to complete the illusion when needed. She would provide a compelling reason for anyone to stop in this out-of-the-way place. It would be unfortunate if someone other than their target were to drive by, but his was not a risk-free business for anyone. Semenov shifted again, fingering the phone and satellite uplink in his thigh pocket. Provided by his employer, it looked like a modified Garmin uplink and was to be used for a single message before moving their captive, and then again as they approached the coast.

He almost never felt anything for his victims unless it was necessary to allow him to anticipate their actions. The application of violence was his trade, one he performed with icy professionalism. He knew any psychiatrist who got the chance would label him something of a psychopath, not that he cared one bit. Two decades of action had left him with an impressive résumé, but no remorse, except when he'd failed to achieve his objective. Failure bruised his ego and he hated that.

Semenov spoke in English, loud enough to wake Golubev. "Your watch." He lifted the night-vision telescope to his eye, focusing on where he knew the road bisected the low hill to his left, and there it was, a pair of green sparks penetrating the pine trees on the ridge. He turned to her, his speech now clipped, in their native Russian. "Vehicle approaching, get into position!"

Golubev's eyes snapped open, instantly alert, reaching for her gear and sliding her new PLK handgun into the grubby down jacket she was wearing. She swung her door open, closed it without noise and tossed the pack to sit on the opposite side of the road, while she herself sat at the road's edge in the position they'd chosen to best present to a vehicle coming from the expected direction. She looked back, signaling ready with a thumbs-up.

Semenov tugged on night-vision goggles and snapped his gun's safety off. He adjusted the spruce bows covering the side of their truck before jogging up the road into his blind where he could approach their target from behind. He expected there would be two agents but ran through his options if there were more. He slid under the netting, comforted by the pine smell from cut branches woven into his cover, satisfied he was invisible from the road. Golubev leaned forward from the tree her back was against, head between her knees, a picture of lost exhaustion. The trap was set.

From behind him came the distinctive crackling of tires driving at speed on gravel. He took a deep breath, relaxing his shoulders, ignoring the dig of stones and twigs on his abdomen and legs. As the sound came level with his blind, he covered his night goggles with one hand to avoid night blindness from the vehicle's light. The gentle squeal of dusty brakes told him they'd stopped. Taking care where he placed his feet, he moved to where he expected there to be blind spots in the truck's mirrors, about twenty-five feet behind and ten feet to the passenger side. Black fatigues rendered him just another shadow amongst many. Adrenaline surging, fighting to keep his hands steady, he waited.

Semenov would have been very surprised if they'd been stupid enough to get out of the vehicle, but these were the professionals he'd been expecting. They stayed inside with the windows shut, but he could hear a querulous voice shouting from inside, no doubt their charge beginning to panic. He caught a flicker of movement in the side mirror, perhaps a face scanning behind. He waited, all movement frozen, smelling the truck's exhaust, waiting for Golubev to play her part.

She gave a masterful performance. Lit by the headlights, she held up a dirty hand to shield her eyes while pushing herself to unsteady feet. Still covering her eyes, she took two short steps towards the truck before tripping over her own backpack to land hard on the road. Semenov winced, knowing how much that would have hurt to carry off convincingly, impressed as always with his partner.

As he would have expected from trained individuals, they stayed hidden while they assessed. While Golubev faked trying to push herself to her feet, the passenger window rolled down about six inches and a woman spoke. "Don't try to get up. Help will come. We can't stop so, we'll go back for help."

Very good, aborting their mission as compromised—what he'd expect from FBI. They would take this Mirza back somewhere secure and try again later. Just as he'd expected. He felt sure they did not suspect a trap but were following the procedure prescribed for them in these circumstances.

Golubev sat on the gravel looking like she was about to cry, staring blind into the headlights. "Don't leave me! I need water! I've been lost for three days." Her performance was flawless.

The backup lights came on and the door opened part way. As the truck moved, a woman's hand appeared, dropping a plastic bag, probably food and a two-liter bottle of water onto the road. *Perfect, now!* Semenov lunged from the roadside, jumping on the running board, left hand grasping the roof rack, shoving the door wide with his right knee. He pressed the MP5's muzzle to the woman's temple, leaning in to be sure he was heard. "Stop the truck now and switch off the engine!" The driver, a large male, took an acceptable second or two to assess before complying. "Throw the keys out the window and place your hands on the dashboard!"

He could hear Golubev's running steps behind him just before she leaned into the cabin to point her pistol at the man's head, controlled fury chiseling the features of both agents to stone. *Yes, a terrible thing to be taken so easily, but at least you won't be dead unless you do something stupid.* Semenov gestured with his chin to Golubev, eyes on the man, gun tight on the woman's head. She ran around to the driver's side, gesturing the man to lie on his belly where she zip-tied his feet together, hands behind his back. Him secure, Semenov secured the female agent by the front wheel of the truck before turning his attention inside.

Success gave him a warm glow, energizing him, forcing a smile onto his face. In the back seat, their charge stared out of wide, red-rimmed eyes, an expression devoid of hope. Semenov's eyes narrowed. There would be no resistance from this one, this rat knew he was finished running. With Mirza secured in their vehicle, he drove the agent's truck into the woods next to theirs, then they dragged the agents from where they lay, ordering them to climb back into their respective seats, lifting them where necessary. He saw flickers of fear in both their eyes, masked, as Golubev returned with her kit and began preparing syringes.

Semenov watched with professional interest and admiration as she mixed her cocktail, mostly Rohypnol, a mixture that would keep them unconscious for some time and leave them with limited memories of the night's events. A small price for them to pay in exchange for their lives. Killing was cleaner, but if he left dead agents, the Americans would never give up hunting him until they were dead. Time to move, no telling how long they had before someone came looking or a local wandered by.

He tugged the concealing foliage from their truck, peeled off the tape and climbed in. Their prisoner was in the back seat and Golubev leaned in from the passenger side. Mirza stared with alarm as she jabbed her needle into his thigh. "What is that?"

Semenov answered for her, not bothering to hide the contempt in his voice. "Ketamine. If it is good enough to put animals to sleep, it is too good for you. But don't worry, you'll be awake soon enough. When you are reunited with the man you betrayed." Mirza had just the time for a look of panicked horror before the drug took him and his chin flopped on his chest. She pulled Mirza to the floor of the back seat and made sure his airway was clear before covering him with gear bags to conceal him from outside view.

She glanced up at him with a professional smile. He shone a light at the truck next to them. The two lolled in their seats showing no reaction. He glanced towards the east. No sign of dawn yet, but it wouldn't be long and they should be far away before first light populated the roads they needed on their way to the anonymity of the highway. Semenov pulled away, powering up the device to send a simple, preprogramed message: *Stopped to talk to an old friend. On our way now.* A few moments later, the device chirped, indicating a successful uplink, so he powered it down. He gave his partner an inquiring glance. She signaled ready and he pulled out to begin the circuitous route that would take them back to the boat.

★ ★ ★

Ericka reached to shut it off when her phone vibrated in her jacket pocket. She glanced at the screen before seeing it was Tim, sliding her thumb to answer. "Shingen's looking for an update, I think it's for you."

Tim's voice was steady but muffled by the low-quality sat phone connection. "It's very bad. I'm sure she doesn't want to hear from me. Chain of command and all."

Ericka rolled her eyes and stood up. "I'll patch her in." Shingen took one ring to answer. "Blackwell here. O'Connell is with me on conference, and we're encrypted. Good morning."

Shingen's tone was glacial. "No, it really isn't. What the hell happened?"

Ericka's stomach tightened at her boss's tone, waiting for Tim to answer. After a few seconds, he spoke. "We found the asset's handlers in their truck about twenty-five miles from their destination in their vehicle, heavily drugged. They still aren't awake. Our medic is trying to wake them up, but they need lab work to identify the drug. No sign of the asset, no blood or any other sign of a struggle. Their truck is undamaged. There's tracks where it looks like the assailants waited, but tire tracks and a hiding spot in the bush are all they left. This was very professional."

Shingen was speaking, asking questions, but Ericka wasn't hearing her. *How the hell?* Not only had he figured out their plan, he'd managed to get real assets in front of them. That meant he'd known for some time. She sunk into her chair. Providence indeed. He'd raised his game and now they'd have to. They'd all but handed Mirza to his guys. That had always been the risk but Mirza was done talking to them until they got him out of that base.

Ericka began hearing Shingen again. "At least they're not dead."

Ericka bowed her head. "Professionals. They're not going to risk an unnecessary murder rap if it went wrong."

Shingen broke the silence. "What now?"

Ericka thought it through before answering. "If they wanted to just kill him, Mirza's body would be there with the agents. I'm betting Dantalion wants a discussion with him before he dies. That's a huge risk, and it's going to take time."

Shingen's tone was disbelieving. "Why would he take a risk like that? You think he's here in the States?"

Time to voice what she'd been thinking for some time. "He's changed. Something's really changed. He's taking risks he never would have before. No layer of detachment. He hates rats to begin with and this one is personal. Mirza has cost him big time. He's going to see personal involvement in his end as worth a lot of risk."

Tim chimed in. "Agreed, we've got an evolving MO here."

Ericka continued. "This could be the breakthrough we need. We were never going to get him technically, now we have a way to bait him out. That's something we've never had before."

Shingen took a few moments before answering as Ericka hoped she would. "What do you need?"

Ericka took a deep breath before speaking again. "We might get lucky on the ground, but with at least twelve hours' head start they could be a long way off, over the Canadian border or getting close to Mexico. Tim, find the agents' phones, send someone to their homes to get their personal mobiles or tablets. I need images of those right now. If I can figure out how he found out where they were going with Mirza it could give us a starting point. Ma'am?"

"Yes?"

"I doubt there's any cell coverage out there. They have to be using a sat phone. We need to get any sat phone transmission records available for the last twenty-four hours anywhere within a hundred miles. There aren't that many providers. We won't get message content but we might get lucky and find transmission location. Maybe even get Dantalion's approximate location. No time for a warrant. If this isn't exigent circumstances, I don't know what is."

Shingen's answer was instant. "Done. Let's get on it!"

Ericka looked down at the keyboard, shoulders slumped as she let out a sigh. There it was. People were just so goddamned used to living half in the virtual world, habit overrode all sense, even with trained agents. She sat alone in the Portland office's lab, laptop hooked up to borrowed forensic machines, cold coffee and half-eaten sub beside her. The first two phones gave her nothing. The FBI-issued mobiles hadn't been powered on within fifty miles of the safe house, they were clean. The problem had come with the male agent's personal iPad retrieved from his home in Portland. The Cellebrite image of his data left no doubt. This very capable software was the class of the field at forensically retrieving data from small devices. The agent had gone on Google maps three days before and looked up directions to drive to the safe house, then written them on a piece of paper that Tim had found in the truck's door pocket.

Someone had been on that iPad for some time, the first

intrusion coming about the time they'd moved Mirza to the States. Most of the malware had been overwritten, likely after each scan, but bits of what looked like an illicit version of Pegasus were still there. Software that allowed the user to remotely place monitoring software on any mobile and monitor all activity on it. Ericka knew with absolute certainty she was looking at the fingerprints of Providence. She stopped to look out the window at the afternoon sun. There weren't that many FBI in this end of the country that he couldn't have found a significant percentage of them and penetrated their personal devices.

From here on, anyone involved in this investigation was going to have to start with new devices with better encryption and strict instructions as to use. Despite near-constant admonitions to never use personal devices for work, many agents did, following deeply ingrained habits. On the upside, there was enough here that she could modify their security software to scan for at least this part of Providence and have some warning of his interest.

He really is a clever bastard! But not that clever. He was too reliant on it. There must be a way to feed him what they wanted without him picking up on it. Ericka giggled to herself as she thought through the various things that would rattle his cage and make him slip up. She stood to walk around the lab, stretching the dull ache from her back using lab tables as impromptu exercise equipment. Fatigue made her long for the chemical aids she had relied on in exile, a pang in her guts sharp like physical hunger. She took a deep breath to force the remembered comfort from her mind, consoling herself with the thought the cravings were fewer and farther between. She was coming back, strength drawn now from purpose.

Grasping the worn wood, she used an ancient-looking chair for a few tricep presses. *Never going back down that hole again. Never!*

She walked back to her equipment, sitting down hard, smiling at the message in her queue. The first blocks of data from the commercial service providers were up on their server. One had complied with the request, but it looked like the other was going to take a court order to get them to release. Her jaw clenched in irritation, but there was no cell coverage where the hit had taken place anyway. Coverage began back on the main highway where their targets would be lost in a sea of other phones that they didn't have time to track down.

Ericka's smile was grim and her palms were sweating. The satellite transmission data had two hits, one right on the location where Mirza had been taken. It looked like it had come from a mobile dongled to a GPS device with uplink capabilities. She could tell it was a short text message, but he'd added a layer of encryption that would take some time to break. Ericka had what she needed so she'd leave that for later. This was confirmation someone had communicated from the scene right at the time it had happened. This was them and now they had a trail to follow. His people wouldn't have bothered to light themselves up and communicate without a reason. Dantalion must need some information from them for contingency planning, perhaps how he was going to move Mirza to where he wanted him.

This was where bureau security protocols had worked against them. Telling the agents not to communicate anywhere near the safe house meant no one would be alarmed at not hearing from agents for long periods of time. That had given his people on the ground a huge head start. The second satellite hit contained another shorter, but equally unreadable message this time from central Washington, but it was already ten hours old. *His team was heading for the coast or more accurately had gotten there seven or eight hours ago.* That made sense. There was no getting him out through an airport. By the time any flight landed, they'd have been waiting on the ground. Same with the Canadian border. The RCMP would be waiting for them. *What the hell kind of boat would get them out of range of the coast guard fast enough?*

She bit her lip. This was going to be tight. She pressed Shingen's contact, dialing Tim in, waiting until they were both on the line before she spoke. "It looks like they're heading for somewhere on the central Washington coast. Must be a boat or some small airstrip. Whichever it is, they could be under way already."

Tim's tone sounded aghast. "Christ, if it's a small boat, there could be hundreds of places to look."

Ericka had no answers. They were just going to have to take a stab at their best guess. "Ma'am, to have any shot at this, we need to get the state troopers into the coastal towns and get any coast guard assets ready to intercept. It isn't like they're going to broadcast AIS." All ships over a certain size were required to broadcast their position on AIS, but it wasn't like criminals cared much what the law was.

Shingen answered, "Don't be too sure. When you've gotten a hook into this guy, it's always been because his minions have done something stupid."

Ericka wasn't buying it. "If we let him decoy us twice in one day, we're going to feel really, really stupid."

Shingen's tone was level, carrying a trace of annoyance. "Then what? Ideas?"

Ericka thought out loud. "Work from the other direction. Get the marine AIS data. Assume all vessels broadcasting are legit. That reduces the pool and we only have to look at radar hits for any non-AIS ships. Contact all the marinas and harbormasters about any boat that's left in the last twelve hours. Assume all observed departures not broadcasting AIS are targets. That might give us a shot."

"That's all we can do." Tim sounded dubious.

"Ericka, given what you think our target's capabilities are, I assume he'll be scanning whatever he can as his team goes. Can you track him doing that?" Shingen sounded hopeful.

She's no dummy. That thought brought the image of Abara's face to mind. Dead two years at the hands of Dantalion's henchman. "Not in anything like real time. If I was him, I would be scanning the whole area anyway, trying to see if any agency assets are close. AIS and GPS spoofing are well within his capabilities."

Shingen's words were broken as if she were very hesitant to speak. "What is your confidence that this conversation is secure?"

Ericka's shoulders tensed up. She never considered he might get that far, but there could be no assumptions with Dantalion. "As sure as I can be, but nothing's one hundred percent with this target."

Shingen paused for some time before continuing, first releasing a sigh. "Our target's former partner has been relocated to that area. We're going to have to move her now anyway. I'm worried any intensified interest in the area might light her up."

Tim swore under his breath as Ericka spoke. *Jesus, this could be how we lure the bastard out.* "Agreed. Given what we've seen here, we were going to have to do that anyway. I know we usually treat relocations on a need-to-know, but going forward, I need to know. For her above all."

"That's not protocol!"

"Our protocols weren't designed with Dantalion in mind. Time to improvise."

22

End Times

Semenov turned his head in disgust at the sound of Mirza emptying the last of his stomach's contents into a bucket below decks. Between the crying and vomiting, it was a wonder there was anything left of the frightened little rat. At least up here in the crisp wind, he couldn't smell it, unlike his unfortunate colleague minding their captive below. He glanced up at the sails, pleased to note the telltales showing near perfect trim, before correcting course by a few degrees.

Keeping absolute EM silence meant they had to use passive navigation and hope the ship they were to meet was where it was supposed to be. At least the thick clouds and drizzle limited air searches. According to the GPS, they should meet up with the passing freighter in less than an hour. He glowered at the dark navigation screen, knowing it would have told him nothing anyway. The ship they were meeting would have their AIS switched off until they were on board and any pursuers were not going to telegraph their presence. There was no help for it but to stare at the horizon and wait.

He could hear Golubev's voice from below shouting at their captive to shut up before she gave him something to whine about. He snapped on the autopilot and walked to lean into the hatch. The seas were enough that even he had to hold on to something to stay upright. His gorge rose at the stench of vomit in the warmer air below and he scowled at Mirza. The one thing he could not stand in a person was cowardice and he wondered how their prisoner had ever functioned in the ranks of the jihadis, being so spineless. "Put this vermin back to sleep! We are close enough now." He knew it was medically dangerous to keep him sedated too long, but their instructions were to have him drugged and in a shipping case to be winched aboard.

Golubev rolled her eyes and gave Mirza a foul look. "Thank you! I was about to go mad with his bellyaching." Mirza's wide eyes watched her as she stood to pull her kit from an overhead cubby. Semenov grabbed Mirza's wrist and shoulder, pinning him while she inserted her needle, oblivious to his screams to be let go. *That will be the day.*

Semenov scanned the horizon aft, field glasses glued to his face, when he heard Golubev's footfalls behind him. They were well outside the twelve-mile limit but he didn't imagine for a moment that would give the Americans pause. *Nor should it. It's not how the game is played and this was a glorious game.* He lowered the binoculars to look at his partner. "That's better!"

She rolled her eyes again and sat down hard on one of the side benches, leaning back to peer off the bow, squinting into the distance. "How long?"

He smiled at her. "Don't start counting the money yet, but it should be any time now."

* * *

"How's he doing that?" Ericka had Shingen on speaker as they both stared at the same thing on their screens.

Ericka shrugged to an empty room. "He's been doing this kind of thing for some time, working for smugglers for a cut. My bet is he's taken every ship's location information from a public source, then added them to the unique identifier on that satellite link he gave his team, then inserted it into the company's server." The data dump Ericka prepared and mapped showed the abductor's location as coming from every single ship within two hundred miles of the Oregon, Washington and British Columbia coasts.

"Any way to figure out which is the real one?"

"Yes, that's easy: none of them. Or he wouldn't have posted the spoof." Shingen was silent so Ericka spoke again. "Unless the ground teams get really lucky, our best shot is going to be when they unload him somewhere. I doubt he went to all this trouble just to shoot him in the middle of the ocean."

Ericka could hear Shingen sigh before she spoke. "Even the navy doesn't have the resources to check all the ships out there. We might have lost him."

"We got lots from Mirza, maybe enough. I hope it's enough."

Shingen sounded puzzled. "Enough to find our target?"

"No, maybe enough to stop him taking his ex-wife when he comes for her." *And perhaps more.* Ericka made a mental note to send what they had to Yusef. She had no doubt when Mirza met his end, Dantalion would make it known how and when to put the fear of Allah into Mirza's colleagues. The thought made her bring Yusef's face to mind and she caught herself smiling.

Semenov hung from cargo netting dangling over the side of the rusted freighter. It was Chinese registered, looking unseaworthy. Golubev had gone aboard first, standing by the railing while the unseen Mirza was winched from the yacht's pitching deck. The men who carried the cargo bin below decks were of a profession where curiosity and questions could be life-shortening. They avoided eye contact, responding to her gestures without question.

He clambered down the side until he was just out of reach of the surging, blue-gray water. No time to waste hanging above the waves, he undid the line securing the sailboat before clambering halfway up where he was confident he wouldn't be plucked off by a large swell. He was wearing a full survival suit so wasn't worried if he did, but it would be undignified to be hauled out of the water by the freighter's crew. Hooking his left hand into the net and steadying his feet, he reached for the transmitter hanging from a cord around his neck. He popped the protective cover off with his thumb and waited until their boat had drifted a hundred yards away, sails luffing.

Just to be safe, he turned his head away as he pressed the switch. There were four charges but he heard a single detonation as the explosives he'd set punched gaping holes in the fiberglass of the lower hull. The *Aya's Hope* disappeared in seconds, taking every remaining trace of their mission to the bottom. Communication equipment and all devices that could hold data had been taped between the charges and the hull, blown to confetti in an instant.

Semenov pulled himself over the railing, staring behind the freighter with a twinge of regret. It had been a lovely boat and all that remained now was a smudge of greasy-looking black smoke dispersing in the breeze. *So it goes.* Soon, he would have money for much better. Before then, he was to preside over this one's end. *Time to prepare.*

Tim could feel the heat from where he stood watching, fifty yards away. Several flares were visible through the blown-out windows, feeding bright red gasoline flames under a ballooning cloud of black smoke. His eyes watered as a gust of wind blew some of the acrid cloud in their direction. He and the state troopers had driven past this spot not an hour ago on their way into La Push. Seems the report of a departing sailboat leaving two weeks of paid-in-advance moorage was the correct lead if more than a day too late. It wasn't like these people were going to risk being caught on a security camera or let the operator see them just to get a few hundred dollars back, but it was a loose end, maybe the only one they'd left.

The burning truck was abandoned halfway down an overgrown access road to the Quillayute River. The trees were scrubby for the area, packed together, all the same height, a tree farm planted after the natural forest was cut. They provided excellent cover from the road, only the smoke had given it away.

Tim walked as close as he could bear to peer into the wreckage, knowing this fire would consume all evidence long before the local fire department arrived. *Good thinking this, burn the evidence but use a timer so it doesn't attract attention until after you're long gone.* This was the work of top-notch professionals. Tim squatted to look at a muddy patch in the potholed, gravel road. It had rained two days before and the dirt showed a single set of tire tracks leading to the back of the burning vehicle. He stood and turned to look back the way he had come. There were no footprints. Several people with a prisoner can't get through mud without leaving some kind of mark. *How did they get from here to their boat?*

Tim waved to the Washington state troopers standing where the old road met the highway, standing there to direct the fire crew when they arrived, sirens just audible in the distance. He shouted to make himself heard. "I'm going down to the river!" The closest trooper waved as Tim pushed his way into the trees on the upwind side of the fire, emerging onto the road about twenty yards the other side of it. The heat was enough to make his face flush, but he ignored the feeling and focused on what he was seeing. He squatted on the edge of the road, pushing ferns from his face, careful not to disturb marks on the wet surface.

Three people, two dragging or pulling a third. On his left, large deep boot prints while on the right they were smaller but the same kind of tread. In between them were a third set of prints that looked like running shoes, smeared as if the person were sliding at times. The tracks went one way, none came back. Twenty feet towards the river were obvious knee prints where the middle person had fallen. *Okay, now we're getting somewhere.* Tim wrapped tape around a tree to keep the evidence undisturbed and made his way along the edge of the road, taking a video from waist level as he did.

As he got to the deeper mud along the river's edge, he took some close-up photos of the boot prints. The tread pattern might tell them where they were made. They would send a full forensic team, but in this part of the country, heavy rain could be expected at any time.

The river here was obviously used by anglers leaving the normal detritus of food wrappers and beer cans, all of which looked faded and dirty like they'd been lying there for some time. Tim pushed his way downstream through brush, mud oozing over his boots, ankle deep. *There it was.* Several straight lines in the dirt, perpendicular to the current —a small, inflatable boat had been left here. That's how they got back to the sailboat without drawing attention, just drift down the river in silence.

It was hard to be subtle dragging a prisoner through the parking lot. People getting out of a dingy and into a sailboat would not have attracted a second glance. Everything thought through, nothing left to chance. Bending low, he scoured the area knowing he would find nothing. People this good took everything with them and got rid of it later. The fact they appeared to have pulled this off with just two of them spoke to that, a man and a woman, a couple to arouse a minimum of suspicion. It was an odd assumption, but people believed a man accompanied by a woman was never up to no good. Many a predator escaped detection, covered by a female wingman.

Loud hissing accompanied by a plume of steam rising over the trees made him look up. That would be the fire department. Taping off the road below the burnt-out truck wreckage, Tim picked his way back through the woods to their cars to call in a forensics team, knowing he was wasting their time. Jaw clenched, he tugged his mobile from his jacket, dialing Ericka. This trail was cold.

As she hung up, Ericka glanced around before walking back into the building at Portland International. She glanced up at the great arched roof covering the area between the parking garage and the terminal, noting rain puddling on the glass, steel-gray skies beyond. She bit her lip as she passed under a ubiquitous security camera. Until they took him down, it was almost as if they'd have to assume his software was watching everywhere it was possible. There was no way he was going to get into everything all the time, but there was no way to tell if he had without doing forensics on each device.

She made a mental note to look into better facial-recognition countermeasures as soon as she was back. Maybe some sort of early warning system that scanned for any software traces his creation left behind as well. Once again with this one, blink and the shape of the board had changed, all the pieces moved, the rulebook rewritten.

Now what? She dropped into a chair that seemed designed, like all airport lounge seats, to be as uncomfortable as possible. She glanced around before unlocking her phone. The few ships they'd been able to search had come up dry, with the unexpected bonus of a shipment of cocaine headed for the Canadian coast, stashed deep in the hold of an old trawler running silent. Mirza was lost along with any knowledge he'd held on to. Ericka had no doubt about his fate and doubted it would be quick or pleasant. Dantalion's hatred of traitors made them something of a calling to him; hard to imagine his fury when it was his own trust broken. *He would have no remorse, but why didn't she? A man under their protection might well be in the middle of being tortured to death!*

Was this the counter to anger, the mental state Seneca and the stoics strove for? Apatheia, they called it, a state in which your negative emotions, they called passions, do not rule you, anger a destructive kind of madness, guilt and regret a waste of time, energy devoted to something that can't be changed. In many ways like Zen, a state focused purely on the present, energy-sapping emotions purged, only then reaching the state of highest potential. Time to talk to Steiner again. Stoicism held that the negative emotions drained you, but the positive ones fueled your potential. But at the cost of empathy?

The barely understandable announcement over the airport's public address snapped her out of her reverie. She'd call on Piggy as soon as she got back. As she walked to board, another security camera caught her attention, this time making her smile.

The return to consciousness came in stages. Mirza could feel his body, but couldn't move—drugs no doubt, a surge of rage accompanying the thought of that Russian bitch and her needles. Rocuronium or something like it, paralysis while conscious. He'd tried to procure some for his jihadi cohorts several years before without success. In silence and absolute darkness, he stretched his perceptions, trying to tell where he was. The air had a dank smell, the tang of metal and sea air, what he thought at first was dizziness was probably the ship's motion. He was still on board. His right arm burned like fire where he could feel an IV taped to his wrist. He wanted to scream as the breathing tube was ripped out by a calloused hand. His shoulders hurt and it was hard to exhale, like he was hanging from his arms. Sharp pain and wetness in his wrists left no doubt. He couldn't feel his feet. He'd been crucified.

He was able to move his fingers. *The drugs must be wearing off.* Panic gripped him and he twisted his body, writhing, jabs of pain in his wrists morphed like electric shocks. He was out for a moment, before the whispered voice brought him back. "Mirza, why did you betray me? After all I have given you, all you could have done without breaking faith."

Speaking into darkness, Mirza spoke, through clenched teeth, his words slurred and hoarse. "Do not speak of faith, infidel!"

The light was hard to perceive at first, but came on slowly—a warm light, heat and sun, the colors of the desert, the sky pure cobalt. Damn him and his love of VR. Mirza turned his head to glance at his hands. In this world he was nailed to a tree, the sound of hissing sand driven by a wind he couldn't feel.

The booming voice came from the sky, dripping contempt. "In this realm, I am God, so I can't be an infidel. That's you. The one who broke faith with me."

Mirza gritted his teeth against the pain. "One day, you will pay for this."

The voice was all around him. "An interesting thought you raise. In the universe He created, is it possible for God himself to sin? You were such a disappointment, Mirza, all that potential lost to blind faith in old gods. You could see what was possible in the overlap between the physical and the meta, but you didn't grasp the implications. Nothing is impossible in a place without laws, morality, or religion—only what you make it."

"Go to hell!"

A quick laugh, the bark of a jackal. "If I do, it will be a place made as I wish it to be."

"The Americans will find you."

"They are irritating that way, yet despite their efforts, here we are." An immense sigh was lost in another wind gust.

Mirza looked to the horizon, seeing the rolling dust clouds of an approaching sandstorm. "Do you think these games, these silly environments frighten me?"

"It has never really crossed my mind to care. I do this for my own amusement. What would make you think I would go to any effort for your benefit? A worm who thinks the garden was built for him." The sky was dimming with dust ahead of the storm, shades of mud added to the blue. "When it arrives, you will face your own demons before you are judged. Before then, there are some things I would like to show you."

The imagery was much lower resolution, aerial footage, the drone's propellers just visible whirring above. He knew this place. In the distance, Al mahal, in Yemen, the town near his brother's home. His stomach sank, lips quivering. The drone rotated, bringing the house into view, surrounded by the orchards that were his brother's livelihood. He could see nothing of Kareem, nor his wife or their children, but the sun was just over the horizon. "No, please, they are completely innocent."

"Except for their misfortune in having an insect for a brother. An onerous burden on its own. But somehow the Saudis have become convinced that Kareem is using his home to build bombs intended for use in the Kingdom.

Communicating with known terrorists. The evidence they have seen leaves no doubt. Very unfortunate."

Mirza tried to move his arms, his reward lancing pain and pulsing wetness on his wrists. "That is a lie! He is a simple farmer!"

The voice was rich with mirth. "In what world is that? In the one I have made he is a jihadi like you. The house is filled with them. Watch!"

The fighters never came into his field of view, but he could hear them, the roar of jet engines approaching from the nearby ocean, echoing from the low hills and wadi. Mirza's vision blurred, tears flooding his eyes, not enough to obscure the flashing explosions. Five bombs detonating at once, the house blown into dust, fragments raining on lush trees for a hundred yards in all directions. As the breeze cleared the air, five overlapping craters gaped skyward where Kareem's home had stood.

Back now to the desert and the voice from the sky. The transition was jarring. "Did you not consider the price when you broke faith? How simple it is to feed 'intelligence' to the Saudis, to tell them what they are so eager to hear."

Mirza shook his head as hard as he could, trying to dislodge the goggles. The tugging on his skin and beard told him they were taped to his face. "Stop!"

"Begging is pointless. All of this happened two days ago. Look again!"

It was night, a helmet camera bounced as the person wearing it ran following several armored soldiers in desert camouflage as they dodged between low bushes in sandy soil. The markings on the helicopter were plain, an Israeli UH-60 Blackhawk, rotors turning as soldiers threw bound captives through the side door. A hand appeared in view, first handing an automatic weapon to a man inside, then gripping the door to pull himself in.

The door slid shut and the video lurched as the aircraft took off in a cloud of dust, banking as the ground disappeared into darkness. The wearer leaned in to the three captives lying face down on the deck, hoods covering their features. One by one, the same hand appeared to pull the cover back, exposing each man's face, taking a close-up of each of them. Mirza's head fell to his chest, but it didn't change the view. All were friends he thought safe in southern Syria where they worked to raise funds for the brotherhood. Now the Jews had them and they would never see the light of day again. Worse, he knew how the Israeli military had found them. His stomach heaved into dry retches.

The demon could read his mind, gloating. "If you hadn't spent so much time talking to them, it might have taken me longer to find them. To be able to send Mossad a dossier on what they were doing and their location down to the meter. Information I took from you. You are a dangerous fool, to everyone around you, an error of mine I will now remedy."

Mirza's arm burned again, more drugs and he was back in the desert. The storm front was seconds away. As it hit, Mirza tried to move his head, a reflex but he was paralyzed again. His world turned dark, a swirling mass of sand, mixed brown and yellow, like looking at the sky from the bottom of a muddy river.

The crowing voice rose over howling wind and hissing sand. "And now comes the test that either opens the gates to heaven or hell. The three questions everyone of faith must answer."

Mirza could see the two shapes, huge but indistinct, always in motion, coming close to stare at him out of black eyes, mouths filled with fire as they questioned him. He would have flinched if he could move. The three questions came as garbled roars, accenting the wind. It didn't matter, he couldn't answer with the drug burning through his veins. He couldn't talk at all.

The tone was scolding, dripping disappointment. "What, no answers? Hell for you it seems. As if there was ever any doubt."

The apparitions floated at the edge of visibility, disappearing for seconds until gusts passed, making the coal-black eyes visible, followed by hulking outlines. A shaft opened below and he was falling. His eyes bugged at the pain as his legs caught fire first. No illusion, the searing heat was real. As the fire traveled up his body, he tried in vain to move, but now he couldn't breathe and his skin was ablaze. He could feel it crackle and split. Then relief. The pain was fading and with it his vision. His world went black one final time.

Semenov stood just below the charred body, extinguisher ready in case Mirza's body flared up again. His victim hung from a wooden cross beam bolted to a steel support rising from the deck. IV tubes and breathing mask hung smoldering in front of the blackened torso, VR goggles melted and fused to his head. The stink made him want to retch but he steeled himself. If he couldn't stand smells like this, he was in the wrong business. Satisfied, the fire was out, he put the heavy extinguisher down hard enough for the metallic sound to echo from the cavernous walls of the ship's hold. Mirza would have to cool a bit before he took him down. A military body bag was laid out behind him.

He was alone. Golubev had administered the initial drugs, then gone on deck to ensure none of the crew came near this end of the ship. She also monitored the satellite uplink, ensuring there was no break in the data stream to their employer. Right now, he expected she was ensuring data-wiping protocols were running before all the gear they had used went over the side. Semenov lit a cigarette, careful to stand back in case any of the gelled accelerant on Mirza's body had spilled. Cleaning up was always the nastiest part of this job, but his willingness to do whatever was needed was why he commanded the price he did. This was far and away the most lucrative job he'd ever done and he knew more would be coming. With this employer, life would never be dull. Time to finish up.

He stuck his head out on deck to ensure his instructions had been followed and the crew had stayed below. Not that they could see much in the inky dark of the cloudy, moonless night, but he didn't want to have to see to loose ends among the sailors. He tilted his head at Golubev, before winching the sagging bag onto the deck. Another glance around to be sure and he unzipped the bag just long enough to stuff two barbels in with the corpse. Semenov wiped the drops from his forehead with his sleeve before he and Golubev dragged the body to the side and pushed it through the open gangplank gate. He didn't hear the splash but didn't expect to over the sound of the ship's engines and wake.

He stood straight, gripping hands with his partner before reaching in his jacket for the flask. Emptying it was the traditional end to every job he'd done since he left the army.

23

Mirror, Mirror

Steiner's smile was welcoming. He put down the book, pointing to the teapot on his credenza, brows raised. Ericka nodded, leaning to shut his door before settling into a chair. While he poured, she glanced out the window at the trees lining the road, seeing the first hint of fall colors paint the leaves, then turned to read the title of the book. "You read Melville to brush up when I'm coming to be shrunk?" She watched for his reaction, seeing nothing.

Steiner was wearing his professional face, sipping before he answered. "Yes, exactly. Let's see if I can do this from memory? 'To the last I grapple with thee; from hell's heart I stab at thee; for hate's sake I spit my last breath at thee!'" He was fighting a smile as he finished. "A familiar passage?"

"Shouldn't you be reading shrink books? First Seneca, now Melville." *Okay, so today's topic is obsession and revenge.* "What's next?"

He shrugged, maintaining eye contact. "Probably *Heart of Darkness*, but we'll see how the next few weeks go."

Smartass. It wasn't like answering honestly here was going to shorten her FBI career. "I'm fine. I'm sleeping and haven't fantasized about killing anyone all day."

"It's only ten." Steiner pointed at his laptop. "I just looked at your tests. You'll forgive me please. You know I have to look to keep those upstairs happy. They'll be pleased you're completely clean and probably don't care about your blood pressure."

No, I'm sure they don't. "It's been a trying few weeks. First Thailand, now he plucks a source out of our so-called protection. I'm not here to be shrunk quite frankly. I need to talk about how he's acting now, the new Dantalion." If she was going to get ahead of him, she needed to be as sure of her conclusions as she could.

Steiner held up a finger, shaking his head. "Sorry, the crazy person doesn't get to decide if she's getting shrunk or not."

Ericka studied his features, unable to read him, trying to quell the sharp stab of annoyance before the smile came unbidden. "Seriously?"

He folded his hands in front of him. "Cheeks flushed, eyes tearing, yes, we are going to discuss anger again. And you do have time for it, like it or not. You cannot fall back into your old pattern of feeding anger to motivate yourself. Answer the question honestly, to yourself at least."

Ericka looked at the floor, biting her lip, knowing he was right but not willing to say it out loud. She closed her eyes, drawing in a slow breath. She'd been having this internal fight for weeks, dying to let the rage flow, but knowing where that path ended each time she'd let it. She felt the unwavering gaze of all those she'd lost, particularly to Dantalion. They expected her to succeed and that would take everything she had. *Dig deep and stay focused, nothing to waste frying in my own juices.* She didn't look up. "Go ahead."

When she opened her eyes, Steiner was staring at her, shrugging. "That's all I needed to do. Force a little introspection. You will take it from there as you choose. As we've said before." He turned to pluck a book from the shelf behind him. "Before we move on, a little Seneca?" She nodded. "A few of his words on the madness of anger: 'forgetful of decency, unmindful of personal ties, unrelentingly intent on its goal, shut off from rational deliberation, unsuited to discerning what's fair and true, just like a collapsing building that's reduced to rubble even as it crushes what it falls upon.'" He let it sink in for a few seconds. "And that is plenty of shrinking for today. Now Dantalion."

"No, wait a moment, decency, fair? You're kidding! Seriously?"

Steiner's tone was firmer than usual, and he leaned towards her as he spoke. "You do need to do a little thinking on this. You maintain that standard not for him, but for you. Remember that evil is not a thing or an entity. It is a series of choices. You do no service to yourself by making the same choices as him, justified by the end and the goal. Redemption for you is succeeding without following his path. Yes?"

Yes. Time for this later, when things in my head quieten down a bit. "I hear you."

"Ahab found his whale but went to the bottom with it. Let's try and do better shall we?"

Ericka chuckled despite herself. "If you're done beating me up now."

The clinical persona switched off and with his smile open, Steiner was eager to talk about her target as always. "What has happened?"

She leaned back in the chair turning to look outside as the sun came out, briefly reviving the colors of summer. *Just blurt it out, parse through the bits.* "It's like he's a different person. He's reckless now. He takes risks the old Dantalion would never have taken. I don't mean he's changed in his fundamental motivations, but he's doing things like he's almost daring us to pick him off. I'm sure our recently lost source is going to come to a painfully creative end if he hasn't already, but why all the risk to abduct him? All the things he had to do to put people on US soil and get Mirza out gave us any number of chances to run him down. They haven't yet, but when he's acting like this, any of them could. So much easier to just have Mirza and his cover team killed."

Steiner sipped his tea, eyes on the ceiling. "Is he just showing off?"

"That's got to be part of it and that's completely in character. But even using this new toy of his has some risk. It has to send its information home. He has to send that information to people on the ground to use. We just have to get lucky once, he has to stay lucky every time. Why is he testing his luck?"

He pointed at her cup, then the teapot, continuing when she shook her head. "Ask yourself this. Why has he never come for his former wife? From his view, a betrayal, and tied to the paralyzing injuries that were probably the trigger that set him in motion. You told me he'd been monitoring her almost continuously before you took her into custody. Why hasn't killing her been at the top of his list? And her new husband?

The wrath of a scorned and belittled narcissist, now shriveled and puny with shame."

Ericka shook her head. "I've no idea. With his new capabilities, I worry constantly he'll find a way before we can move her. What do you think?"

"I believe she's in terrible danger. I suggest the reason he's never come for her is he felt diminished, not a complete man. He was ashamed for her to see him reduced as he was. All the dominance and fear derived vicariously, through the action of others, isn't enough for her just desserts. He wasn't going to approach her in a wheelchair to finish her off, nor watch while someone else does it. But now that's changed. Now, he has recovered to some extent, he will want to kill her and he will want to do it in person."

Ericka bowed her head, squeezing her eyes shut. "So, it's all about a swinging dick now?"

Steiner's gaze was intense. "Yes, precisely. For her end, that is exactly what it is about. She humiliated him with his business partner, and he will blame her for the accident that crippled him, if that's what it was. He ends up, probably sexually dysfunctional, but certainly diminished to his thinking. It is like the motivation for so many spousal homicides. You, of course, know when women are most likely to be killed by their male partners?"

She was painfully aware. "Yes, at the moment they try to leave the relationship."

He put his cup down to gesture with both hands. "Precisely! With his narcissistic ego, that moment of rage is permanently felt, eternal for him. So, he has bided his time to savor the moment. To do this right by his thinking, he will do it personally, whatever the risk of consequences. This may be how he chooses to end himself as well and, I suggest, explains what you are observing in his actions."

Oh yes. Ericka's hand shook with excitement. "And there's our opportunity. He can't take her somewhere or come here for her without taking huge risks. This is where we get out in front of him!"

"You might not have much time. The other thing that will govern him now? After all his successes and your inability to catch him, he will now feel he has a reputation to defend. That matters hugely to him. Take his threat of another spectacular hit very seriously."

"What about towards me? He went to a lot of effort to get me back." She looked at Steiner, waiting.

Steiner raised a single brow. "Surely that's obvious. You challenge him and that intrigues him. The undivided attention of someone like you inflates his ego. After your extended 'leave' from the FBI, he may fancy you are secretly something of a follower, someone who can carry his legacy. I expect he is genuinely pleased you are back and have taken up the chase. Twisted as it may be, he likely feels a real connection to you. He may have no others."

"I'll have to give some thought to that." Ericka smiled at Steiner, holding out her cup for more tea. *Time to float the idea that had been rattling around in her brain for a few days.* "Do you think his old partner, Bromwich, is in the same danger?"

Steiner's brow furrowed and he hesitated. "I thought he was dead."

Ericka smiled at him, enjoying the banter. "What if he wasn't? What if, one day, this AI monster of his found some indication his old partner was alive and in WITSEC or something?"

Steiner pressed his lips together, shrugging. "I'm not sure what you're getting at, but as an intellectual exercise it is my professional reputation that he would 'lose his shit.' But I'm not following you? Are you confident you can manipulate this Providence of his?"

She shook her head. "I have no certainty I could do that, but I might be able to fool the person interpreting the results."

Steiner's eyes narrowed as he stared at her. "Go on!"

"What if we dig up poor Mr. Bromwich again, get a high-res 3D scan of this skull, get the very best reconstruction we can. We have lots of photos of him. Set him up somewhere where a low-res camera will catch it in a still."

"Why would he be looking for Bromwich?"

Come on, Piggy, clue in. "He isn't, but I'm pretty sure he tries to keep tabs on me. If we're in the same pic, he can hardly fail to notice."

"To what end? More bait?"

"No, so he's so enraged he can't think straight."

Steiner stared at her for some time before speaking, eyes wide. "Ericka, my dear, this is why I worry about you."

He leaned back in his chair, lifting his feet onto the desk beside the keyboard. *What a glorious feeling it was to be able to do that simple thing.* Despite the stab of pain in his lower back, he could feel his face flushing, excited like a child. Things were going to be very different from now on. The program displaying on a monitor to his left chimed for attention, a glance telling him someone was scanning, attracted by what he was doing. Reaching over, his feet still up, he placed his software into passive mode. It would automatically take up the hunt again, searching for new routes to the data it wanted or trying the same ones again later, determine if the scan that had stopped it was part of a defensive reaction. Providence was infinitely patient. It would passively gather whatever it could, looking for its target, then probe to see if there was a way to place monitoring software on nearby devices.

He smiled, wondering if the world's security services realized how often he employed the strategy of stealing the software of one to use against the others. Once they deployed a new cyberweapon, they were releasing it into the wild where its components could be copied and studied. When the creators of Stuxnet deployed their creation against Iran, it had been a game changer for everyone. This powerful worm had the ability to travel from computer to computer, hiding and doing nothing but propagate until it found its target, moving quickly when new vulnerabilities were discovered, able to cause actual physical damage to connected devices. It had spawned any number of imitations and improvements, including his own, some of which toiled at the heart of Providence.

Sun flooded the room with yellow light, the shadow of dancing palm fronds projecting on the far wall. Now he was walking again, the balmy climate of Myanmar was much more to his liking. The money he paid the local military commander kept him free of any official interest. Generous transfers of crypto directly to exchange accounts on another continent, paid through a legitimate intermediary, ensured he had the colonel's unstinting support. It was still prudent to walk just at night in places that had been scoured for security cameras. It would be dark in another hour.

He stood to stretch, leaning against the wall. Painful but necessary if he was to have the mobility he needed. The prescribed regime was bringing him back, and he was now able to take slow walks without aid and without pain. A machine chimed. He craned his neck noting Providence had resumed its search, finding the unfortunate secrets that brought him followers, often unwilling at first. It had found a mobile associated to his subject. *Excellent! As soon as your device updates some of its software, Providence will begin to install and we'll see what you've been up to.*

Israel's security service always had the very best software and this was no exception. Software able to penetrate a mobile phone without having physical access. Once installed, it turned the phone into a life recorder, able to monitor all communications, web searches, purchases and of course, location, every detail of the owner's life open to whoever controlled the software.

His improved version was built into Providence. What it found could be available to the highest bidder, or perhaps for his own use. That they would find him eventually, he had no doubt, but before then his grand finale would leave a lasting impression and lay the groundwork for what came after him, the unseen promised land indeed.

He toggled the display on another screen to view Providence's offerings on Claire for the day, a ritual he never missed. Doing so never failed to bring the same physical reaction, an intoxicating blend of volcanic rage and resolution of purpose, a mix that brought with it the familiar reaction of new and better fantasies of how she would suffer. The experience left his heart thumping against his ribs, vision darkened and a sheen of tingling sweat all over his body. There was just one way to salve the gaping wound her treachery had left and each time he felt the hunger, it motivated him to redouble his efforts. The time was getting close, all the sweeter, more intense for the years he'd waited. Once his final work was completed and events in unstoppable motion, then, at last, it would be time.

Where were the FBI and the US Marshals finding these idiots? Did they think he was stupid, or perhaps they didn't care and they just went through the motions of trying to protect her? They followed instructions to power down anywhere near, but as soon as they were outside the designated perimeter, they powered up and connected. WITSEC was usually administered by the US Marshals and the fact that this one had a stream of FBI visitors entering and leaving a 'dark' zone where no one was hooked up told him all he needed. Agents recruited from a generation that couldn't survive without a connection to the virtual world made his task all too easy. *Where could they recruit agents who'd never joined social media, never posted a picture online, people who left him nothing to harvest and use to track them?* That, and he knew Claire. She loved her own pretty face far too much to undergo the kind of cosmetic surgery that would have any chance against Providence's facial-recognition abilities.

There, that was her, standing in the cosmetics section of the pharmacy for far too long, taking off the hat and sunglasses to preen in the mirror, almost dead center of the security camera's field of view. *And that, Ericka, is what makes your job so terribly difficult.* People live in the overlap between the physical and the virtual without ever giving it a thought, no idea of the traces they leave, no one around within sight they feel safe, strangely ignorant of their presence in the virtual world. Claire was no fool. Even a moment's thought would have told her the store's security cameras created digital records, often stored somewhere they could be found and taken before being overwritten. Offsite monitoring meant data traveled and even if encrypted, it was left vulnerable by the idiot security kid who stored passwords and keys on his phone. All these tools running at the direction of an AI. There was almost nothing it couldn't see given time.

Chirping from a third monitor brought him back. This was what he'd been waiting for, one of the last pieces about the man who was the hapless target of Providence's unrelenting gaze, a man who was buried deep in the Chinese bureaucracy. He bit his lower lip as he read, then gave a snort of laughter, well pleased at what he saw. Yes, that would do nicely, more than enough to convince him to part with access codes. The man could never tolerate any of Providence's findings coming to light. The stain on his family's name would take generations to expunge, if ever. Nothing like a bit of cultural sensitivity to enhance results.

He glanced out the window. Almost dark enough, but time for one last look, to see if his little gift to Ericka had been delivered. *A well-earned gloat over a vanquished enemy.* It was a time-honored ritual he'd enjoyed for as long as he could remember, all the sweeter when he could deliver it in an environment of his own creation. He hoped she would grasp the irony.

A jolt of pain in his back made him reach behind to hold the area of the surgical scar while he lowered himself into his chair, gritting his teeth as he reached for the desk-mounted controller. No signal yet, Ericka hadn't activated. It would give him time to plan.

"Why don't you just write, 'moved NFA, return to sender' on it and follow where the post office takes it?" Ericka stared at Shingen, fighting the urge to snarl at people who asked stupid questions. She stared at her supervisor, watching her struggle with her answer.

Shingen scowled, staring for a few seconds before turning to look out the window. When she spoke, her tone was cold. "The question was, can you track the signal? I don't need the sarcasm."

She wasn't getting anywhere antagonizing her boss, but the constant requirement to justify every step she took made Ericka's blood boil. "No, not unless he really screws up." She leaned back in Shingen's uncomfortable, but impeccably fashionable chair. *Springing for her own office furniture by the look of it.* "I expect he sent a new pair because I wrecked the old ones trying to analyze how they work. Is the lab still looking at them?"

Shingen shook her head, glancing at her laptop. "They just finished. As expected, nothing on them that tells us anything. No threats or contaminants. Same as the last time: a commercial set that someone's modified to scan the wearer's face, and a tiny three-sixty camera mounted on top to record the wearer's POV. Can't tell how it's wired without cracking it."

Ericka leaned forward, peering at the screen. "Looks like he used a different model to start, but more interesting that he keeps wanting to talk. The shrinks all agree he's changing as he goes. Last time he wanted to boast, it was right before he stole an airliner in flight. We're going to have to listen to him very carefully."

Shingen's expression was neutral, but Ericka could see her fight an eye roll. "Yes, obviously. But again, are we in a place now where we can use this thing to track him?"

"Not a chance, but given how this set is wired, this time you'll be able to see what I do. We can duplicate the video stream."

"Well, that should prove very interesting."

Semenov looked down to where his thickly muscled legs protruded from the white, resort-supplied bathrobe. A small lizard made its way up the cracked concrete of the balcony, using the rough surface like a scaled-down version of a free climber. Soon it would be time for the beach. He stood and stretched, staring out over drooping coconut palms at the brilliant blue water and gleaming white sand of the Caribbean beach.

Cuba suited him. Excellent cigars, coffee and rum. Best of all, no American tourists to spoil the quiet. Many of the resort staff had Russian names, the legacy of Soviet military presence decades before. They gave the place a homey feel. The old resorts of Varadero were not as fancy as the newer ones crowded with tourists, but here a false name and generous tips were all that was needed to ensure the peace and quiet of anonymity. A man with the legions of enemies he'd accumulated treasured any place he didn't have to watch his back.

Tipping back the last of the thick, sweet coffee, he tossed

the robe on the bed before rooting in his bag for fresh trunks. As he tugged them on, he saw the blinking light of the satellite dongle. Swearing, he reached for his mobile. He'd barely been here a week. He clenched his jaw as he waited for it to hook up, eyes scanning the message as it appeared. It was sent in the clear without encryption of any sort. None was needed, the content was innocuous and the transmission data was probably already gone from the network. *Aunt Ingrid is dying. She only has two months to live. You need to come home.*

Semenov understood what it meant, the terms were prearranged. He was going back to the United States and his employer had decided the day that someone was going to die. He shrugged and walked to the door of the suite, picking up his battered straw hat, stuffing his feet into sandals. After that last one, he didn't need the money for a while, but the adrenaline rush of the adventure would always draw him back. Operating on the home soil of the mighty American security apparatus right under their noses was just too much fun, but not today. He could afford another week before going home for his briefing.

As he walked onto the white steps, the sun's heat washed over him like being deluged in near-scalding water. Time for a swim.

24

Countdown

Ericka waited in the dark and absolute silence, hands resting on the arms of her chair, not gripping, no sweaty palms this time. The VR headset had some weight to it but it wasn't uncomfortable. *Such a difference from the first time.* This time there was no effort to repress the fear because there wasn't any. Most surprising of all, the anger was gone and her mind felt empty for it, lighter. No having to discipline her thoughts or mentally shout down voices in her head, no feeling a need to gather her resources, just the silent detachment of a great cat waiting under cover for her quarry to come close enough.

Preparation too had been different, reading and clearing her mind, no running scenarios in her head and worrying that he might get the better of her. Seneca was right—anger and hate, however they might feel justified, created an impenetrable clutter that sapped the mind's abilities. She had to take him down and this was the only way.

Ericka was alone in the lab, but knew that Tim, Clarke and Shingen were sitting in the next room, leaning into screens that would duplicate a flattened version of what she would see in VR, hearing everything she did. She'd managed to piggyback the feed into the headset's screens. These and the data stream itself would be recorded for later. Ericka knew there was a risk Dantalion would take the opportunity to lecture her about things the observers didn't know, but that wasn't important now. Ending his rampage was all that mattered and everything else was a distraction—at worst something she would have to deal with when this was over. There would be no concealing things from the others for self-preservation, she was all in.

An imperceptible sound, perhaps a hiss, told her the headset was active and receiving data. Ericka shifted, sitting a bit straighter, ready to confront the monster. It was more than just the absence of fear and anger. She was anticipating resumption of the hunt, almost eager to tease the clues from whatever show he had ready this time. She folded her unseen hands in her lap just as the screens started emitting visible light.

Ericka sat in undefined darkness, the only thing visible a familiar seated shape, gray tones, as if lit from a hidden source above. The image in front of her wasn't familiar from their previous encounters, she'd seen it in her travels. Several arms' lengths in front of her was a flawless digital rendering of Guillaume Geefs' *Le génie du mal*, a sculpture of Lucifer she'd seen displayed in a Belgian cathedral. The depiction was perfect, capturing in exquisite detail the almost beautiful seated male figure, shrouded in bat wings, chained and looking down, holding a crown and a broken scepter. The image exuded the intense melancholy of the original, complete with a single tear on the left cheek. *Is he feeling sorry for himself now?*

Ericka knew it was coming but it was startling, nonetheless. The statue sighed, lifting its head to stare at her with featureless, marble eyes, giving her the barest hint of acknowledgment. It paused for a few moments, then the head turned while the right hand descended, extending to point over to her left, palm upturned. Like a theatre where the lights come on to reveal the set and actors, she could see a vast chamber with metal walls, possibly the hold of a ship. In the center stood a man with his back to the camera, head tilted as he stared up at a crucified figure. The hanging man's face was obscured by VR goggles, but she knew the naked figure was Mirza, spikes piercing his wrists, sunk into the wood, which was fastened to a steel support. The stocky figure in front of Mirza took a step forward, doing something she couldn't see, but Mirza's body erupted in flames and he screamed as his back arched.

Ericka tore her gaze from the scene to focus on the statue, finding its eyes were locked on hers, red light from the inferno dancing on its wings. She had to quell a surge of nausea before forcing herself to speak in an even tone. "Do you think cruelty to a helpless captive impresses me?"

"Not unless you inflict it yourself, though I know you have different tastes than I do." The voice was the same self-satisfied, rich baritone. A fleeting smile crossed the statue's features, animated and given life by the familiar expressions of her quarry. "Believe me when I say those I meant to benefit were duly impressed. Nothing like a good motivational video by an influencer to fashion the broader working environment towards optimal productivity."

Don't give him the satisfaction of further reaction, stay cold and hard. "And why is showing it to me worth the trouble of sending me new gear? I trust you know, I'm far beyond intimidation by you."

The smile broadened. "If you weren't, I don't think I'd bother talking to you at all."

Ericka hoped her avatar reflected the steel she put in her features. "So, you've shown me how management works in your organization. The improvements in taste and avatar design are duly noted. What do you want?"

The figure leaned back, head tilted forward, mockery delivered with fake concern. "Don't you want to know how I found him? Maybe engage in some synergistic feedback seeking to improve future outcomes? Perhaps, I should offer my services as a consultant to incompetent police forces. Spend some cycles and bandwidth on best practices and circle back next time performance lags?"

Bastard! Her gut muscles tightened and she had to dig deep for calm. "Don't be too smug! Just because you've imitated stolen bits of software you didn't write and bodged them together isn't a sign of genius, Einstein. This Providence thing is like a pickup truck slapped together from junkyard parts by drunk hillbillies. It's easy to spot."

The response was as bizarre as it was startling. The marble statue tilted its head back and roared with laughter, a cackle that could have come from the throat of any jackal on the Serengeti. The figure wiped its face at something that wasn't there and for a moment she was able to picture London in VR gear. He seemed to compose himself. "Perhaps so, but you didn't think of it, much less build and conceal it."

Touché! Indulging him wasn't getting anywhere. The kind features of an old woman played across her mind's eye, making her jaw clench. "What do you want?"

He leaned back into a familiar pose, fingers steepled in front of his face. "The usual. To taunt you for not catching me and monologue about my greatness. I'm getting predictable." Ericka didn't respond. After a pause he continued. "To speak with the only peer I have. The world continues to change as I predicted and now I have opportunities I knew would come."

Ericka's stomach churned with nausea from listening to him, but she couldn't let the opportunity pass, any telling detail he might give her. "Go on!"

He glared before speaking. "Doesn't the utter dependency alarm you? It should, or at least your masters. The complete loss of reference to objective fact. The sheep have become so utterly dependent on the digital extensions of their world, they don't really perceive where one ends and the other starts. They can't drive, fly an aircraft or steer a ship without navigation aids and trust them over their eyes. They rely on unverified nonsense on social media for information. They unknowingly record every decision or interest they have by subscribing to services that regard everything they do as a saleable commodity. They fondly imagine that they make informed decisions when they are in fact manipulated through almost every choice they make."

Plenty of truth to that. "And why do I need to be lectured on this by you?"

The statue did an impressive eye roll. "Because you aren't seeing the possibilities. Do try and rise from your current role of government running dog and see beyond the blinkered views of those holding your leash. The masses live half in and half out of the digital world, the new reality if you like, but they don't perceive where one ends and the other starts. This unseen overlap opens up endless possibilities for someone as enterprising as I am. Dominance in one leads to mastery in the other."

Good, the narcissist looking for glory and adoration has a big mouth. *Goad him.* "And yet, you're constantly on the run. We very nearly put a bullet in you and you survive in the bosom of criminal gangs for whom you have nothing but contempt. You survive by luck and pat yourself on the head for brilliance. Impressive!"

The flash of rage was crystal clear on the statue's face. He probably didn't intend to reveal that and was quiet for a few moments, perhaps gathering himself. "You've mocked me once before and had to eat your words." *True enough.* "You'll see what I mean in due course."

Ericka smiled, wanting to be sure the facial scanning picked it up for him. "Empty boasts. You're on the run. Everyone is looking for you now. It's just a matter of time."

The somber head dipped. "But not before one more display of what I mean. And prepare a few things for what comes after. Perhaps not even then."

He was losing interest, staring again at the image of Mirza's burning body, before turning towards her. *Time to push some buttons and end this.* "Let's talk about the real world for a minute then, shall we, Mr. London? Enough with the dark-web-demigod bullshit. What we're looking for is a very little man with an ego-inflating handle. You're sitting in the dark somewhere, hiding, paying people to protect you, and one day this fantasy of yours is going to end with your door battered down and stun grenades. Look up, I'll be there!"

Ericka waited just long enough to see the look of stunned rage before she broke the connection. She sat for a few seconds in the dark of the headset, seeing Mrs. Donnelly's face but controlling the toxic rage. *Restrain the pleasure at goading him and return to the icy focus that would end this. Such feelings were for later, they were no use now.*

She tugged the headset off, blinking in the light, flinching as she stood up, not dizzy, but unsteady. She gulped for air as the door opened and Tim, Clarke and Shingen walked in. *They're looking at me like I'm crazy.* Tim handed her a bottle of water and she gulped it. Ericka looked at Tim. "So, how'd I do?"

His expression told her he'd talk to her later. "If he has a dog, I wouldn't want to be it right now."

Shingen stared at her, arms folded. "We'll debrief later but that wasn't really according to plan."

Ericka glared at her, then looked down before speaking. "You can't choreograph this. That wasn't done because I wanted to take a poke at him. It was calculated to try and wound him a little. He can slip when he's angry like anyone else."

Steiner was eyeing her with a little too much professional interest for a public setting. Ericka frowned at him and he seemed to get the hint, turning to fiddle with his pen, doodling in the margin of his notepad. She looked to find Shingen was also staring at her from the head of the boardroom table. Ericka's commanding officer had made the drive from DC to their lab and said little since she'd arrived. Tim and Clarke seemed to find the view out the window more interesting than the meeting itself. Her team were dressed casually, each drawing a disdainful look from Shingen, who like her predecessor was a stickler for decorum. Steiner wore a suit. Outside of his home, she'd never seen him wear anything else.

Shingen turned to Ericka, her smile looking forced. "Okay, let's hear it."

Ericka glanced at Steiner before speaking. "In a nutshell, we're going to bait him into doing something stupid. Nothing technical. While we have some idea how this Providence system of his works, we've got no confidence we can defeat it at this point." She glanced at Tim and Clarke, drawing confidence from their concurrence. "It's not about the trap, it's about the bait. Dr. Steiner's insight into this subject has been spot on since the start. He believes and I agree that a combination of events gives us an opportunity."

Shingen looked at Steiner, brows raised. "Doctor? I hadn't realized you'd joined our profiling unit?"

Steiner smiled as his head dipped, his face reddening a bit. "I have not, but I do believe I have something to contribute to this investigation." He waited for Shingen's approval. "This target is enormously intelligent and highly strategic, but his narcissism is completely out of control, making him vulnerable. He knows, standing alone with the enemies he has accumulated, his end is inevitable and looming. I believe he will feel the compulsion to do two more things before he is arrested, or more likely killed. The first is he will be preparing a spectacular, look-at-me final event and perhaps hope to die on his feet committing it. His comments to Ericka about how easy manipulation has become provide some guidance as to how he thinks he might accomplish this. Expect this to be something in the order of magnitude of his previous crimes, such as the hijacking."

Shingen's eyes narrowed, lips pursed. "And?"

"He will feel an irresistible urge to kill his former spouse and do it personally."

Shingen was looking to Ericka, hand raised with fingers splayed. "And the opportunity?"

Here it goes. "He's going to worry he will get taken down trying to do either one at the expense of the other. If he thinks he has to do both, he'll have to cut corners and take risks. Anticipating whatever hit he has in mind will be difficult, but we know where his other target is and he is going to have to come to her."

Shingen looked aghast, mouth open as she shook her head. "You want to use his ex-wife as bait?"

Ericka shook her head, smiling. "Not quite. We could never be sure enough of her safety. We use the one person in the world London hates more than her, his old partner Bromwich."

Shingen looked from face to face, scowling like she was being toyed with. "Who is a little bit dead, last I heard."

Tim chimed in. "Not as dead as he could be. Still some life in him."

Ericka spoke over him, throwing him a quick smile of apology. "Not dead in the overlap, to use our target's phrase. For all his disdain of the great unwashed, he's a hypocrite. He depends entirely on his technology to see the world and that's a weakness. We bring his old partner back to life, try to take our target down when he makes his move. Relocate Claire at the same time, while his focus is on Bromwich's shade. We have to move her anyway, no extra risk."

Shingen's brow was furrowed, her expression puzzled. "What, you think you can CGI something that will fool this Providence thing of his?"

No, I'm absolutely sure I can't do that. "Not sure enough."

"Do you think he knows where we have his ex-wife?" Shingen's eyes narrowed.

"I'm absolutely certain of it. There are traces of his software on webcams in the area where she is and on the phones of some of the agents who administer her."

Shingen's mouth dropped open, eyes wide. "Then why is she still alive?"

Steiner raised his hand to interject. "Because while he was recovering from his injuries, he felt diminished, unmanned, less than he was. He wasn't going to wheel up in a chair and shoot her. Now he can walk to whatever limited degree, she is in immediate danger. Now, he can stand over her as she dies, which heals his wounded ego. That is all that matters to him."

Ericka leaned over the table, resting on her elbows. "She's going to need guarding twenty-four seven from here on in. After he took Mirza right out of our hands, we take no chances."

Shingen stared at Ericka. "And we're sure we know how he did that? Any chance of a mole?"

Ericka looked to Clarke who'd been tasked with answering that. Clarke tapped the folder in front of her as she spoke. "It's never one hundred percent, but there's no sign of inside activity potentially a data breach."

Shingen turned back to Ericka. "So how?"

"He kept finding him by inferring where Mirza probably was based on agent activity. Once he found him the first time, it wasn't hard to guess where we'd take him in the short term, a military base. From there, he kept watch and got lucky when someone he knew was an agent went looking for directions. The team he had in the field were pretty exceptional, probably ex-special forces of some kind. He directed them somehow, then covered their traces as they made off with Mirza. We never got close until they were long gone."

Shingen looked down, shaking her head. "All one man? It doesn't make sense. How?"

Ericka pressed her lips together, drumming her fingers on the table. "Lots of hired help. People to assist him to create his toys, muscle on the ground, but he's the head of the snake. If we can make the chop, everything else around him falls apart. I can't imagine anyone else gets to steer his AI."

Shingen's head tilted, not liking their options. *That makes two of us, but it is what it is.* "So, tell me how you're bringing the unfortunate Mr. Bromwich back to life and pressing him into FBI service."

Tim gazed at their commander, having already carried out the first part. "First, we have exhumed him for the second time, this time to get a high-res digital scan of his skull from which we've printed a plastic copy." Shingen's eyes opened wide, but he continued before she could speak. "That combined with the photos we have of him when he was alive, will allow us to create and age an almost perfect likeness. Good enough to fool facial-recognition software of any sort from a still."

Shingen's brows furrowed as she turned back to Ericka. "And why would he be scanning for someone he thinks is dead?"

Ericka couldn't help the smile. "He won't, but he will be scanning everything he can about his ex-wife. When Mr. Bromwich contacts her, he'll fill his pants."

Shingen's expression was skeptical, just short of an eye roll. "For about fifteen seconds 'til he realizes he's being baited."

"That's exactly what we expect, but it won't stop him using

Providence to run it down, if only for intelligence purposes and entertainment. When he does that, he'll find the message came from Bromwich's own phone with its globally unique MAC number."

"And where did we get that?" Shingen glanced from one to the other.

Clarke answered. "The California Highway Patrol had it stashed away in exhibits. It was marked for destruction, but that hadn't happened."

"And it will take him another ten seconds to think about where we might have gotten it from."

Ericka turned to Shingen, shoulders tense as she waited to explain the last part of the plan. *This one was really no dummy.* "When he hacks it, it will show that access to the phone was gained using Bromwich's fingerprint." She waited a few seconds for drama. "Which we got from his old company's security system and 3D printed on latex. It's an early generation of fingerprint reader. We've tested it and it works." In Ericka's view nobody but an idiot used biometrics. It wasn't like a password. If it gets stolen, you can't make up a new fingerprint or retina.

Shingen was smiling now. "You don't think he'll think of that?"

Steiner leaned in to speak. "I expect that he will, but he'll never be absolutely sure of the answer. The way he is 'wired' so to speak, he will have to run this to ground and the one way to do that with certainty is to confirm his information on the ground. His rage and animosity will make it irresistible once he thinks there is even a small chance Bromwich is alive."

Shingen turned back to Ericka. "And this old fossil of a phone will even hook up to the cell net."

"No, it probably won't. Far too old for that, but it will hook up to Wi-Fi and that gives some kinds of connections plausibility." Ericka glanced at Steiner, brows raised as he clearly wanted to speak.

"All traps work because of how badly the quarry wants the bait. This snare depends on his fury blinding him to some degree."

Ericka spoke over him in her eagerness to get this to work. "We'll use our physical avatar where we want him to think Bromwich is hiding. Make sure security cams pick it up. Once Dantalion has images in hand and assures himself the data hasn't been altered, he'll have no choice but to consider the remote possibility he might be alive."

"And if it doesn't work?" Shingen's eyes narrowed as she stared at Ericka.

Still doesn't quite trust me. I wouldn't either. "At the very least, it gives us cover to move Claire, which we have to do anyway. If it doesn't lead us to arrest, then we think of something else and keep trying 'til we get the bastard. What else can we do?"

Shingen glared down at the table, lips pressed together, taking her time before speaking, sighing several times. "I'll go upstairs for approval. Start getting prepared."

Hong Jun dreaded these sessions, a fear that left him shivering, his chest hammered by heart palpitations, but he'd let the monster in and there was no escape now. Not just into his home, but also into his country's newly completed BeiDou satellite navigation system. It had happened so quickly. What started out as a bad gambling addiction had opened a door just such a crack that a monster had pushed through. It was an addiction fueled by grief and alcohol after the death of his wife.

He was in debt beyond any hope to pay, and the gang's enforcers had made it very clear, it would not just be he who paid the price. His seven-year-old daughter in the care of his parents—all three would be the first to pay the toll. He had believed their lies that he could wipe his tally clean with one simple act; use his privileges to reset the audit functions in the BeiDou control system. Essentially, put something in the watchdog's water so it sleeps while the intruder does his work.

Jun had thought they simply wished to steal data about the locations of certain ships and know if they were being tracked, likely smugglers. Unlike western navigation systems, BeiDou had a two-way signal allowing the system to determine the position of anyone using it. Far too late, he was made aware who he was really working for and that his new employment would not be ending any time soon.

The VR headset arrived in a box wrapped in plain paper, found on the doorstep to his apartment after three hard raps on his door alerted him to the delivery. As cold air flooded over him, he kept his eyes down, knowing better than to be too curious about who'd delivered it.

His voice sounded like a rodent's squeak, making him wince as he spoke. Worse, it echoed off the virtual walls, the reflected sound all the more pathetic even to his ears. "I can't keep doing this. If I'm caught, my life will end in a cell." The gray concrete of a prison yard flashed in his mind, and he had to fight to choke down the sob.

The rich baritone dripped contempt. "A firing squad is possible for treason in China. Perhaps you will be lucky." The apparition drew back into the shadows, still now as a statue, a man made of polished stone with immense bat wings, a western symbol but one he knew well.

Jun stumbled over his words, his English not keeping up with his scattered thoughts. "They are investigating again, they know something is wrong. There were men in the facility asking questions and looking through records. They might find what I have done. We have done this too much."

The head tilted back and to one side, the forced sigh managing to carry both disdain and impatience. "Yes, I'm sure they will eventually, but you will not live long enough to tell them the details. This is your final task. Do you need reminding?"

Jun shook his head, his stomach in knots at what he knew was coming. "No, I don't."

"It seems to me that you do." The monster's right hand curled in an almost casual gesture.

Jun winced at the instant flood of light. He was looking down at a playground, one he knew well, a place he knew his mother would bring his precious Chu Hua to play after school while she chatted at a bench lined with elderly women. The drone's rotors were visible overhead. His guts lurched as he peered down. There she was, nearing the top of the slide, talking to the child above as she waited her turn. "Stop please!"

The sneer was audible as the scene faded, replaced by the gloom of the immense hall they had begun in. "If I need to remind you again, I will start with your father. Are we clear?"

Jun's eyes welled up at the thought. "I understand."

The demon let the silence continue for some time before speaking, giving him a slight nod. "Listen very carefully!"

★★★

"How do they look on video?" Ericka leaned in behind Tim to look at his screen. They were the only people in the lab. Displayed was a few seconds of Tim sitting on a bench outside with a man who looked very much like the late Clyde Bromwich, suitably aged and staring away from the camera.

"Looks fine, just not the kind of guy you can have a good conversation with." He turned his head to give her a twisted smirk.

"Idiot! And? Facial recognition?"

Tim shrugged. "All the facial-recog software we have is producing a match with known pics of Mr. Bromwich. It works, but we can't let our creation appear on video for more than a second or two. It looks just flawless in a car, especially when the neck pivots."

Ericka smiled at Tim, squeezing his shoulder. The trick was going to be getting London to find it on his own without setting off suspicion. They needed a visceral reaction and they needed data to feed him that was flawless. "I've got his old phone ready to go, wired into a laptop. I've it set up to record any intrusion, but I need you to have a look in case I've missed anything. Have you heard from Shingen about the move?"

Tim pivoted his chair away from the battered desk to look up at her. "She hasn't told you? They're leaving her there for the time being. The brass thinks we have a better shot at keeping her safe with enhanced security there, than trying to move her or hide her somewhere else. They might be right."

Ericka gritted her teeth, irked that Shingen wasn't including her in all aspects of the plan. "Yes true, given time, he'll find her again but thinking we were about to move her might have induced him to try for her now." It also made using the Bromwich fake almost useless. They couldn't risk baiting him into a murderous attack if she was actually there. The plan hinged on getting Claire out before he knew it.

Tim was staring at her, leaning back, obviously waiting for her to explode. "We might still be able to use it."

"Only to try and distract him once he's made his move. We can't be part of inducing him to attack!" Ericka pressed her eyes shut to force calm.

Tim waited, expression neutral at being told the obvious. "All we can do is be sure they make a proper job of the security detail and watch for any hint he's on the move. Unless he makes a move somewhere else, we're going to have to wait him out."

Waiting for him is always a mistake. She flopped back into a chair before speaking. "The last team he sent were serious professionals, but it isn't like he can insert enough people onto US soil or hire locals to overwhelm the security teams and local police both." Ericka could tell from Tim's look he was worried about her but trying to hide it.

Tim reached for his coffee, wincing as he took a sip. "No, he can't. Nor can he do anything really clever without possibly lighting himself up. He's made too many enemies, everyone's watching."

"I just wish the shrinks agreed on where London's head is at. Steiner's of the view he'll try for Claire whatever the odds."

Tim shrugged and stretched, his shirt taut around the bulk of his shoulders. "Fucking witch doctors the lot of them."

"Is Shingen thinking to leave her there permanently?"

Tim shrugged. "Not that she mentioned but I'm not on her consult before deciding things list."

25

Scent Rolling

After days of ceaseless noise and vibration, the interior of
the hand-built submarine went silent and all Semenov could
hear were waves washing over the fiberglass hull. The air
stank and Golubev sat scowling at the Colombians perched
on the ladder, preparing to open the hatch. Semenov forced
his cramping shoulders to relax, taking deep breaths to slow a
racing heart. He was not lacking in courage, but he would be
very glad to get out of jury-rigged monstrosity. Most narco-
subs couldn't fully submerge and were really low-profile
vessels, but American deployment of maritime drones had
forced the cartels to up their game. This one was black and
piped its exhaust under the bottom to cool it to avoid a bright
infrared signature. His eyes had bugged when he had come
on board and been told this fucking septic tank with a motor
could submerge for hours at a time.

Of course, none of this concerned his employer to any
visible degree. Semenov risked a glance at the man, hoping
not to catch his eye. Little fear of that. Since they had left the
Baja coastline, London, or Dantalion as he'd always known

him, had sat hunched over a computer, often wearing a VR rig, almost never speaking and rarely looking up at all. If the five days of living inside this submerged coffin had any effect on him, he gave no sign. It occurred to Semenov that being in complete isolation, immersed in writing code might be a normal state of affairs for him and where he was mattered to him not at all. Each night, his client had told the captain to run on the surface for a time so he could connect to a satellite, then he would return to his perch as absorbed as before. Semenov had not seen him sleep.

Golubev caught Semenov's eye, shaking her head before rolling her eyes as the crew struggled with a stuck hatch. The last member of their team, his old comrade Arseny Baranov, lay on an inflatable camp mattress, appearing asleep. With a flurry of curses, the hatch swung open to a sound like fiberglass cracking. He was glad they were not going home on this same tub. An overpowering sense of relief flooded over him as a puff of fresh salt air drenched his face. Not waiting to be invited, he shouldered one of the crew out of the way, clambering to the top of the ladder so he could scan the nearby beach with night vision. It was a rare, clear night for this part of the Oregon coast and Semenov could see nothing but low surf breaking on an empty beach.

A glance at his watch gave him the GPS expected coordinates. They were just offshore, two miles south of Cape Lookout, Oregon. Once on land, he and Golubev would walk to where their vehicles should be waiting before returning to the beach to pick up their client and equipment. Any sign of trouble and Baranov was to get him back to this deathtrap and get out before American vessels could respond.

Semenov slid down the ladder like the practiced sailor he

was before scowling at the crew, impatient to get the inflatable raft up the ladder. He couldn't imagine what his client had paid the cartels to use one of their precious subs as a taxi, but it wasn't his concern. He walked over to kick Baranov in the leg, speaking in Russian. "Wake up idiot, we're here."

His employer was still seated, stuffing his computer and other equipment into a pelican case, which he snapped shut before standing and tossing it to Baranov to carry. Using the cargo netting attached to the inside of the hull, he pulled himself to his feet. His wince of pain was quickly concealed, but Semenov saw it. He waited a few moments before speaking. "All is in order. We will be ready to go ashore shortly."

The scarred head snapped up and their eyes locked. Even though Semenov was a veteran of many gunfights and battles, the gaze of this man always made him flinch, like encountering the fixed gaze of a rabid animal. He didn't answer. Dantalion smiled, starting for the ladder, his gait unsteady.

Yusef's voice made Ericka picture his broad smile, surprised at how her mood at once lifted. She flipped the app for encrypted voice on her mobile before answering. "Always, a pleasure, but I hope you're not still working at this hour."

The timbre of his deep voice made her think he was smiling. "There is never a time I'm not working I'm afraid. This isn't the American public service you know."

The banter was a welcome respite, making her shoulders drop down a notch. "We're always hiring. Do feel free to submit your CV through appropriate channels."

That drew a laugh. "Yes, I expect after our target plucked that toad Mirza from the FBI's protective bosom there will be a number of vacant positions. I watched the video. I do not mourn his passing, but that was gruesome even by this one's standards."

Ouch, jerk! To make it worse, she was sure that Mirza hadn't given up all of his former master's secrets either. "So, are you calling for a reference in support of your application, or to tell me you have him hogtied in a cell?"

"Neither, but I have some interesting news."

"Please!"

She heard him draw a deep breath and sigh before speaking, picturing his familiar thoughtful look. "First, we believe London has moved his base again, back to somewhere in China. We've no idea where, but it would have to be tucked in one of the cities somewhere, likely with some sort of gang protection. We have some intercepted traffic between gang members to that effect. Most interesting is a reference to helping this person they are protecting get to Mexico. I believe he may have already left, perhaps some time ago."

Ericka's heart jumped a beat, then started pounding. *He's on his way, getting somewhere close, planning to have Claire brought to him.* "No details, I take it?"

"Just that he is expected back soon."

"Do you plan on informing the Chinese police?"

"No, they are filled with gang sources. He'd be tipped off in an instant. He could also be protected. Better we wait, I think."

Ericka had been just about to say that. "Thank you for that. We are about to start an operation to lure him in. Seems it may be working."

Yusef paused for a moment. "You're using his former wife as bait?"

Clever boy. "Not quite, but I'm sure he knows where she is."

"My best wishes for success." Yusef paused, hesitation in his voice slowing his speech as he continued. "The other news is far more intriguing. We received a storage device from someone claiming to be a relative of Mirza's. The note said Mirza had told him to send it to us if he should die violently or disappear."

Ericka's eyes bugged open as she sat up, her breath catching. "And? What's on it?"

"I don't know. It's encrypted and has defied our efforts to break it so far. The amount of data is small. I am, of course, wary of letting loose some sort of malware once we do. I have no way to verify it actually came from Mirza as opposed to another of London's tricks."

Yes. That would be completely in character. "Are we getting a copy?"

"I am still waiting for permission."

"We'll get to work on it as soon as we have it." Ericka nibbled her lip, thinking. "What does your gut tell you?"

She could hear him fumbling with his phone before speaking. "I think Mirza was a clever little bastard, more than I credited him, and this kind of revenge is in character for him. If your current operation doesn't result in stopping London, we should give this our undivided attention. Who knows what he was holding back?"

Ericka had the same read on Mirza. If Mirza'd had the ability to retaliate from the grave, he'd have done it. "Thank you. Stay in touch. I feel like we're very close."

"I agree. You shall have my prayers for your success."

Ericka sat up as Shingen strode into their office, gait stiff, face blanched as if drained of blood. From the corner of her eye, she saw Tim and Clarke pivot in their chairs. When Shingen did not sit, Ericka stood to speak. "What is it?"

Shingen leaned on the edge of a desk, head bowed for a moment, her dark hair shot through with the gray of a lifetime's stress. Her head snapped up to lock eyes with Ericka, her expression barely controlled anguish. "You were right—we should've moved her."

The knot in Ericka's stomach was instant. "Claire? What's happened?"

Shingen's head turned to look to the side, breaking eye contact. "She's gone. Did a runner past her own security."

Clarke looked aghast, her eyes wide with disbelief. "How the hell?"

Shingen was clearly forcing herself to meet Ericka's gaze now. "She waited for the one time when shift change meant there was only one team on site. Took off in her car without saying anything. The team followed until their car stopped, bleach in the gas seized the engine. By the time backup got there and they found her car, she'd ditched it. No sign of her since."

Ericka squeezed her eyes shut, speaking without opening them. *That poor woman, no end to her suffering for her marriage to this monster.* "He must have got to her somehow, panicked her." She opened her eyes to find Shingen's expression had changed to surprise, brows raised.

"Yes, he did. The team going in found a thumb drive in her computer, just a short video on it."

Tim interjected. "That computer was supposed to be air-gapped!"

Shingen stared back. "It was. They also found the drone that delivered it."

Ericka's shoulders sagged, sighing before speaking. "What did he say to her?"

Shingen's grip on the desk tightened, knuckles turning white, then she stood straight turning to one of the computers, bending to sign in. "Have a look."

Ericka fidgeted while the secure server processed Shingen's credentials. As the media player appeared on the screen, she sat down, leaning in to stare. The video showed the silhouette of a tall, lanky man, his face in shadows, his gait shambling as he approached the camera. The figure waited for a few moments, shoulders hunched, terribly thin, radiating palpable menace. When he spoke, the voice was familiar if gravelly, unfiltered by the usual array of electronic synthesis. "Claire, my dear. We must meet one last time. I have always known where you are, never stopped watching you, but the time was never right. Don't delude yourself that they can protect you. No one can protect you. I will be there presently." The shape was still for a few seconds, gave an almost imperceptible bow and the clip ended.

"Jesus Christ!" The words burst through Ericka's lips before they'd even formed in her mind. *No wonder she ran. In protection for years and no police or intel service seems to be able to touch him. Claire would've thought him willing to die there just to get to her, such was his hate. She probably didn't even have a destination. Just pure panic.*

Shingen was shaking her head. "It doesn't make sense. I see

why he'd want her to run away from her own protection, but how's he going to find her?"

Ericka looked at Tim as she answered. This was going to have to happen really fast. "Because she doesn't think they can defend her. He'll find her the same way we will. There's no such thing as off-grid for long. His Providence could spot her first, so we have to have people closer to her than he does. He can't have more than a handful in the area. Let's get our shit together and get moving."

Shingen met Ericka's gaze without flinching. *She knows this is on her, she needs us to dig her out.* "What do you need?"

Ericka paused to think it through. "All the ground assistance the locals can give us. A place to work out of, maybe the state troopers and at least one helicopter to get to her before he does. A company or military plane to get us into Aberdeen without connections."

Shingen was all business now, visibly pulling herself together. "Good hunting. Keep me posted. What about a public missing persons notice?"

Ericka had already thought of that and shook her head. "No, if anyone spots her and posts something, he'll see it before we do." She walked over to her locker, pulling out her go bag. She turned to Tim and Clarke. "Let's head for the airport. Shingen, could you please ask Dr. Steiner to stay near a phone?"

Ericka stepped out into cool evening air, dropping to sit on the concrete steps while she waited for the others. She pictured Claire's face, remembering the fear etched into her perfect features, even back then, two years ago. Now she was somewhere in the Pacific Northwest, alone and on the run, with almost no resources. It was going to take everything they had to get to her before he did.

How had she gotten here? A question Claire had asked herself hundreds of times over the years. He must have been watching her all along, despite the FBI's assurances she was safe. She hadn't been safe since the day they'd met but she was far too long in realizing that fact. Frank London had been charming, intelligent, successful, if a little full of himself. A great catch. No real warning signs at all until it was too late and she'd paid the price almost every day since.

She stared into the deluge through eyes that felt filled with sand, scanning between the trees across the road from the bus shelter as if he might be lurking in the forest waiting for her to walk too close. She tugged her hood forward to conceal her face, heedless of rain diluting her tears. *Will there ever be a time without fear? Do I have to pay for my mistake forever?*

Claire hadn't slept in the thirty-six hours since opening the video, his message to her. As she brought it to mind, her reaction was the same, fighting to quell her heaving stomach, face down as the raindrops spattered mud on her boots. Frank never gave up, never forgave, never content to leave the smallest slight unanswered, imagined or not. How did he find her? It was nothing she'd let slip, she had no one to slip to anymore. There was only one answer. He was inside the FBI or able to track them and those idiots led him right to her. She would have to get away from them, pull her small savings as cash, run as far away from phones and cameras as she could. Hop between small towns, cross the border, try and find somewhere completely off-grid and hope someone eventually took him down. She'd need a gun too. If he found her, she was going down fighting. *Not much of a plan.*

All those years, too afraid to leave him, too comfortable in the life his wealth gave her. *What was I thinking?* She'd seen the eruptions of volcanic rage when someone crossed him, endured them herself when he'd caught her chatting with any other male, a gilded cage shared with a rabid animal. *Hardly the first woman to endure years of an abusive relationship, but wow, can I pick them!* She squeezed her eyes shut, chest tight as she remembered. Claire had no doubt if London hadn't been so badly injured killing her lover, he would have come for her next and put her in the ground.

Then the short happy time with Brandt Cole, a man with his own flaws but who shined by comparison to his predecessor. At least until he ran, fearful of Frank, unable to endure protective custody. *Coward! I guess for better or for worse is open to a bit of interpretation.*

Claire lifted her head at the sound of the arriving pickup splashing through puddles as it pulled to a stop in front of her, brakes squealing. Standing, she pulled her hood back far enough she could look around. No police, her abandoned car must still be on the overgrown logging road where she'd left it. The middle-aged woman driving leaned over to open the passenger door. Blond and husky, she wore an unnecessary pair of sunglasses perched on her head. "You need ride?"

It was hitchhike or walk, the Greyhound was way too risky anyway. Claire forced a smile, nodding. "Where are you headed?"

"Port Angeles."

That would do for a start. Claire dropped onto the worn bench seat, pulling her bag between her knees. "Thank you, that would be great! I don't think the bus is ever coming."

Across from her, the driver smiled, staring at her drenched clothes. "I'm Emma. Does it ever stop raining here?"

Weird, she sounds Russian.

26

Hunters

Claire must have thought this place a kind of living hell.
Aberdeen, Washington, was a coastal industrial town, a
paradise for lovers of the outdoors, a wasteland for a socialite
climber finding herself indefinitely confined to witness
protection. An industrial hub in a coastal rainforest. They
had arrived at Bowerman Airport in the small hours, heading
immediately to facilities borrowed from the Washington
State Patrol, waiting for the last of the agents from Seattle
and Portland to arrive. All wore civilian clothes made blocky
by body armor. The heavy sound of a helicopter's rotors in
landing cycle made the windows vibrate.

Ericka pulled off her sunglasses as a gust of wind spattered
the lenses with the opening salvo from the next raincloud.
Rolling gray overcast filtered all light, giving everything an
almost metallic tint. She shivered as she glanced around the
enclosed vehicle yard; it was all sodden as if it hadn't dried
out in months. One of the cover team joked that all forms of
recreation here involved either killing something or burning
fossil fuels, or both. The seven agents on her team were staring

at her, several with narrowed eyes. *The one that went batshit and jumped the wall.*

She ignored them, glancing at her mobile as it buzzed the arrival of a message. Ericka glanced at Tim who was staring at her, brows raised. She shook her head and turned to look again at the advancing clouds. They were just going to have to wait it out.

Semenov spared a glance at the door leading to the room he'd helped set up and equip, wincing at the thought of what must be going on in the darkened room. A man who'd chosen a lifelong path of violence, even he had limits. He fancied himself a mercenary warrior in the time-honored tradition, albeit one for hire to whoever met his price. His boots drummed on the deck's bare wood as he went outside to keep an eye on the road. He closed the door behind him, not wanting to hear what he knew was coming, his nose wrinkling as if at a foul smell.

He turned up the collar on his dark green jacket against the wind, glancing to where the other two waited in concealed positions, locations calculated to place anyone entering the property under withering crossfire. This would only end one way if they were found, but none of them would go down without a fight. He knew their employer would never be taken alive.

The rented cottage perched atop a low sandy cliff, nestled amongst cedars and pine. The featureless roar of distant surf competed with dripping rain falling into countless puddles. Their inflatable boat was concealed under a tarp behind beach dunes not far above the high-tide line and could be ready to go on a minute's notice. The property had a private trail down. It would be a short ride if they were pursued or their ride wasn't waiting, but he had great faith in his employer's abilities. He sat, the old porch chair creaking, concealed by heavy bushes growing in front. Propped against the wall next to him were a pair of shovels and three large bags of lye. Amateurs used lime, but lye did a much better job of dissolving teeth and bone. Time for a cigarette—action might come at any moment.

Semenov and his team had been there for two weeks waiting, baffled at their employer's promise that their target would deliver herself nearby shortly, and then she had. At least close enough that sedating her and bringing her back was the work of minutes. He wasn't sure what it was, maybe the atavistic fear etched into the face of a stunningly beautiful woman, but his taste for this employer's adventures had come to an end. Honor and professionalism demanded he complete his mission, but this would be his last one for this ghoul.

Semenov flipped his cigarette butt into a puddle, hearing a short hiss, before pulling out his tablet to scan the sensors he had set up around the property.

Ericka held her mobile in front of her, pressed to her chest to protect it, on speaker so Tim could listen. She cocked her head, straining to hear over rain pelting her hood, oblivious to the cold. Tim leaned in so their foreheads almost touched. "Tim's here, on speaker, go ahead."

Clarke's voice had the robotic sound of a weak connection, her speech pressured with excitement. "We've lucked out.

There's only one it can be. There aren't many towers there, so the data block was small."

Before Ericka could speak, Shingen interjected. She hadn't realized her boss was on the call. "You've got all the warrants in place?"

Jesus! What the hell is the matter with her? Without thinking, she growled her answer through clenched teeth. "We don't need a warrant! Give your head a shake! What have you found?" Tim's eyes stared into hers from a foot away. He shook his head and Ericka closed her eyes to squeeze the heat from her mind, pushing the jinni back into its cage.

Clarke talked over Shingen's indignant 'excuse me!' "The telecoms handed basic tracking data over without one. Someone's in with the judge now getting full authorization for everything we need."

That last would be for Shingen's benefit. Ericka pictured O'Brien's hulking form, a silver-tongued behemoth, leaning forward to impress the need for urgency on a bemused judge. It almost made her smile. "And?"

"Three burner SIMs hooked up to local towers for the first time since Claire ran. Two are still hitting them. Triangulation has them in public places in the main shopping area to the south. Unlikely candidates, they're right out in the open. Probably local drug dealers. One signed on briefly just north of town and made a call to somewhere in Ontario. Tracing that. Then it signed on again forty-five minutes later, even farther north, and did what looks like telephone banking. Neither are where the car was found. The locations are a bit vague, sending them to you now."

Ericka was beginning to hope. "That's all we've got. Jesus, I didn't know you could still do telephone banking." But burners usually didn't support apps so it made sense. She was reminded of her earlier impression of Claire; she's no idiot despite having made a career of acting the bimbo. "Anything else?"

Clarke was almost gushing with excitement. "He's scanned some of the Bromwich pics and the phone. He's taken the bait."

The surge of warmth rose to engulf her. Ericka tilted her head back, her voice far too loud. "Yes!" Her mobile chimed call waiting. Ericka started, catching her breath when she saw Yusef's number display. "Keep us posted, gotta run." She disconnected, not bothering to engage the encryption. "Go, Yusef, we're in the field and you're on speaker. We think London has his ex-wife."

"Then this will be timely for you. We've managed to decode some of Mirza's legacy I told you about. We can see some of London's traffic. Enough to track one of the satcom services he's hacking. He must use more than one, but we got a weak location trace on one signal sent about a week ago." Yusef's voice trailed off like he'd become distracted.

Ericka had to force herself to breathe. "And?"

A few seconds passed before Yusef spoke, his voice catching like he was puzzled. "You're transmitting in the clear? I have your location as the north end of a place called Aberdeen, Washington? Yes?"

What the hell was he on about? She forced the emotion from her voice to speak clearly. "Yes, correct."

"It isn't very precise, but his last signal is very near, so close you're overlapping. London's right on top of you. He's there!"

The bastard is toying with us.

★★★

Tim rubbed his beard as he glared at the list on his mobile, too long to check them all even with local police helping. This area of the coast had hundreds and hundreds of vacation rentals and empty summer homes where they might have taken her. It made him feel like an idiot. He'd assumed London's men would try for Claire when they moved her, take her somewhere distant where he could take his time. The brazen plan of getting her to run and then coming onto US soil himself was unexpected. Ericka and Steiner were right— he'd changed, no way he'd have been this bold before.

It would take long hours they didn't have to seize rental data from all the various services to even look for possible hits. Even then, the target would have taken steps to camouflage his efforts. They'd almost no chance of finding data to point the way.

Tim scanned his list again before glancing at Harris— the agent driving—seeing her focused on the driving rain drumming on the windshield. SA Brenda Harris of the Portland office clutched the wheel, eyes narrowed in concentration, her short blond hair and muscular build giving the impression she was ready for whatever would happen. He shifted his weight, turning to peer out at the now building surf, gloom deepening as the evening approached. *We're going to have to get lucky.* Continue to eliminate all the condos, no way they wouldn't get noticed bringing their captive in. The same applied to smaller properties near the beach; they were packed in way too tight for any privacy. Keep looking at the rentals on larger lots, back away from the strip, preferably well-treed. There was no time. If London managed to find Claire soon after she ran, he'd had her for most of a day. Tim's stomach knotted at the thought. The first six properties they'd tried had come up dry.

He forced himself back to the list, starting with the largest lots. He scrolled with his finger, stopping as one caught his attention, oceanfront, four-point-five acres, cottage right above the beach, private, secluded location. He expanded the listing service ad to look at the photos. The place was perfect: treed, long, gated driveway, showing as not available now, presumably rented. *Worth a look.*

Tim spoke to the driver as he traced out their route on the app. "Harris, keep following the one-oh-nine north, when you get across the Copalis River, go past Ocean View, stop before the intersection with Copalis Rock Lane. We're getting out for a look on foot before we go in." He turned to the two agents in the back. "As soon as we stop, break out the heavy weapons and night vision. We're doing this in the dark."

The light under the forest canopy was even dimmer, but all to the good for what he was planning. Tim waited while Harris got out of the gray SUV, checking her pistol and ammunition. She fluffed up her raincoat to conceal the armor from casual glance. Tim stepped to the back of the vehicle, boots splashing in pooled water as he did. The men were unpacking gear under the shelter of the rear hatch, rifles and ammunition laid out ready for use. "We'll only be a few minutes. Be ready!" Seeing the thumbs-up, Tim turned to walk down the shaded lane. Harris joined at his side, walking close to give the impression they were a couple. The sign to the narrow, paved lane said it was private. *Not today it isn't.*

About two hundred yards in, the driveway to their target

property appeared. The gate was open, but the cottage wasn't visible, obscured by thick forest and fading light. The low rumble of distant surf pierced the hiss of rain, muted by the trees. Tim took a deep breath, calmed by the salt air and tang of cedars. He froze inside as he saw it, turning to look down the road, speaking under his breath in case there was a mic. "Camera on the tree by the gate. Looks new. Don't stare that direction." A standard game cam set back in the trees to watch the road, not the driveway. Then he saw the second one, recognized by its shape, pointed at the gate. *Got him! He's here.*

As soon as they were well past the gate, he reached for his radio. *No, they'll have a scanner. Maybe even an IMSI-catcher to detect cell phones.* Walking back too soon could also tip them off. He turned to look at Harris. "Head back to the highway through the woods. Use the sat phone to call in backup. Tell Ericka I'm as sure as I can be. I'll keep watch here."

She said nothing before slipping into the trees, picking her way back to the main road.

He knew she couldn't see him as he stood in the shadows. The intense light shone on Claire twisting against her bonds as the last of the drugs wore off. She was naked on the old stretcher, feet cuffed to the corners, her hands together over her head anchored to the frame. Her eyes were squeezed shut and one of Semenov's crew had draped a sheet over her, which struck him as an odd mercy from hardened mercenaries. Eyes locked on her face, he moved towards her making sure his steps were loud, ensuring she knew he was close. Tears dribbled past

Claire's compressed eyelids and her lower lip quivered. *She knew*.

He raised his hand over her face, close over her neck, hoping she would feel the body heat and was rewarded with a gasp and the sight of her writhing to get away. He drew the sheet down, exposing her, savoring the beginning of the show he'd promised himself for so long. His hand ran along her smooth abdomen, cupping a heavy breast, squeezing, pleased that she twisted away as though scalded.

Smiling, he stood back, examining the collection of knives he'd laid out on the table next to her, selecting a use for each. Standing out of the light, he'd thought about forcing himself on her but couldn't bear the thought of the humiliation if he was unable. There could be no moment of triumph in this for her, no final mortification to add to what she'd done. This was his time for which he'd risked everything.

He selected a small forward-curved knife, a *karambit*, one designed for slashing, hooking a finger in the metal loop at the hilt's base, cold steel in his hand making him draw a sharp breath. His heart began to hammer the wall of his chest. Face flushing, he turned to stand beside the stretcher.

He stopped, unable to move, frozen to the floor as he met the gaze of Claire's large green eyes. Managing astonishing dignity and courage for where she was, her features were set as she spoke, her tone level. "If you think I'm going to beg you, go fuck yourself!"

His chest tightened, making his breathing short, almost gasping. Having her had always been about possessing the prize of her beauty, a marvel for all to see, a living tribute to his entitlement. It had made the shame, public disgrace, so much the worse when she'd spurned him for his partner.

While she played at the part of the bimbo when it suited her, he was no less aware of the mind and determination that were the real Claire. She had a role to play, testifying to his triumph and she lived the benefits of her bargain. Claire was his and she was a source of his pain, an agony he had generously shared ever since.

"Good, this will be far more satisfying with a bit of fight in you. Remind me of what you've done."

Claire's lip curled with the contempt of long familiarity. "I'm shocked you had the courage. After these years of hiding in the dark and paying others to do your dirty work. What happened? The man I knew was a fucking asshole, but he at least had a set! Welcome back."

Oh, you will pay for that. He stepped forward grasping her neck, watching while she steeled herself not to cringe, her eyes focused unblinking on his, cheeks flushed red, resigned but no hint of fear. Those eyes, for all her beauty, the body of a goddess, it had always been her eyes. It was he who squeezed his eyes shut, turning away. His nose began to run and tears pressed past his eyelids. He couldn't catch his breath, bent over, hands on knees to prop himself up. He stood to see her staring at him, eyes holding a hint of triumph. Lips curled in a snarl, he threw the knife scything through the air, so it passed an inch from her head, rewarding him with a flinch, but that was all it was, nothing but a reflexive instinct.

He grasped Claire's chin, leaning in to stare from a handbreadth away, their breath mingling in violent intimacy. "I can make you beg."

She spat back her words. "Not without a group of hired thugs. You had to rent several sets of balls to even try!" He backhanded her across the face, gasping at the pain in his hand, but satisfied to see blood trickle from her nose. Her voice dripped contempt as he held his smarting hand. "Don't hurt yourself, you pathetic child!"

He swung to pluck the largest knife from the table, his vision red, almost unable to see, then started at the heavy pounding on the door behind him, Semenov's voice shouting. "There's trouble. We must go now!"

Golubev's voice crackled in Semenov's headset, jolting him alert. "Something has tripped two of the motion sensors. One on the property, one across the road, nothing on the cameras except a couple walking past the gate a few minutes ago."

Semenov stood, lifting his tablet from the window ledge, toggling through the video. The couple seemed innocuous at first, then the man stared straight at the camera. There was a quick conversation and then it seemed to him they were studiously ignoring the property. He hadn't gotten this far by not listening to his instincts and now they were screaming. He pushed in his earpiece while toggling to connect to the police scanner they'd set up in town. Yes, no doubt about it, the state troopers were mobilizing and setting up roadblocks north and south. "You and Baranov fall back and cover the road. We are going to have to move. I'll get our client."

Semenov could hear the snarl in her voice through static. "Fuck him. I'm not rotting in an American jail for that sick bastard. Baranov, meet me at the vehicles."

"On my way."

Semenov thought for a moment of joining them. Loyalty to the mission weighed on him, but not as much as his own skin. It wasn't devotion that made him run inside the cottage to warn his employer. He simply thought the boat was a better bet. And if he escaped, he wanted to get paid. *Perhaps, Golubev and Baranov would draw off the Americans for long enough.*

Tim crouched under a dense stand of shrubs, ignoring that he was sitting in a puddle, soaked to the skin. When he'd heard the sound of people moving through the brush, seemingly not caring about cracking branches and rustling bushes, he knew they'd been made. He could just make out the driveway in the gloom as he crept forward, stopping when he could make out the outline of covered windows lit from within, no sign of movement. He took several deep breaths to steady himself. His backup was still at least fifteen minutes away.

Tim stepped into the lane, straightening, pistol out and pointed at the ground, acutely aware his adversaries could well have night vision. The sudden, intense bright of the headlights stung his eyes, freezing him for seconds before he dove back into the underbrush. An engine's roar preceded the old pickup truck passing by where he'd been standing. There was just enough light to see there were two people in it, one man and a light-haired woman. *Fuck, he's got her.* Radio silence was over. "He's got her, on his way up to the highway. Try and block him off!"

Harris responded. "He's past us, heading north on one-oh-nine."

Tim gritted his teeth, but there was no way out for them going north. *He will probably kill her before he's taken.* "I'll go into the cottage and secure any evidence. Get after him!" If they did take him alive, better if all the evidence wasn't bricked up. He stood in the clearing, able to see the brick driveway and cottage with its covered porch. He held his breath listening but there was nothing but the incessant rain driven by a rising gale. There was a second car, an old Subaru.

From behind it, the roar of waves was louder. Someone could still be in the cottage, but more likely they'd gotten out towards the beach. Too risky to go in the building alone. Keeping near the edge of the bushes, he circled the parking area towards the cabin. *That's a woman's voice. Are they still in there?* Another look and he stepped onto the bricks, keeping the car between himself and the building. If it was Claire in there, he couldn't wait, the target could kill her any second. Rain splattering into puddles didn't hide the distinctive sound of the heavy footstep behind him. His stomach cramped while a chill crept up his spine. *One of them had gotten behind him.* Tim closed his eyes and bowed his head. *Up to you now, Ericka.*

He held the knife to her jugular, twisting Claire's head to make the cut, his eyes focused on hers, eager for his reward, the fear, his due. She stared back, unflinching, daring him. *Why couldn't he do it?* Those eyes, every time they locked in a stare, it was as if his hand froze. He rubbed his chin as the idea occurred to him, seeing her eyes narrow with suspicion. "I have a better idea. It seems you've formed a rather poor impression of me and it wounds me."

"Oh, go fuck yourself!"

"I pay idiots to do that for me. It's why nothing ever goes to plan."

"Just get it over with, coward. Then you can boast how you killed a woman tied hand and foot. All by yourself. No one to help you. Or call in one of your thugs to do it for you and pretend you did."

His shoulders relaxed as he made his decision. It would be much better this way. He smiled and finally, she quailed. "Don't flatter yourself, bitch! Dead, you would miss the last one, it will be my best yet. I want you to live to see it." Her expression said she thought he was just toying with her. "But, before I go, I will take something that is rightfully mine, something you and that fucking toad, Bromwich stole from me." She gasped as he grabbed a handful of her thick hair, twisting it to stop her moving. "Your beauty of course!" He leaned over, slicing into one cheek, across her nose, the tip grinding bone, ending in the cheek on the other side. Something far beyond the talents of even the best plastic surgeon. Her shriek was cut short, turning to a gurgling sound as blood from her nose gushed into her throat.

He stood back to admire his work, smirking as she writhed to one side, turning her head to spit out blood so she could breathe. Good point, all this would be spoiled if she drowned. He unclipped the cuffs from the carabiner, leaving them on while he pressed a wadded towel to her face almost tenderly. "Keep the pressure on it or you'll bleed to death. If that bastard Bromwich is truly alive, send my regards and tell him I look forward to seeing him soon." He started at the gunshot from outside, lunging towards the door.

Semenov's voice carried from outside sounding, level as always. "We must go. It is now or never!"

Semenov made his way down the trail using only his small headlamp. He glanced over his shoulder to ensure his client was still with him, equipment case slung over his shoulder. The man looked unconcerned, without emotion. *Fuck, and people call me a psychopath!* He swallowed hard as they made it to the boat. Dangerous surf had built with the rising gale and they would be very lucky to make it to their ride, presuming it was where it was supposed to be.

It was as if the man could read minds. "They are waiting for us. They don't get paid if they leave, and I have motivated the man who owns it in other ways to see that I live."

Semenov shook his head, pulling on his dry suit, before they dragged the small inflatable to where the spent waves spilled up the strand. They hauled it down until a surging wave hissed past, floating it. The engine started on the first try. The boat bucked as they passed through the surf zone, breakers drumming the hull, throwing spray. Then they were through into the darkness.

Ericka pushed past the state troopers, flashing her badge, leaning into the cab of the truck. The air still had the tang of gunpowder telling her the shooting had ended just minutes before. Dark amidst the downpour, vehicle headlights penetrated to cast small swaths of light. He had put up quite the fight if the number of bullet holes were any indication. Choking down her elation, she had to see. Both were dead, she'd heard on the radio as they approached, Claire his final victim. The passenger window was shattered.

Ericka leaned in to where the woman's head hung across her chest, her body held in place by the seat belt. Her stomach churned at the smell of blood and bullet-ridden intestines. She held her light so she could see the face under the lank hair, sick they hadn't been able to protect her. The face she saw made her gasp, words bursting through her lips to the cover team. "That's not her. I don't know who this is."

"What the hell?" One of the state troopers from the dark behind her.

Ericka flipped her light up to the driver's face. Vacant eyes stared out over heavy features sporting a trimmed beard and several scars. Ink protruding from the neck of his shirt looking like noxious weeds growing up from his torso towards his face. Whoever this thug was, it wasn't London. *A decoy, or were they just idiots trying to escape? Where is Claire?* She spun to look at her team. "We need to ID these people. Some kind of hired muscle or mercenaries."

The answer came from behind her, she didn't see from who. "On it!"

The need for radio silence was gone. Ericka fumbled for her mobile, oblivious to the relentless downpour soaking her, dialing Tim. Several attempts went unanswered, leaving her queasy with rising panic, staring at the phone as dribbling rain distorted the screen.

One of the state troopers spoke as he approached. Ericka noted the sergeant's stripes. His fixed gaze and grim expression made her swallow. "Your protected civilian is alive and on the way to hospital with significant injuries." He paused as if to gather courage. "Officer down, one of yours."

God no, Tim. "Alive?"

The sergeant looked away for seconds before restoring eye contact. "Barely, he's not expected to live. Get in!" He pointed towards a police SUV. "I'll take you."

The short drive south blurred into a formless collage of sirens, rain thundering on the roof, blue and red flashes flickering on wet trees streaming by in the black. Ericka was frozen inside, mind dead, detached from her surroundings, oblivious to the speed, like she was watching a video filmed through an impressionist's lens. A sudden turn put a wheel in a pothole, jolting her back to reality as the vehicle careened down the lane and into a driveway. She glanced at the sergeant, who gestured ahead with his chin. The trees near the cottage flickered with red light reflected from several emergency vehicles crowded together.

Ericka opened the door and jumped out well before the vehicle came to a stop, almost stumbling, recovering to a dead run, focused on the ambulance with its rear door open. She splashed through deep puddles ignoring the cold wet, focused on the man lying in the gurney in the back. She could see enough of him to know it was Tim. One of the state troopers moved to stand in her way, but a shout from the sergeant behind her cleared her path. "Let her through!"

One of the medics moved to the front, making room for Ericka. She sat down hard on the bench to the side of the stretcher, mud and water pooling under her boots. Tim was as white as frost under harsh LEDs, blood already pooling to the lowest part of his body, eyes shut, oxygen mask still in place where they had intubated him. His jacket and shirt were torn open, his chest bearing witness to the medic's frantic efforts to save him. Shot through the right lung. They had tried to patch the wound to let him breathe, red and pink stains on the sheet a testament to their failure. Burnt patches of skin displayed their efforts to restart his heart. They had to try, but Ericka knew from the position of the exit wound, he'd never had a chance. *Shot from behind. Fucking cowards.*

She held his hand while staring at his face, wondering

what had happened, trying to press her emotions down for another time and failing. Her hands shook, tears tickling her cheeks as they streamed down her face. *No one approached armed suspects alone. He must have thought Claire was about to be killed or lost it at the prospect of avenging his aunt's death. Jesus, Tim why didn't you wait? You didn't have to die like this.* She'd never know, never know anything except that evil bastard had taken another life, this time the last person alive she considered family, a brother. The weight of grief crushed her.

Voices penetrated her mental fog, drawing her back, listening now to the conversation going on behind the ambulance, catching the tail end. "There's no other way they could've gotten out. We must have missed them by minutes. Call them again!"

Time for grieving later. If there was still any chance to catch the monster, time to focus. She jumped down to speak to Cooper, one of Tim's team. "What? Tell me?"

The man looked away, rain streaming down his face, clearly reluctant to disturb her mourning. "Easier to show you." He walked to the remaining suspect vehicle, a rusty Subaru, gesturing to an area of the ground with his light. The rain hadn't washed away all of the blood yet. "This is where we found him." Cooper flicked his light to the side of the car, holding it there while she leaned to peer into the pool of light.

It took Ericka a few seconds to realize what she was looking at. They weren't scratches, they were writing. A sharp piece of stone lay underneath where Tim must have dropped it. He'd scratched the word 'beach' into the lower door. She stood to stare at Cooper. "You've called it in?"

He nodded. "The coast guard is moving boats out, but

there's no point sending choppers until the weather clears. Can't see a damned thing. No radar contacts. If they had a boat, it was small. It's really blowing out there. Not survivable in a small boat. No traces on the beach so far."

Ericka wasn't listening. She strode down the trail, stumbling through clumps of wet beach grass and brush, her light a small headlamp. She stood on the last small dune before the land gave way to a wide beach. To her right, lights of searching officers played across the sand, crisscrossing beams appearing solid in the downpour. The thunder of constant breakers blended into a solid roar, a wall of white noise. Wind-driven rain stung her face, washing tears to trickle unnoticed into wave-compacted sand.

A state trooper emerged from the gloom, her features just visible in Ericka's light. The officer gestured towards the waves, shaking her head. "Two sets of washed-out tracks. If they went out in that, they're dead. Their bodies will wash up soon enough."

Ericka turned away to stare back out to sea, unable to see anything but the flickers of rain crossing the beam of her light.

No, they didn't drown. He's out there somewhere. This one has so many lives, I've lost count. I will find you. None of this goes unanswered. If it ends me, so be it. Maybe even better that way.

27

To Know Your Enemy

It was Steiner's hand squeezing hers that brought her back. Ericka looked up to where he sat across the table, smiling at him while pulling her arm away. *No time to let feelings go now. No telling where that would end.* The scene replaying in her mind was a time years before when Tim had introduced her to his aunt, the formidable Mrs. Donnelly. Certainly, no letting that one play out now. Pulled from her reverie, she turned to look out O'Brien's office window at the lights of DC. The three sat around his desk nursing drinks in silence, the bourbon in front of her untouched. She turned from the window to find both men staring at her with narrowed eyes. *And well they should.* Ericka had gone through Tim's funeral and memorial service without showing a hint of emotion, she'd made sure of it. *Time for that later.* She needed to get back on the hunt before she exploded.

O'Brien broke the silence. For the first time Ericka could remember, the lawyer's usual jovial demeanor was gone, replaced with a somber expression on a face aged ten years in a day. He was taking this very hard. "Okay, there's never a good time during something like this, so now's as good as any. If you go, they may treat your immunity agreement as void."

Steiner's pale skin was red and blotchy. Ericka had never seen him react like this. "To say nothing of its effect on you."

She looked down, shaking her head, refusing eye contact for the moment, afraid the stab of anger in her guts would be visible. "Thank you, but I really do have bigger fish to fry, one in particular."

O'Brien sighed, having a generous sip of his whiskey before speaking. "I get that, but you still have to think about after. In a more practical view, if you go renegade again, you'll lose the resources that might be the way to get what you want."

Ericka pictured her coming conversation with her supervisor. Shingen had to see sense. "That would be bad, but I still have to go. That data the Pakistanis got dropped on them is the best lead we have and there's every possibility Dantalion doesn't know we have it. This is the only way they'll share it."

"Obviously, they want you to crack it and catch the bastard while they take credit for it." O'Brien's tone broadcast his irritation. "Maybe your brass will let you go and this won't be an issue."

"Time will tell, but you both know what I'm going to do." Ericka glanced at Steiner. "So, let's talk psychology for a change of pace. What happened in that cottage? Was that Dantalion or London?"

That brought O'Brien's characteristic smile back to life. "Yes, Dr. Steiner. Perhaps my memory is wrong, but I don't think that set of events unfolded exactly as you called it?"

Ericka took a sip of the bourbon, feeling it burn its way down while she watched Steiner compose his thoughts, taking a moment to give the lawyer a dirty look. Steiner laced his fingers across his belly before answering. "I'm not sure that is a useful way to approach the issue, Ericka. I think it is a reflection of his years living almost entirely in the virtual world. Regaining his mobility perhaps did not give him all he'd hoped for. He's lived so long in the shadows, he wasn't prepared to face the horror of the real thing. Remember, underlying much of what we call narcissism are cowardice and insecurity, the need to always convince yourself you are what you know for certain you're not."

O'Brien sounded puzzled. "For years, he's had others kill, rape and torture for him and record it so he can live it as intimately as possible."

Steiner leaned forward, shaking his head, one finger raised. "His earlier crimes were carried out by others, feeding his wants with sight and sound, not engaging the more visceral senses, not an elaborate video game anymore."

Ericka leaned back to look at the ceiling. It had to be more than that. "Maybe, he did love her at some point in the past, in his own twisted way. Maybe he just couldn't bring himself..."

Steiner pursed his lips, staring at his immaculate nails. "More likely, he realized once he got there that he couldn't stand what would possibly be his final act to be perceived as so petty, so weak. He had to have a woman tied up by others to carry it out. His savage wants to torture her and his ego collided. You've read Claire's debrief? To his thinking, he took back what she'd deprived him of, a possession rightfully his, the status her beauty conferred on him by being his. She had already wounded his ego with the affair, a wound amplified all out of proportion by his psychopathy after he became paralyzed. When she mocked him, she may have saved her own life. He may have felt obligated to prove her wrong, show her he is what he considers himself to be. Have her see it."

O'Brien stared, brows raised. "Very good, that makes perfect sense and fits what we know. This incident aside, if I'm understanding your general theory of him, he will continue to be reckless from here on. Now, with the small added bonus that she will see whatever he's got planned, yes?"

Steiner smiled at him. "See, you are wasted lawyering. You could have done something useful with your life."

O'Brien's eyes widened. "Funny how every time I get most of a bottle of whiskey in me, I start to sound like a shrink."

"You two are like an old married couple these days." Ericka smiled at them in turn. "But if you're right, we need that data cracked now. He could move at any time."

Steiner wasn't finished. "And afterwards, Ericka, what then? Are you done?"

She glanced at O'Brien before answering. "If I read that agreement right, I'm out to pasture as far as the FBI is concerned."

O'Brien's expression fell, becoming somber, his lips pressed together before speaking. "All jokes aside, where *do* you go from here?"

Ericka swallowed as she looked away. "I don't know. I crossed the line. I'm still working out where that leaves me."

"Who drew the line?" O'Brien peered at her, not blinking.

"Sorry?"

"Which line? The law? Religion? They all have lines and they're not all in the same place. Which?"

What does it matter? "Mine."

"Then walk back and stay back."

Steiner smiled as he spoke. "Seneca would approve the advice, though I don't think he liked lawyers either."

Ericka glanced between the two men. This would have to wait for another day. "Before I get moving, a final toast, an oath if you will." She held up her glass. "To Tim, your death will not go unanswered! None of them will." All held their glasses up before draining them.

When Ba Lian Ming asked his associate to speak face-to-face, this was not what he'd pictured. The VR headset had arrived some time ago, but this was the first time he'd used it. Still, this was amusing, seated on a cushion in a Buddhist temple across from a shadowed form, a shape that looked a lot to Ming like some western demon. It really was very good, an environment so compelling he fancied he could smell the incense and feel the night breeze through the temple's open sides. He looked at the hulking form, noting the feathers in his wings fluttered as he shifted his weight. "You shouldn't have gone to this trouble just to entertain me."

It was the first time he'd heard this Dantalion's voice and he wondered if it was real. "No trouble at all. These environments are something I enjoy creating, the ability to play at being a god in your own little universe." The demon's head tilted to one side. "You are wondering if everything is ready?"

"My associates are very eager to proceed. There will be an opportunity in five days. They inquire constantly."

As the apparition turned his head, light played over almost delicate features. Ming could see a faint smile twisting full lips. "As long as I have a list of the assets they will use, I am ready to proceed with two hours' notice. If they would like a demonstration, an appetizer, I would be more than happy to demonstrate the technology in advance."

"They will be pleased. I'm never sure where you are but, once this is done you must expect the entirety of my country's cyber-intelligence community to come after you like a pack of wild dogs. They do not work under the same constraints as the western services and have near-complete control over the national portion of the internet. Move swiftly, my friend. There will be no clemency for this."

Now this thing was staring at him. "Mercy is neither given nor expected but thank you for your warning." The form dissolved like smoke in a gentle breeze, leaving Ming alone in the temple. He smiled to himself as he had a last look around the virtual before pulling the set off. If this succeeded it would be the coup of a generation, profitable beyond belief.

Allama Iqbal International Airport looked more like a grand hotel than a terminal. The brick building sported exquisite Islamic arches before melding into a more modern, functional design. Ericka's clothes stuck to her in the sweltering heat as she stood in front of the arrival terminal ignoring the shouted entreaties of taxi drivers hawking their wares.

Yusef's voice came from behind her, his smile containing real warmth as she turned. It was the first time she'd seen him in uniform. "Welcome to Pakistan, please let Achmed take your luggage."

Ericka turned to look up at one of the largest men she'd ever met, his bulging chest and shoulders strained the fabric of his uniform, his smile displaying an incomplete set of teeth.

She handed him her bag, about to apologize for its weight before he lifted it to one shoulder like she'd packed it with feathers. She turned to Yusef.

Yusef gestured towards the mass of drivers and porters. "My apologies. The ramp was blocked and we were obliged to wait here. This is why I wasn't in the terminal when you arrived. Please follow Achmed closely."

She stuck close behind the behemoth as the man plowed through the mass of people without breaking stride. Those not getting out of the way quick enough for Achmed's tastes were tossed aside, one ending up on the ground, the flash of anger on the man's face gone when he saw who he faced, remembering pressing business elsewhere. Achmed said something to him in Urdu that made him quail and step further back.

Yusef held the door and gestured her into the back of the large BMW. Achmed sat beside the driver, scowling at the masses as they drove as if hopeful of trouble. Ericka turned to look at Yusef on the seat beside her. Her clothes were crawling on her after several connecting flights, but it would have to wait. "Any progress on the decryption?"

"Yes, some." He paused to stare at the traffic. "It was as if we were meant to be able to open it, but that it would not be easy. You haven't told me how it went with your supervisor. Are you here as Special Agent Blackwood or Ms. Blackwood, formerly of the FBI?"

Ericka looked away smiling, remembering her meeting with Shingen. Her boss hadn't looked pleased when people much farther up the food chain had made the decision. "They are still suspicious about why you wouldn't share a copy, but as long as I can pass on our results, they're content."

Yusef's eyes rolled as he shook his head. "Not my doing and I'm sure you can appreciate the politics between us and your country now we are more aligned with China as we are."

"Your agency's reputation doesn't help."

Ericka saw a brief flash of annoyance, instantly masked. "Our methods are dictated by the resources we have and the enemies we face. No one seemed bothered by them when we handed over Mirza to your colleague or upset with what we get from captured jihadis."

Ericka flinched, looking at her folded hands, needing to avoid eye contact, Mirza's name reminding her this was her first op in many years without Tim. "We'll have NSA and Homeland intel support if we need it. I don't mind getting out of the States for a bit."

Out of the corner of her eye, she could see Yusef was staring at her. He grasped her wrist as he spoke. "O'Connell was a good man and an outstanding agent. I grieve his loss."

He was more perceptive than she gave him credit for. Time to change the subject before she dropped into that hole, too much to do. "Thank you. Where are we going?"

"Not far. We have a field office at the air force base on the other side of the runway. My team is set up there."

Ericka paused for a moment, drowned out by the roar of a commercial jet as they drove under the flight path. "Do they have all we need? We can still send a copy to the States to get the extra horsepower to crack the encryption."

Yusef shook his head. "Not needed. As I said, they wanted us to open it." He was gazing at her, eyes sparkling. "But not by infidels. The keys that are unlocking it are based on scripture, not random numbers. I am confident we will have access to all of it shortly. As to what we do with it, that is where you come in."

What was he playing at? "Go on."

"What Mirza has given us seems to be a map of sorts, showing the message routing and communications protocols between London and his clients and lackeys. We can't get at message content, but we have started identifying who he's talking to and when."

But to do what? This can't be just some dirt he's dug up on someone using Providence and he'll want to top the hijacking from two years ago. Since then, all he's been doing is hunting down people he thinks have betrayed him and helping smugglers avoid arrest. "Who've you identified?"

"A number of Chinese gangsters, people in thrall to gangs, various people in Chinese industries. Several who work on their global navigation system."

Ericka nibbled her lip as she stared out the window while they slowed to pass through the base's gate. He liked to do a proof of concept on a small scale first. That was worth looking at. "When he stole our drones and steered your fighters away, did you figure out how he did that?"

Yusef's brow knotted as if puzzled. "No, not with any certainty. He managed to get into the aircraft's navigation somehow, but we could find no evidence of the precise mechanism. Why?"

"Humor me. Can I have access to that data? Your aircraft use the BeiDou system, yes?"

He was frowning, pausing to choose his words. "Yes, we do, but those planes retain very little data and we found no sign of malware. Everything was working perfectly. What are you thinking?"

It was just a guess at this point. "He's been messing with AIS and various nav systems for some time. It will be something using that technology. It's worth another look. This could happen very fast. We don't want to just sit there watching it happen again."

"And?"

"He likes aircraft for the same reason jihadis do. A hijacking or a plane crash gets everyone's attention. The only shrink I trust thinks it's all about going out with the biggest bang he can. He may not care about surviving the aftermath. We need to expect he could be a lot more reckless."

Yusef toyed with his watch. "And he knows the forces arrayed against him. He will be moving quickly."

Hong Jun sat in fascinated horror as he watched it happen. None of this was his doing, which was likely the singular reason he wasn't in a cell. He'd never known how this Dantalion had gotten his code inside a self-contained network. All he'd been required to do was reactivate two user accounts for people who used to work there and modify the system's audit functions after each incident. The actual events were either done with someone else inside or this monster had gained the ability to reprogram parts of the system remotely. It was probably both. Hong choked down the wave of nausea, resisting the urge to look around the open work area lest it attract attention.

Almost all of the previous incidents looked like little more than assisting smugglers by fooling the navy into navigation errors, then manipulating AIS to hide the smuggler's vessels. All Hong had to do was ensure the security system didn't pick up the manipulation. This time looked very different. The area of coverage was farther out to sea and these looked like codes for military aircraft. He closed his eyes to contain the tears.

Yes, there was no way around it. One way or another this would be the last one. They would never stop searching until they found who did this. The loss of face for the country and party would beggar belief.

28

The Calm

Ericka looked up from her screen and out the window of her small, borrowed office. The uniformed analysts sat in rows like a classroom, all focused on their tasks, the ops room cavernous around them. It looked like an old, converted aircraft hangar. After two days, she found herself impressed by the analysts, both their abilities and dedication, each processing huge amounts of data. She stood to walk between them before making her way to Yusef's office to conference with the American teams. As she emerged, ceiling fans running full speed ruffled her hair, a welcome wave of cooler air washing over her. She strolled behind the rows of specialists, stopping to look over shoulders, offering words of encouragement. At first, they had seemed surprised, apparently more used to their organization's rigid military hierarchy.

Ericka dropped into the chair across from Yusef's desk. Now, several hours after sunset the air conditioning was finally catching up. Her clothes stuck to her and she drank constantly from her bottle. He turned his screen to face her, clicking on the conferencing system. Voices coming from the speakers had the metallic sound that signaled encryption, but clear enough she could distinguish between Clarke from the FBI, Maxwell from Homeland and Kumara from the NSA. Yusef hunched over his desk staring at his notepad, as if trying to force himself to focus. The officers' barracks they were using offered fleeting naps more than true rest. Ericka found she had to will herself past fatigue.

The pitch of Clarke's voice betrayed her frustration. "Our data's all over the place. I've put together what we have so far, but there's got to be more to it. He's definitely in China somewhere, in the west probably. We have a series of transmissions between our target, two known gang leaders, one or more people inside administration related to the BeiDou system. We can't get any sort of content yet and have no prospect of cracking them any time soon. Plenty of transmission data between these gang guys, and any number of other Chinese nationals. The lower we go down the totem pole the more likely we are to get content, but he's supplied the people he cares about with his best encryption."

For Yusef's sake Ericka spoke to make it clear what she'd told her colleagues. "What I need now is everyone to scour whatever retained communications we have between these people from other investigations, flunky to flunky, all databases, geofence it for China, then go through what's left for the last year to see if there's any indication of what's to come. Less focus on trying to break into the current stuff. Look for evidence of early planning. We have a large, dedicated team here to do the legwork so we can handle the volume."

Kumara's voice sounded hesitant. "We've provided what we have but we've had to edit and scrub to protect how we obtained them."

Ericka shifted her weight to lean into the screen. *Say it to be sure.* "Anything new from Five Eyes?"

Kumara's voice rose in pitch. "Nothing. We're not holding anything back. You have everything we have."

Maxwell piped in. "We've done the same with intelligence partners. You're getting a lot of low-level gangster stuff, but we've no way to filter for relevant content other than go through it manually."

Ericka fancied she could see Clarke's scowl as her erstwhile protégée spoke. "We got some of these same Chinese gang members during the Anom bust. Everything in the clear, but it's mostly drugs and smuggling."

Ericka stared out the window at the darkened base, toying with her bottle as she thought. Anom was an FBI sting where they'd convinced hundreds in the criminal underworld to buy into a supposedly police-proof communications system that the FBI themselves controlled and sold, ending up with millions of intercepted messages between them.

She could tell from Yusef's expression that he was about to stir the pot again. His tone was firm. "Is it time to share this with the Chinese? They may well know who's who in this."

Ericka's stare was fixed as she shook her head. "We've been through this. We've no idea how far he's penetrated the Chinese services. Any direct contact will tip him off."

The tension in Kumara's voice made her words sound like a bark. "To say nothing of tipping off our adversary about our capabilities. That was our agreement."

Seeing Yusef's frown, Ericka cut him off before he could speak. "Yes, no one's handing them anything at this point. If we find the Chinese are about to be hit, we'll tell them. No contact except a warning. Yes?" Yusef looked away. After a period of silence, she spoke again. "Send us the next block of data when you have it. We're about two-thirds of the way through the last one. Anything else?" No one answered. "Talk again tomorrow then. 'Til then." She closed the window and leaned back in her chair, eyeing Yusef.

Yusef lifted his teapot, brows raised in inquiry. She smiled while he poured, wondering which of the many kinds in his tea chest this one was. As she reached for her cup, one of the lead analysts knocked on the doorjamb as he stood outside.

Yusef glanced up at him. "Yes?"

Rail-thin, no more than thirty, his eyes red with exhaustion, he looked nervous as he spoke. "One of the analysts has found something she would like you to see."

Ericka answered. "Something happening?"

The man glanced at Yusef before answering. "Yes, there seems to be increased traffic between some of the primary targets, but nothing we can read. What Lieutenant Mak has is related to past gang activity. As you requested."

Ericka gulped her tea, gasping as the scalding brew went down. "Let's see what she's got."

Mak stood in the doorway for a moment before Yusef gestured her to the seat next to Ericka. She was petite, large eyes darting between them, jet-black hair tied tight behind her head. Yusef looked at Ericka as he spoke. "Lieutenant Mak is part of our foreign intelligence directorate, formerly of the Shanghai police where she worked in digital intelligence with the gang unit. English please, Lieutenant. What have you found?"

Mak's delicate fingers played over her keyboard. When she was ready, she looked up, sitting erect, speaking in flawless but accented English. "Thank you, sir. What I have found is nothing related to our main target, but upper members of several gangs communicating and planning together."

"And why is that of interest to us now? Don't these gangs normally cooperate?"

Mak shook her head. "No, usually, they try to knife each other any chance they get. They also seem to be in communication with people in the Communist Party though we don't have content, just transmission data. Communication with party officials is not unusual either, but in the context of what the gang members are saying is very odd. These are gangs Dantalion has associated with in the past, done work for them."

Ericka turned her chair to face Mak. "Do we have any message content at the gang member level?"

"We do, much of it received in the first block of data from your government. They are discussing dividing up business for various kinds of crimes in new territory."

Yusef shook his head. "That hardly sounds like news."

Mak turned back to face him. "In Taiwan."

"Yes, and?"

"None of these gangs operate in Taiwan. The island has its own gangs."

Ericka felt the beginnings of a tickle in her guts. "Any time soon?"

Mak looked at Yusef. "Yes, that's what got my attention. They are talking like it's about to happen soon. And about which government officials they'll have to pay. Officials in the Communist Party, the mainland government."

Yusef's brow was knotted, his smile puzzled. "No invasion is imminent. Sorry I'm not following you?"

Mak shook her head. "No, all that is happening now is

the usual aerial incursions into Taiwan's air defense zone. They've been doing that all week."

Is that what he's up to? Ericka could feel the hairs rise on the back of her neck. "Anything from Dantalion at the same time?"

"Yes, there is traffic before and after with several of them we believe is his, but no idea about content."

Ericka squeezed her eyes shut, her heart starting to race. "Yusef, the night the American drones were stolen, your planes were using BeiDou for navigation, correct?"

"Yes."

"And your phones showed your correct position, while your plane's nav system was way off, almost steering you clear of your targets, correct?"

"Correct."

Mak was shaking her head. "I'm sorry?"

Ericka gasped, sweat trickling down her back, tripping over herself to get the words out. The BeiDou system was different from the western GPS systems and GLONASS in that it was two-way and could, if properly equipped, identify the device using the system. She continued talking over their questions. "What if he's inside the BeiDou system and can select areas of the world or even individual devices and feed them an error?"

Mak shrugged. "He appears to have been doing something like that to help clients smuggle for some time. I—oh!" Her eyes were wide.

Yusef's eyes narrowed as he frowned. "What does that give him?"

Ericka held up her wrist displaying her Garmin watch. "Think it through! GPS is passive, BeiDou can do more. It can receive the location of the device using it, convey messages. He can tell where his targets are and steer them in real time!"

Yusef was looking down, shaking his head. "That's how he steered our fighters without leaving a data trail."

That's it. Got you, you bastard! His big event. "Precisely! If he gets the Chinese air force to fly over Taiwan, it could start a war, one the People's Republic will never let themselves lose. I think the comms you found are the gangs planning the aftermath, their reward for setting this up, hiring him to do the work."

Yusef was gulping for air. "It's no secret some parts of the Chinese government think Taiwan should be retaken now. If this triggers the war they want, they are in a position to reap the spoils. If it fails, it will be a terrorist act, the last triumph of a known cyber-terrorist."

Ericka took several deep breaths before answering. "Which means they will try to kill our target either way."

Yusef's gaze held Ericka's. "Now it is time to warn them. No need to violate our agreement with your government. The Chinese don't need to know how we did it."

"I'll let my superiors know."

Mak spoke as Ericka was dialing. "We're too late." She turned her screen so they could see the alert. It was in Urdu. Seeing Ericka shake her head, Mak translated. "Possible Chinese attack on Taiwan under way. Military aircraft over Kaohsiung. Taiwanese Air Force and ground batteries engaging."

Major Yeung Feng of the People's Liberation Army Air Force stared out the cockpit of his J-11 fighter, scanning below, trying to see a hole through thick clouds blanketing the sea. The aircraft was an improved version of an older Russian design, not a newer stealthy type. They wanted to be seen. That was the point. This was their territory and they could fly here whenever they liked, Americans be damned. Behind him in loose combat formation, flew twenty-two identical fighters, escorting ten H-6 bombers, the fourth such mission this week.

Yeung scanned the horizon behind, thrilled to see the gleaming warbirds reflecting low morning sun as dawn broke. He scanned his navigation screen. Seven more minutes to the edge of the breakaway republic's air defense interception zone and no sign yet of their adversaries. Any minute now he expected to see the American-made F-16 fighters appear on radar, but today for some reason they were keeping their distance.

Puzzling, there must be substantial headwind at this altitude. By his watch, they should have reached the point where they would turn around minutes ago, but satellite navigation still had them some distance away. His threat assessment alarm went off, they were being tracked on a targeting radar. *There they were, just late to the party today.*

Yeung turned to glance at one of the bombers flying below and to his left, keying his mic to give the order to turn for home. His words turned to a gasp as the lumbering aircraft's right engine exploded, sending the fuselage spinning to the left and leaving a black smoke trail arching down before disappearing into the clouds. A second alarm in his headset gave him an icy stab in the guts followed by gentle vibration as his aircraft deployed flares designed to divert heat-seeking missiles.

His years of training kicked in. He hauled the fighter into

a tight right-hand turn, his G-suit tightening around him like a snake's coils preventing blackout, a missile's smoke trail flashing by tens of meters away.

Gasping to force air into his lungs against the Gs, Yeung craned his neck to look above and behind just in time to see his wingman turn into a fireball as another missile found its mark and detonated. Behind him, skimming just over the clouds were three Taiwanese fighters, the gaping shark mouths of their air intakes unmistakable even at a distance. He drew a deep breath, then squeezed the mic button to make the call. "Return fire and regroup. Head home and protect the bombers." Switching frequencies, he squeezed again to call base. "Under attack, several losses. We are returning fire and regrouping to return to base."

The reply was almost inaudible. "Acknowledged. Turn towards naval units for cover. You've drifted..."

Static smothered the rest of his commander's words as Yeung had to turn again, this time to avoid cannon fire from a trailing F-16. *They really did want a war. All right, Tom Cruise, let's see what that American antique can do!* He inverted his fighter, hauling back on the stick to dive towards the ground, dropping into the clouds, the world outside smothering gray as rain drummed on his canopy. Righting his aircraft, Yeung pulled out of the dive, hoping proximity with the surface would create enough radar clutter to avoid a missile lock. He started a tight left turn to rejoin his group when he dropped out of the clouds, expecting to see the open waters of the Taiwan Strait. He gasped, eyes bugged wide, his last-minute turn avoiding the skyscraper by less than a wingspan, leaving him banked at ninety degrees above streets clogged with traffic.

How? This looked like Kaohsiung! They should be tens of kilometers from here. Yeung banked to the west, out towards the open ocean visible to his right. No wonder they were shooting at them. Why hadn't someone warned him? The navy in the strait must have seen them overshoot. *Did they think we had orders to attack? Were their comms working?*

He regretted the momentary distraction. His fighter shook like a rat in the mouth of a terrier as cannon shells ripped open his left wing, setting the fuel ablaze. *Just waiting for me to get over the water.* Yeung yanked the ejection handle, buffeted first by rushing air as the canopy disappeared, then squashed down by a giant hand as the ejection seat's rocket fired, his vision going dark. It was the tug of the opening chute that brought him back, tasting blood, unable to breathe through his nose. Jolting pain stabbed his neck as he looked up to confirm his chute had deployed. A Taiwanese F-16 flashed by close enough he could see the pilot peering at him. *Qù nǐ made!*

Looking down between his feet, the wind's wave patterns made it clear he was going to land well away from shore. Better he drowned here than live on as the idiot who started a war with nothing more than his own stupidity.

29

The Storm

"You need to contact someone way high up in the state department right now! Maybe the secretary of state." Ericka's eyes were squeezed shut, her forehead in her hand as she leaned over her mobile. No one on the other end was speaking first, Shingen, O'Brien, Kumara and the head of the NSA, General Yamashita, all paused for thought or were struck dumb. *There's no time!*

"Yamashita here. You have to be absolutely sure and be ready to produce the data. Coming from us, the Chinese aren't going to want to believe it. They're going to think we're trying to stall them so we can get assets in theater to assist Taiwan."

Ericka had anticipated this, gritting her teeth at the thought of how little hard evidence she had. "We don't have anything direct. Everything's circumstantial. All we can show them is he's been manipulating their navigation systems and that he's communicating with Chinese nationals, gangsters, BeiDou tech people and some lower-level party functionaries."

"O'Brien here. By now the Chinese will know their planes

actually did end up over Taiwan. They know they didn't order it. It may not be that big a leap to get them to buy it." *Thank you, O'Brien!*

Kumara interjected before Ericka could respond. "They may not be willing to be seen to lose this, even if they do realize it was their fault. They will want to win the fight however it got started."

Ericka raised her voice to cut in before anyone else could speak. "That's exactly why they need to hear this before it goes far enough it gains a life of its own."

"Yamashita. Agreed. What are the Pakistanis doing? The Chinese may listen to an ally."

Okay, they're listening, they get it. "The same thing we are. Working up the food chain far enough to find someone the Chinese will listen to. They concur with the analysis."

Someone else tried to speak, but Yamashita cut them off. "Okay, decision made, I'm on it. I'll need a full intelligence package with all you have. When can I have it?"

Ericka hadn't realized she'd been holding her breath and her words exploded out. "Already done and waiting to transfer."

The first part had gone as planned. Now whether this became a war or just a nasty incident was up to various national leaders, each with their own agenda, like writing a book and getting someone else to write the ending. His hands shook, adrenaline surging through him. Again, he had done what no one else could, what nobody had come close to. Ignoring the pain in his back he stood, eyes never leaving the array of screens projected inside his headset. The next stage was critical. By now they should have some idea of what he'd done, but the question was, could they correct it in time?

He glanced at the time, wiping the tickling sweat from his forehead. He'd have to move soon. The Chinese state-sponsored hackers and intel people were no fools, and he'd likely made himself visible to others. The active control he'd used this time had left a trail, thirty more minutes and he would cross over the western border through Nepal and on to his next haven. *Probably his last, but that didn't matter anymore. When one's end is certain, what else to do but make the best of it?*

Time for the last reprograming. It would be triggered from another location, but he would confirm it from here, another set of errors in the BeiDou system. By then, they would know someone had corrupted it, but it would take time for them to fix. They would know their satellite guidance was unreliable. Knowing the problem didn't change the fact that the Chinese military needed it working to deploy some of their most advanced weapons. If they fired them now, they had no idea where they'd go. If Taiwan or their allies fired first, they were sitting ducks and they knew it. If the Chinese navy moved closer to Taiwan so they could be ready with less advanced weapons not needing satellite nav, Taiwan would perceive a further threat and would fire first. Interesting choices for everyone. *A Mexican standoff in the Taiwan Strait.*

I expect you've figured it out by now, Ericka, but what are you going to do about it? How's that for a legacy? Worthy of your contempt now, Claire? Closing his eyes, he released the searing rage, letting the rushing wave crash over him like the narcotic it had become, certain knowledge of pain and fear in others was the only way to feed his own hunger, sate a need gnawing inside him for as long as he could remember. When it passed, his shoulders sagged and he sat, almost weak, hands trembling.

The die was cast and it was time to go. He set his equipment to encrypt, trusting his associates to carry out the further step of burning everything. It didn't matter now, but he had a reputation to uphold, leave no trace, no clue how he'd done it. That and the gangs in charge of incineration had more to lose from his data coming to light than he did. *And, Ericka, there is just a chance you do have Bromwich and that means we have unfinished business. I don't think you do, but without knowing how you fooled Providence, I can't take that chance. I hope you get this in time.*

"Did you send it?" Ericka flopped into a chair in Yusef's office, her chest tight as she stared at him. She clutched at her laptop, not sure how much she would share, not quite believing what she'd seen. She pushed the door shut with her foot. There were fewer analysts on the floor; many were sleeping for the first time in days.

Yusef's skin was pallid, eyes red with fatigue. "My government has sent it to the Chinese government and we have sent it directly to our contacts in the Chinese military. They already had the same package from your government. From the sound of it, I'm not sure it will make much difference. I don't understand the thinking."

"It makes perfect sense." His eyes locked on hers, his head tilting, waiting for her to speak. "Plenty of them have wanted this war for some time. They may not have started this, but there's going to be plenty of them happy to take the windfall and run with it. And it doesn't matter how it got lit, some kinds of fires are really hard to put out."

The corners of his mouth ticked up into a wry smile. "Classic Dantalion. Hack the minds, not just the machines. He knew if he could get it started, neither side will want to finish it if they think they will look like the loser."

Ericka gripped her computer, biting her lower lip. "Dantalion now, is it? From his perspective, it's another colossal win. He's reached out of cyberspace and got two nations shooting at each other for nothing. It's based on the principles he's worked all along. Look for the flaws in the people. There was a time when it was possible for people to hide their deviancy and their sins. Now we create so much data every day, someone can always find out what everyone else has been up to. Dantalion collects sins for compulsion and augments blackmail by knowing what to offer his targets to bring out the very worst. Suddenly he's got disciples. He's succeeded at least as much from his psychopathy as he has his technical genius. This hit shows just how spectacularly well it's worked."

Yusef gestured with his chin at his computer. "One thing that we sent they've used already. They think they've managed to track him."

Bullshit! They couldn't really track him or they'd have him now. Ericka's hands slid on her computer leaving a damp trail, as if clutching it tight made the precious contents more secure. It was going to be an awkward conversation when it came, but not quite the time yet. "Do we know what's happening in the Taiwan Strait?"

"Last we heard, there had been a few more aerial skirmishes with losses to both sides and the Chinese were moving several squadrons of missile cruisers into range of the island. Our intelligence group says they are going to have to get quite close to degrade Taiwan's air defense network. The Chinese can't trust their own guidance system so they are trying to reprogram their weapons to use GLONASS. I expect they don't trust your government not to introduce an error into GPS. Your country's navy is also moving into the strait. Our people theorize they intend to act as a buffer, but the Chinese think they may be moving to support Taiwan. This could go either way."

Ericka relaxed her grip on her machine. Now was not the time, but it would come soon. She stared at the tiled floor, controlling her breathing to maintain focus, ignoring the nausea that welled up as she inched towards the precipice of self-control. She felt the brooding eyes of all her dead, knew what they expected, true redemption the only way to silence them. *Not much longer now.* When Ericka looked up, Yusef was studying her and she answered his unspoken question. *Yes, I am on the verge of exploding, but I won't.* Nothing to dull her focus, no split agenda, she would get it done this time.

Rear Admiral Xú Donghai of the People's Liberation Army Navy lowered his binoculars as the last debris from the Taiwanese F-16 tumbled into the sea, leaving a trail of black smoke, the impact producing a puff of steam and spray no bigger than a whale's spout. No parachute. He had listened as the signals officer warned the fighters off and had himself given the order to launch missiles, bringing three fighters down, forcing the remaining two to dive towards churning seas, skimming the surface, heading for home. Ordering death was the focus of his job, but never something to be done lightly.

Glancing around the bridge of his flagship, a Type-55, Renhai-class destroyer, he took a moment to gather himself before studying his task force's deployment. The screen showed the collection of twenty-three destroyers and frigates maintaining correct combat spacing as they made a slow fifteen knots down the strait. The rough seas and lowering clouds gave the water a treacherous look. Four submerged submarines moved to cover the north and south of the main island should the Americans seek to move significant assets into the strait. His task would require a very delicate touch. For now, the Taiwanese navy was staying out of range, letting the air force shoulder the load.

Glancing at the vessel's captain, Lín, he tugged on an overcoat, then shoved the hatch open to step onto the outer deck. Xú needed to clear his head and think without having to school his features against the crew and the inevitable political officer tasked with watching him. Long experience gave him perfect balance against the rolling deck as he strode to the railing. The ship's bow sliced through gale-driven waves, throwing up a constant mist of seawater that he could taste when he licked his lips, the steel railing cold in his hand. He steadied himself to scan with binoculars. The nearest two of his ships were clear but the farther ones were indistinct ghosts, dark gray silhouettes on wind-whipped cobalt.

Out there somewhere in the gloom were three American Arleigh Burke-class destroyers cruising a few miles offshore of Taiwan, their targeting radars off, their intentions unknown. They weren't hiding though. All three were broadcasting

AIS, something inconceivable for military ships with hostile intent. *They want us to know they are there and that they're American.* Some of his superiors feared the ships were simply the vanguard of the American navy coming to Taiwan Province's aid, but they weren't acting like it. *More likely they were hoping their presence would prevent escalation. Time would tell who was right.*

While it was now clear to all in his government that this conflict had been precipitated by error, they would not allow it to end with a military defeat or a further assertion of independence by the island province. The loss of face from either result would be attributed to him now. Xú had known it the second he'd read his vague orders. He was to reassert his country's right of navigation. If attacked, he was expected to win. The great fear of the Chinese admiralty was that their new weapons would be shown to be ineffective against American technology, resulting in a reduced ability to dominate China's coastal waters. Best if the contest never happened, but his hands were tied. Sun Tzu would agree. He was to order a squadron of ships to steam for the line marking the edge of the Province's claimed territorial waters and cruise along the boundary, daring attack. A gust of wind brought rain, stinging his face. With a final glance to the horizon, then the sky, Xú pulled the hatch open and stepped in. He would lead from the front and command the squadron himself.

Rear Admiral Rashaad Coleman, United States Navy, stood behind the weapons officer, gripping her chair as a large wave made the ship pitch. She turned to look at him, shaking her head. Smiling his thanks, he walked the rolling deck to the bridge's front windows where the wipers were not keeping up with rain and spray, standing next to the deck officer. Commanding from the USS *Howard*, he could just make out the other two ships of his tiny squadron, cruising ahead of him, running line astern. His flag, the *Milius* and the *Benfold*, were all Arleigh Burke-class destroyers out of Japan, America's best but they were outnumbered by China's latest but untested ships.

"Sir!" One of the comms officers lifted his hand over his equipment.

Coleman turned to look. "Go!"

"The two surviving F-16s just landed. They're reporting no survivors from the other three."

"Thank you." Even if they'd ejected, they wouldn't have lasted ten minutes in these waters. His heart thumped against the inside of his chest, reminding him he'd forgotten his blood pressure pills. No one ever said this was a stress-free job but the last few days had been something. A regular patrol with light stores of armaments on board had become a very different operation when China and Taiwan had started shooting down each other's planes, followed by a hastily assembled armada of missile boats appearing in the Taiwan Strait.

His orders didn't help. *Remain on station in the Taiwan Strait taking all necessary steps to deter hostilities. Initiating incident was the result of a cyber-terrorist attack on People's Republic navigation systems. At this time, weapons authorized against Chinese naval assets only if fired upon, not in defense of Taiwan armed forces.*

Coleman had discussed the orders with his captains. "Not sure what the hell this means? Are we supposed to do a goddamned song and dance routine to distract them?" Since then, he'd ordered the ships to load weapons but keep their targeting radars switched off to avoid the Chinese thinking they were about to get shot at. Until Fleet Command gave him a better idea what they wanted, he intended to cruise up and down near the Taiwan coast, just outside their waters, trying to look determined but unthreatening.

"Sir, incoming message from Taiwanese coastal units. Their long-range radar indicates seven Chinese vessels have broken off from the larger group and are heading directly for us."

Here we go! Coleman concentrated on his tone, forceful and calm, no quaver. "Thank you. Sound general quarters please." The high-pitched whistle sounded over the intercom, preceding the announcement signaling all sailors to move to battle-ready positions, but not yet indicating imminent combat. He watched as the bridge crew tugged on body armor, noting the furtive looks his people exchanged. *Well, they might. This could well be a short and miserable experience.*

Yamashita sounded as calm as if he were discussing gardening, even as his voice was distorted by encryption. "Anything else we can offer?"

Ericka shook her head as she spoke before remembering he couldn't see her. "There's no more evidence we can send. If they still don't believe he got inside their system, it's because they don't want to accept it. The evidence is clear and compelling."

Yamashita paused and she wondered for a moment if the connection had dropped. His voice was hesitant when he spoke. "I agree, but we need to give them everything we possibly can. We appear to be heading towards a naval engagement with the Chinese navy with very few assets in range."

Damn! The only thing left was the crash but that was more of a good guess than anything else. Ericka ground her teeth, finding it impossible to sit still. "We didn't put it in the first package because we weren't sure when we compiled it. Hell, we're still not sure. The crash a few weeks ago that killed those party officials near the Tibetan border was likely a Dantalion hit. If they can audit BeiDou records for that time, it may give them some confirmation, but we have no direct evidence, no data to offer them."

Before Yamashita could respond, Yusef cut in. "I don't expect any of this will make any difference. They know what happened already, whatever they are acknowledging publicly. Our attaché reports they are already arresting the people we identified for them."

Yamashita sounded resigned. "That's what the state department thinks too. All we can do is wait and hope they take the off-ramp we've given them."

Coleman sat in the captain's chair facing sideways along the bridge when the call came from the weapons station. "Taiwan's shore batteries appear to be readying to fire."

Before he could respond, the communications officer spoke. "They are signaling us they believe an attack on us is imminent. They will fire if we are fired upon."

This could spiral very rapidly. Coleman ran through his options, enamored of none of them. "Please forward my request that they do not fire on our behalf. We are not in danger and can defend ourselves." He turned to the surface weapons officer. "SWO, confirm?"

The officer leaned into her screen, pausing before she answered. "Confirm. No evidence the Chinese ships are readying surface weapons. They appear to be running active air defense radars and point defense. They are on an intercept course, but there's no indication they intend to attack. Recommend battle stations and go hot on the air defense systems. AWACS says, there are some aircraft near the Chinese coast." These larger American aircraft carried powerful radars and loitered outside of combat zones.

"Any chance they're missiles?"

She squinted at her screen for several excruciating moments, shaking her head as she began to speak. "Negative. Definitely not YJ-18s, much larger, profile's all wrong for missiles."

Coleman scowled in thought. The Chinese probably weren't going to see his powering up their air defense systems as a threat. "Tell all ships to go to battle stations, defensive weapons only." Leaving themselves without the ability to counterattack was definitely not according to the manual, but there was nothing normal about this.

Xú lowered his binoculars, continuing to stare ahead. It wasn't as if using them allowed him to pierce the uniform wall of gray ahead, but it was better than sitting and fidgeting while he thought things through. They were abeam the waves now, causing the ships to roll while an occasional larger wave boomed on the hull like a kettle drum, accompanied by the sound of rattling equipment, standing crew members shifting for balance. A glance around the bridge showed him set jaws and eyes fixed on the task. They were an untested service using equipment that had never seen combat. Today could tell the tale.

As Sun Tzu had written so many centuries ago: 'Success in warfare is gained by carefully accommodating ourselves to the enemy's purpose.' The real adversary here was the American navy. So long as he did not provoke them into firing on him, he could carry out his mission without losing a ship. The Americans themselves were fond of establishing freedom of navigation in contested waters by cruising their warships through it. They were not going to shoot at him for doing the same, or let their lackeys, the Taiwanese, interfere with him. All he had to do was restore face for his political masters, prove they had neither lost nor given anything up and they were back to the previous uneasy stalemate, awaiting the right time.

Xú raised his voice to issue his orders. "All ships are ordered to come twenty-five degrees to port to intercept the boundary without crossing it. Verify all positions using alternate navigational means." He waited for acknowledgment, feeling the ship lurch as it turned, waves now quartering on the port bow, a much smoother ride from here on in. He heard the threat-assessment alarm before this weapons officer spoke. He stood and turned towards the station, brows raised in inquiry. "The Americans?"

"No, sir. We are being targeted by shore batteries on Taiwan. Likely Hsiung Feng III by the radar profile—the American ships appear to be maintaining a defensive posture."

Xú shook his head, glaring at the screen showing the US ships. *Control your dogs or we are both going to suffer!* No help for it. If they wanted a war, he would have to oblige them. "Power up offensive weapons and target the Taiwanese shore batteries and known military assets!"

Coleman's knew his mouth was hanging open as he listened to his stations report in. *What kind of fucking stupid was behind this decision?* "How many?"

His SWO was shaking her head, her expression aghast. "Tracking twelve missiles outbound. Hsiung Feng IIIs, all heading for the approaching Chinese squadron. They'll pass over us. The Chinese navy are powering up weapons, dispersing into offensive posture."

No, not on my watch. They can have my commission later if they want it. These kids are not going to die in a swinging dick contest between foreign countries squabbling over something that happened before any of them were born. "Order all ships to track those missiles and shoot them down!"

"Sir?"

"You heard the order."

The deck officer's expression was tense, visibly weighing his words. "Sir, are you confident that command is within our orders?"

Good call kid, but this isn't really a war, it's the fallout from a terrorist incident, that's how we have to deal with it. "I am, or I wouldn't have given it. We're not going to discuss it. In case I'm wrong, the consequences will fall on me alone. We're not going to kill anyone on either side, just do what we can to stop them doing it." Coleman waited for any further challenges to his order. "Now, please!"

"Aye, sir." The SWO leaned into her console, coordinating with the other ships.

On the deck outside, missile launchers pivoted into ready posture. Coleman turned to the comms station. "I'm going to need to talk to Fleet right away."

Familiar vibrations shook the deck milliseconds after the roar of launching missiles announced his order had been carried out. Coleman leaned near the window, peering out just in time to see several of the weapons blast from their launchers, disappearing almost instantly into low clouds, thick columns of smoke dissipating in the wind.

Xu's head snapped up, not believing what he'd just heard. "Say again, please!"

The weapons officer's attention remained focused on his screen. "All three American ships have launched missiles."

He might have miscalculated. His heart raced, making his breathing quick and shallow. "How long until impact?" They'd never be able to survive a combined onslaught from Taiwan and the American ships.

The officer's mouth dropped open, hesitating while squinting at his screen. "They're not shooting at us. I think they've launched at the Taiwanese missiles." Xú held his breath for a few more seconds while he waited for his officer to speak. "Yes, confirmed. They're shooting them down."

Xú was careful not to show any emotion to the bridge crew. *A bold move, my American friend, whoever you are, but the right one. An American who could play Go rather than chess. How unusual.* "Stand by on defensive systems. Some will get through."

★ ★ ★

Coleman stood behind his SWO. "Outstanding work!" The officer's screens showed several successful intercept tracks from all three American ships.

She looked perplexed. "One got through, but the Chinese point defense systems nailed it. It was really close."

"Admiral, Fleet for you!"

Coleman sighed. Time to pay the piper. He clapped his SWO on the back as he walked away. "In my ready room, please. Any more launches from Taiwan, bring them down. Any change in posture from the Chinese ships, you know where to find me."

30

Calling Card

Ericka had a moment of wondering where she was before the disorientation cleared enough for her to hear the knocking. As soon as it was clear the shooting was over, she'd closed her eyes for a nap, plunging into a deep sleep. Several times in the night her messaging system had woken her. She pivoted her feet onto the floor, looking up to see Yusef standing in the doorway, staring at her. Smiling at him, she pulled her boots from under the cot, tugging them on before speaking. "Sorry, how long was I out?"

He smiled. "Seven hours. Don't apologize. I was asleep too, but there is news."

"Yes?"

"They didn't get him. The word from the Chinese is they missed him by hours. They are rounding up everyone remotely connected to this, but once again the serpent has eluded everyone. There will be show trials aplenty, but they will be very glad to be able to blame this on an absent foreign terrorist. The military engagement appears to have ended where it must. All forces have disengaged."

Ericka glanced at her laptop, which lay on a table just out of arm's reach. She could see the message light blinking. If Clarke had what she suspected, then this was finally over. *Going to need some time to be sure.* "Give me a few minutes to clean up and I'll meet you in your office. There's something we need to speak about. Yes, thanks for coffee." He raised one brow, smiling as he left. She tugged the computer onto her lap, nibbling her lip as she read. No question what it was. The endgame was here.

Yusef looked up as she walked in, his eyes studying her. He knew something was up, but she doubted he knew what was coming. He waited while she got settled, pouring her more coffee then pushing the cup to the edge of his desk. Ericka clutched the laptop on her knees, planning how to say this so it wasn't misinterpreted. Straight up was the only way. No compromising this with her own interests like she had the last time. "I'm sure I can figure out exactly where he is now."

Yusef spat a mouthful of coffee, setting off a prolonged coughing fit. "You did that on purpose!"

"I didn't but if I'd thought of it, I would've."

Yusef had several gulps from his cup before continuing. "Why are you keeping me in suspense?"

Careful, this can't sound like a bargain, or worse, blackmail. Her mouth felt dry, forcing the words out. "I need to ask for a favor."

His eyes narrowed and he sat forward, posture more erect. "And is one tied to the other?"

Ericka leaned in, elbows on his desk. "Not at all. I only mention it as I want you to take the time to consider what I ask before acting on the location."

"So, no strings?"

"None at all. Let me tell you to clear the air before we go further. He's here in Pakistan. In the tribal areas. I can nail it down any time."

Yusef flushed, eyes watering as he struggled with control. "How long have you known? Are you talking to him?"

He was wondering if she'd been holding out on him. Time to defuse this. "Just now, since I woke up. A few days ago, he sent me a message through the FBI, to one of my old dark-web handles, purportedly something he wanted me to pass on to his former wife. That was bullshit. It was a pretense to send me a message. With all that was going on, no one looked, much less spun it down. Once they found it, my people sent me bits throughout the night. Combined with what we had from Mirza it won't even be difficult."

Yusef's stare remained hard. "Why has he suddenly become so careless?"

"Surely, it's obvious. He isn't ever careless. He knew it would be enough that I could find him quickly. It's an invitation."

Yusef squinted, clearly not believing her. "Tell me how you know this?"

"The content of the message threatened to kill someone who's been dead a long time, someone we were at pains to bring back to life."

Yusef shook his head as he spoke. "He wants to bargain?"

He just wasn't seeing it. "I suspect he knows I faked his enemy's re-emergence. It's his way of telling me he's aware of what I did." Ericka paused, but Yusef didn't respond. "It's an invitation to me to find him."

"For what?"

"I don't know what he wants."

"And the favor?"

"You know what it is. Before you kill him, take me close, give me time. He's not going anywhere. He's run out of places to hide."

Yusef looked at his hands as he toyed with a pen, his expression softened. He looked relieved. "You want to kill him yourself."

"No, I really don't. Your forces can do that."

He looked puzzled as he stared at her. "Do you have any idea what it is like up there? I'm sure we can get you in, but you're never coming out again. Sorry, a western woman alone, an FBI agent would be a prize of great value to them."

"I have no idea what it's like up there or why he's there. I don't care. I have no idea what these tribal chieftains see in him. He hardly presents as one of the faithful."

Yusef snorted his contempt. "They are not devout themselves. They playact at it when it suits their purpose, but they are whores for gold. As long as he pays them, they will protect him, the faith's teachings be damned."

Ericka was not surprised. "Will you do it?"

"You're avoiding my question. Why?"

She couldn't do this without his help, she'd have to tell him and hope for the best. "I have done things, terrible things I can't forget. You, of course, are familiar with the western concept of redemption? Of atonement? I need the answer to a question and only he can answer it for me. With him dead, I'll never know."

"A question about what?"

"About me."

"I don't understand. You are not a Christian woman. Why

do you need to seek forgiveness from a god you don't believe in?"

Ericka stared into his eyes for a few moments. He was a remarkable man, constantly surprising her. "I need to forgive myself."

"I'm not compromising our ability to kill him."

Ericka's vision blurred as tears flooded her eyes. "I'm not asking you to. If they need to take the shot to get him, forget I'm there. Do what must be done."

Yusef's eyes began to brim as he answered. "There will be no warning. Once you give us the coordinates, permission and orders will take a few hours at the most. We have drones from the Chinese now. I expect he and anyone near him will end in a rain of missiles. You won't even hear them coming."

She squeezed her eyes shut. "He will end as he should. Do you really not understand? Isn't there an equivalent in Islam? *Tawba*?"

He smiled, shaking his head. "I think you misunderstand the concept. In Islam, *Tawba* is about remorse and repentance, sometimes restitution. It is not an excuse to commit more sins by taking revenge under a façade of restoring balance."

It was Yusef's great talent that he could see right into people. "As you say, I am not a believer."

"No, an adherent to stoicism, you once told me."

Ericka spoke slowly for emphasis. "I'm not going to kill him, but I may die with him. I accept that. There's no other way back for me."

Yusef linked his fingers over his belt, staring out his office window, before leaning into his computer, typing for a moment. "I have read a little of your philosophy. Here is a quote from Seneca that has stuck with me from the moment I read it: 'There is no person so severely punished, as those who subject themselves to the whip of their own remorse.' Yes?"

The familiar black pitch bubbled up. She thought it exorcised, but here it was again. Ericka gulped a few breaths, forcing it back down. *Deal with that later if there is a later.* "Yes. Will you do it?"

Yusef was several minutes staring at his desktop, silent, eyes unblinking. "As long as there is no compromise to our ability to eliminate him, then I will. May God go with you."

Ericka waited until the helicopter was gone, dust settling around her, no light but the waning moon and brilliant stars, so cold her breath misted in front of her. The sun would be up in two hours, and she had a way to go. Her GPS showed her at five-point-three kilometers from the cluster of buildings she'd identified, a number of small structures on a hillside, one larger surrounded by several smaller ones, likely no more than stone huts. The only intel available said it had once been used as a processing station for opium before its owners had been arrested or chased away, their crops burned. She scanned her surroundings for threats, holding her breath as she listened, heart pounding against her ribs.

As soon as the sun was up and the pilots could confirm their targets, they would fire without warning. The Chinese-made Wing Loong II drones had infrared capability but shooting into their own territory, the Pakistani military had to be sure. That gave her the window she needed.

The sky was clear, cold, and the altitude combined with them to make the stars brighter than she'd ever seen them. A good night to die if need be. With not enough light to see by, Ericka pulled on night-vision goggles, peering ahead in the eerie green light. As desolate as it looked, the area was hardly uninhabited. Her arrival in a Pakistani military helicopter would have been noted and she'd no doubt unseen eyes would soon be on her. She was less than ten kilometers from the Afghanistan border, such as it was. In this area both governments regarded it as all but ungovernable. The rocky path was clear enough, so she set out at a brisk walk, flinching at how well the sound of trodden rocks and gravel traveled. She would make it there if he sent people out to bring her in, presuming she was right about the invitation.

With three kilometers behind her, panting at the exertion, she sensed their presence before she saw them, shadows near stones that came to life, walking to block her way. Ericka tugged off the night vision and stood waiting. She spoke no Pashto so she had little choice but to wait and see what they had in mind. Her breathing was regular, her heart slowing now she was still. There was no chill, no goose bumps, nothing. She was cold inside, truly unafraid. She almost smiled, fully prepared for the end if that was what was to be. It was very liberating.

One man stood in the center of the path, his features dark under the traditional turban, eyes lost in dark pools cast by heavy brows. Heavily bearded, his mouth showed no expression as he regarded her. He said one word, distorted by his heavy accent, his tone making it a question. "Dantalion?"

Ericka nodded and he held out his hand, gesturing towards her pistol. She undid the belt and handed it to him, staring at him. Someone behind her pulled the night goggles from her head, pocketing them as she turned to glare. She fancied she saw a hint of a smile on the man's face. Two others approached her, hands outstretched to frisk her, the one to her right reaching for her breast. *Oh, that will be the fucking day!* She launched a lunging kick at his solar plexus, dropping him to the ground as he gasped for air, before pivoting to face the other in a fighting stance.

The rest of them seemed to find their colleague's plight very funny, laughing at him, pointing as he struggled to regain his feet, bent over, sucking for air through his teeth. The leader barked a command, his words clearly telling them to shut up. Discipline was restored though the man she'd planted gave her a sour look that spoke of future trouble.

As she approached the buildings, they were backlit by the glow of the coming sunrise, the first hint of light and color painting the sky as the stars retreated. On the roof of the largest building, silhouetted against the sky, a lone figure stood motionless, hunched, hands clasped in front of him, waiting. She stopped, looking up. *Here at last, finally it's over.* Ericka forced her jaw to unclench, relief flooding through her, making her almost giddy. The familiar voice was soft but clear. He said something in Pashto, gesturing to bring her up. Two ladders later she stood on the roof, hearing the men clambering back down behind her.

He stood near the small hutch, protection against wind and sun, piled full of blankets and cushions. In front a low table stood piled with several small laptops connected to a cluster of equipment and at least one satellite dish. It gave the impression of having been thrown together in great haste. She stopped to stare, hardly believing it, staring at the monster she'd chased for so long, forcing down the wave of rage, feeling the eyes of her dead fixed on her every move. Tall, gaunt, unarmed, still he radiated palpable menace. As Ericka stepped forward the thin wood sagged with her weight, creaking under her as she moved.

"Do be careful! My current accommodation is not up to my usual standards." He stood behind the table, staring without expression for several moments. *Sizing up the real me compared to the digital one he's known.* "You do really impress, Ericka. You understood the invitation, quickly used the scant data I gave you and came—" he gestured "—knowing how unlikely it is you will ever leave."

Keeping her voice calm and level was easier than she expected. "Who says I want to leave? I'm done chasing you. It's rather lost its challenge."

That drew a chuckle. "You needed a proper look at the one you could never beat, the one who always slipped out of reach. The one you were never going to best. That must really hurt the colossal ego. Don't deny it. It takes one to know one."

Ericka couldn't keep the sneer from curling her lips. "Spare me your bullshit! I got you. Blinded by Bromwich still alive. Try and deny it!"

His head hung as he smiled again; his admiration seemed genuine. "The data was flawless, I admit. Not the tiniest error. I was forever thinking how you'd done it. My facial-recognition scan fooled by a physical recreation was all I could think of. Astounding work, and yes Providence was completely fooled. Instead of using data to fool the physical, you altered the physical to manipulate the virtual. Your finest work, my dear."

She gritted her teeth, forcing her words through them. "How?" *Damn him!*

There was enough light to see the subtle smile, still dark

enough to conceal underlying expressions. "Same way you keep catching me out. You're too trusting of your own minions. Two years ago, before you first found me you exhumed Bromwich to confirm he was dead, wondering if he was me. Yes?" He stared, watching her writhe, anticipating her response.

The gasp exploded from her chest, her vision dull as she fought down the rage. "How the hell did you find out about that?"

The short laugh was followed by a visible wince of pain on his features. "Try not to kill them if you get back, but some cretin in your organization actually filed the exhumation report with public records."

He wasn't lying. She cringed inside, gasping at the thought that he was here for no other reason than because he wanted to be here, playing out a final act he'd written himself. "If you knew, why did you invite me?"

"For the same reason I've let you live several times when I could've killed you. For the same reason I have told you before. I want the company of a peer now, and you're the only one I've ever found."

"So you've said. Why now?"

There was a hint of impatience in his tone. "Surely it's obvious. I've been a thorn in the side of far too many powerful people, every day could be my last. If you survive, you are the witness to my legacy. Just because I'm dead doesn't mean this is over for you or anyone else. The things I've set in motion don't need me now. The fire will burn on its own. For me, the far more interesting question is why are you here? What do you want Ericka? What do you think I can give you?"

There were several answers to that swirling in her head.

Standing here now, I don't know which one of them is true. His face was lit by the first sunlight. She turned to stare at the bright red sliver of light coating the jagged skyline like blood, mountaintops draped in scarlet. *Out of time. Any minute now. This will have to do.* She turned to stare at him, unable to resist. "Thus, I give up the spear." At first, he looked puzzled, then his eyes widened, glistening, he knew the quote. His expression was almost grateful.

Ericka turned back into the sunrise, staring into the sun, blinding her to everything else, no answers to the questions after all. The last sensation would be the warmth of sunshine on her face. *This would be balance enough.*

Yusef was right. She didn't hear them coming. Flares of white light, concussive explosions all around, sound with such energy, like being slapped in the face by a massive, unseen hand, piercing shrieks of dying men drowned, then silenced. The missiles missed the central building, but the shockwave collapsed the un-mortared structure, the floor heaved up, buckling her knees before disappearing beneath her. Breathless from the explosions, first a brief sensation of falling, blinding pain in her leg and then nothing but the darkness of oblivion.

31

Equilibrium

Her first awareness was stabbing pain, like a knife through her thigh, warm and wet, pooling on top of her leg before flowing around each side to meet behind her hamstring, dripping to the ground. Ericka opened her eyes, inhaling so hard the gasp was almost a scream, her leg's lower half twisted, bent under a slab of rubble. She bit her lip against the pain, trying to suppress the moan, but it came out a shriek that echoed back from several directions in the dark. Groans burst through compressed lips as she levered herself on to her elbows, feeling her leg. Blood oozed from the wound, not the pulsing, arterial jet she feared.

From behind came the sounds of crumbling bits of debris settling, raising more dust. Her eyes were caked with it, forming a gritty mud as it mixed with tears, filling her nostrils and lungs, triggering agonizing coughs she couldn't suppress. She could see nothing. Something that felt like corrugated metal rested on stones touching her head. The small emergency pouch of water in her vest served to rinse her eyes and wash the dust from her throat without slaking the terrible thirst.

Ericka leaned back, trying to find a position that reduced the pain of the fracture without jagged rubble digging into her spine, finding a moment's respite. Her eyes adjusted. She could see faint outlines of light around random stones. She hadn't expected to live. Help would be here soon, she would survive. Deep breathing helped. Her eyes popped open, looking at the debris around her, more light getting through from above as the sun rose. She'd heard nothing, but something gripped her, tightening her bowels, forcing her awake. She knew. He was still here.

Gasping, she reached up, gingerly sliding the metal to one side, opening up an area a few feet across to dim light. He was staring back at her, silent, unmoving, within arm's reach. The lower half of his body buried, trapped the same as her. His upper lip curled back but he said nothing.

A bubble of scalding rage welled up. "What does it take to kill you? Truly, the devil takes care of his own."

A slight smile accompanied a small snort of laughter. "Indeed, he does, Ericka, indeed. I might say the same thing, seeing as you survived as well." His face contorted with pain and he bent, a hacking cough taking him so he spat phlegm and blood before looking up, wiping his mouth with his wrist.

She wasn't done with him. "The commandos will be here soon, try not to die before then. I have plans for you."

He smiled. "I'm sure you do, but I too have men. What if mine are here first?"

The deep laugh bubbled out of her, sending stabbing pain through her chest. "Then they'll die here with you. This is where it ends."

His features softened as he managed an agonized chuckle. "As well it should, as it must. This is how it had to be." The edge to his tone said he was taunting her again. "I wanted to see you again before you assume my mantle."

There was no controlling the rage as it erupted from inside her. "You bastard, I'm nothing like you!"

He was quiet for a time before his expression became somber. "This has been a long time coming, inevitable. I wasn't going to be taken alive, but with all the world's digital might arrayed against me, my end was only a matter of timing. As much luck as anything else. I wanted to control the time, to meet my end at the hands of the only opponent I've had worthy of the name. After all, I made you who you are!"

Ericka couldn't help the taunt. "Who says you'll end here? Maybe you need to go back, trussed up like a fucking pig to rot in a cell 'til you die."

"It is a mercy I ask after all I have done for you."

"Half my team is dead, my best friend, an old woman who never harmed you. What the hell are you talking about—mercy?"

His gaze was intense, eyes unwavering. "I showed you your true self, allowed you to blossom without the restraints you'd imposed on yourself. You took it and ran. I gave you the vision, the clear sight to look in the mirror without telling yourself lies about what you saw."

"You think I'm like you. You really do."

He spat his words at her. "You are exactly like me! You used my tools, stole money from gangs, used my software to do it. You carefully planned to kill those two men. Savored it even. Enjoyed every minute. No fleeting moment of uncontrollable rage there. You can't walk back from that. All you can do is own it, not be afraid to embrace who you are. You betrayed everything you thought you were. Judas doesn't get to spend the silver, then say sorry and walk away. Some things can't be undone."

Ericka glanced down, not able to look at him. "Nothing can be undone, just choices made in the present."

"You don't believe that nonsense."

"I do, actually. Time, I lived it, isn't it?"

His lip curled into a sneer. "Don't be too pleased with yourself. Sanctimony doesn't become you after what you've done. Only with me dead are all your dirty little secrets gone. If you let them take me, we are going down together. Did you think I wasn't watching while you took your revenge? Recording? Maybe they'll let us share a cell."

Ericka leaned back, pressing her eyes shut, unable to deny much of what he was saying. Her search for her sister's attackers was over. She'd have never found them without him and she'd have gone into the ground trying. But it was more than that. Her fear was gone now. Fear of what she was, fed by what she'd done. Fear that she actually was like him. Unintended, that was his final gift. She'd once convinced herself that everything she'd done was righting a wrong suffered by others. It wasn't true, but she wasn't like him at all. The knowledge drained the darkness. Seneca was right, evil is not a tangible thing, not an entity to be fought, just a series of choices, decisions. Evil vanishes when the right ones are made. She was free of her past the minute she truly started down a new path.

It couldn't be revenge or to punish, only to restore balance. Delivered without remorse, just grim necessity. She tugged the knife from inside her jacket, turning the gleaming blade in front of her eyes, the handle smooth, hilt warm in her hand. Not her first kill, but the first time made without festering rage, mind devoid of dark thoughts smothering her spirit. She would do this, eyes open staring into his. She had to do it for the same reason she'd been the one to bring him to ground. No one else could. That made it a duty, not mere vengeance.

His eyes focused on the blade's curved edge without blinking, then flashed to hers, gleaming with the pressure of boiling rage. Ericka reached out with her left hand, grasping a handful of his collar, hauling him to her within striking range.

He swallowed hard, eyes focused on hers, back to glowering with the same malevolent rage as their first meeting. It was as if he could see her thoughts, step into her mind. "Don't flatter yourself, Ericka. My being gone doesn't change who you are. Ending me is a shallow victory at best. For me, it ends here today, but for you this will never be over, ever."

No way he's getting away with that shit. "Your cabal, your legacy? Just rats to be flushed out, exterminated like the vermin they are. Barely worth getting out of bed in the morning to chase them."

His lips curled into an evil imitation of a smile. "Yes, I'm sure, but that's not what I meant."

"These are your last words, make them count!"

His eyes blazed with pride and arrogance, Dantalion's rage searing through London's haggard features. "I have hidden something in a place no one will ever find. In many places, at the same time. A thing that ensures my legacy lives on. When the time is right, when it detects what it needs, it will emerge. A dormant seed awaiting rain to bloom and surge back to life. When it happens, there will be no mistaking it."

Before she could speak, his hands flashed up, grasping hers, the clammy grip of a thing already long dead. Ericka recoiled inside, maintaining her grip on the knife. Without haste he pulled the blade to him. She didn't resist. The wicked, curved tip slid into the flesh of his neck just above his collarbone, the motion almost casual. Hot blood jetted out, bubbling over her hand as he gasped, spitting crimson to dribble down his chin, dripping onto his chest. His eyes held hers, still flaming with rage and hate, holding her focus until she felt his grip slacken. His hands dropped to his lap, a puppet with its strings cut, leaving her hand holding the knife buried to the hilt in his flesh.

She let go, leaning back, still staring into his eyes, Dantalion's gaze vacant. As she watched life bleed from him, his face transformed. No longer twisted by the volcanic anger beneath, his features relaxed, losing age, his face becoming smooth as malice drained away. Dantalion faded, leaving just London's scarred face, the visage of a different man who might have been, the empty shell a final testimony to a life that didn't have to be.

The demon was gone.

Epilogue

It was impossible for her to identify what was unique about the scent of the North Pacific, its unrelenting purity, the all-pervading miasma from each lungful of brisk ocean air. The smell of these waters was certainly part of it, as were plants nurtured by the thick fog and wind, the riot of growth existing everywhere soil and water combined to permit it. But it was more than that. It was as if the sun, still low on the horizon, penetrated flesh, burning out the accumulated pitch weighing down her thoughts, smothering her. Her muscles lost their rigid stance, her pace slowed, breathing deeper now. She felt clean inside for the first time in memory, purged.

Ericka turned, craning her neck to look back the way she had just come, seeing the white edge of lapping surf wipe away tracks in the sand made by her moments before. Cedar trees hung silent in the morning calm obscuring the trail leading to where she'd left the battered zodiac. Nothing behind her now, it all lay ahead. A slow progression up the beach, shoes hanging from one hand the better to feel the sand between her toes with each unhurried step. The first hint of the day's breeze pushed strands of hair into her eyes, locks stiff with salt from last night's swim.

The string bag slung over her shoulder carried all she needed for the day and some things she would never hope to need again. It was these items she pulled out as she found the spot she'd picked out the day before. The edge of the reef was close to shore here. The turquoise of the beach ended, giving way to darker blue beyond. It was the perfect spot, deep water in a place no one ever came anyway. She walked up the sand out of reach of the gentle waves and took out the tablet and phone. Both devices were paired to the small device linking them to an orbiting network, but not for much longer. She sat on the grasses above the sand, waiting until the device chimed contact, a satellite overhead.

Long practiced fingers slid over the tablet's smudged surface, loading several packets of compressed code, one final check and they were on their way. Software in many locations, all thousands of miles from her, ran simultaneously, encrypting and overwriting data, leaving nothing to mark her passing. In a few hours, all evidence of her location would be gone as if she'd never existed. Other things she preserved for a time now hard to imagine. Now to mourn her dead, say goodbye to those she'd never see again, a process she'd denied herself.

The sun had warmed the phone's glass, but its touch was repulsive. Time for a last message to those she cared about, Yusef, Steiner, O'Brien. *My dear friends, I'm afraid this is goodbye for some time, but not forever. When I'm ready, I'll be back. When I can look at myself in a mirror. When I'm whole again, redemption complete. Ericka.*

The message on its way, she powered down the uplink, confident the software she'd activated moments before would briefly take one of the satellite company's servers offline while it purged all record of her device. Nothing would lead anyone here.

And now for the best part. Ericka smiled, skin tingling with excitement as she pulled the roll of tape from her bag, attaching the mobile to the tablet with four torn strips. It would be best if her construct was as flush as possible. She knew she had an idiotic expression on her face as she waded out, flinching at the icy water, stopping when it was thigh-deep, spent waves tugging her legs. She waited as the set passed and the swells were at their weakest, she had one shot at this. Ericka held the tablet in her right hand, her left in front, the classic pose of a disc thrower, knees bent to make her toss as low as possible.

Ericka put everything she had into it, eagerly counting the six times the tablet skipped off the surface before disappearing. She'd hoped for seven, but fortune had other plans. Her disconnection from the world was complete. Several deep breaths and a sigh before turning for the beach, retrieving her things before walking a little further.

The sun-faded hammock was where she'd left it, covered by a dark nylon tarp, shaded from the midday and afternoon sun, the slight rise giving her an unrestricted view of the water where waves were starting to build in earnest as the sun churned the day's wind into motion. Leaving lunch and water in the hanging bag, she pulled out a book, one of several by the same author, read before, now waiting to be understood again: Seneca, *On the Shortness of Life*. Time to mourn, to start afresh, time to rebuild. She ran her fingers over the rough paper, then pursed her lips with a slight shake of her head. Maybe not today, perhaps not tomorrow either.

The book open on her chest, she squirmed deeper into the hammock, forcing her eyes to stay open a while, drinking in the colors of the Kyuquot Sound summer before drifting into a dreamless, untroubled sleep.

Author's Note

Before beginning, I should warn that this note contains many spoilers. First, a few words about Dantalion. People ask, do criminals like Dantalion exist? I have constructed him from the psychopathy and acts of the many criminals I have dealt with over the years so in that sense he is quite real. Nothing he does is beyond the talents of high-end hackers or state-sponsored groups. Most high-level hackers spend their time trying to steal secrets, money or to simply show that something is possible. In short, they are rational actors with understandable goals. In this book and *The Hacker*, I explore the consequences of a true psychopath in possession of the very best of dark web and hacking tools. In *The Exploit*, far from merely hiding and feeding his horrible lusts, Dantalion has had a taste of glory in the aftermath of his remote hijacking. Now, he must have more. The glory-seeking narcissist part of his psychopathy comes to the forefront of his behaviour and motivation. The literature contains many examples of serial killers who become completely enthralled with their own fame, often taunting police for their inability to stop them, sometimes becoming obsessed with those pursuing them.

Dantalion's crimes in this book are a manifestation of that kind of progression.

The Exploit is entirely a work of fiction, but the technologies depicted are either real or a short step ahead of current capabilities. I continue to emphasize social engineering in Dantalion's technical exploits as that is how it often occurs in the real world. By this I mean the combination of bribery, manipulation, and extortion of people within a target organization who have the credentials to open the door. It is often the easiest way in and the hardest to defend against. No organization is immune from it and so-called 'zero trust' environments take a great deal of resources to administer; everyone has only the access they need and is subject to constant requirements for authentication and monitoring. Essentially, everyone is assumed to be a liability absent constant proof they are not. And yet, still the hackers get in.

All of the technology in *The Exploit* is in the public domain. As with *The Hacker*, I concentrate on what the technology can do, sometimes sacrificing detailed accuracy as to how it does it to preserve the narrative flow. I postulate new ways existing technology or near-horizon capabilities might be used.

I will begin with the American drone program. As with many of Dantalion's hacks, it begins with an extorted inside man allowing the attacker to get past any 'air-gapping' (complete physical disconnection from any network). Once connected, Dantalion loads his malware and stays connected long enough through a device on his mole, here an apparently analog watch. Does he need to go this far? Maybe not. The drone program has been hacked several times through badly secured network architecture and even a simple keylogger, which records whatever is typed on a keyboard, including passwords. Iran claims to have taken control of an American drone in flight and has provided some evidence they were successful. This is disputed by the drone's owners.

Dantalion uses his access to the Chinese BeiDou satellite navigation system to steer intercepting Pakistani fighters away from his hijacked drones. Currently only China and Pakistan fully use the BeiDou system for military purposes. As it turns out, Dantalion has a mole in there too. He might not need it. The world's militaries and intelligence organizations constantly seek ways to undermine each other's systems the better to foil their adversary's abilities to direct weapons to targets. Dantalion might be able to steal the technology to penetrate the systems without creating all of it himself.

Clearview AI has been around for a number of years. It is a commercial system allowing a client to seek a facial match for a known image against all photographs in the public domain, social media, news, advertising, public events, everything. Who has not posted a picture of themselves to some public place on the internet or been caught when someone else posts an image of an event? Unless a person has been living under a rock, deep in a remote mountain range, chances are Clearview AI could find them. It is such an enormously powerful tool, some governments have tried to restrict its use.

Pegasus has been the subject of significant news coverage since I wrote *The Hacker*. This hugely capable software is installed on a target's mobile, permitting the user, amongst other things, to take control of nearly all a phone's functions: read emails, texts, and social media, listen to calls, turn the camera and microphone on, and determine GPS location. It can be installed when a link is clicked, a call is made, a social media app is used, or a message is sent, to name a few. It evolves over time using new 'zero-day' exploits, new flaws in software, as they are discovered. It is said to be restricted to legitimate use by government agencies and police, but there are many allegations its use has gone far beyond that, now including organized crime groups. Once deployed 'in the wild' code may be stolen, as I have postulated Dantalion doing.

AI-focused cyberattacks are another recent feature of high-end hacking. All tech is vulnerable to be misused and AI is no different. It may be used by criminals to guess passwords, neutralize standard security software, use deepfakes for social engineering, carry out reconnaissance of the target's technology and activities, feed legitimate AIs false data and run faster-than-human automated attacks.

In *The Exploit*, I combine several of these new technologies into Dantalion's tool called Providence, short for the masonic 'Eye of Providence' or the all-seeing eye of God. I postulate him using dispersed processing, hidden in a number of facilities with huge processing power such as crypto mines. With it, he can find people, set automated processes to gather information about where they are and what they've been doing, gather a complete dossier on someone using his own version of Pegasus, then plan his attack. I would not be surprised to learn that such conglomerate tools exist in state-sponsored labs and agencies already.

Could a cyberattack be used to start a war? It seems to me that it could. If adversaries are equipped and spoiling for a fight, it would take little to light a fire that would be hard to put out. Once begun, it might be very hard to stop, particularly given the speed at which modern weapons are deployed and the damage they can do. No one wanted World War One to turn out the way it did, but a single pistol shot set in motion the events that got it started. In the 1980s, World War Three almost got started when a computer glitch nearly led to the Soviet Union launching a nuclear counterattack in response to an American attack that wasn't happening. Is it so far-fetched to suggest a well-timed digital nudge that got real shots fired couldn't do the same? Especially when modern military hardware is so dependent on its own digital tools to work properly. Military decisions must be made on data and data can be manipulated, often with no time for real-world investigation as to its accuracy.

It once again goes without saying that the police investigators depicted here are completely fictitious and not based on real officers, and the events in this book are not based on any particular case or cases I have dealt with.

Lastly, I'd like to thank the people whose talent and dedication have contributed to this book; my beta readers too numerous to list, my agent, Ian Drury, for his review of the first version of the manuscript, my editor, Greg Rees, along with all members of the Head of Zeus team for their thorough polishing and creativity, and Doug Collins, for his insightful technical review and comments. Any technical errors that remain are my fault entirely or are me taking artistic license trying to create a better story.

My heartfelt thanks to my family, particularly my wife Tiffany, for listening to me while I thought my way through this book and for her thoughts on the manuscript as it developed. I have dedicated this book to her and my recently passed Uncle Pat. He was there when this all got started, working as a systems engineer for IBM in the very early days of computing when you couldn't learn it or be taught it as they were literally creating it as they went along. He is sorely missed.

Daniel Scanlan

About the Author

DANIEL SCANLAN is a Canadian former prosecutor of twenty-seven years experience, including extensive work on cybercrime, digital evidence, and smuggling cases. He wrote the non-fiction *Digital Evidence in Criminal Law* and was a contributing author to *The Lawyer's Guide to the Forensic Sciences*, winner of the Walter Owen Book Prize. He lives on Vancouver Island and enjoys ocean kayaking and hiking. When not outdoors, he is reading and will read almost anything, except books about lawyers.

Follow Daniel on @DanielMScanlan and
danielscanlanauthor.com